BOILING THE OCEAN

— The America Incorporated Saga —

MIKAEL CARLSON

WARRINGTON

Danbury, Connecticut

Novels by Mikael Carlson:

– The Michael Bennit Series –

The iCandidate

The iCongressman

The iSpeaker

The iAmerican

– Tierra Campos Thrillers –

Justifiable Deceit

Devious Measures

Vital Targets

Revealed Secrets

Decisive Endgame

– Watchtower Thrillers –

The Eyes of Others

The Eyes of Innocents

The Eyes of Victims

– America, Inc. Saga –

The Black Swan Event

Bounded Rationality

Boiling the Ocean

BOILING THE OCEAN:

Attempting something too ambitious or effectively impossible due to its broad scope.

For all my fellow veterans

CHAPTER
ONE

LIBERTEUM

New York University Medical Training Facility
NOHO Geographic District
New York City Municipal Corporation

Michele knows that they were lucky to make it off that SpeedRail. The employees blocking the door were more likely to alert the PSS than to step aside and let them pass. Yet, that's what they did. It was a short yet dangerous walk from that station to the New York University Medical Training Center.

Rykos was in bad shape by the time they arrived. The underground trek from the crypt under Old Saint Patrick's Cathedral nearly killed him. Farron contacted his friend and persuaded him to perform the emergency surgery. The medical student was the best option available and did a remarkable job.

"It's going to be a while before he's conscious," Farron warns as he shuffles up to her seat at Rykos's bedside.

"I know," she says, accepting the coffee he offers.

"Medical Post-Graduate Jekshun should be back anytime now," Farron says, continuing the one-sided conversation.

Michele nods, glancing at the informational display showing Rykos's vitals. The time in the lower corner is the only indication of how early it is in this windowless recovery room.

This facility is a trauma center that trains the next generation of corporate doctors and nurses. Farron explained when they arrived that the medical trainees practice on hundreds of corpses before they touch a live human.

Urches don't have the luxury of modern medical care. The high-tech bed Rykos is resting on is as foreign to Michele as a flying saucer loaded with little green men. The display shows the information collected from the army of sensors attached to Rykos. Tubes running into his abdominal wound secrete a hormone solution that promotes recovery.

Michele has refused to leave Rykos's side since he emerged from surgery. Her first choice was to take him to their last remaining stronghold. Farron insisted they come here instead, and it saved his life. The doctor trainee informed them that Rykos wouldn't have survived had she not acquiesced.

"What happened to Rykos wasn't your fault," Farron says. "His father shot him. Nobody could have predicted that."

"I know," she mumbles.

Jekshun arrives and immediately checks the information on Rykos's LED display. Jekshun is clinical in his demeanor and dispassionate in his discourse. Satisfied with what he sees, he turns to them.

"What's the prognosis?" Farron asks.

"The bullet tore through his small intestine but missed other organs. I repaired the damage and am treating him with antibiotics to fight sepsis. He lost a lot of blood but is young and in good health. He should make a full recovery."

"Thank you, Jekshun. I mean it," Farron says as Michele breathes a sigh of relief.

"Consider us even."

"Agreed."

"When will he wake up?" Michele asks.

"In the next hour or two, although he'll be groggy. I'll sedate him enough for you to move him."

Michele's head jerks. "Move him? What do you mean?"

"I mean that you can't stay here. Instruction resumes tomorrow. It'll be the talk of the university if anyone finds out that I performed surgery on a hero of the corporation at the request of a patrician and a wanted terrorist."

"Where do you expect us to go?" Michele asks.

"I don't know, but you can't stay here."

"That's unacceptable!" she shouts. "You need to find a place for him to recover."

It's an emotional reaction, not a rational one. The tensions of the last twenty-four hours have frayed her nerves. Jekshun did them a huge favor, but that doesn't mean she'll let him toss them out on the street. It's a death sentence.

"It doesn't work that way. I know who you are and what you've done. Don't think that I'm doing any of this for you. I returned a favor to Farron. Otherwise, I would have turned you in when you arrived. Maybe I still should."

"Do that, and you'll find out what it's like to be one of the cadavers you carve up."

"I don't appreciate threats," Jekshun says, straightening his posture and thrusting his chin forward.

"Neither do I."

"Okay, calm down, everyone," Farron interrupts, earning hostile glares. "He's right, Michele, we can't stay here. Training classes aside, it's only a matter of time before the PSS figures out where we went after leaving the SpeedRail station. Can he be moved safely?"

"It's not ideal, but yes. Abdominal wounds are serious injuries. Before the Great Collapse, a gunshot wound like that wouldn't have been survivable. Ten years ago, a move would have killed him. But now, he can be moved without causing more damage."

"Thank you, Jekshun," Farron interjects before Michele can protest.

The two men shake hands. "Sure. I'm meeting friends for breakfast. It's a Sunday tradition. If I don't show, they'll ask questions. I'll be back early this afternoon with a gurney," he says before leaving.

"You should be a little more grateful, Michele," Farron advises after the door closes. "He's risking his life. More importantly, without him, Rykos would be dead."

He's right, but she's in no mood to admit it. "What favor did you do for him?"

Farron grins. "Let's just say that greasing wheels has always been a hallmark of the rich and powerful."

"So much for corporations ending corruption," Michele says, shaking her head.

"Greed is as much a part of humanity as the need for water and oxygen. It can never be eradicated. Now, the more pressing problem – how are we getting out of here?"

There aren't many options. Traveling with Rykos through the underground is impossible. That leaves street transportation. The Keatings are under investigation by Intercorpex, so using one of Farron's conveyances is an unacceptable risk. That leaves them only one option.

"Can you get word to the Emissary?"

"Sure, but what do you want me to say?"

Michele glances at Farron. "You said they get cadaver deliveries here. Ask him if he has been to any funerals lately."

CHAPTER
TWO

AMERICA, INC.

The White House
Corporate Governance District
Washington-Arlington Municipal Corporation

The Bureau of Corporate Security agent manning the lobby desk of the West Wing nods as Fiolla passes him. He's only there for show. Computers monitor access to the building via biojacks, and a platoon of heavily armed BCS agents is posted nearby to deal with intruders.

Instead of heading toward her office, Fiolla turns left down a corridor leading to the colonnade connecting to the executive residence and entering the Eagle Room. Another BCS agent clears her for entry, and she's escorted to an elevator. He gestures her out when it reaches the third-floor solarium, and yet another agent waves her forward. One thing is clear to her: The extra BCS agents on duty aren't here for Valen's protection.

Valen is still a threat to the woman who replaced him despite being removed from his position. Zeykala can only temporarily hold the CEO position unless the corporate charter is amended. Naturally, that's what she's lobbying the board of directors to do. Until then, Valen is eligible to resume his duties. That must be keeping Zeykala awake at night.

"Thank you for coming up to see me, Fiolla," Valen says, standing and offering her a seat opposite his. "Coffee?"

"Yes, that sounds wonderful, thank you."

He pours it from the service himself. Unlike her previous visits to the residence, there is no wait staff tending to his needs.

Valen hands her the cup before retrieving a disruptor that he sets on the table before sitting down. This device is smaller than the last one he used. It renders directional microphones, eavesdropping devices, or any manner of audio espionage ineffective. Anyone listening won't hear their conversation and will instantly know why.

"I figured the BCS would have confiscated those."

"They took two of them. I had three," he says with a grin. "They won't come after it because they won't want to admit that they're eavesdropping."

"Sir, words can't express how sorry—"

He holds a hand up to stop her. "It's not your fault. Even I didn't foresee what Hammond did."

The chairman is Valen's long-time ally and had several opportunities to end yesterday's hearing. Instead, he allowed a vote and broke the tie, ultimately removing Valen from power.

"Do you know why he turned on you?"

Valen shrugs. "Zeykala got to him. I'll eventually figure out how."

"With all due respect, sir, you're taking the betrayal well. I would be livid."

He smiles and places his cup and saucer on the table. "Every great general loses a battle or two, Fiolla. It doesn't mean the war is lost. The board will eventually come to me with a reinstatement offer."

That's a bold proclamation, even for an ardent optimist. Zeykala is only one of Valen's political enemies. Fiolla can't conjure up a scenario where he returns to his former position. Gross incompetence is a damning reason for removal. Nobody recovers from it.

"How? Why?"

"I trust you, Fiolla, but it's better if you don't know. Your position at the White House is already in jeopardy."

Fiolla nods despite not understanding the logic behind that decision. "Why am I here, then?"

Valen leans forward. "Dark events are about to transpire. I need you not to lose hope. We're still in the fight."

"Okay. What do you need me to do?"

"Your job. You're widely respected and have more influence than you know. Zeykala needs a steady hand within Corporate Affairs to allay the concerns of the subsidiaries. She'll try to turn you into an ally. Play along."

"I'll do my best," Fiolla says, unconvinced Zeykala will keep her in the White House.

"I know you will," Valen says as they stand and shake hands. "There's one more thing: Virtari is a dangerous man. Stay far away from him."

* * *

Virtari waltzes into the Oval Office and makes himself comfortable on one of Zeykala's sofas. His relaxed posture causes her to grimace, but she stifles her objections to his behavior. She needs allies right now, including the cantankerous

Bureau of Corporate Security director. Determined not to let him know that it bothers her, she quietly moves around her desk and sits on the opposing sofa.

"Well?"

"Fiolla is having coffee with Valen in the Solarium. I warned you that she'd remain loyal to him."

"Yes, I *know* what you told me, Virtari. I don't need to be reminded of it like I'm an eight-year-old who forgot to make my bed."

"Apologies, Chief Executive."

There is no sincerity in his words. The head of the BCS is never sorry about anything he does or says.

"What are they talking about?"

Virtari shrugs. "Does it matter?"

"Virtari, you pride yourself on being the supreme collector and purveyor of information. It might be *useful* to know if they're plotting to slip rodenticide into my morning tea."

"Rat poison isn't what you should be worried about," he says, stretching his arm out along the back of the sofa. "The board's decision to remove Valen is unpopular. Your top executives started a riot on Corporate Hill that took dozens of my agents to subdue."

Zeykala frowns at the unpleasant memory marring an otherwise marvelous day. Following Valen's removal, vocal dissent escalated into violence that embroiled the chamber in conflict. The board members were evacuated, and the uprising was squelched, but it should never have occurred in the first place.

"What's your point?"

"You're the chief executive officer, so I shouldn't need to explain this. You need to win them over."

Zeykala's jaw tightens. Employees and subsidiaries work for her, not vice versa. Unfortunately, the director is right. She is filling this position temporarily, and mass firings of senior executives will only cause more problems.

"I need Fiolla to get with the program. I know you don't like her, but her relationships with executives can help us soothe their bruised feelings."

The comment causes Virtari to let out a sarcastic laugh.

"Bruised feelings? Is that what you think caused that melee? Zeykala, the highest levels of corporate leadership were ready to tear Shareholder Hall down to its foundation."

"It was an emotional reaction," the CEO snaps.

"Fiolla is Valen's best hope to earn their allegiance when he attempts to oust you. And she's having coffee with him."

Virtari's cynicism may be an asset as the Bureau of Corporate Security director, but it annoys Zeykala. He frequently uses it to advance his agenda. He despises Fiolla and will say whatever it takes to get her terminated.

"If you bothered learning what they were discussing up there, we would know," Zeykala says, rising and straightening her tunic. "Inform me if a plot is uncovered. Until then, Fiolla gets the opportunity to prove her loyalty. Understood?"

"Yes, ma'am," he says, contempt dripping from his voice. "There is one more thing. We assumed complete command of the Liberteum manhunt from New York Public Safety and Security. Chief Executive Safmor and Acting Chief Guardian Dzamko are cooperating, if not enthusiastically."

The NY PSS and the BCS have a long and storied hatred of each other. The contention over the Liberteum manhunt has only increased the animosity that began with the Catharsis and grew during numerous quli riots.

"Finding Liberteum is your top priority. This transition of power will go smoother if they are eliminated quickly."

He nods as Zeykala circles back to her desk and stares at the tablet sitting on it. "Have you spoken to Intercorpex about Talya Bettancourt's status as *prima*?"

"As of right now, that's still in limbo," she says, not glancing up.

"Shalius Covington still maintains that he is majority shareholder," Virtari says, goading her to be more proactive.

As the board was determining Valen's fate, Intercorpex experienced market volatility issues. Their claim that the cause was due to patricians' trading patterns has been refuted within the ranks of the elite. Administrator-General Raimius hasn't issued an official statement on the disruption's cause despite the exchange being offline for the first time in its history. The event shocked the corporate world and raised the ire of the patricians.

"ICX will determine what to do about the market anomaly. The questions over who is *prima* will be settled then. Are there any other *security* concerns you would like to discuss?" Zeykala asks, determined to change the subject.

"No," the director says with a smirk. "Rank and file employees are still processing the Intercorpex closing and the change in leadership. Your address tonight needs to set the narrative before they form their own opinions."

Again, he points out the obvious. "Let me worry about messaging. You need to maintain order. I expect the qulis to take advantage of Valen's removal by pressing one of their ridiculous agendas."

Qulis are America Incorporated's problematic manual labor force. The derogatory moniker came from the term "coolie," which was used in the nineteenth and twentieth centuries to denote unskilled native laborers in India and China. "Quli" became an oft-used slur in the early days of the First Reconstruction, when many workers were of Asian and Latino descent. Now, it's the modern vernacular for the entire lower working class.

"I'll keep them in line."

"See that you do," Zeykala warns before her BCS director slinks out of the Oval Office and heads back to the hole in the Pentagon he came from.

CHAPTER THREE

LIBERTEUM

The "Motor Pool"
Hell's Kitchen Geographic District
New York City Municipal Corporation

Haven stares at the man in silence. They took a considerable risk to grab the piece of trash at the epicenter of guardian activity. The area around One Guardian Plaza is covered with cameras and flush with personnel who can respond to any incident. Disguised as qulis, they lured him to the utility van and snatched him without anyone realizing something was amiss. It was easier than they thought it would be.

Once in their custody, Haven removed his biojacks without anesthetic. They abandoned the vehicle far enough away to avoid unwanted attention and traveled underground to the Motor Pool. All this in the name of settling unfinished business.

"Don't look so scared. If you cooperate, this will be over before you know it," Haven says, breaking the long silence.

The man bound to the metal chair in the center of the room shivers with fear as he stares wide-eyed at Haven. What a coward. Michele could never understand why he detests these people so much. This is one of the reasons. They're sheep who deserve to get slaughtered.

"W-what do you wh-want from me?" the guardian asks, barely able to form the sentence.

"Information," Haven says, pulling up a chair and taking a seat in front of him. "But before we get to that, let me explain a couple of things. First, I have extracted your biojacks. Yes, we know where they are, and, yes, we removed all three of them.

"Second, this room is lined with copper wire. No drone hovering over the city will pick up audio in here. Nobody will hear you scream—and you will scream if you don't tell me everything I want to know."

Nyvar prepares medieval-looking tools on a beat-up table nestled against the left wall. The guardian watches him heat a spike with a blowtorch His quivering worsens when he returna his attention to Haven.

"Wha-what inf-information? I don't…I don't know anything."

"We'll get to that. Your name is Petruccho. You're a captain at One Guardian Plaza's Real-Time Crime Control center. Is that correct?"

"Yes," he croaks.

Haven stands and smacks him hard against the cheek with the back of his hand. The satisfying sound reverberates in the small room, punctuated by Petruccho's whimpers as blood trickles from the corner of his mouth.

"You work at the RTCC and have the audacity to say you don't have any information? You're in the middle of the largest security operation since the Catharsis. Captain Petruccho, when you lie to me, I will hurt you. If you continue lying, I will hurt everyone you love. Do you understand?"

He nods, swallowing hard. It's a good bluff. Haven doesn't know who his family is or where they live. The advantage of being a feared terrorist is that your enemies believe you are capable of anything. He wasn't bluffing about the screaming part, which Nyvar is patiently waiting to demonstrate.

"Please, d-don't hurt my family."

"That will be up to you," Haven says, sitting back down. "What is your current assignment at the RTCC?"

"I-I command the…the section that muh-monitors drones and static cameras. That's all."

Haven nods and Nyvar presses the red-hot spike against the man's hand. He howls in pain as his skin chars. The smell of burnt flesh wafts around the room as the captain sobs. Nyvar removes the spike and shakes his head before returning to the table to reheat it.

"Don't test my patience, Captain. I don't want your job description, so I'll rephrase the question. What are you looking for on the feeds?"

"We're searching fa-for the terrorists," Petruccho whines.

"See how easy this is? The terrorists left in two groups after the raid you conducted on the church crypt. One group fled using a SpeedRail and detonated a bomb in Library Park Station," Haven explains with personal satisfaction. "That second group concerns me. Where did they go?"

He starts to talk and then stops. Haven shakes his head and moves behind Petruccho. He grasps him under the chin and yanks his head back. Nyvar has upgraded his tool for the next round. He approaches with a white-hot iron poker and waves it in front of Petruccho's face. The captain follows the glowing instrument with his eyes until it stops in front of his right eyeball, causing him to recoil in horror.

"No, no, no…please," he pleads, tears streaming down his cheeks.

"Tell me what I want to know."

"They got on a SpeedRail," he blurts out.

"Not likely. Take the eye," Haven commands.

"It's the truth! It's the truth," he bawls. Nyvar cocks his head at Haven and relaxes for a moment.

"You are saying that an urch, a patrician, and a kid all got on a SpeedRail that they know is covered in surveillance and monitored in real-time?"

"Ye-yes, we have the video. There were four of them. They got on at Prince Street."

"Four of them?" Nyvar asks.

"Koltayne," Haven says with a sigh. "He was providing security. I guess he didn't die when the building blew. Michele must have turned him."

"Traitorous bastard," Nyvar mumbles.

Haven grabs Petruccho's face. "Where did they go?"

"University Square. We…we don't know where they went from there. One of them appeared badly wounded."

Haven releases his grip. Nyvar frowns as he returns to the table. The man loves playing with his toys. The more pain they bring, the more he covets them. Michele never let him ply his trade, but Haven's rules are more liberal.

"Tell me one more thing, and I will set you free, Captain Petruccho," Haven says, pacing around him for effect. "Did the PSS interview the employees who saw them on the SpeedRail?"

"The BCS took over the search for Liberteum," he says, his voice higher at the prospect of his imminent release. "I don't know if they talked to them…they aren't sharing information."

"That's typical. Very well. I appreciate your cooperation."

Haven stops behind the captain, grabs his head with his left hand, and yanks it backward. His other hand pulls a blade across his exposed neck, severing both carotid arteries and his larynx. The piece of scum gasps and looks at his torturers in horror as blood sprays in long streams from the wound.

"I thought you said you were going to set him free."

Haven wipes the knife on the captain's uniform top. "I did. I set him free from a life of servitude to his corporate master. I never said I would let him *go* free."

Nyvar grins. "What now?"

"It sounds like Ivy was still alive when they left that train. They needed to find a doctor."

"The PSS or BCS would have checked the medical centers."

"There aren't any in that area, and Michele wouldn't have risked taking him to one anyway. Freejacks are reported, and Rykos is a hero of the corporation. He's recognizable."

Biojacks are one of the methods corporations rely on to subjugate their employees. The basic ones provide location monitoring, entry access, and a means to complete financial transactions. The more advanced ones monitor health status and serve as redundant backups. To slip out from the grip of the corporation, biojacks need to be removed, making someone a "freejack." The corporation views this as a crime worthy of immediate termination. Every urch understands the result of being captured.

"So, where'd they go? Valhalla?"

Haven considers what's near University Square when it dawns on him. In his mind, he runs through the obstacles of reaching it. The city is swarming with guardians and BCS agents. Drones are monitoring the entire city, and static video monitored by their computers will flag even minor things for an army of analysts to sift through. It's a huge risk to leave the Motor Pool again, but he needs revenge.

"Her stronghold is somewhere in Midtown. Michele doesn't have any safehouses near University Square, but Farron might know somebody that could help them. Do we still have those guardian uniforms we stole for phase three?"

"Yeah, why?" Nyvar asks.

"Tell Tielur and Symun to gear up and prepare a vehicle. We're going hunting."

CHAPTER FOUR

AMERICA, INC.

NYCMC Executive Center (NEC)
Municipal Governance Geographic District
New York City Municipal Corporation

The heavy oak doors swing open and reveal the cavernous space that's home to the chief executive officer of the New York City Municipal Corporation. Once upon a time, Ilaria coveted the idea of occupying the ornate space that symbolizes power and success. Before marrying Teman, she was on the fast track to a high-level executive position. He was a strapping young guardian with a promising career, and they set out to become the ultimate power couple.

Instead, she got pregnant with Varella, and one of them had to leave the workforce. It ended up being her. Rykos was born three years later, further delaying her return to the corporate world. Now that he has graduated, Ilaria is eager to pick up where she left off.

"Oh my God, Ilaria! What are you doing here?" Safmor says with genuinely enthusiastic surprise in his voice.

"I'm visiting you."

He stands, and they share a hug. It's a serious breach of professional protocol but forgivable for long-time friends.

"I'm thrilled to see you, but why aren't you at the hospital?"

"Teman is resting, and Varella is with him."

She has always been daddy's little girl. Their marriage is deteriorating, and Varella is siding with him. The friction over his job has taken a toll over the years, but their disagreements over Rykos have caused the most damage. She wouldn't have guessed her wanting to return to the NYCMC would drive an even bigger wedge between them. Teman has never raised a hand to her before, even during arguments worse than the one before Rykos's commencement. It was the reason they weren't speaking before he was captured by Liberteum and tortured.

"I'm sorry about what happened to him. I plan on visiting as soon as I can break free from my duties."

"Thank you. Would you happen to have any news about my son?"

Safmor directs her to a pair of sofas tucked into the corner of his office. He avails himself of the tea service before joining her. Like Ilaria, he never developed a taste for coffee. He hands her a cup and keeps the other for himself.

"Lemon and a little honey…just as you like it, I believe?"

"Yes, thank you."

The pair shared countless late study sessions at NYU when they were in the executive program and longer hours as junior executives following graduation. She knew that Safmor had a crush on her all those years. Their relationship changed from close friends to cordial acquaintances after she started dating Teman. When they married, the future CEO begrudgingly moved on. His marriage ended with his wife's tragic death six years ago.

"Is that why you came over here? I'm sorry if you aren't getting updates. I'm afraid we haven't found his…we haven't found Rykos yet," he corrects himself, not wanting Ilaria to hear that her only son is probably dead. "The BCS has taken over the search for Liberteum. It's a stressful time at One Guardian Plaza."

"My being here actually has nothing to do with Rykos," Ilaria says, forcing a half-smile as she changes the subject. "I was hoping to revisit our conversation from Career Day."

"Ilaria, I hardly think this is the appropriate time to—"

"I can't control what happens with Rykos. I need to look at my future. Human Resources is soulless and won't have any compassion when they confer my next assignment. If the order hasn't already been drafted, it will come any day now."

"You're putting me in a difficult situation, Ilaria."

"You're the CEO. You should be used to that by now," she says with a brilliant smile meant to lighten the mood.

"You know I adore you, but with everything that has happened to your husband and son…."

"My husband was tortured by animals who want to destroy our way of life. He may have shot my only son," Ilaria says, now fighting back her tears. "Both men in my life have been taken from me, in one way or another. I need something that provides meaning again."

"I wish it were that simple," Safmor says, leaning forward. "Rykos was in the company of known terrorists. How do I justify that when I'm inevitably questioned about appointing his mother to an executive position?"

Ilaria matches his body language. "He was rescuing his father, nothing more. That's how you justify it. Ultimately, it's your call regardless of who questions you. You know that you need me in this building."

Safmor places his tea down on the small table beside him. He's obviously flustered and knows she'll keep pressing him no matter what excuses he offers. It's an advantage of knowing someone for her entire adult life. She's convinced he'll agree once she pushes the right button.

"I know no such thing," he says after a pause.

"Yes, you do. We wouldn't still be having this conversation otherwise. I'm the asset that you and the NYCMC *need* right now. Tell me I'm wrong."

"I would never impugn your abilities," he concedes. "Had you not had children, you'd be sitting in this office instead of me. You were always the stronger executive."

"But I did have children, and you're here because you earned the position. But the world has become more dangerous and unpredictable. The executives in Washington are going to start searching for scapegoats if things don't improve. Who do you think they'll come for first?"

His look says it all. The BCS taking over security operations in the city is only the beginning. An executive with a fraction of Safmor's intelligence would realize that.

"It's a risk."

"Most things in life are. No candidate is better for director of Business Development than I am, and that position is open."

Safmor flashes a grin. Business development was Ilaria's specialty before Varella was born. As a junior executive, she launched initiatives that catapulted numerous subsidiaries to record growth. Her boss took the credit, but everyone knew the successes were hers.

"That's a fast-track executive position. You'd be jumping the line," the CEO argues.

"Do you want to groom a replacement or have an ally you can count on?"

His eyes shift up and to the left. She found the right button.

"I've always hated debating you," he says. "I will make the by-name request to Human Resources."

"Thank you, Safmor. You won't regret it," Ilaria says, unable to hide her enthusiasm.

Safmor shakes his head. "You might. You have no idea how bad things are in this city."

CHAPTER FIVE

THE PATRICIANS

Lyris's Domicile
Battery Park City District
New York City Municipal Corporation

The announcement that somebody is at his door must have come as a surprise. Lyris has been in exile since being relieved of his Intercorpex duties. Even his most loyal subordinates at the Wall Street NOC are avoiding him. The shock is understandable when he answers to find Denali Keating and his manservant standing there.

The two men are shown in. The Battery Park domicile is nice, although almost Spartan for a man with Denali's wealth and impeccable tastes. Lyris's nicest piece of décor wouldn't be fit to decorate a coat closet in his Connecticut estate.

"Can I offer you anything? Some tea or coffee?" Lyris asks.

"No, we won't be staying long. I came by to congratulate you on your exemplary performance yesterday. I was beginning to doubt that you had the guts to shut the exchange down."

"I wish I could take the credit. I didn't shut it down – my replacement did."

"Director Wyeth was carrying out your order – a very impressive display of loyalty on his part, I might add. He took a great risk following that directive with Raimius standing fifteen feet away. I wish I had been there to see the look on the bastard's face."

Denali knows more about the workings of the Wall Street NOC than Lyris could ever imagine. He has moles everywhere. By executing the order, Wyeth sabotaged his career. His fate is now tied to Lyris, and Lyris's fate is tied to Denali. It's enough to make the patrician smile.

"Wyeth is a good man and a valuable asset to Intercorpex."

"He will be a valuable asset to *you*," Denali says.

Lyris perks up. "You still intend to ensure that I become administrator-general?"

"I'm a man of my word. You have proven your worth, Lyris. Nothing says more about a man than how he performs under pressure. You were tested and proved your mettle. The reward is coming. You'll be running Intercorpex by the middle of the week."

"The regents are replacing Raimius?"

Lyris obviously can't believe anything would happen that fast in a bureaucracy as large as Intercorpex. That's because it doesn't.

"There is strong support for his removal among the regents, but their input won't be required."

"I don't understand," Lyris says, not connecting the dots.

Denali presses his lips together. He's being cryptic by design. The former executive director doesn't need to know what's coming. It's better for everyone if he doesn't.

"You're not meant to," Denali says, nodding at Abbot, who proceeds to open the door. "Things are going to move quickly, Lyris. Events will transpire that cannot be foreseen or planned for. Rely on the same good judgment you used on Saturday, and you'll be fine. You're about to become administrator-general. Prepare yourself for what that means."

CHAPTER
SIX

RYKOS

New York University Medical Training Facility
NOHO Geographic District
New York City Municipal Corporation

My eyes open, and I see nothing but white. It's a little disconcerting until I feel the pain from my abdomen shoot up my spine and register within my brain. Nope, I'm not dead.

"I thought we lost you," a female voice whispers from my side.

I turn to see Michele sitting next to the bed. She takes my hand in hers and squeezes it. Another jolt of electricity shoots through me. That one was welcome.

"You're not about to say something cliché, are you?"

I smile. "Like I must be in Heaven because I see an angel?"

"Yeah, like that."

"No, I won't be that boring. I have learned something important since I've been with you, though."

"What's that?"

"I'm exceedingly hard to kill."

Michele allows herself a brief laugh. "You learn fast not to take that for granted. How are you feeling?"

"Uh," I say, glancing down at my stomach. "Like I've been shot."

"How would you know what that feels like?"

I cock my head. "How would you? Have you ever been shot?"

Michele releases my hand and stands. She lifts her shirt and shows off her toned midsection and the pair of round scars on her left side. The bullet traveled right through her.

"The underground is a dangerous place. Scars are badges of honor in the urch population."

She lowers her shirt and I playfully frown. I want to ask if there are any more that she wants to show me.

Michele scoffs. "You're definitely feeling better."

"What happened to Haven? Did the PSS get him?"

"I'm not sure," she says, sitting. "From what I've seen on corporate news, it looks like he escaped. He killed a lot of people in the process."

"That figures. And my father?"

Michele shakes her head. "I'm sorry, I don't know."

I sink deeper into my pillow. I don't know how to feel about that. We went through hell trying to save him. It was a huge risk for Michele…and for me. Then he shot me. Whatever happens from this point forward, I don't know if I can ever forgive him for that. He was lucid enough to call me a traitor. He knew what he was doing when he pulled that trigger.

Part of me hopes that he didn't make it out of that crypt. It's selfish to say that, but it's how I feel. I wanted to save him from Haven. I thought it might build a bridge across the rift that had grown between us. I couldn't have been more wrong.

I return my stare to the ceiling. For the first time, I realize this doesn't look like any underground space I've ever been in. Either Valhalla is a palace, or I'm somewhere else.

"Where the hell are we?"

"NYU's medical training facility. Jekshun patched you up."

"Who the hell is Jekshun?"

"A friend of Farron's who owed him a favor."

I try to turn my torso. The shooting pain makes me think better of it, and I settle back into the bed.

"University Square? How did we get up here?"

"SpeedRail," Michele says.

I study her face. She isn't kidding.

"Are you crazy?"

"A lot of people on that train thought so," she says with a grin. "I'll tell you the story later."

"I'm looking forward to it. I don't remember a thing."

"You were pretty out of it. We're safe here for the time being. Unfortunately, we can't stay."

I look back down at my abdomen. "I hope you don't expect me to walk because that's not happening."

"Farron's making some arrangements for us."

I take Michele's hand. "Thank you for helping me with my father. You didn't have to. I don't understand why you did."

Michele presses her lips together. She wants to say something but doesn't. Finally, she forces a smile.

"How can I put this in a way you'll understand? I made an investment in you that I hope pays off someday."

The door swings open, and Farron glides in. He has cleaned up since their escapades in the crypt and looks refreshed.

"I hope I'm not interrupting…whatever this is," he says, seeing us holding hands. "You look a hundred percent better, Rykos."

"Looks can be deceiving, but thanks."

"Michele, I made the necessary arrangements with the Emissary. We should be good to go when Jekshun returns."

"Who's the Emissary?" I ask.

"An old friend."

Another cryptic response. I want her to give me a straight answer but decide not to push her further. I don't have the strength for that conversation…yet. It's going to have to happen soon. I'm tired of being in the dark. My fate is now linked to Michele and Liberteum, whether I like it or not. I need to understand what I've gotten myself into.

CHAPTER SEVEN

INTERCORPEX

The "War Room"
ICX New York Exchange
New York City Municipal Corporation

Late morning here means it's the end of the workday in Zurich. Not that it matters. The commissioner-general is practically welded to his desk. Jurghen was a brilliant chief inspector before being promoted to the highest office in ICS Security. He's politically astute, although not overt in displaying that acumen. Zyree has always trusted him because he supports his subordinates. Well, almost always.

"Are you kidding me with this? Did you slip and hit your head or something?" Zyree shouts at the display on the wall.

The commissioner-general gives him an indignant look. Zyree doesn't care if he's hurting feelings or breaching protocol. Zyree was shot at yesterday, and not all of it came from the terrorists. Jurghen is treating the incident like business as usual.

"I'm going to assume you sustained a concussion in that explosion. Otherwise, I can't think of a single damned reason you'd talk to me that way," Jurghen scolds in his thick German accent.

"I can think of one – anger. You're releasing the woman who tried to kill me!"

"I read your report and Chiana's statement."

"Let me guess – she claimed she was engaging a terrorist and not shooting at me."

"Yes, that's exactly what she wrote," he says, lifting an eyebrow.

"She's lying. Watch the video from the PSS. The terrorists in that room were already neutralized."

"The video was corrupted," Jurghen says, taking off his thick glasses. "The footage couldn't be recovered."

"It was fine when I uploaded it to our servers."

"Well, it isn't now."

Videos don't magically corrupt themselves. There are safeguards preventing it and high-tech tools that recover lost data if it happens. Jurghen knows that better than anyone. Something is terribly wrong.

"Besides," he continues, "according to Chiana, he arrived after the fact and saw you attacking her."

"He charged into that room with us! He knocked her…Jurghen, please tell me you aren't taking her word over mine."

"You are both respected chief inspectors with vastly different accounts about what happened. Considering the lack of corroborating evidence, I'm not adopting either of your stories as the official narrative."

Zyree runs his hand through his hair. Jurghen has made up his mind, and there's no point in arguing with him.

"What happens to Chief Guardian Chiana?"

"She will be released by New York's Public Safety and Security on her own recognizance and ordered to report back to Zurich."

"Unbelievable," Zyree mutters, believing she should at least be escorted.

"I want you out of New York too, Zyree. There's nothing more for you to do there."

"You want me to leave with Haven still running around? He is one of ours. It's our responsibility—"

"He *was* one of ours. The Bureau of Corporate Security has assumed control of the manhunt, and no, he's their problem. Do you have as cozy a relationship with them as you do the PSS?"

"No. Their wives don't even have cozy relationships with them."

"Agreed, and since the exchange is offline due to reckless trading by the patricians, there's nothing for you to do there."

"Yes, I'm sure it was only reckless trading," Zyree says in a tone heavy with sarcasm.

"Do you have hard evidence to suggest otherwise?"

The commissioner-general is too professional to accept insufficient explanations during an investigation. Inspectors have a natural nose for sniffing out lies and propaganda. Corporations may rely on them to control employees, but ICX inspectors are wired to recognize lies and uncover the truth.

"What happened to you, Jurghen?"

His face turns bright red with anger. He inhales deeply and exhales before leaning in to the camera.

"I think you need some time off, Zyree. Instead of coming to Zurich, go back to one of the islands in the Caribbean Corporation and work on your tan. Take Malkor with you. I'm sure he could use the break, too. You need to get some perspective on things. I will get debriefed by Chiana and will recall you when I can stomach talking to you again."

Jurghen disconnects the VidLynk, and Zyree pushes deeper into his seat. He rubs the growing stubble on his chin. Part of him wishes he had never left the Caribbean following the Secaucus data center attack that started this mess. Instead of finishing a cushy assignment down there.

"I don't suppose there's any chance on you taking Jurghen up on that vacation?" Malkor asks from the side of the room, getting a disapproving look from Zyree. "I didn't think so. So, what's the plan?"

"The world's going straight to hell, Malkor, and everybody is either pretending it isn't or blaming someone else for it. Nobody has an interest in solving the problem."

"What does that mean for us?"

"It means we're going to get lunch," Zyree says. "Then we're going to start fixing the problem."

Zyree is done playing around. He's been shot, knocked unconscious, almost incinerated twice, engaged in countless firefights, and nearly killed by a colleague. Now he's dealing with a formally supportive boss who has suddenly taken leave of his senses. Something is going on, and he's determined to get to the bottom of it. It's what good chief inspectors do.

CHAPTER
EIGHT

THE PATRICIANS

The White House
Corporate Governance District
Washington-Arlington Municipal Corporation

Talya has gotten comfortable in this room. She wasn't invited to spend much time here during Valen's tenure as chief executive. That's one of the many reasons she wanted to remove him from power. Zeykala isn't a strong replacement, but at least she responds to the *prima* patrician's guidance. No matter what Shalius Covington claims, a Bettancourt will always be the largest shareholder of America Incorporated.

Both women are studying reports on their tablets when Director Virtari strides into the Oval Office with one of his minions after being admitted by an assistant outside the door.

"What is it, Virtari?" Zeykala asks without looking up.

"We have news about Liberteum. With your permission…."

The CEO nods and Virtari opens a secure VidLynk on one of the wall displays.

"This is Special Agent Caylem. He was the BCS's liaison to the White House under your predecessor. I reassigned him to command the manhunt in New York. Go ahead, Special Agent Caylem."

"Thank you, sir. "While assuming control from the PSS, we uncovered this video footage from a SpeedRail. It is timestamped shortly after the raid on Old Saint Patrick's Cathedral."

Talya joins Zeykala in watching the surveillance footage. She can't believe what she's seeing.

"Please tell me that the terrorists didn't escape a secure cordon using mass transit."

"That appears to be the case, ma'am," the agent confirms.

"Your wonderful New York Public Safety and Security hard at work," Virtari says to Zeykala.

"How are we finding out about this now?" the CEO asks, anticipating Talya's next question.

"It has taken time to assimilate—"

"The guardians are dragging their feet," Virtari interrupts. "They don't want to cede control. Catching the terrorists that killed over a hundred employees and dozens of their comrades takes a back seat during a turf war."

"Special Agent Caylem, I want you to sift through every shred of information the PSS has on Liberteum. If a guardian so much as blocks an agent's way to the restroom, remove them from duty. Understood?"

"Of course, ma'am."

Talya turns to Virtari. "Who are the people in this video?"

"One of them is a confirmed member of Liberteum. The woman was captured on surveillance video during the raid on the Chinatown urch rave. The kid next to her isn't known to us, but we're searching."

Zeykala nods. "And the other two?"

"Stop the video and enhance facial recognition," Virtari orders. "You're going to love this."

The computer complies, freezing the faces of the two men and matching them with photographic records. They appear within seconds, complete with full biographic data. When Talya reads the names, her mouth hangs open.

"You've got to be kidding me," Zeykala says.

"I'm afraid not. The two men are Undergraduate Rykos, hero of the corporation and son of the NYCMC's chief guardian, and Farron Keating, patrician of the *gentez-majorez* and son of—"

"Denali Keating," Talya mumbles. "Intercorpex was right. The Keatings were involved in the Wall Street attack."

"The evidence points to that, yes," Virtari says.

"These employees around them – did any of them sound the alarm or try to stop them?"

"No, ma'am. They surrounded the terrorists but let them walk off at University Square."

The patrician feels her face flush as a surge of anger rips through her. Why would they do that? Employees know it's their responsibility to report suspicious activities and intervene when practical. Considering that information on Liberteum and the events downtown were broadcast widely, passengers on that train had the duty to do both.

"Virtari," Zeykala says, "track down every one of those employees and find out why they didn't fulfill their obligation to the corporation."

"Yes, ma'am."

"Any theories as to why they got off at that particular stop?" Talya asks, still reeling at the employees' inaction.

"It's possible that the crowd on the train spooked them. Rykos appears injured. That corroborates PSS reports that Chief Guardian Teman shot his son before the terrorists fled. They could have been searching for medical attention."

"That family is insane. Why University Square?"

"We don't know. There are no medical facilities nearby. Maybe they have an underground stronghold there."

"Find them," Talya orders Virtari. "Start with the university area. Tear the place down if you have to."

Virtari glances at Talya before nodding. He signs off the VidLynk and leaves the two women alone in the room.

"Orders to Virtari should come from me," Zeykala says, her voice low and even.

Talya glares at her. "Then show some backbone and get that idiot Safmor on a VidLynk. If he can't get his PSS to cooperate, find an executive up there who can."

CHAPTER NINE

AMERICA, INC.

NYCMC Waterside Advanced Trauma Center
Gramercy Geographic District
New York City Municipal Corporation

"Hello, Mother."

The sterile tone those words were delivered in is what causes Ilaria to turn before entering Teman's room. This level one trauma center is one of the most advanced in the entire sphere of influence. Accident victims are brought to this facility from as far west as the Mississippi River to receive the best medical care the corporation can offer. The people who accompany them are emotional wrecks, not detached and distant.

But that's how Varella can best be described. Ilaria embraces her daughter in the corridor outside Teman's room. It's not reciprocated. Their eldest child has never been the warm, loving type, but her frigid demeanor is worse than usual.

"I rushed over as soon as the physician contacted me. How is he?" Ilaria asks, now feeling a stab of guilt for being away.

"He's been asking for you," she says, her tone meant to pile on the guilt.

"What did you tell him?"

"The truth – that you were at the Executive Center instead of here with him."

Ilaria closes her eyes and nods. Her marriage is complicated enough. Varella could have been gentler with that information. Instead, she poured gasoline on the fire.

"Thanks for nothing, Varella."

"What? Did I lie? He deserves to know the truth."

"It's far more complicated than that."

"I don't see how," she says, wielding the indignant look she perfected as a teenager. "My father was beaten to within an inch of his life, and you're trying to get a job. And you say I'm the ambitious one."

"I…it's not that simple!" Ilaria shouts, failing to stifle her anger.

"Why? Because he killed Rykos? The penalty for treason is death."

"Don't talk about your brother that way!" Ilaria snaps.

"He…was…a…traitor," Varella says, leaning forward and glaring at her mother. "Just because you don't believe it doesn't make it untrue. He deserved to die."

Ilaria takes a deep breath, fighting the urge to shake some sense into her. Varella and Rykos despise each other, but that doesn't matter. They are a family.

"I can't believe you would say that."

"And I can't believe you won't. Then again, I shouldn't be surprised. Rykos always was your favorite."

Varella turns and walks away from Ilaria after the parting shot. Her mother doesn't stop her. She nods at the guardian posted at the door, and he admits her. Teman is resting inclined in his bed. He's still heavily bruised and swollen. The treatments are working, but he still looks like death warmed over.

He stares at her through hollow, defeated eyes. That's her impression, at least. She can't imagine what he went through in that crypt or what it did to his mental state. She doesn't know if it's from the torture or the news about her.

"You're…you're applying for a job at the Executive Center," he says, his voice raspy and jaw struggling to move.

That answers her question. It's also the first words he's said to her since his capture. Their relationship has never been exceptionally loving, but this is ridiculous. There is no "it's good to see you" or "I'm sorry." She is only greeted with a sentence that was more of an accusation than a statement of fact.

"And you shot our son."

"He was…a traitor."

"He's your son! And stop talking about him in the past tense."

"He *was*…my son. Liberteum…tortured me. He joined them."

"Rykos helped rescue you, Teman."

Her husband shakes his head. Ilaria pulls up a chair, acutely aware that the Waterside Trauma Center has a version of the Maester system called Hippocrates. It manages all the facility's functions including monitoring and forwarding questionable conversations to the PSS for review. She needs to be careful with the BCS controlling One Guardian Plaza.

"How…do you know?" he struggles to ask.

"Because I asked him to find you. Your guardians never were find Liberteum's location, so I asked for his help. If I hadn't, you'd be dead."

"You sent him…to his death."

"You pulled the trigger. I need to live with the consequences of my decision. So do you. I'm clinging to the hope that he's alive until I know he isn't."

Teman closes his eyes and settles his head deeper into his pillow.

"I don't…want you working for Safmor."

"You don't get to make that decision."

"I'm your…husband."

Ilaria rises and moves the chair to the back wall. She doesn't know if their marriage can be saved. They have twenty years' worth of unresolved issues. Now he may have killed their only son. There is no getting over that, even if she manages to forgive him.

An executive position gives her the excuse to bury herself in work and focus on anything other than their dysfunctional family. She gave up her career for Teman once before. She won't do it again.

 "You are, but I'm no longer charged with raising our children. Accept that. I officially start when Human Resources finalizes my administrative assignment."

"No…you can't."

Ilaria sighs. "I can, and I will. I accepted that you always placed your job before your family. Then you destroyed our family. Now you'll see what it's like to be the second-most important thing in someone's life."

She doesn't look back as she leaves. Ilaria still loves her husband, but he's a hollow shell of that young, strapping guardian she fell for. Their marriage is nothing more than a legal union that she no longer feels compelled to sacrifice for. Those days are over. She is taking control of her destiny now. Whether that will include Teman is something that will need to be decided.

CHAPTER

TEN

LIBERTEUM

New York University Medical Training Facility
NOHO Geographic District
New York City Municipal Corporation

For most of Haven's life, walking into a building was among the most routine and mundane things he could do. It was as simple as walking through a door. Once someone goes off the grid, that singular act takes on a new meaning. He felt it when he walked into the office to initiate the Secaucus explosions. He feels it now.

A holographic generation appears behind the reception desk when Haven enters with his three men. He shakes his head. Everything is automated in this world, even in training facilities. It explains why employees are so helpless.

"Can I help you?" the attractive female holograph asks with a pleasant smile.

"Yes. Where are the medical training rooms?"

"This entire facility is dedicated to training," she says in a helpful voice. "There are designated areas for each medical specialty."

Haven looks at Nyvar, who shrugs. "How about surgical?"

"Down the main corridor, then left, then right. Just follow the signs. Unfortunately, the training center is closed. You will have to return tomorrow."

"Are all the rooms empty?"

"Classes don't begin again until tomorrow morning," the hologram confirms. "Please return at that time."

"Do you have monitoring in this building?" Haven presses, not seeing any evidence of a surveillance system.

"That is privileged information," she says.

"And we are guardians conducting official business as part of an ongoing investigation. Does this building have monitoring capability?"

The woman freezes for a moment before coming back to life. "This facility has a version of Hippocrates for diagnostical training purposes. There is no video or personnel monitoring unless specifically requested by the instructors."

Haven knows educational institutions have a system similar to Hippocrates but can't remember the name. Not that it's important. The system here isn't reporting activity, and that's what matters.

"Thank you. We're going to go check some things out."

"You're welcome, Guardian."

Nyvar grins and shares an incredulous look with Haven before they exit the foyer and follow the corridor.

"The hologram was helpful," Nyvar says as they follow the signs to the surgical center.

"Employees are trained not to question authority," Haven says, "and they write the software. Don't expect it to act differently."

"Do you really think Michele brought Rykos here?"

Haven checks his handgun and positions himself to open the door to the surgical training center. "Let's find out. Ready?"

The men nod. He presses the access button on the wall and the double doors swing open. They burst through them, swinging their weapons left and right to find nothing but an empty corridor.

"Check the rooms."

Nyvar and Symun check the surgical quarters one by one. Haven keeps his weapon pointed down the hall, and Tielur provides rear security while they work. The wing seems empty, but Haven can't stifle the feeling that they aren't alone.

"We have company," Tielur announces.

"What do you think you're doing?" a voice bellows from behind them.

Haven spins and aims, causing heavily armed men dressed in all black to train their rifles on him. He lowers his weapon and relaxes, causing his men to do the same. Nyvar offers a quick sideways glance. He also knows this is trouble.

"What does it look like?" Haven snaps, trying to stay in character.

"Nobody told us there were guardians in the building," the leader of the four-man BCS detail informs him.

"Does that surprise you? Our two organizations hate each other."

The agent's mouth curls up as he relaxes. His team lowers their weapons and walks toward them. Haven shakes the leader's hand when they meet in the middle.

"Who sent you here?"

"I could ask you the same thing."

"I assume you're looking for Rykos and the terrorists. You know the BCS took over that investigation…so why are you here?"

"Didn't they teach you at West Point never to assume?" Haven asks, putting his limited knowledge about the BCS and their training to good use. "If we were searching for terrorists, it wouldn't be dressed like this."

The lead agent looks over his uniform. Guardians performing daily duties wear more ceremonial than functional clothing, armed with only a handgun. Haven is beginning to regret leaving their rifles behind for the sake of appearances.

"We'd also be better armed," Nyvar adds.

"So, why are you here?"

"The RTCC dispatched us in response to an employee complaint. We still do that, unless you're taking over those responsibilities too."

He doesn't react, as though the snide comment was unexpected. "An employee complaint registered in an empty building?"

"That's why they sent four of us to investigate instead of two. Logical, right?"

Haven spots something about the look the agent gives him. There is no trust in it. He finally smiles, but it's all wrong.

"Well, thank you for your initiative, but we'll take it from here. You and your men can leave…maybe even use the extra time to shave."

The comment catches Haven off-guard. Guardians are clean-shaven and meticulously groomed. Haven and his men are neither. The game is up. The agent twitches his trigger finger. That's all the warning that's needed.

Haven raises his weapon and fires two rounds just beneath the agent's body armor. He swings his gun to the right and blasts that agent in the face at point-blank range. The red mist and brain matter turn the gleaming white wall of the corridor into a work of modern art.

Nyvar dispatches the other two BCS agents with similar speed. The BCS team never knew what hit them. Symun and Tielur move to cover positions in case they have reinforcements nearby.

"You should have quit while you were ahead," Haven advises the lead agent writhing on the ground.

He stops moving and stares back at him with fiery hatred in his eyes. Haven trains his weapon on the man's forehead and smiles. It's the last thing he sees before a clean hole is ripped through his forehead.

"Grab their weapons and ammo. We need to search for Michele and get out of here before more of them arrive."

Armed with their newly acquired firepower, his men continue the search. Something feels wrong. Long passageways are dangerous in a gunfight. They can duck into rooms off the corridor but will find themselves pinned down. If Michele is here, she has the advantage.

A man appears from around the corner at the far end of the corridor. He begins walking toward Haven with his hands up. All four of the imposter guardians train their rifles at him.

"Please, don't shoot! I'm just a post-grad here."

"The woman, the patrician, and the injured kid. Where are they?"

"They're just around the corner…they made me help them!"

"Yeah, right," Haven grouses, firing a shot clear through his forehead.

His face doesn't even have time to register surprise. His legs give out, and he crumples to the ground. Alive one second, a corpse the next – just like every employee in this world should be.

The four men surge down the hallway and stop at the corner. Nyvar peeks and catches sight of Michele before she spins on the balls of her feet and trains her weapon in his direction. Then all hell breaks loose.

CHAPTER ELEVEN

RYKOS

New York University Medical Training Facility
NOHO Geographic District
New York City Municipal Corporation

The gunfire causes me to lift my head off the gurney. I catch Nyvar ducking back around the corner before another man appears and fires his rifle. The tug of projectiles in the air around me forces me to bury my head deeper in the pillow.

"It's Haven," Michele shouts, causing Farron to grimace as they wheel me down the corridor faster.

"What? Aw, hell!" Koltayne exclaims.

The corridor opens into a wider vestibule with a pair of extra-wide elevators. Farron activates the sensor and rushes to the minimal safety of the side wall. Koltayne wheels me to the opposite wall and slams the gurney against it. Michele takes position next to Farron, who fires while she reloads.

The elevator chimes its arrival. We're unable to move without exposing ourselves, and we let the doors close. The building is empty, so it isn't going anywhere. That's something, at least.

I can't see much, but everyone stops firing. Haven has us pinned down. The PSS will respond, so time is not on anyone's side. It's a game of chicken. Losing is a matter of who blinks first.

"Quite the predicament you're in, Michele," Haven calls out. "If you try to get on that elevator, it'll be the last thing you ever do."

"Maybe I should just surrender then," she responds, getting a menacing glare from Farron.

"It will go a lot easier for you," Haven warns with a laugh.

"I'm open to ideas," Michele says, looking at the three of us.

"This is it for me," Farron says, sliding a fresh magazine into his weapon. "We don't have the ammo to fight it out."

"I'm down to five rounds," Koltayne adds after checking his ammo count.

I stare at the ceiling. It would be a shame to survive getting shot by my father to die at Haven's hands. I focus on the three nozzles above me. Modern buildings don't use water sprinklers anymore. This is better. We can't run, and we can't fight, but we can be clever.

"Fire," I say, getting looks from the trio.

"We don't have the ammo—"

"No, we need to set a fire. The suppression system is heptaflouropropane. It's a chemical-based mist that neutralizes oxygen. It will reduce visibility long enough for us to get in the elevator."

Michele looks up and then peeks down the hall. Small spouts are spaced about ten feet apart. "You're a genius. Farron, how do we activate the fire suppression system?"

"Start a fire?" he offers with a shrug.

"We can wait here all day, Michele," Haven shouts. "You're outgunned. Don't make this harder than it needs to be."

Michele ignores the warning and points. "Koltayne, check and see if anything is in that trash bin."

"Half full."

"Good. Do you have a light?"

Koltayne digs in his pocket and produces an old stainless steel butane lighter. I have no idea where he got that relic.

"Won't the elevators be locked down once the system activates?" Farron asks.

"Hopefully, they return to the basement," I say. "We're heading in that direction anyway, right?"

"It's a risk."

"Do you have a better idea?" Michele asks. Farron shakes his head. "Light it."

"Time's up, Michele. Say 'hi' to your father for me."

Koltayne lights a few pieces of paper. The fire in the receptacle picks up fast after he drops it in. It won't provide much of a smoke screen, so this will come down to the suppression system. Farron bolts to the elevators to activate the sensor. He retreats as bullets pepper the door. That was close.

"We can still see you," Haven sings. "A smokescreen isn't going to save you.

"Koltayne, focus on getting Rykos loaded. We'll put down fire until we're empty."

"That won't take long," Farron mumbles.

"It doesn't have to."

The doors to the elevator open. "Go!"

The fire suppression system kicks in, and the gas does its job instantly. Visibility up and down the corridor decreases to almost zero. I can hear Haven and his guys coughing. Michele and Farron hold their breath as they fire, forcing Haven and his men to retreat.

Koltayne rushes me into the elevator. Michele and Farron join us after their last rounds are fired. Haven and his men fire wildly. Farron spins and drops to the car's floor, grasping his arm as the doors close. The digital display announces the fire alarm by flashing red and white. It signals that we're returning to the lowest floor.

"Hurts, doesn't it? You okay?" I ask Farron as he climbs to his feet.

"Do I look okay?"

Michele pulls his hand away, revealing a large scratch. "It just grazed you, you big baby. You'll be fine."

The doors open, and we cautiously pile out into the basement. Koltayne sweeps the corridor ahead. This place will be crawling with guardians and BCS agents within minutes, and the fire lockdown won't hold Haven long. Michele wheels me through a series of maintenance passages that connect the campus's buildings and catches up to Koltayne in an underground parking garage.

"Lady's choice," he says.

"We take the ambulance," Farron says. "We'll have a better chance of passing through roadblocks. Can you drive?"

"I've never done it before," Koltayne admits.

"You'll figure it out," Michele says. "Farron, ride up front with him. I'll get in back with Rykos."

We load up, and Koltayne swings the vehicle out of the underground garage after a brief tutorial. Sirens from PSS vehicles wail around us. There's a lot of noise and activity, but nobody stops us. A few moments later, we're out of immediate danger.

"Head east toward the old meat-packing district," Farron says, navigating as Koltayne maintains a death grip on the wheel.

Koltayne complies, clumsily steering us down the street and making turns as Farron directs. When he hits a straightaway, Farron turns in his seat to face the rear.

"We need to link up with the Emissary," she says.

"It's too big a chance. If we get caught with him…."

"I know the risks, Farron. It's our only workable plan."

"Who's the Emissary?" I ask.

Nobody answers as a PSS vehicle speeds past us. I'm not going to get an answer. Sore and still woozy, I rest my head on the pillow as Koltayne tries to drive without killing us.

I'll find out who he is soon enough, I guess. We were fortunate to get out of the training facility alive. Close calls are becoming a habit I could do without. I hope that Haven got caught in their net but am certain he didn't. We were lucky, but not that lucky.

CHAPTER TWELVE

AMERICA, INC.

The White House
Corporate Governance District
Washington-Arlington Municipal Corporation

Fiolla knows this can't be good. The Oval Office is filled with Valen's enemies, which she assumes has been the norm since Zeykala assumed the mantle of corporate leadership. The problem is that she isn't one of them and was still invited.

Every pair of eyes stares at her. She subconsciously straightens her posture and forces herself to cross the carpeted floor into the heart of the gathering. Fiolla stops in front of Valen's old desk and stares at its newest owner as she takes a deep breath.

"You wanted to see me, ma'am?"

"Yes, thank you for joining us. For anyone unaware, this is Executive Fiolla, the White House liaison for Corporate Affairs."

The group nods except for Director Virtari, who offers a hostile glare that he doesn't try to disguise. He made it clear during the melee that followed Valen's removal that he has unfinished business with her.

"We require your expertise. Virtari will explain the situation."

He clears his throat before rising from his seat. "BCS analysts pieced together information earlier today that led to the whereabouts of a key Liberteum leader at New York University's medical training facility. Agents were dispatched and made contact with four men dressed in guardian uniforms. While they were verifying their credentials, the imposters opened fire and killed them."

"That's horrible," Fiolla says, meaning it. Despite despising the BCS and the man running it, those men had families that will mourn their loss.

"We're still trying to determine what happened after that."

"There's no video?"

"The building is a training facility. The Hippocrates system only functions during instructional hours. There was no surveillance."

"The terrorists escaped?"

Fiolla's question is innocent, but Virtari interprets it as a personal affront to his competence. "If the PSS had provided actionable intelligence sooner, we would have moved in with a larger force."

"Fiolla, it appears that public safety has been dragging their feet transferring operational control of the manhunt to Virtari's agents," the CEO says from behind her desk.

"And you want me to help facilitate that?"

Zeykala shares a grin with her BCS director in a way that strikes Fiolla as two people sharing a private joke. The problem isn't that she doesn't get the punch line – it just won't be funny.

"No, we are capable of handling that. I want you to blame the PSS for the murder of the BCS agents."

Fiolla feels the blood drain from her face. "What? That's ridiculous. You just said the guardians were imposters."

Zeykala's face hardens. "If you will all excuse us, I need to talk to Executive Fiolla privately. Virtari, please stay."

The executives beat a hasty retreat from the office after acknowledging the command. Virtari stares at Fiolla like a lion watching its prey on the savanna. She isn't offered a seat on the sofa, so this will be an uncomfortable conversation.

"Fiolla, you assured me before Valen's hearing that your loyalty was to the CEO of America Incorporated. Do you remember that conversation?"

"Yes."

"Good. That saves me from having to remind you. I hope you meant what you said. Despite what you may think, I believe you have a bright future here."

"Thank you, ma'am."

"Don't thank me yet. You excel at your job, Fiolla, and your words carry weight. The problem is that I question your loyalty, and that's not something you want me to annotate in your next performance review."

Fiolla wants to tell her where she can stick it, but that would end her career. Valen told her in the Solarium that he needed her to keep her job in the White House. He's her mentor, and she will oblige even if it means lying to the chief executive officer.

"I meant what I said. I serve America Incorporated."

Fiolla catches Virtari rolling his eyes. It will take actions, not words to convince him. Even then, he'll still harbor doubts. BCS agents are born skeptics, and their directors are known to be neurotic.

Zeykala purses her lips before nodding. "We'll see. Coordinate with Public Affairs to release this footage. Instruct them to blame the New York Municipal Corporation's Public Safety and Security."

"Of course, ma'am. If I may ask…what's the desired result?"

"First, the NYCMC seems to have forgotten its place. Municorps serve the parent company by administering living environments. Second, and more importantly, because I said so. To serve the corporation is to serve me. Do you have a problem with that?"

"No, ma'am," Fiolla says confidently, despite having a big problem with it. "I'm only seeking to confirm the desired objective."

Zeykala nods, offering a weak smile. "The PSS may not respect Virtari's authority, but they will respect mine. *That's* the desired objective."

"I understand. I'll get right on it."

"I know you will. Make it convincing. You are the Corporate Affairs liaison and have a reputation for fixing problems. If you can't compel AME News to report what's needed, I'll begin to question whether your services are required here."

CHAPTER THIRTEEN
INTERCORPEX

Lyris's Domicile
Battery Park City District
New York City Municipal Corporation

Two feminine voices can be heard from outside the bathroom. Lyris heard the door chime sound, and he assumes Nevala answered it. None of that was disconcerting until he recognized the second voice. Now he's strongly considering locking himself in here.

Nevala is not the jealous type, but she has perpetual insecurity about their relationship. He hasn't done much to assuage that. Another beautiful Asian woman appearing at his domicile without warning or explanation will only exacerbate her anxiety.

"Let her in, Nevala," Lyris says, seeing the standoff at his door after emerging from the bathroom.

Nevala steps aside, wearing her suspicion on her sleeve as Chiana enters.

"This is Chief Inspector Chiana with ICX Security. She handled my Zyree problem. Or was *supposed* to."

"Nice place. Who's your guest?"

"I'm Nevala, personal assistant to Administrator-General Raimius."

"And you're here with Lyris. How cozy."

"Now that the introductions are over," Lyris interjects before things get ugly, "what are you doing here, Chiana?"

"I was just released from PSS detention and knew you would want to see me before I report to Zurich."

Chiana intended to make that sound suspicious. Nevala folds her arms and welds them across her chest.

"Why were you detained?"

"I tried to kill Chief Inspector Zyree. Do you have something to drink around here?"

Nevala cocks her head at Lyris. He obliquely suggested that during their stroll through the gallery, but he didn't anticipate her failure. She doesn't strike him as someone who settles for getting less than what she wants.

"I'll get you one," Lyris says, heading for the liquor decanter on top of the credenza.

"Why would you try to kill another chief inspector?" Nevala asks.

"Because Lyris asked me to while we were sharing some quiet time."

The former director winces. When he returns with a glass of Irish whiskey, Nevala's accusatory stare nearly freezes him in place. "I need to speak to Chief Inspector Chiana alone."

"Oh, I don't think so."

Chiana flashes an amused look as she removes her black security jacket to reveal a tight undershirt that hugs her magnificent shape. Lyris lets his eyes linger a little too long as she drapes the garment over the back of the sofa and makes herself comfortable.

"What happened in the crypt?"

"We were breaching the terrorist stronghold under the church. They were firing from crypts, so we moved down the main corridor behind a track-mounted shield wall. I went in with Zyree and a guardian to clear a burial chamber. Once the deed was done, I saw an opportunity to eliminate him and took it."

"And failed," Lyris says, not worrying about offending her considering the strife she's causing with Nevala.

"The guardian we were with blind-sided me. If Chief Inspector Zyree was easy to kill, he'd have been dead long ago."

Lyris shakes his head. "Now what?"

"Zyree requested a formal inquiry into my conduct. I have already ensured that the corroborating evidence was…corrupted."

"What evidence?" Nevala asks.

"Guardians have cameras on their body armor. Zyree obtained the footage from the man in the room and forwarded it to Zurich with his report. It was intercepted and purposely degraded."

"How?"

"Loyalty is earned in my business. In this case, a good friend at the Cyber Operations Directorate took care of it."

"None of that explains why you're here," Nevala says, searching for the explanation she still hasn't received.

"I've thrown up some obstacles, but they won't hold forever. The commissioner-general will learn the truth, and then I'm finished. I'm going to need your help."

Lyris frowns. He has problems of his own. Raimius relieved him from his position as executive director of global operations. His future at Intercorpex is hazy. Denali Keating is his last hope, but he can't divulge that to Chiana. Trust only goes so far.

"I would love to help, but I'm not in a position to exert any influence on Jurghen."

"That's too bad," Chiana says, rising from the sofa and grabbing her jacket.

With her back to Nevala, she makes a show of putting it on for Lyris's benefit. He gets one last look at every curve before they get hidden away beneath the synthetic fibers of her uniform.

"You're going to need me, Lyris. You might not know how or why, but you will. Once I report to Zurich, I will no longer be of any service to you. Loyalty has value, but in this case, it also has an expiration date. It was nice to meet you, Nevala."

Nevala sits on his couch without a word once the door closes behind Chiana. Silence can be an effective weapon, and Nevala wields it like a katana.

"I can explain that," Lyris blurt outs too eagerly.

"Can you?" she asks with a hint of sarcastic innocence.

"We had an unspoken agreement that Zyree's removal would be in our interests. That's it."

"I see." Her body language conveys a different message than her words.

"She's ICX Security, Nevala. The ability to crawl under people's skin makes her good at her job. She sensed you didn't like her and irritated you on purpose."

"She's right. I don't like her and don't trust her. Why did you hide that from me?"

"It wasn't on purpose," Lyris explains. "Zyree is a pain in my ass, and Chiana won't be promoted to commissioner-general over him. It seemed like a solution to both problems."

"And by failing, she created a bigger one. If Denali makes you AG after Raimius is gone, you handed her the only leverage she'll ever need against you."

"Having a loyal ally running ICX Security will be useful."

"Lyris, allies only work together so long as their interests are aligned," Nevala says, taking Lyris's face in her hands and looking him in the eyes. "What happens when they aren't?"

She holds his gaze long enough to drive her point home before turning and leaving the domicile. As the door closes behind her, it dawns on him that she wasn't talking about Chiana; she was talking about herself. Nevala has always been loyal, but she just put him on notice about what happens if he dares cross her.

CHAPTER FOURTEEN

THE PATRICIANS

Keating Family of the Gentez-Majorez Estate
Greenwich Geographic District
Southern Connecticut Municipal Corporation

Denali settled on having a late lunch served on the back patio. Or an early dinner. It doesn't matter what his staff calls it. He's a patrician who can tell his chef to make him a meal whenever he pleases. It's Sunday, and he wants to spend at least part of this beautiful spring day outside his study.

The heavy doors swing open, and he expects it to be his meal being brought out by a pair of servants. He was wrong. The commander emerges and strides up to him, looking tired and agitated.

"Lacune, I never see you outside the ops center unless you're bearing bad news."

"I'm afraid that trend is about to continue, sir. We've managed to locate your son."

That gets Denali's undivided attention. "Where?"

"The PSS has footage of him on a Brown Line SpeedRail heading north from lower Manhattan."

Denali wrinkles his brow. Farron doesn't use public transportation, but that isn't something he would characterize as "bad" news.

"So what?"

"He was identified alongside the leader of Liberteum, Registrant Rykos, and another man. They have the means to link the Keating family with the Liberteum terrorists."

Okay, *that* is bad news. Denali stands and moves to the marble railing so he can stare out at the Long Island Sound. It was inevitable that the rumored connection with Liberteum was confirmed. It just wasn't supposed to happen this soon. It also shouldn't have been that easy.

"Why was my idiot son on a SpeedRail with her?"

"We don't know. My source in the PSS claimed that Rykos appeared injured. They also have after-action reports that claim Chief Guardian Teman shot him during his rescue at Old St. Patrick's."

"He shot his son?"

"Apparently."

None of that explains why Farron was at that Liberteum stronghold. He was supposed to distance himself from Michele, not stand next to her during a PSS raid. Denali needs to know why he's doing this and has failed to maintain contact.

"Where is he now, Lacune?"

"We don't know, sir. They exited the SpeedRail near NYU and disappeared."

Denali scowls. The family doesn't have any assets in that area. He has no idea where his son could have gone.

"Our teams near the church during the PSS raid didn't spot them?"

"They must have used underground passages. We had no presence down there."

"Damn tunnel rat urches," Denali grumbles.

He tightens his jaw. Farron is going to have a lot of explaining to do. His son's involvement is integral to his plan. He can't understand why the entitled brat is being so cavalier when he's destined to inherit unlimited power.

"Thank you, Commander. Keep me informed."

Lacune steps off as the meal arrives. Denali has lost his appetite. First, it was Farron's enchantment with Fiolla, that young executive at the White House. Now he seems to still be overly chummy with the leader of Liberteum. What is it with this generation? They are so weak and impressionable.

Denali decides to leave his meal and go for a walk. A visit to the garden will help him think and hopefully improve his mood. There are a lot of variables to his plan. Moves and countermoves. He didn't expect his son to be one of them. It's something he will have to deal with. The first warning he gave Farron seems not to have resonated. The second one will need to leave more of an impression.

News: Details emerge of the shootout at NYU: NY PSS accused of attacking corporate security ... Intercorpex Global Index (IGI): No Data ***MARKETS CLOSED*** ... Corporations applying pressure to ICX administrator–general for outage statement ...

CHAPTER
FIFTEEN

INTERCORPEX

Former Liberteum Safehouse
Tribeca Geographic District
New York City Municipal Corporation

Zyree pushes the door open and eases into the high-end Tribeca domicile. Patricians have no home automation reporting, and the BCS disabled the security system. The sensors on his new biocomp aren't picking up movement. It pays to be cautious, so they clear each room. The place is empty.

"Do you know what hell will rain down if the BCS catches us here?" Malkor asks.

"Do you think I give a damn? Besides, they have bigger problems."

The two men take separate paths around the open floor plan. Farron's trendy guest domicile is nice despite still being under construction. Complete with box trim, crown molding, expensive marble, and a high-end digital entertainment system, it's a comfortable space despite being unfinished. Zyree bets it's far better than Liberteum's usual accommodations.

"What are you looking for? Any valuable evidence was removed a long time ago."

"There's more to investigating than just searching for evidence. You need to understand motives. Finding them helps to get in the heads of your adversaries."

"And you think walking around one of Farron Keating's bachelor pads helps?"

Zyree slowly continues his walk. This is a brilliant place to hide. Teman ordered subterranean security sweeps, so Michele found herself a refuge aboveground. This building would never have been checked even had the PSS started street-level searches.

"Would you ever have looked for them here?" Zyree asks.

"Sure...after searching every other building on this island," Malkor says with a grin.

This place still has energy. Zyree can't describe it, but he can feel it tickling his nervous system. He moves over to the window and looks down at the street below. He has no doubt that Michele enjoyed this same view. After a spending the sum of her life in the dingy and confined spaces of the underground, the change of perspective would have been irresistible.

A message pops up on Zyree's contacts from ICX Security Headquarters in Zurich. The communique is addressed to all inspectors. He scans the directive sent at the request of Administrator-General Raimius and lets out an exasperated sigh.

"Is he serious?" Malkor asks after reading his message. "New York has been victimized by several major attacks from terrorists who, for those keeping score, are still at large. Yet, somehow, Raimius thinks it's a swell idea to host a meeting of the world's most powerful patricians here?"

"Apparently."

"That's moronic. Why not hold the meeting in Paris or Rome?"

"He's desperate to restore confidence in the exchange," Zyree explains. "It has to be at Intercorpex Headquarters."

"You don't sound surprised."

"Stupidity doesn't surprise me anymore. The higher up the food chain you go, the worse it is."

Zyree meanders down the hall to the bedrooms. Everything has been removed. He scans the walls and notes the data displayed on his augmented contacts. Nothing was hanging on them.

Malkor is impatiently fidgeting in the living area, paranoid over a possible encounter with the BCS. Satisfied that he's seen all he can, Zyree closes his eyes and stands motionless. He focuses on the energy…the feeling.

"I can't get a handle on them," the chief inspector says, opening his eyes after a few long moments.

"Handle on whom?"

"Liberteum."

"They're terrorists, boss," Malkor says with a sneer. "What more is there to understand?"

"A lot."

"They completed their mission when they took down the exchange. And you know what? It wasn't the apocalypse they hoped for. Society is more resilient than they thought. Good for us."

There was no shortage of experts who maintained that ceasing trading for a single day would have a cataclysmic effect on the world economy. Some corporate news outlets speculate that the shutdown's impact hasn't been felt yet. It doesn't matter who is right…it feels incomplete.

"Maybe Liberteum doesn't plan on stopping at that."

"Zyree, I love you like a brother, but you're starting to sound like Raimius."

"Do you remember what Liberteum means?"

"Free them."

"That's right," Zyree says, moving to the kitchen counter and leaning against it. "As in liberating humanity from the bonds of corporate servitude. What if Liberteum has a bigger plan to 'free the people'?"

"Did this empty domicile tell you that?"

Zyree ignores him. Things don't add up. Terrorists kidnapped Rykos but left his friend Balin behind. Then they let him go instead of killing him. They tried to hack the exchange but could easily have used the gas mains in the old Broad Street Station to flood the NOC basement with fumes and blow it up. And then there's Michele letting Zyree live. Liberteum is capable of killing thousands or tens of thousands of people and hasn't.

"Let's assume you're right," Malkor says, interrupting Zyree's train of thought. "How would they do it beyond crippling ICX?"

"Taking down our current system isn't fundamentally different than destroying a pre-collapse government. The first thing you do is divide your opponents."

"The bombing in Secaucus pitted Intercorpex, the patricians, and corporations against each other."

"Yes, although I don't think that was their only intent. Step two is creating a crisis."

"They did that by taking the exchange offline," the junior inspector says, nodding. "And the next step?"

"It's the one I'm worried about: Force leaders to make unpopular decisions."

"Turn the people against those in power," Malkor says, getting with the program. "That could get ugly fast. What's the final step?"

"Present an alternative."

"You mean like anarchy?"

Zyree shakes his head. "Nobody wants to return to that. Whatever they have in mind, Rykos is a key part of it. I just don't know how."

Of all the mysteries surrounding Liberteum, his involvement is the most baffling. Did he join them, or is he being used? Was this always part of the plan or a coincidence? He hopes that he can ask Michele someday.

"Do you really think a small group of terrorists can change the world? I mean, it'd be like—"

"Boiling the ocean?"

The business term fits. "Boiling the ocean" is an old expression that employees used when executives had them undertake a project or task that was too complex or grand in scope. Liberteum's mission is both.

"Yeah, something like that."

Zyree looks around the room. The realization hits him like a sledgehammer.

"All you need to boil an ocean is to light the world on fire. If you wanted to create global chaos, how would you do it?"

Malkor shrugs.

"Can you think of a better target than a meeting of patricians?"

He shakes his head. "No way. Not possible. Intercorpex Headquarters will be a fortress."

Malkor is right. That campus will be the most secure location on Earth. Then again, the exchange was thought to be impenetrable. Liberteum has already turned impossible feats into reality.

"We're done here. Come on."

"Where are we going?" he asks, relieved.

"We can't stop Raimius from packing the dynamite, so we'll need to stop Liberteum from lighting the fuse."

CHAPTER SIXTEEN

AMERICA, INC.

NYCMC Executive Center (NEC)
Municipal Governance Geographic District
New York City Municipal Corporation

Ilaria has been in this building a thousand times, including six hours ago. Most days, she's seen corporate minions going about accomplishing their daily tasks. Even on high-stress days, there was nothing more than an elevated buzz in the building. This is different. The staff is harried, and she is walked directly into the CEO's office.

"Thank you for rushing back so quickly, Ilaria," Safmor says, moving around his desk and stepping into the middle of his office to shake her hand.

"I came over as soon as I could. What's going on?"

"I'm afraid I need you to start your new position early. I know that this is a difficult time, so if—"

"Let's begin," she says without a moment's hesitation.

"Are you sure? I'm sure Teman wants to spend time with you after what he went through."

"Teman understands duty to the NYCMC better than anyone."

She knows she sold the lie. Ilaria doesn't believe her husband understands duty despite having used it as an excuse for twenty years. Abandoning him at the medical center was a horrible thing to do, and Safmor won't understand why without a lengthy explanation.

"Very well, then let me be the first to welcome you aboard. Send him in," Safmor says after turning his head. Seconds later, an older uniformed guardian enters. "Ilaria, please allow me to introduce Constable Dzamko. He's the acting chief guardian until your husband is well enough to return to his post."

"Constable," she says, shaking his hand.

"Ilaria is our new managing director of Business Development."

Director Ilaria. She smiles at the thought of her new title. It's something she looks forward to hearing people use.

"Congratulations, ma'am," Dzamko says as they sit on the sofas. "We have a serious problem. Three hours ago, the Bureau of Corporate Security was investigating a lead into the possible whereabouts of Liberteum at the NYU Medical Training Facility when an incident occurred."

Ilaria's heart jumps into her throat. The word "incident" is used in common vernacular to marginalize the seriousness of something bad. As a business development executive, she wouldn't be here, even in an advisory capacity, unless this had something to do with Rykos.

"Why were they there?"

"The RTCC uncovered SpeedRail video surveillance of Liberteum's leader, a henchman, and two others. One of them was Farron Keating."

"As in the son of Denali Keating?"

"Yes."

"That's a little surprising. And the fourth individual?"

Dzamko shifts his eyes over to Safmor, who exhales sharply. "Facial recognition identified him as your son."

"So, Rykos is alive," Ilaria whispers, closing her eyes after the initial shock.

"We should have known sooner. Our computers flagged the incident, but we didn't have the manpower to review it following the massacre on the SpeedRail."

"I understand. Thank you for the information, but what does this have to do with the BCS?"

"The four of them got off at University Square," Safmor explains.

"The terrorists couldn't walk Rykos into a medical center for treatment," Dzamko adds. "We think one of them had a contact at the medical university who performed surgery on your son during the three-day break."

"Do you know who operated?"

"Medical Post-Graduate Jekshun."

"Did you interview him?"

Dzamko shakes his head. "He was found dead in the corridor."

Ilaria deflates at the news. Every time she resigns herself to losing Rykos, he pops back up. She needs this emotional ride to end, preferably with him safe at home.

"Who killed him, the BCS or Liberteum?"

Dzamko casts a wary eye at Safmor before turning back to Ilaria. "Neither. According to the Pentagon, we did."

"I don't understand."

"This will help. Gotham," he commands his office assistant, "turn on the main display."

Unlike most executives, the CEO of the New York Municipal Corporation keeps the digital assistant's name. She doesn't know how or why "Gotham" was chosen, but that's been the name since the system was installed.

The large display inset into the wall comes to life tuned into AME News. The chyron tells the story better than the reporter: *New York City Guardians Kill BCS Agents at NYU Med.*

The report runs raw body cam footage of men conversing with the PSS. An instant later, you see a guardian pull out a weapon and fire. The video changes as the agent falls to the ground. The final shot is of the guardian standing over him.

"To recap," the reporter summarizes, "one medical trainee and four corporate security agents are dead, apparently at the hands of the New York City Municipal Corporation's Public Safety and Security. As of this time, there is no statement from the PSS refuting the allegations, and both the Pentagon and the BCS's New York field office have yet to comment.

"This is a fast-moving story, and we will bring you updates as we get them. To discuss more on the impact of this incident and what it means, we turn to—"

"Gotham, mute the display."

"Please tell me your people didn't do this," Ilaria pleads.

"They didn't," Dzamko confirms.

"Then the BCS faked the bodycam footage?"

"No, the RTCC authenticated the video," Dzamko says. "I'm saying that those men aren't guardians. Sir?"

"Gotham, display the video segment transferred from the RTCC," Safmor commands. "Fast forward to time index…seventeen eleven. Play at one-quarter speed and enable motion control."

"The uniforms are ours," Dzamko says as the video inches along, "but look closely. Your husband is a strict man, Ilaria. He insisted rules be followed without exception. What's wrong with this picture?"

The video pauses with the "guardian" standing over the agent. Ilaria leans closer to the display.

"He isn't clean-shaven."

"Correct. Now, he could have been working extra shifts and not had time, so we dug deeper. That led us to this."

Dzamko calls up an official PSS file. "This man's name is Haven. He's listed as a deceased inspector with Intercorpex Security. We know him better as the deputy of Liberteum behind the SpeedRail massacre and the man who captured and tortured your husband."

Ilaria is shocked beyond words. She's staring at the face of evil. The facial recognition is a one-hundred percent match. These men were imposters, and the BCS is lying about it.

"Safmor, you need to tell the BCS."

"We did. They didn't respond."

"Then get a correction out to AME News!" Ilaria exclaims.

"We did that, too," the CEO says, settling deeper into the sofa. "It was sent to Public Affairs as soon as we made the match. They ran their story anyway."

"Hostility between the PSS and BCS is no secret to executives, but it's not something employees know much about," Dzamko explains. "I believe our new CEO is using this incident to keep the BCS in charge of our security."

"By lying?"

"Yes, and it doesn't end there. They're also blaming Teman."

The surge of anger causes Ilaria's face to turn bright red. The consequences will be severe if they succeed in making Teman a scapegoat.

"What? He's in a hospital bed! How could he possibly have anything to do with this?"

"According to Director Virtari, he left standing orders not to cooperate with the BCS, and those instructions are being followed by most of the PSS."

"That's insane."

Safmor leans forward and steeples his hands. "I know it is, you know it is, and Dzamko knows it is…but the employees will believe it."

"Okay. How do we fight this?"

"We can't, at least not directly. We're not going to win this round no matter what we do."

Ilaria crosses her arms. "I don't accept that. I don't care who's in charge down in Washington. We cannot let them usurp our authority to satisfy their lust for power."

Under normal circumstances, those words would be considered subversive. Right now, Ilaria doesn't care.

"I told you she'd be right for this job, didn't I?" Safmor says to Dzamko, eliciting a nod. "We'll continue to plead our case, but you're here for a specific reason: I need you to visit AME News and tell them the truth."

"About this?"

"About everything. Tell them about your son, Teman, what you know of Liberteum, the PSS, and what I just showed you. Tell them all of it."

"What good will that do? AME News works for the parent corporation."

"The truth is ugly, but it's on our side. They need to recognize that," Dzamko says.

"Chief Executive Zeykala gives the orders, but the employees who work at AME News aren't unthinking slaves to the propaganda machine. At least, not like their corporate masters think they should be."

"You want me to use my business development position to get in the door and find a sympathetic ear. Got it. What if I find one?"

Dzamko joins Safmor in leaning forward. "Bend it."

CHAPTER SEVENTEEN

THE PATRICIANS

The White House
Corporate Governance District
Washington-Arlington Municipal Corporation

Zeykala folds her hands in front of her on the desk and stares hard into the camera. She's used to being stern and commanding, but not when her image is being broadcast live to millions of employees.

"We're still trying to determine the circumstances surrounding the murders of our corporate security agents in New York. Be assured that we will not rest until those responsible for this tragic incident are held accountable. Know that our thoughts and prayers are with the families of those brave corporate protectors."

She looks down at the desk as the words hang in the air. Zeykala has no idea whether those men had families. The BCS agents might as well be grown in a lab considering the way they are cultivated and groomed. Employees need to be sympathetic to their sacrifice, and families suffering a loss has the required psychological impact.

"In light of these events and the ongoing terrorist manhunt, I'm declaring an emergency in the New York City Municipal Corporation. All employees within its geographical limits will be expected to adhere to curfew and travel protocols. I sincerely hope that these temporary measures will help us return to normal business activities as soon as possible.

"These are difficult times that we will overcome. Today's tribulations will make us stronger tomorrow than we were yesterday. America Incorporated will continue to be the standard by which all other corporations are measured. That is my solemn vow. Thank you."

"And...we're out," the AME News producer says once the red light over the camera clicks off.

There is some polite clapping from the executives lining the walls of the Oval Office. The new CEO was hoping for more enthusiasm about her positive speech and got this anemic response instead.

"Bravo, Zeykala, bravo," Talya Bettancourt mocks, emerging from behind the group while clapping slowly and deliberately. The room falls silent. "It's almost like you were meant for this position."

"Everyone, stop what you're doing," Zeykala barks. "Give us the room. You can pack your equipment after we finish."

The executives head back to their offices, and the AME News crew shuffles out into the hallway. Talya impatiently waits as the last of them leave. When the door finally closes, she rewards the world's most powerful CEO with a scolding look a parent gives misbehaving children.

"You know, it pays to be polite to your staff. A 'please' or 'thank you' helps maintain morale."

"I'm here to run a corporation, not coddle employees."

"Suit yourself."

"What can I do for you, Patrician Bettancourt?"

"Patrician Bettancourt? It's *Prima* Bettancourt, and you can start by explaining why you didn't make it clear that I still hold that title."

The *prima* patrician is the largest shareholder of any corporation. They are determined by Intercorpex and are certified either by the board of directors or CEO, depending on the corporate charter. The larger the corporation, the more power the *prima* has within the community of elites.

The Bettancourt family has held the most shares of America Incorporated since trading began. It was a shock to everyone in the chamber when Shalius Covington marched into Valen's hearing and announced he had acquired enough stock to displace her. It's also why Intercorpex's determination about those trades is so important – upholding them would mark a seismic shift in power from the Bettancourts to the Covingtons.

"I've been a little busy," Zeykala says as Talya moves to the window to stare out at the Rose Garden.

It's an hour before twilight, and the angle of the sun casts long shadows in the garden. Talya has no interest in admiring the view. She knows how to avoid the psychological games that executives play and doesn't want to have a conversation with a desk between them.

"Then perhaps you require a refresher course in prioritization."

"Intercorpex hasn't reopened the exchange, nor have they determined the status of trades made during the anomaly."

"Yes, I'm aware of that," Talya snaps.

"I don't have the power to name the *prima*. That is the exchange's responsibility."

"I distinctly remember you once railing about the power Intercorpex wields over its member corporations. You accused Valen of cozying up to them, yet haven't taken a single step to begin liberating America Incorporated from the exchange's grip."

Zeykala hates having her words thrown back at her. That's precisely why Talya used them.

"I'll have more leverage once my appointment to this office becomes permanent. Then I will do *exactly* as I said I would."

"You don't need leverage to do the right thing. You have a reputation for getting things done, Zeykala, so why am I doing all the work?"

"I got Valen removed. It was unpopular with the executives, and I need their support to—"

"*I* got Valen removed," Talya interjects. "And the executives will fall in line because *you* are their chief executive officer, not because you beg for their support."

"I'm not begging for anything."

Talya narrows her eyes. "Aren't you? I need you to be an effective CEO, not a popular one."

She has maintained an effective working relationship with Zeykala because they have shared ambitions. She got what she wanted with Valen's removal: this office. Now she needs to remember why Talya installed her here.

"You're right. I've neglected your rightful claim to be *prima*. I promise to give it the attention it deserves."

Talya is undeterred by the sudden change of direction. "By waiting for ICX to make a decision?"

"By rectifying the wrong done to your family. I will petition the board of directors to take up the matter when they convene. Even if Intercorpex doesn't negate the trades, they can choose not to recognize Shalius's claim."

"I'm glad we could reach a consensus," Talya says, now having gotten what she wanted. "Good evening, Chief Executive Zeykala."

The *prima* strides out of the Oval Office knowing that the new chief executive is imagining how her back would look riddled with bullet holes. It doesn't matter. Zeykala is a useful idiot. So long as she plays her part, she can envision whatever she wishes. Talya has her own ambitions to tend to.

CHAPTER EIGHTEEN

LIBERTEUM

"The Motor Pool"
Hell's Kitchen Geographic District
New York City Municipal Corporation

Weapons maintenance is Haven's time to think. The mindless work allows his thoughts to wander, only they continue drifting back to the same thing. They took a massive risk going downtown and barely escaped the medical training facility with their lives. That would sit better with him had they achieved their mission. Instead, he lost another opportunity to finish Michele off once and for all.

"Haven?" Tielur says after poking his head into the small room that once served as a shop office. "You need to see this."

He doesn't complain about the request despite leaving strict instructions that he was not to be disturbed. He knows his men. The summons means it is something important. Haven rises from the small, sturdy table and follows his subordinate into the garage.

This structure has been in disuse since the collapse. Unlike much of Manhattan, the Hell's Kitchen area of the city hasn't undergone an urban renewal. That suits their purpose. This facility once held a fleet of delivery or utility vehicles and is the perfect place to hide their ground transportation assets. So long as they use the underground accesses, there is no reason for the PSS to ever come looking for them here.

"We found this guy poking around outside," Symun says while holding a gun to the man's head.

"Kindly tell your man to remove his weapon," the impeccably dressed man says in a British accent that makes him sound more distinguished than he is. Having dealt with him several times, Haven thinks he's more likely from Staten Island than the British Isles.

Haven nods, and Symun holsters his weapon. "What are you doing here, Abbot? Running another errand for your master?"

"I serve at the pleasure of Denali Keating and the Keating family. Some of my duties are more…unsavory than others," he offers in his typical condescending manner.

"Can we just kill this piece of trash?" Nyvar asks.

"Yes, that would be a sound tactical decision. Unleash your capricious bravado and further antagonize your bourgeois benefactor by eliminating his most trusted confidant. How could that possibly go wrong?"

"What?" Nyvar asks, not understanding any of Abbot's snobby words.

"And in what way have I disappointed his highness?" Haven mocks with a bow, mimicking Abbot's accent.

Abbot doesn't appear to take any offense. "I think you know. Our arrangement called for certain actions to be taken in a certain order. Now that the exchange is offline, your antagonist is supposed to be dead. Yet, that has not happened."

Haven wants to snap the twerp's neck. Denali has an army capable of handling that task but knows Michele is wily and street smart. She's a survivor, and killing her was never going to be as easy as snapping a finger. That's why Haven was instructed to finish her.

"It's proving to be more problematic than I thought."

"I would not have guessed that a hundred-pound girl could overpower a mad dog like you—twice, as I understand. She is either a formidable adversary, or your skills aren't as advertised."

"It's actually been three times now, not two. She'd be dead if Farron didn't intervene."

"Yes, well, I suppose an entitled young patrician would be quite the challenge for a seasoned, former ICX inspector in a gunfight. He has been trap shooting once or twice."

"Is that why you're here, Abbot? To ridicule me? Because if Denali has something to say, perhaps he should climb down from his ivory tower and tell me to my face."

"Well-respected patricians of the *gentez-majorez* do not keep company with rabble. That's why they employ men such as me."

"I don't like being treated like a pawn on some rich man's chessboard," Haven says, moving to within inches of Abbot's face.

To his credit, the manservant doesn't flinch. In fact, he looks amused. Threats of physical violence won't spook him.

"We are all pawns, Haven. That is the world in which we live and the world I believe you are attempting to destroy."

The terrorist grins before walking over and leaning against one of the parked vehicles. "Is Denali going to dispose of me once I'm no longer useful?"

Abbot chuckles. "Michele is a crusader. You, on the other hand, are a wild animal. He knows you will meet your fate on your own terms—perhaps in a hail of gunfire during some epic last stand?"

"Right. Why are you here, Abbot?" Haven asks, tiring of this conversation.

"I have been entrusted to inform you that the meeting at Intercorpex is tomorrow at nine a.m. I am to report whether you are ready to proceed as planned."

"The meeting is Thursday at eleven," Nyvar insists.

"No, it isn't. The meeting is tomorrow, and you will execute the plan exactly thirty minutes after it is scheduled to begin."

"I don't understand. That's not what AME News is reporting."

"You're like a dull instrument, Haven – deadly, but not all that sharp. The administrators at Intercorpex aren't going to announce the actual date and time of such a critical meeting knowing that homicidal terrorists are still on the loose."

Haven presses his lips together, annoyed that he didn't identify such an obvious misdirection. He doesn't like being called dull, especially by this pretentious prick. When this is over, Abbot had better hope they don't meet again.

"We'll be ready."

"Excellent. I will inform Patrician Keating. This is now your primary mission and sole focus. Do not draw unnecessary attention to yourselves. Once you have finished, you may murder and rampage through the city to your heart's content."

Haven bristles at the orders. He abhorred taking them from Intercorpex, Michele, and even her father. He keeps his objections to himself because Denali Keating is providing the opportunity of his dreams – revenge. In just over twenty-four hours, he will strike a blow that will never be forgotten. There's just one order of business to worry about.

"What about Michele?" Haven calls out as his men escort Abbot to an exit.

"She is no longer your concern. We will take care of her."

CHAPTER NINETEEN

AMERICA, INC.

The White House
Corporate Governance District
Washington-Arlington Municipal Corporation

Fiolla looks around the theater as she makes her way down the center aisle. The small cinema features red walls with rectangular gold inlaid designs and tiered seating for about forty people. Other than being fitted with state-of-the-art sound and video equipment, the décor and style of the room strike her as authentically pre-collapse.

"I'm sorry I'm late, sir," she says, easing herself into the red upholstered seat next to his.

"It's okay. Shhh." He presses a finger over his lips as he returns his gaze to the big screen.

The film he's watching was filmed in black in white. It's a far cry from the color-corrected, ultra-high-definition, propaganda-laced drivel emanating from Hollywood in the Corporate Age. Captivated by the movie, Valen pays Fiolla no attention for a few minutes before finally speaking.

"I'm sorry, I love that part. Have you ever been in here before?" he whispers, now only half-watching the screen.

"I never knew it existed."

"This is one of the best perks of being CEO. I'm going to miss it."

"I didn't know you were a movie fan, sir."

Valen shakes his head. "I'm not—at least not of anything from this era. That's the perk I was referring to: I have access to the film vault."

"What are you watching?"

"*Mr. Smith Goes to Washington.*"

"I've never heard of it," Fiolla admits.

"I'm not surprised. It was released in 1939 and is on the banned list." She gives him a disapproving look. "Like I told you – perks. It's about a naïve politician who goes to Washington to fight corruption in the government."

Fiolla nods, understanding why it's on the banned list. "Some things never change, do they?"

"No, they don't. Speaking of which, do you have any news for me?"

"Intercorpex scheduled the summit with the patricians for tomorrow morning at their New York headquarters. The media announced it for later in the week as a security measure."

Valen nods slowly but says nothing.

"What's bothering you, sir? You aren't yourself. I mean, even considering the position you're in."

"There's some—" He stops abruptly and grimaces. "What's everyone saying about Zeykala?"

"That she's a tyrant. Executives in the subsidiaries are upset at the prospect of having to work with her."

"Zeykala's nickname used to be 'Iron Face,'" he says with a laugh. "It was chosen because she never smiles. She's cold, calculating, and ran her company with dispassion. She achieved results at the cost of universal hatred for her. That reputation was why the board passed her over for CEO."

"And now everyone's worst nightmare has come true."

"It was my fault," Valen says quietly, staring at his hands.

Fiolla knows that Valen takes responsibility for everything that happens to the corporation. This is taking it a bit far. There's no way he could have known what the terrorists had planned or how the board of directors would react to it.

"What do you mean?"

"You're a top executive in America Incorporated, Fiolla. If I tell you more, it could put you in grave danger."

"I already am in danger."

He studies her for a long moment, and she holds his gaze. Valen doesn't use words like "grave danger" lightly. Most executives would walk away, but she has already taken sides in this political tug-of-war, for better or worse.

"All right. Everything that's happened – the failures against Liberteum, the attacks on Intercorpex – I brought them on myself."

"I don't understand."

He leans back in his chair. "Only three people in the world know what I'm about to tell you, and two of them are dead. Three years ago, five specially trained BCS agents were dispatched to the New York underground. They were under deep cover as urches, and their mission was to infiltrate Liberteum and gather intelligence on the group's activities. Four failed, but one of them succeeded."

"What?"

"I have someone on the inside, Fiolla. The asset has been in place for a while."

"You…." She stops, too stunned to speak.

"It's okay. Ask the question."

Fiolla swallows hard. "You knew about the Secaucus and Wall Street attacks before they happened?"

Valen nods. "I know Liberteum's entire plan, but my complicity is deeper than that. I provided my asset with what Liberteum needed to breach the PSS's emergency operations center and seize control of the PSS drones."

Fiolla's jaw hangs open. What he's admitting to is nothing short of treason against the same corporation he was entrusted to lead. Worse, she's now an accomplice. He meant "grave danger" when he said it.

"And the recent 'anomaly' that forced the exchange offline?"

"Intercorpex was hacked by Liberteum. My asset pushed to move up their timeline to coincide with the board meeting."

That's what his e-note meant. During his hearing in front of the board, Valen sent her out of the room to ascertain what exactly was going on. When she informed him about the strange market activity, he simply stated, "I know."

There is nothing more trying on the soul than conflicting emotions. Valen lied to her. Even if he had valid reasons, he's supporting terrorists. With an infiltrator reporting their location, the group could have been eradicated with one VidLynk to the Pentagon. Instead, he created a monster.

"Why would you do that?"

"Because I'm the naïve senator from this movie," he says. "Intercorpex is accumulating power. The patricians are exerting more influence than ever before over the corporations. There is only so much we can do to combat that."

"And you chose to fight that by consorting with terrorists?"

"No, I seized an opportunity. Unique problems require unconventional solutions. When the asset provided us with their plan, I knew I could use Liberteum against the exchange and the patricians."

"That's not a good enough reason to justify working with murderers."

"It is when you see the big picture."

"Said every tyrant in history," Fiolla says, her angry tone seeping into every word.

Valen frowns. "Yes. Fiolla, corporations and the elites have been fighting for power since we rose out of the ashes of the Great Collapse. Intercorpex was created as a buffer to prevent the system from collapsing again. Unfortunately, they abuse that authority. All that's needed is an administrator-general with ambition, ruthlessness, and an excuse to exercise full dominion over the world."

"You're talking about Raimius."

"The board of regents could historically be relied upon to act before an AG became too powerful. Then Raimius came along. He's a brutal dictator, and everybody, including the regents, fears him. To expedite his departure, drastic measures had to be taken."

This doesn't sound like Valen. At least the Valen she knows. He's always been in control. Why would he believe Raimius has political ambitions that he can't handle?

"That drastic measure ended up costing the lives of countless employees," Fiolla says, turning her attention to the movie.

He gives her a sideways glance. "Don't for a moment think that burden is easy to bear."

"Who infiltrated Liberteum?"

Valen leans back into his chair. "I don't know his name. It was withheld as a security measure. All communications are over GlobalNet, and contact is sporadic, at best. I haven't heard from the asset since before the last attack."

"Sir, what you did is—"

"Treasonous?"

Fiolla sighs. "I was going to say 'irresponsible.' Why are you telling me this now?"

"I've always trusted you, Fiolla. That's why I never exposed your unauthorized and inappropriate relationship with a patrician."

For the second time in this conversation, her mouth hangs open. She manages to close it and fashion some sort of plausible denial.

"I-I'm not sure—"

"Lying isn't your strong suit, Fiolla. Don't try. I know about you and Farron Keating."

Her cheeks burn as red as her hair as the initial shock of his revelation turns to embarrassment. "How did you find out?"

"It doesn't matter."

"Why didn't you…?"

"Turn you in? Why should I have? You both did a good job of keeping the secret, even from the BCS. I know a thing or two about keeping things from people. I'm telling you now because I can't ask you to trust me without proving that I trust you."

Fiolla lowers her eyes. She hasn't earned that trust. She passed sensitive information to Farron. Valen probably doesn't know that, or they wouldn't be having this conversation. He's not the only one with secrets.

"I brought you into the fold to help make America Incorporated a better corporation. It didn't work out quite as I expected, but there's still some fight left in me. I'm going to need your help to see this thing through."

Fiolla closes her eyes. What choice does she have? She is already a target for Virtari and Zeykala, and this information only implicates her further. He was counting on that. He has always been a great manipulator. She just learned firsthand how great.

CHAPTER TWENTY

RYKOS

"Valhalla"
Unknown Geographic District
New York City Municipal Corporation

My eyes click open, and I see Michele standing above me. She gently squeezes my shoulder. I feel a hundred percent better than I did at the medical center, but the last thing I remember was being shot at and fleeing in an ambulance. Seeing her is the first indication that I'm not in a corporate prison.

"How are you feeling?"

"Remarkably well, considering. What day is it?"

"Tuesday, very early morning. You spent most of yesterday unconscious. We figured that the best thing was to let you rest."

I look around the room. It's nicer than the accommodations at Broad Street Station and much cleaner than the crypt they were holding my father in. It doesn't compare to Farron's domicile, but most places don't.

"Where are we? I mean, are we safe?"

"You're in Valhalla, and there's no safer place for us in the city."

"I thought the Alamo was the safest."

"The Alamo was the most defensible. This place is the most secret, and that's its strength. I can give you the tour if you're up to a short walk."

"It beats lying here."

I ease off the bed. My abdomen is sore but not as painful as I would have expected. I stand and check my balance. So far, so good.

"Any news on my father?" I ask.

"No, Jasper hasn't been able to find anything definitive. There is an acting chief guardian and no reports of needing a permanent replacement. He could still be alive."

I nod. Life is a series of equations. On one side, my mother knows my father's fate, and I don't. On the other, she doesn't know about mine. It would be nice if we could balance that at some point.

The hallway is short, and I stop when we reach the end. I gaze around the room in amazement. It must measure about twenty feet wide and forty feet long. The illumination is provided by overhead LEDs and blue inlaid lighting along the walls. The back portion of the room contains workstations for the hackers, and the front features a planning area and passageways. One of them is the opening to the spiral staircase that must lead to whatever is above us.

"Whoa. Are you kidding me with this?

"Not bad for a bunch of tunnel rats, right? This is our operations center. It's the focal point of a self-contained habitat complete with bunk rooms, a full kitchen, lavatories with hot showers, and a computer network that's better than some corporations can manage. It's Liberteum's crown jewel and the last place we have left."

"This is home for you?" I ask.

Michele offers a smile. "It's the only place I have ever found peace."

"We chalk that up to the massive electromagnetic field surrounding us," Jasper says from his workstation.

He gestures at the two walls with computers and displays. Adiz just glares at me. I don't think he likes the idea that I'm here. He may have a good reason – I seem to attract unwanted attention wherever I go.

"Will Haven find us here?"

"He knows we're here but can't do anything about it. Even with a sizable force to storm this place, good luck getting to it."

"Why? Where are we?" I ask.

The question goes unanswered. A man dressed in full religious regalia emerges from the spiral staircase. My eyes open wide in surprise. He is among the last people I expected to see down here.

"I will never get used to that stairway," the Emissary breathes, recovering from the descent. "And that was the easier of the journeys."

"Let's just say we have divine protection," Michele whispers.

"Cardinal Michael-Castello?"

"Undergraduate Rykos! It's good to see you up and about, my son. I was concerned about you."

"It's just Rykos now, but that's…that's not…what are you doing here?"

"I'm a humble shepherd tending to the black sheep in my flock," the Emissary says. "You have many questions, but I lament that time doesn't permit me to answer them right now. Michele, I apologize for the early morning visit, but the BCS completed yet another search of the sanctuary and crypt yesterday evening."

"They were here again?"

"Unfortunately. They seem to assume that the church is hiding you. I can't imagine why," he says with a mischievous smirk. "Every religious structure in Manhattan has been searched multiple times. Their frustration grows each time they leave."

"Thank you, again, Emissary. I'm very sorry that we have inconvenienced you."

"Not at all, my child. There is one more thing I must inform you of. A meeting has been scheduled at Intercorpex headquarters here in Midtown."

"What kind of meeting?" Rykos asks.

"A summit," Michele answers. "Patricians, Intercorpex leadership, and corporate executives have all been invited."

"We heard about it," Farron interjects as he enters the operations room from a passage. "It's scheduled for Thursday."

Farron walks up and kisses the man's ring. That's not something I expected a patrician to do, even for clergy.

"It is good to see you again, Farron. You are correct that media outlets are reporting that the gathering is Thursday. However, a trusted congregation member has informed me it's being held today."

"Today," Michele mutters, staring at the wall behind the cardinal.

"I thought you should know. If I learn more, I will endeavor to relay it to you. Unfortunately, I must return to the sanctuary. I'm likely under passive surveillance, and a prolonged absence will raise enough suspicion for them to take a more active interest."

"Thank you, Emissary."

"Thank you, Your Grace," Farron parrots. The holy man nods to us in a gesture of reverence.

"Rykos, I hope we find time to talk. I know you are shouldering a terrible burden. I believe God has a plan for you. Your presence here warms my heart."

I can't resist a smile. "Thank you, Cardinal. I look forward to it."

The Emissary disappears up the poorly lit spiral staircase as Michele starts pacing in the center of the room.

"Why is he called the Emissary?" I ask Farron in a hushed voice designed to not interrupt Michele's train of thought.

"He was a lowly priest in a local parish when Quarren and his wife fled America Incorporated for the underground. After Michele was born and his wife fell ill, Quarren became desperate for help and went to him. Instead of turning him over to the authorities, Father Michael provided what support he could.

"To avoid endangering him should he ever be caught, Quarren coined the code name. Even when he was promoted to head this diocese, Cardinal Michael-Castello has always helped Michele and her father with their cause."

"Okay, so if this place is so secret, why would he risk coming here? How did he get here undetected?"

Farron smirks and points at the ceiling. "Because he works right above us."

"We're in another crypt?" I ask, eliciting snickers from the hackers. I realize the stupidity of the question after I ask it.

"No, we're two hundred feet below Saint Patrick's Cathedral."

"Two hundred…Midtown? How is that even possible?"

"The wonders of the New York underground," Farron muses.

"Pre-collapse, the church installed a standing column well geothermal heating system to defray energy costs and reduce carbon dioxide emissions from burning fossil fuels," Michele explains after she stops pacing. "When the system needed replacing two decades ago, my father and the Emissary—newly frocked as the Cardinal of New York—decided to utilize the qulis to help build this while the work was in progress."

"You're telling me that above our heads is the main house of worship for every religious executive in the city?"

"Brilliant, isn't it? Ground-penetrating radar will never find this place. There are no blueprints that a computer can dig out of the municipal corporation's archives. As I said, this is the safest place for us in the city."

"Qulis built this?"

"Laborers worked nights to widen a pilot hole for a shaft into that spiral staircase. The entrance is so cleverly hidden that you could tear the cathedral down and miss it. Once they reached this depth, it became a mining operation that took years to finish."

I shake my head in amazement. Qulis are the lowest class in the corporate world. Employees treat them like bottom-feeders who are barely a step up from the urches. Their autonomy means that they are rarely monitored and unworthy of attention. It's the only way building this place would have been possible.

"I never realized that Liberteum and the qulis cooperated so closely."

"The enemy of your enemy is your friend," Michele advises.

"Not always," Farron says, his face turning grave. "Is there any chance Haven knows about tomorrow's meeting at Intercorpex?"

"If the Emissary can find out the real meeting time, so can Haven."

"That's what worries me. If he knows about it…."

Michele nods. "He's going to hit it."

"How do you know?" I ask.

"You know Haven well enough by now," Farron says. "He's the harbinger of death and destruction. That much power concentrated in one location is an inviting target."

"So, what are we going to do?"

"Nothing."

"Nothing?" I ask as my face contorts in disbelief. "Are you kidding me? You're going to sit back and let those people die? That makes you no different than Haven."

"What do you expect us to do? If we had the people to stop him, which we don't, it would still be a long shot. We barely escaped the Alamo with our lives trying to rescue your father, for as much good as that did."

"Coward. Maybe you don't care how many people die so long as it serves your purpose."

Farron's eyes flash with anger, and I step toward him. I may not be a fighter, but I know I can take him.

"Settle down, boys," Michele says, stepping between us before turning to me. "It's not cowardice, and we don't want mass bloodshed. That's the reason Haven left us in the first place. If he attacks, it will seriously damage our cause whether it succeeds or not."

"More reason to do something."

Farron shrugs. "I'm fresh out of ideas. If you have one, let's hear it, Rykos."

I rub my forehead. This kind of brainstorming is what Mollae was good at. It's what will make her a great executive. She could talk seemingly without the need for oxygen. The night we…. A thought pops into my mind.

"I have one," I say, regaining the attention of everyone in the room, "but you aren't going to like it."

CHAPTER TWENTY-ONE
AMERICA, INC.

The White House
Corporate Governance District
Washington-Arlington Municipal Corporation

These security briefings are tedious, and it's way too early in the morning for one. Zeykala digs her fingernails in the fleshy ball of her thumb. The jolt of pain registers and increases her alertness, but the effect is short-lived. Valen personally oversaw preparations for several high-profile meetings, but she feels the details are beneath a CEO's station. There are far more important matters to handle.

"We are assuming primary responsibility for facility access," Special Agent Caylem says, navigating the display to show the campus's ingresses. "There are two main entrances, two service entrances, and three pedestrian access points. A detail will man each along with a representative from Intercorpex. They assigned ICX Security inspectors to our roving patrols and stationary posts on the grounds. Intercorpex is handling all security within the walls of the complex's buildings."

"Who's the scene commander?" Virtari asks from his seat next to Zeykala in the Situation Room.

"I'm personally assuming command of our agents for the duration of this meeting. I have temporarily reassigned responsibility for the Liberteum manhunt to another senior agent."

Special Agent Caylem strikes Zeykala as competent and methodical, but he exudes the BCS swagger that most executives find infuriating. Sucking up is practically a sport in today's corporate environment, but the way he does it smacks of arrogance. She doesn't need the finer details of who is running what up there.

"Underground access?" Virtari asks.

"Maintenance and utility tunnels along with a vehicular tunnel for the East Side Autoway. The tunnels will be heavily monitored with sensors and static video, and autoway traffic will be diverted."

"What about aerial coverage?"

"Six drones are tasked for perimeter defense, with two more operating at higher altitudes to provide a strategic overview. Three more are dedicated to monitoring the river in the unlikely event of a water approach. In the event—"

"It sounds like you have things under control up there, Agent Caylem. We'll be in contact if there are any further questions."

Zeykala nods over at the communications specialist, who ends the VidLynk. Virtari looks annoyed at the interruption, but the CEO couldn't stand another minute of the briefing. The BCS director will just have to get over it.

"I take it you're satisfied?" Virtari says with a sneer.

"You're the experts. The perimeter looks impregnable…unless they manage to infiltrate it. Then what?"

"We greet the intruders with two heavily armed quick response teams."

Zeykala rolls her eyes. "You have an answer for everything, don't you?"

"I find it helps to be prepared for every eventuality, like when some idiot schedules a high-profile conference in the same city victimized by two terrorist attacks and a running gun battle."

"Raimius wants to hold this meeting at their headquarters as a sign of strength."

"He's a moron," Virtari says, leaning back in his chair.

Zeykala rests her elbows on the table and steeples her fingers. "Normally, I would agree. In this case, it's a smart move. If Liberteum attacks, he can blame us. If they don't, he shows the patricians and the corporations that everything is under control."

"He can show strength in Zurich. It's the birthplace of Intercorpex anyway."

"Yes, but no longer its brain or beating heart."

Virtari smirks. You must be channeling Valen. That's something he would say."

Zeykala would usually consider that an insult. Given Valen's reputation as a strategic thinker, she'll view it as a compliment. Virtari rarely offers one.

"Valen liked playing games," she says, standing. "I don't. Make sure all the security arrangements are in order. You may trust your agent, but I don't. I need your involvement to ensure nothing goes wrong."

"And if something does?"

The CEO narrows her eyes. "Then people who make an enemy of me will find out firsthand just how soft Valen was and how much I'm not like him."

CHAPTER TWENTY-TWO

INTERCORPEX

The "War Room"
ICX New York Exchange
New York City Municipal Corporation

Malkor enters the war room, and Chief Inspector Zyree swings his feet off the war room conference table. The blood rushes back into them, causing uncomfortable pins and needles. He glances at the time on the display: a quarter to eight in the morning.

"Hey, boss, when was the last time you slept?" Malkor asks, handing him a cup of coffee.

"I caught a few winks last night."

"I mean in an actual bed."

Zyree shrugs before taking a sip of the warm, heavenly brew. "All I would have done is toss and turn anyway."

"What bothers you most – Chiana being released after trying to kill you, the meeting at headquarters with Liberteum still a threat, or not being involved in the security preparations?"

"All of the above."

Malkor pulls out a chair and sits. He stares at the map of Midtown Manhattan glowing on the conference room's main display. It's the same one Zyree has been staring at for hours without yielding insights. He instinctively knows every security arrangement without needing a briefing. What he can't figure out is what Haven will do to render it all useless.

"The complex will be locked down tight. Do you think Liberteum will take a shot at it?"

"No, but Haven might."

Malkor cocks his head. "Aren't they the same thing?"

"Maybe once upon a time. Now, I'm not so sure."

"Chief Inspector Zyree, this is the switchboard. You have an incoming audio-only VidLynk," a pleasant-sounding female voice announces over the speaker system.

"Since when does anyone contact you through the NOC?"

"Since never. Who is it?" he demands.

"I'm sorry, Chief Inspector, no name was provided. The request was marked urgent. Shall I make the connection?"

"Go ahead."

"Ortan?" Malkor asks. "Sounds like something he might do."

"Nope. Too subtle. This is Zyree," the chief inspector announces when the VidLynk is established.

"Hello, Chief Inspector."

Zyree straightens in his chair at the sound of the familiar voice. "Rykos?"

"Yeah."

"We thought you were dead."

"I almost was, courtesy of my father."

Zyree nods at Malkor, who is analyzing the waveforms for manipulation. Voiceprints can be spoofed, but Zyree's instincts tell him he's the real deal. No information about Teman shooting his son has been released or circulated.

"How did you know where to find me?"

"It was an educated guess. Are you alone?"

"Inspector Malkor is here with me. He can be trusted. My turn. Why are you contacting me? You know that I can trace this VidLynk."

The main display with the map glows to life with a new image. Rykos stares at them with a petite brunette at his side. She's far more beautiful in ultra-high definition than in surveillance images or the dim lighting of a SoHo basement.

"Because if you had a quantum computer and ten years to run the backtrace, you still wouldn't find the origin."

"Michele, right?"

"Good memory, Chief Inspector."

"No thanks to the blow to the head that your buddy gave me."

Michele offers a mischievous grin. "I'm sure Rykos is sorry about that, but the other option was killing you."

Zyree wants to ask why they didn't but thinks better of it. "I'm going to assume that the most-wanted terrorist in the world doesn't make random social calls to her pursuers. I also assume you're not arranging your surrender, so what do you want?"

Michele looks over at Rykos before staring back at the camera. "To warn you that Haven is going to attack today's meeting at Intercorpex."

"The meeting is Thursday," Zyree says, probably too quickly.

"Let's not play games with each other, Chief Inspector. Even if I was fishing for information, you didn't sell the lie."

Zyree glances over at Malkor and catches him shaking his head. He's either impressed or undressing her with his eyes. He prefers to think it's the former because this woman is good. The only thing in the world more appealing than a beautiful woman is a *smart,* beautiful woman.

"Okay. Why are you telling me? Isn't Haven one of yours?"

"He was."

"But not anymore? Why not?" Malkor asks.

"Because he's a murderous psychopath who tortured my father and has already tried to kill her three times," Rykos says, his voice seething with hatred.

"You have blood on your hands, too, Michele," Malkor retorts.

"We all do in one way or another, don't we, Inspector? You can choose to believe me or ignore me. That's your prerogative. I know Haven, and since he has a history with Intercorpex, you know him too."

"I do," Zyree says, staring at the ground. "I helped bury him after he…died."

"Then you know what he's capable of. Haven murdered dozens of people in cold blood after fleeing the church just because he could. He won't pass up the chance to strike the summit."

Malkor turns to Zyree with a raised eyebrow. He must think it's creepy that his boss came to that conclusion fourteen hours ago.

"Why do you care?" Malkor asks. "How many guardians died during your attack on the exchange?"

Michele lowers her eyes as Rykos's face hardens. "That was regrettable. I don't want to see people die."

"Says the terrorist," Malkor says under his breath after a scoff.

"I know what you must think of me. If I liked killing just for the sake of it, we wouldn't be having this conversation, Chief Inspector. Your colleague would be attending your funeral instead."

"Touché. I'm not handling security for the event. How do you expect me to stop Haven when the entire PSS can't find him?"

"I don't expect you to thwart the attack. I want you to prevent it from happening."

Malkor snickers. "And how are we supposed to do that?"

Michele looks off-camera. Zyree doesn't know if she's seeking assurance from someone else or having second thoughts about providing information. When she turns to Rykos, he offers a reassuring nod.

"I'm going to give you the location he'd launch it from."

* * *

Zyree races to the elevator as fast as his legs will carry him. Malkor is contacting their superiors in Zurich, so it falls on him to inform Intercorpex leadership. The new director of global operations is in the best position to sound the alarm.

"What floor, please?" the disembodied voice asks when he steps into the elevator car.

"Office of the director of global operations."

The doors close, and the elevator lurches upward before abruptly stopping. Zyree grabs at the walls to steady himself. The lights are on, so the power wasn't lost. Being fully automated, the computer-controlled lift contains no floor buttons, not that it would matter.

The chief inspector mashes the emergency call button and waits. Nothing happens. He jabs the button with a ferocity that does nothing to alleviate his frustration.

"Hel-lo," Ortan announces after the small display in the elevator comes to life.

The man's computer prowess is only surpassed by his obnoxiousness. Ortan is one of the most intelligent and socially awkward men Zyree has ever met. His mobility is aided by an exoskeleton he's used since losing the ability to walk following an accident.

"Ortan, did you stop the elevator?"

"Computers control everything, Zyree. I speak in ones and zeros. When you understand their language, you can make them do anything."

"That's…terrifying. This isn't a good time."

"You're not even going to ask about how I am or what I've been doing? I'm hurt," he says, flashing an exaggerated frown. He has a flair for the dramatic.

"Damn it, Liberteum just contacted me with information that the patrician meeting is getting targeted."

"Why would Liberteum—"

"Start the elevator, Ortan."

"Did they contact you via VidLynk?" he asks, doing his maestro thing as he moves information around the displays in his room.

"No, they sent a carrier pigeon. Start the damn—"

"When?"

Zyree sighs heavily. There's no point in arguing with him. This elevator isn't going anywhere until Ortan gets what he wants.

"It came in through the switchboard ten minutes ago."

"Did you trace it?"

"The origin was geolocated to a science station in Antarctica. They warned us that a backtrace wouldn't work."

"It wouldn't work for mere mortals, maybe. Luckily, you have me, and I have Huldufólk."

Zyree closes his eyes and shakes his head. Ortan and his magical computer-controlling elf. He's spent way too much time in Iceland.

"If you can trace the call, do it, but if you don't get this elevator moving right now...."

"Touchy, touchy. You have no appreciation for my work, Zyree."

The elevator springs back to life like nothing happened.

"Thank you. Did you have a reason for contacting me?"

"Yes, but it can wait. This is more important. I'll contact you once I know something," he says, disappearing from the display as the elevator reaches its destination.

Zyree rushes out and makes his way down the corridor to the largest office in the building. He uses his biocomp to swing the doors open as he bolts past the seated admin, who shouts the usual protestations. She swiftly gives chase as he barges into the office.

"Chief Inspector! The director is in a meeting!"

"I can see that, but Lyris is here, so it's unimportant."

"Zyree! How the hell did you get in here?" Lyris asks.

"Security override."

"My door has an override?" Wyeth asks as Zyree makes his way over to the desk.

"I'm a chief inspector with ICX Security, Director. I can override every door in this building."

"What do you want?" Lyris barks.

"I have intelligence that leads me to believe there is going to be an attack on the meeting at headquarters."

Lyris shares a look with Wyeth. Zyree knows that his nemesis despises him, but he would never characterize him as an alarmist. Zyree single-handedly ended the threat during Liberteum's second attack. If he believes there is a threat, there is one. Wyeth knows that as well.

"What do you know, Chief Inspector?"

Zyree launches into a briefing, omitting details about where the information came from. He doesn't want to spend hours explaining why a terrorist contacted him; he'd much rather be working to stop a more dangerous one. The two men aren't happy with that reasoning.

"This is worthless without us knowing your source," Lyris says. "Tell us."

"I don't work for you, and even if I did, I still wouldn't tell you."

"Will you tell me, Chief Inspector?" the new executive director asks.

"With all due respect, Director Wyeth, I don't work for you, either. It's a source in a position to know. Malkor is filing a formal situation report to ICX Security. I'm here to inform you. A flash warning needs to be issued to the people on the ground up there."

"You have no proof. Only speculation," Lyris says with a dismissive wave.

"Gee, Lyris, when have I heard those words before?"

The direct insult about his handling of the Broad Street attack hits the mark. Lyris takes a step toward Zyree, his fists clenched.

"Stand down, Lyris," Wyeth warns. "The two of you can beat each other to a bloody pulp on your own time. Chief Inspector, how sure are you of this threat?"

"I believe it's imminent, Director."

Zyree owns this now. If Michele is wrong or his instincts fail him, he will likely have just committed career suicide. Even that path is better than the alternative.

Wyeth moves back around his desk and opens a VidLynk channel. "Can I help you with something, Director Wyeth?" the automated assistant asks.

"Contact Director Virtari of the Bureau of Corporate Security for America, Incorporated."

"I will attempt to establish a VidLynk," the disembodied voice relays.

"Are you heading up there, Chief Inspector?" Wyeth asks.

"No, I plan on preventing the attack. This warning is in case I fail."

"Don't let me keep you," Wyeth says, looking up from his display.

"Director," Zyree says with a nod before shooting Lyris a hostile glance.

Zyree rushes out of the office. He's lost precious time doing these "check-the-box" activities. A single report sounding the alarm should have been enough considering the criticality of this meeting. Unfortunately, that's not how Intercorpex works. It's not how the world works. It never has been and probably never will be.

CHAPTER TWENTY-THREE

AMERICA, INC.

AME News Broadcast Studio
Midtown Geographic District
New York City Municipal Corporation

The seven o'clock news is the most-watched hour of television in America Incorporated. For the East Coast, it's the last thing employees see before heading out to work. The middle of the sphere will watch it while they are getting ready for the day, and the West Coast watches while working out or drinking their morning coffee. That makes its AME News anchor one of the most known faces in the corporation's entire sphere of influence. The worst part is that she knows it.

"Thank you for agreeing to meet with me, Journalist Kassaya," Ilaria says as she takes a seat.

The journalist's office is small but comfortable, at least by executive standards. Ilaria notices that her chair is slightly lower than her host's and she suppresses a grin. Even news anchors play the corporate power game.

"What brings you here?"

"Chief Executive Safmor asked me to come," Ilaria says, wearing her best smile.

"Ah. You drew the short straw."

"Not really. I think of it as pulling the long straw in a fist full of short ones. I don't consider you an enemy."

Her smile turns more genuine at the honesty. "That's refreshing. Congratulations on your new position. Your husband must be proud."

Proud. If there's any word to describe how Teman feels about her working for Safmor, that isn't it. Under usual circumstances, Ilaria would put on a brave face and hide that issue. In this case, telling this journalist the truth may help her achieve what she came here to do.

"Not exactly. Teman is barely talking to me. Our marriage is not in a good place right now."

"Oh, I'm…I'm sorry. You'll have to pardon my reaction. That's not what I expected to hear. You two seem to have the perfect marriage."

"Everything in this world is more about appearances than truth, isn't it?" Ilaria asks, letting the comment hang in the air. "Teman's displeasure with my working at the Executive Center is the least of my problems. In fact, I'm angrier with him than he is with me."

"Why is that?" she asks, sipping her tea.

Ilaria takes a deep breath. "Because he shot my son."

Kassaya nearly chokes. "Did I just hear you right? Wh-why would he do that?"

"Because Rykos was with Liberteum when Teman was rescued."

Kassaya sets her cup down. There's nothing more satisfying than shattering the illusion of the world to someone who thinks they have it all figured out. For a journalist, news that the chief guardian tried to kill his son because he was associating with a known terrorist group is about as earth-shaking as you get.

"Director Ilaria, maybe you should start from the beginning."

Ilaria smiles, fidgets, and then begins her long recount of the events leading up to this moment. She doesn't hold back on the details when she explains her drinking, the strain over her son's abduction and rescue, Teman's physical abuse, sending Rykos on a mission to save his father, and what little she knows about what happened in the aftermath. Nothing is off-limits. Even with minimal interruptions and questions, reaching the fake story about the BCS agents' murders takes more than a half-hour.

"That's one hell of a story," she says when Ilaria finishes. "Your son…is he…?"

"Best case scenario? With Liberteum. I don't like to think about the worst case."

Kassaya presses deeper into her chair and settles against the headrest. "Does corporate security know about that yet?"

"You mean, how am I working for the NYCMC if my son is affiliated with a terrorist group?" Ilaria asks with a weak smile that gets rewarded with a nod of affirmation. "The PSS conducted Teman's initial interview and is sitting on the information. The BCS hasn't interrogated him and won't until after this big summit at Intercorpex."

Kassaya breaks eye contact and stares at her desk. A minute goes by before she leans forward. "Ilaria, I believe every word you said. While your story is compelling, to say the least…they will never let me report any of it."

"I know. Even if I had a mountain of evidence, it doesn't fit the corporate narrative, and AME News is beholden to its masters in Washington. I don't expect you to do anything with what I just told you."

The comment catches her off-guard.

"Then why tell me all of this?"

"Because it bothers me that you can't report it, and I'm guessing it bothers you, too."

"Why would you think that?" she asks, growing suspicious of Ilaria's motives.

It's Ilaria's turn to lean forward in her chair. That's the opening she needed to make her pitch. If she's wrong about this woman, this whole conversation will have been pointless. Here goes nothing.

"I watched your interview with Executive Fiolla the day of the attack. You ambushed her because you knew she was lying. You were about to box Chief Executive Valen into the same corner during your subsequent interview before you were warned not to."

"Was it obvious? Or is this woman's intuition?" she asks.

"I was on the executive fast track before I got pregnant with my daughter. I'd like to think I earned that because I was smart and perceptive."

"And you left the corporate workforce instead of your husband?" she asks, shifting the topic away from herself.

"Teman was a respected guardian who many thought could run public safety one day. It turns out they were right. Policy mandates that one parent leave their occupation, and…."

"It was never going to be him," she finishes, knowing all too well that this is a male-dominated world.

"The joys of being a woman in the modern age."

"That's why I never married or bothered to have any children."

It's refreshing to see a larger-than-life journalist have a human moment. What everyone sees are only their public personas. Ilaria wanted her to open up. She never realized how much they see the world in the same light.

"I don't regret my life or my choices but I do resent the choices made for me. Someday, I hope to help change that corporate policy."

"Do you think having a woman as CEO of America Incorporated will have any impact?" Kassaya asks.

Ilaria smiles. This conversation has moved past trying to convince her to become an ally. Kassaya feels like a friend.

"I think it will make matters worse. Like you, Zeykala didn't have children. Unlike you, she was too ambitious to ever consider having them. Her ego would never let a family distract her from the climb up the corporate ladder."

"That's treasonous talk, Ilaria," Kassaya warns.

"It's the truth, and there isn't nearly enough of that in this world."

She gives her a broad smile. "No, there isn't, is there? Assuming I can find out anything about the allegations against the PSS—"

"You won't, and you'll have an uncomfortable conversation with the BCS if you ask questions. As I said, I just wanted you to know the whole ugly truth."

Ilaria stands and offers her hand, which she rises and graciously shakes.

"Thank you for this."

"You're welcome. The world is coming unglued, Kassaya. The Valen hearing was a coup, the tension between the PSS and BCS is about to boil over, the patricians are rumored to be militarizing, Intercorpex wants to rule the world, and Liberteum wants to destroy the system. Sooner or later, you're going to get an opportunity to show employees the truth, not what the parent corporation wants. I hope you'll consider giving it to them when the time comes."

"That's asking a lot," she says, exhaling deeply.

"Yes, it is. The consequences would be…well, we both know. I feel like big changes are coming. The people will need to hear facts, not propaganda. All I ask is that you be open to the possibility."

"'The people.' That's an interesting word choice. Don't you mean the corporate employees?"

Ilaria gives her a wink. "Thank you for taking the time to meet with me, Kassaya."

CHAPTER TWENTY-FOUR

LIBERTEUM

"The Motor Pool"
Hell's Kitchen Geographic District
New York City Municipal Corporation

Haven emerges from the lavatory and strides across the floor to join Nyvar, Loghun, Symun, and Tielur in the middle of the motor pool. His boots tapping on the concrete echoes through the cavernous garage. The four men stop talking and try to stifle snickers that eventually erupt into laughter at his appearance.

It's been a while since the former Intercorpex inspector wore a uniform. He would have preferred the Bureau of Corporate Security's tactical gear. Those designers recognized the need for shock value and made it both functional and imposing.

It stands in stark contrast to the sissy parade uniforms that guardians wear. Even his old ICX Security uniform didn't have the air of authority the BCS tac gear conjures. Haven thinks he would have made a great BCS agent if he didn't despise everything they stand for.

"I didn't think you knew how to use a razor," Nyvar chides, prompting him to stroke his now hairless face.

The key to success isn't making mistakes; it's learning lessons so they aren't repeated. They all should have shaved before donning guardian uniforms to go after Michele. Failing to do so almost cost them their lives. Mission success today hinges on their believability, and appearance is everything. That means his facial hair had to go, even if he doesn't like it.

"Old habits die hard. Where are we at?"

"We've reviewed and recited all details of the plan. The equipment is prepped and checked. We're ready."

"Good. We've been together a long time, so I won't bore you with a motivational speech. The five of us are about to strike a hardened target against some of the best-trained forces in the world. The difference between success and failure will be measured in seconds. Loghun, Symun – you guys have to be precise with your timing. Delays will be catastrophic. If you fail, Nyvar and I die.

"We won't let you down, boss," Symun assures.

"What if things go wrong?" Tielur asks.

"Improvise. Be determined and resourceful. You all know the plan, the rally points, and the exfil routes. You know how to get this done and get out."

"Roger that," Loghun says.

"We're about to do today what Michele and her father couldn't in years. This blow will be fatal. This repressive society will collapse like the house of cards it is. When it does, we get to watch as the world burns to ashes."

So much for no motivational speeches. The four men let out a testosterone-laden cheer. They have more in common with the warrior cultures of the past – Spartans, Huns, Vikings – than they do the corporate pansies who run this world. It's how Haven knows they'll succeed. Modern security forces may be formidable, but they aren't as motivated or dedicated as these men.

"It has been an honor knowing each of you. There's a chance that this will be the last mission for some of us. For anyone who doesn't return, I pledge that your sacrifice will not have been in vain, even if it costs me my own life."

They all know what is at stake and respectfully nod at Haven. The men are beginning to load into the two vehicles when Nyvar pulls their leader aside.

"Shwarx is all set for rear guard detail. He's new but trustworthy."

The PSS raid on the crypt was more costly than Haven could afford. He lost a lot of good men who were irreplaceable. This plan has changed because of it, but it's still workable. Not that he has any choice. Denali Keating made that clear.

"Shwarx is too green to be of any value, and we need to secure the motor pool. Have him meet us at rally point echo if we haven't returned."

"All right. Let's hope that isn't necessary."

"Where is he now?" Haven asks.

"On the roof providing overwatch for our departure. He said drones are covering the whole city."

"No doubt. I'm not worried about it. We have valid transponders and passable BCS uniforms. We'll make it across town. Let's get loaded up and go break the system."

CHAPTER TWENTY-FIVE

RYKOS

"Valhalla"
Midtown Manhattan Geographic District
New York City Municipal Corporation

I've never seen Michele act this fiery with her own people. Not that I've known her that long. Outside of dealing with Haven, who's a psychopath, she treats the other members of Liberteum with respect. I don't know if this is frustration or something else.

She is glaring at Adiz, who is seated along the far wall of Valhalla's operations room. Even Jasper looks like he wants to find a dark corner to hide in. If looks could kill, we'd be dragging their bodies out of here.

"You've been telling me for months that you had a way into the network," Michele shouts at him from three feet away. "You've been pushing to launch this phase for a week. Now that it's go-time, you're saying we're not ready? I thought you said you have a way in."

"I do, but—"

"But what, Adiz? Phase three requires a distraction. If Haven attacks the conference, it might be the only opportunity we get."

"I'm well aware of what's needed," Adiz argues. "The way in I was planning to use has been shut down. Nobody wants to move forward more than I do, but the secondary port is too risky. The odds of failure are too high."

"How high?"

"Eighty percent, and that's an optimistic estimate."

"Unbelievable!" Michele exclaims in a tone a few octaves higher.

Jasper swallows hard. "The secondary interface can be traced back to us. It's a near certainty that our firewalls won't keep them out of our network. Within minutes, Valhalla's location will be compromised."

Michele rubs her chin in obvious frustration. The handful of people in Valhalla all watch, none daring to say a word. The operations room is bathed in uncomfortable silence that begins clawing at their sanity.

"Guys," she says after wresting back control of her emotions, "we've been working on this for years. We are about to squander our chance."

"Intercorpex has the most protected computer network on the planet," Jasper says. "Archangyl is more than just a computer network defense system. It's a citadel. It has layers of defenses an attacker needs to breach to reach anything vital."

"It can't be that good," I argue. "You beat it when you were at Broad Street."

"That was different," Adiz interjects. "We tapped directly into their network. We can't do that this time. Archangyl is a near-artificial intelligence that adapts to threats against it in nanoseconds. It plays aggressive defense by deploying virtual decoy networks when an intrusion is detected. Then it will reorder file systems and create fake servers to confuse and trap an intruder. The system stalls for time while simultaneously tracing the source of a hack before it's shut down."

Michele was hoping to turn Haven's probable attack into something positive. I don't think she has the manpower left for whatever deception is needed. There certainly aren't enough people here to defend Valhalla if it's uncovered. Not that I understand how they could find it this far underground.

"So, we could be exposed here if we proceed?" I ask.

"If we act rashly, yeah. Valhalla piggybacks corporate fiber optic lines. They might not know our precise location, but they'll know the general area. They will shut everything down until they find us. It would be a siege that we could never outlast."

"Michele," Jasper says, "we've been reverse-engineering Archangyl for months with dummy attacks to understand how the system reacts. We've learned a lot. We'll find its Achilles' heel, but we need more time."

"More time for what?" Narik asks from behind us as he's escorted in from his confines in the bunk room.

He looks like hell. Like most patricians, he's always been well-groomed and impeccably dressed. Now he's neither. His hair is unkempt, his face unshaven, and he has bags under his eyes from lack of sleep. I'm sure the thin mattresses here aren't as comfy as the overstuffed one at his uptown brownstone.

"Archangyl," Michele says, taking the lead on delivering the bad news, "is proving more difficult to breach than we thought. We're delaying phase three."

"Wait? No, no, no," he says, shaking his head. "I overheard you say that Haven is going to attack Intercorpex today."

"That's what we think," Farron says, speaking for the first time.

"Then you need to execute the plan."

"The risk is too high that Valhalla gets compromised."

"I don't care. Take the chance. Launch the attack," he orders, acting every bit the petulant patrician used to giving instructions and expecting them to be carried out without question.

"No," Michele says, folding her arms.

"What do you mean, no?"

"There's no hidden meaning in the word, Narik. I will not compromise this facility or my people on a long shot."

"This is what we've worked for!"

"Success is what we're working for. Everybody here knows the stakes. I won't jeopardize all that work without having a reasonable chance—"

"Did you forget who helped you get this far?" Narik asks, applying the only leverage he has. "You'd be nothing without my support."

"We didn't forget that you pulled a gun on Michele," Jasper interjects, joining the fray.

The two men glare at each other, but there isn't much of a defense for that. I'm sure the Covingtons' support was important, but I wonder if Michele thinks it was worth the cost. Considering that he's been chained to a bunk, I bet the answer is no.

"I happen to agree with Michele," Farron says, weighing in. "It's too much of a risk."

"Incredible!" Narik exclaims, theatrically throwing his hands in the air. "You risked everything to save Chief Guardian Teman. You doubled down on the stupidity when you took Rykos to NYU to save him. You take risks when it suits you. This is our chance to act, and you're blowing it."

Michele is on the verge of losing her temper. She gets right into the patrician's face, causing him to lean backward.

"Doubling down is an old term. I took calculated risks to help us achieve our objective. You want to gamble and hope for the best. I will not do that. Accept that you're not in control here."

Narik thrusts his jaw out. He's indignant at the realization that she's right. What I don't understand is why he's in such a rush. What are a couple more days or weeks if it's the difference between success and failure? There is so much more going on here that I don't understand. That is going to need to change, and soon.

CHAPTER TWENTY-SIX
AMERICA, INC.

The White House
Corporate Governance District
Washington-Arlington Municipal Corporation

She doesn't know what compelled her to watch this. The summit is starting soon, but she is drawn to this footage. Fiolla has seen dozens of Valen's speeches in her time at the White House. This one wasn't remarkable for its wording or eloquence. It was nothing more than remarks to a group of graduating registrants.

The only thing special about it was one of them in attendance. Rykos was named a hero of the corporation for political reasons. Of that much, Fiolla is certain. It was also the reason that Valen chose to address Dinsmore Academy. Rykos has since become radicalized, and her former boss has been ousted from office. Part of her is struggling with the reasons.

"Rosie, fast forward to time index ten fifteen," Fiolla commands her digital office assistant. She doesn't need to watch the nostalgic remarks of the chancellor or optimistic musings of the valedictorian.

"Playing," she responds in her odd English accent.

"We left behind the wars and poverty that consumed the old world," Valen says from the podium. "We matured from the violence and corruption that were once commonplace in it. You are free from the yokes of suffering and despair that monarchs and presidents, despots and tyrants thrust upon their people. We unlocked humanity's true potential."

Fiolla swipes her hand to stop the video playback. Is that true? Are people *really* free from suffering and despair? Are modern executives that different from the political leaders of yesteryear? The American Congress likely fancied themselves superior to the Roman Senate. Politics is politics. It doesn't matter if you wear a toga, a suit and tie, or an executive tunic.

"We will never bow to their threats or cowardly attacks," Valen says after Fiolla restarts the video. "We have faced them in the past and will eliminate them in the future. Their legacy will be that of the corrupt ideology they idolize: abject failure."

Fiolla pauses the video again and rubs her forehead. Those are bold words, but he never backed them up. He knew their plan. He knew how to defeat them. He watched from Washington as Liberteum almost crashed the market. Intercorpex called it an "anomaly." People were told these lies without hesitation. Whose ideology is more corrupt?

"Turn off the video, Rosie."

Lies and deceit. They are a cancer that has spread through humanity. There is no honor. No pride. No joy. There are only the lies they tell each other. Valen is a liar. So is Farron. Add to that Talya Bettancourt, Zeykala…the list is endless.

Fiolla has never felt this way before. She's ashamed of the corporation she sacrificed for and worked hard to serve. Now she's complicit in its lies. Valen entrusted her with a secret. He wants her help in finding his way back to power. The tyrant running America Incorporated would burn down the White House to stop him. Is he any better than Zeykala?

She used to think so until he admitted that this whole crisis was partly his doing. He allowed Liberteum to conduct an attack in one of their most important cities. What kind of CEO allows an enemy of the corporation to operate freely solely for political gain?

Fiolla wishes things were good with Farron. He's an expert at dissecting political motivations, and his dispassion for America Incorporated guarantees objectivity. But she can't call him. Nothing has felt right since the exchange went offline. The man who claims he wants to marry her and wasn't using her has gone silent. It can't be a coincidence.

She stands and paces around her small office. The world is going straight to hell. Her faith in the corporation, the system, and its leaders are following it. Has she been blind this whole time? Are the men that Fiolla admires most playing her as a pawn? There are so many questions, so few answers…. She lets out a deep sigh, not knowing how things could possibly get any worse.

CHAPTER TWENTY-SEVEN

INTERCORPEX

"The Motor Pool"
Hell's Kitchen Geographic District
New York City Municipal Corporation

Electromagnets became the most common way to secure doors when home automation systems were developed before the collapse. Computers simply enable and disable them when commanded by cutting their power. America Incorporated programmed that capability into biojacks based on an access profile. It is an elegant way to ensure an employee can only enter authorized areas.

The other security upside is that forced entry is near impossible. Over twelve hundred pounds of force would be required to physically defeat the steel door Malkor is currently working on. Zyree cannot cut power to the decrepit building, so plan B will have to suffice.

"This is a bad idea," Malkor mumbles as he sets the small, black EMP generator on the lock.

"You say that every time we do something."

"What does that tell you?" he grouses.

The electromagnetic pulse generator creates a transient disturbance that radiates outward from its epicenter. With a press of a button, electronic devices are rendered worthless. Every corporation on the planet bans their use by anyone except security personnel.

"It tells me you're getting old," Zyree says with a smile, knowing he is nearly ten years older than his partner.

"Or that we're about to kick a hornet's nest filled with heavily armed terrorists...by ourselves," Malkor concludes, pausing to glance over his shoulder at Zyree.

"We don't have the time to wait for the cavalry. It's on us."

"If you say so. This thing isn't going to blink out our biocomps, is it?"

"Nah. It only has a three-foot range. But it will likely make you sterile. You don't want to have little Malkors, do you?"

The junior inspector offers a disapproving look as he joins Zyree ten feet away. With a press of the remote, he activates the device. The metallic click on the door is the only sign that the lock has been defeated. He draws his weapon.

"If we're wrong about this, we got played by a hot terrorist. We probably won't live to see the sunset if we're right. Gee, what do I hope for?"

"That we shoot them before they shoot us," Zyree says, conducting a press check to ensure his weapon is loaded and ready to fire. "Let's go."

The "motor pool," as Michele called it, is what's left of an old shipping facility near the tunnel under the Hudson River. It's the perfect place to hide in plain sight. Zyree imagines they could watch from the roof as PSS agents screen vehicular traffic entering and exiting the island.

The two men enter the structure and pause just inside the doorway. Malkor eases the door closed to avoid announcing their presence. The building is pitch-dark, but Zyree's contacts display no immediate threats. Once their eyes adjust to the darkness, they move stealthily through the dingy maintenance area.

This place has been abandoned since the collapse. It should be coated with an inch of undisturbed dust and littered with rusting equipment. That's not the case. The garage is spacious enough to park a couple dozen vehicles. Eleven are here, ranging from passenger conveyances to utility trucks. That explains how Liberteum managed to attack the data center circuits across the river in Secaucus. If they had access to vehicles and procured valid transponders, they would have freedom of movement aboveground.

Zyree gives the halt signal to Malkor and points at his eyes with his index and middle finger. He indicates the direction of a closed door. Malkor nods, and they skulk through the garage knowing countless men with rifles could be hiding anywhere in here. He gives a three-count using his fingers and swings the door open swiftly and quietly. The chief inspector charges into a shop area, moving off along the back wall while sweeping his weapon side to side.

Malkor goes the opposite way, doing the same. They stop after a few paces and listen. Their entry wasn't silent. Anyone here undoubtedly heard them. Malkor gives him a shrug.

Zyree's thoughts wander to the bodies of the patricians found in the Bronx. He ruled out Liberteum being involved because of the logistics involved. Now he's not so certain. While it doesn't make sense to leave them staged there, even for the propaganda value, they clearly had the means to do it.

His biocomp detects motion and displays the threat to his contacts before his brain registers the movement his eyes see. Both inspectors react a split second before a man steps out from behind a van and unleashes a salvo from his rifle. The shots sail wide of Malkor as he dives hard for cover behind a cargo truck. The second fusillade stitches the concrete block wall behind Zyree as he drops to a knee. Aiming with the aid of his biocomputer, he squeezes the trigger three times in rapid succession.

The three bullets all hit their mark. The first two strike the man square in the chest, and the final one rips through his head, leaving a trail of pink mist in its wake. The terrorist crumples to the ground in a heap, his eyes open and staring lifelessly ahead.

"Tango down," Zyree announces.

Malkor is back on his feet and crouched, shaking his head. He's okay, but that was too close for comfort. Zyree recalls his training: If you see one, think three. Using arm movements, he signals Malkor to sweep the right side of the garage while he heads left.

They creep along the walls, carefully checking between and underneath parked vehicles. The pair meets at the front of a large roll-up door on the bay's far side. Their weapons are at the high ready despite their confidence that the man they killed was alone.

"Clear," Zyree says when he is close enough to avoid shouting.

"Same. They may already be gone."

"Or they're hiding somewhere in the bowels of this building waiting to ambush us."

"I don't like either option," Malkor says, shaking his head. "We can't search this place on our own. This is a pre-collapse building. Who knows what's underneath it?"

"Agreed. We know we're in the right place, at least. I'll contact the PSS. Look around and see what you can find. Stay alert," he orders Malkor before commanding his biocomp to establish communications with One Guardian Plaza.

Zyree explains the situation to a cynical dispatcher, who reacts to his request for assistance with a healthy dose of skepticism. It's not until he relays that a target was neutralized that she agrees to send a unit over.

"Uh, boss," Malkor says, emerging from around one of the vehicles seconds after Zyree disconnects the comms to the PSS. "We have a major problem."

"What do you—" Zyree stops when he notices a pair of corporate security uniforms draped over Malkor's arms.

His heart jumps up into his throat. Things just went from bad to worse. Haven doesn't need to storm the ramparts. With those uniforms, he has the keys to the castle.

CHAPTER TWENTY-EIGHT

THE PATRICIANS

La Parisienne
Corporate Governance District
Washington-Arlington Municipal Corporation

It's not every day that Talya Bettancourt, the esteemed *Prima* of America Incorporated, asks anyone to meet for breakfast. She considers everyone below her station in life, including patricians of the *gentez-majorez*. Yet, here he sits in a well-appointed chair in this fine eatery, watching the most powerful woman in the world stride to his table.

Talya sits without a word and places a napkin on her lap. A waiter immediately fills her coffee cup with an aromatic brew before departing with a bow. She takes a sip before turning her attention to Shalius. He stares back at her. Talya wanted this meeting, so she can go first.

"Why aren't you at the summit?" she asks.

"Why aren't you?"

"My interests lie in Washington. I have no interest in how Intercorpex portrays this outage."

Shalius nods. Talya didn't want to leave him here, even for a day, without the ability to counter whatever move he made. He relishes having that power over her.

"Why did you want to meet?"

"I thought it was time that we talked one-on-one."

"I didn't think this was a social call. I'm not sure what needs discussing."

"I think you are. We've known each other for decades, Shalius. Our families share a history that predates the Great Collapse. You know me. So, I find it difficult to believe you would think that I would sell my shares when the exchange went haywire. You took advantage of the situation."

"I exploited an opportunity."

"At my expense," Talya says, taking another sip.

Shalius offers a slight shrug. "It's just business, Talya. It isn't personal."

"It is to me." She leans forward. "I will always be America Incorporated's *prima*."

Shalius smirks and matches her. "Except you aren't."

Talya leans back and nods. "You come from a naval family. I understand that your ancestors served in the military. I know you understand the meaning of sacrifice, commitment, and honor. Yet you exhibit none of those traits."

She has some nerve to lecture him like that. The Bettancourts are takers who have owned for so long they've forgotten how to build and create. It's why America Incorporated has stagnated. Talya is the last person who should be evoking those cherished qualities.

"It's funny how those with power and influence demand sacrifices from everyone except themselves."

"I don't want this to end up bloody between us," Talya warns.

"Is that a threat?"

She shakes her head slowly. "It's the end result. The Bettancourts built this corporation. I will not stand and watch you seize control of it."

"Bold words, Talya. Are you familiar with the story of the Spanish Armada?"

"Should I be?"

"The Spanish Armada was an enormous, one hundred and thirty-ship naval fleet deployed to invade England in 1588. There were eight thousand seamen and eighteen thousand soldiers manning thousands of guns. It was called the 'Invincible Armada' until it got outfoxed by the English and battered by a series of storms. It lost over sixty ships in its defeat before limping back to Spain."

"Is there a point to this?"

Shalius smiles. "They believed they were invincible because they were bigger and more powerful. They thought they couldn't lose. The English didn't defeat them. Neither did the weather. It was their hubris that did them in. You should read more history, Talya. It may prevent you from repeating its mistakes."

She drains her coffee and sets the cup gently down on the bone china saucer. She dabs her mouth with the napkin before laying it on the table.

"A great story, expertly told, Shalius. You left out the most important part, though. Spain's King Philip II assembled the flotilla to oust Queen Elizabeth I from her throne. He failed. What makes you think it will end any differently for you?"

Shalius doesn't have an answer for that. When she leaves, he stews over letting her get the best of him. He knows better. This is a high-stakes game. He needs to learn to stop underestimating his adversaries even when he thinks he has the better of them.

CHAPTER TWENTY-NINE

INTERCORPEX

Assembly Hall is a legacy left over from the previous tenant, the United Nations. It was completely rehabilitated and infused with cutting-edge technologies after America Incorporated gifted Intercorpex the space. Lyris despises it because it values form over function. Designed to make patricians at home, Assembly Hall is brimming with gaudy woodworking and expensive marble that woefully contrasts with the design of the post-modern ICX campus.

The adaptable usage concept was the one thing the architects got right during the renovation. The desks and work areas have all been removed for this meeting, making space for additional chairs installed to accommodate the expected audience. The rows of seats are arranged gracefully in arcs around an elevated stage, providing a superior view of the podium. There is little doubt that each will be filled when the summit commences.

"We're very happy you could attend, Lyris," Marggerie says in an upbeat tone as she approaches his perch along the wall. Regents Borix and Vijai join them, and handshakes are exchanged.

These are the three most powerful and influential regents in Intercorpex. They were savvy enough to use a tour of the damaged NOC to meet with Lyris and advance a far more dangerous agenda: enlisting his support to oust Raimius. The former executive director of exchange operations senses that they are about to make their move.

Despite their varied backgrounds, they are united in the singular ambition to end his reign. That cooperation will end when it's time to name a successor, as there isn't a single regent who doesn't covet the administrator-general position. They don't know that they aren't the only ones with an eye on it.

"I appreciate you extending me an invitation," Lyris admits, "although Raimius won't be happy to see me. I'm persona non grata in this building."

"You were decorated for exemplary performance," Borix says in his thick Russian accent. "You *belong* at this meeting."

"Raimius doesn't have the authority to control who regents invite to a summit," Marggerie adds.

"By the end of the day, he won't have any authority if things go according to plan," Vijai says, earning smirks from his peers.

"You have the votes to remove him?"

"We have interest," Marggerie responds, "and that's enough for now. Once we convene, we can persuade the other regents to fall in line. Raimius has enemies, and his lack of leadership in the wake of those horrendous attacks will prove compelling."

"There is a growing sentiment that new leadership is in order," Vijai says, piling on, "even if it's only spoken in whispers."

"If that's the case, why do you need me?"

"Raimius is intimidating. Some regents won't vote to remove him unless they know it's a sure thing. Your support will be crucial to swaying the uncommitted," Borix adds.

"What Lyris is politely asking is what's in it for him?" Marggerie explains to her fellow regent. "Isn't that right?"

Lyris has no doubt that she's the one most aggressively angling to replace Raimius. Marggerie is intelligent, cunning, well-connected, and political enough to pull it off. She's not Raimius, but they're cut from the same cloth.

"I wouldn't label this a quid pro quo," Lyris says, measuring his words. "But business transactions are conducted for the benefit of both parties."

"We understand. It would be inappropriate to finalize any details here," Vijai says, "but you will be well taken care of."

There are audio recorders and cameras peppered throughout this facility. In a packed room with many interesting conversations ripe for eavesdropping, the odds that they're being monitored are remote. Had Raimius known Lyris was coming, Intercorpex Security would have been tasked to track him. Despite the odds, the regents have no reason to be reckless with their words.

"You're asking for a leap of faith," Lyris says, playing dumb.

"Yes. Given your current status, what do you have to lose?" Borix muses.

He has a point. Lyris is on the outside looking in. This could be a ploy by Denali Keating to test his resolve to become administrator-general. He doubts the esteemed patrician would bother, but Denali is full of surprises.

"The regents will be meeting after opening remarks," Borix explains. "Raimius's removal was omitted from the official agenda for obvious reasons."

"It's rare we all get to see each other in person. It will provide for interesting discourse."

The regents reside in corporate spheres of influence spanning the globe. Most were originally proconsuls—corporate liaisons to Intercorpex responsible for ensuring exchange rules were followed by their respective corporations.

They meet regularly, so traveling to a single location is not only prohibitive but unreasonable. As a result, meetings are held via VidLynk. Since they set the strategic direction of Intercorpex, what's discussed in those conferences never becomes public knowledge unless they want it to.

"You're all here?"

"Present and accounted for," Borix beams. "To my knowledge, that hasn't happened in decades. Attendance never surpasses seventy-five percent, even when a new administrator-general is selected."

"Ladies and gentlemen, please take your seats," Nevala, acting as the emcee, announces from the lectern. "Opening remarks will commence in a few moments."

The elites in the room break from their conversations and begin to find chairs. As is protocol, the patricians of the *gentez-majorez* are seated up front, with the lesser patricians in the rear. The regents sit in reserved seats in the front row, while the senior exchange employees are sitting in two large galleries set into the walls near the stage. Everyone else is relegated to standing in overflow rooms with large displays showing a live feed of the meeting.

"We'll be seeing you later, Lyris," Vijai says with a warm slap on the shoulder as he steps off with Borix towards their seats. With a wink, Marggerie follows them.

"Ladies and gentlemen, corporate executives, distinguished patricians…it is my great honor to introduce Raimius, administrator-general of the Intercorporational Exchange."

Nevala yields the podium as Raimius walks out with a throng of Intercorpex and America Incorporated executives in tow. He's greeted with polite but not overly enthusiastic applause. The executives flank either side of the lectern as the clapping quickly subsides.

"Thank you. It's an honor and privilege to address such a gathering of esteemed global community members, although I wish it were under different circumstances. We understand the gravity of the moment and welcome the corporate leaders and the heads of great patrician families of the *gentez-majorez* and *gentez-minorez* joining us today.

"You are all invested in Intercorpex's success as the world's premier and most important marketplace. We understand that recent events have shaken your confidence, and this gathering is designed to address and alleviate your concerns.

Together, we will overcome our shared challenges and map a trajectory for this proud and important organization."

There is another round of polite applause. The men and women in this room aren't here to watch them unveil a new trading platform. The exchange is offline, and they're losing millions of Bytecoin. Lyris is surprised they bothered to applaud at all, much less with the enthusiasm that Raimius expected.

"We want answers, Raimius, not platitudes!" a voice cries out from the audience. A ripple of agreement sweeps through the room.

"You deserve answers," Raimius responds, off-script. "You all deserve them. You're entitled and empowered to hold accountable those responsible for the attacks that ravaged us and the anomaly that affected our trading.

"To provide those answers, Chief Executive Safmor and senior directors of the New York City Municipal Corporation have joined us today. Special Agent Caylem of America Incorporated's Bureau of Corporate Security will brief you on the terrorist threat we face. Finally, our top engineers and developers will explain our network resiliency and reaction to the trading activity that forced us offline."

"Trading activity? Are you kidding me!" one of the patricians shouts.

"They weren't real trades!" another screams, with countless others parroting their concerns.

Lyris shakes his head. Raimius didn't bring experts; he brought scapegoats. He plans on passing blame to save his own skin. It's an audacious play to keep his position, assuming he can pull it off. If the regents are to be believed, he won't.

"I have heard the rumors circulating about what happened on Saturday. We will dispel those rumors here today. I will not be satisfied until you leave here with full confidence in our hosts, our security, and the Intercorporational Exchange itself."

The hecklers remain quiet through the polite applause. Raimius probably thinks he's winning them over and has no idea what's coming. This is likely the last day of Raimius's tyrannical reign.

The mere thought of that causes Lyris to grin.

CHAPTER THIRTY

LIBERTEUM

ICX Headquarters
Midtown Manhattan Geographic District
New York City Municipal Corporation

The truck is rumbling down Forty-fourth Street when Nyvar suddenly slams on the brakes. Haven braces himself against the dash and glances up at the crimson traffic control indicator. Urches rarely engage in activities that the mindless zombies aboveground take for granted. Driving is one of them.

Haven stares at the gleaming glass tower directly in front of him. Next to that is the marble façade of Assembly Hall and the greatest concentration of wealth ever gathered. It's the current epicenter of world power. He smiles, thinking he must have done something right in a past life.

Nyvar makes a left turn north onto Intercorpex Plaza. Haven watches the campus pass them on the right. He visited this building a dozen or so times when he was an inspector. Now he will make one more appearance. Nyvar steers the truck into the auxiliary main entrance. Haven checks the mirror and watches Symun, Tielur, and Loghun continue rolling north toward their staging area. Everything is going according to plan.

"What do you want me to do?" Nyvar asks after a uniformed member of ICX Security steps in front of their vehicle with his hand outstretched.

"Not run him over. Obey all commands. Remember who we're supposed to be."

"Roger."

"What is all this?" the guard demands after the truck stops. He's looking up at Nyvar while pointing to the back.

Haven climbs out of the cab and moves around the front of the vehicle. "We have extra construction barriers for the front of the building."

"I can see that," he says, glancing at the flatbed. "We already have vehicle deterrents in place."

"Yeah, I noticed them. We were dispatched here to reinforce the temporary perimeter."

"On whose authority?" a BCS agent asks, walking out of the guard house while his ICX Security counterpart pulls out a transponder reader. "I don't recognize you."

"You wouldn't. I arrived in the city this morning from Philly. As for authority, the order came from Director Virtari."

"And not through Special Agent Caylem?" the agent asks.

Haven stifles any reaction. He's flying blind here. Not knowing the command structure will be a dead giveaway of the ruse. Special Agent Caylem could be in charge, or it could be the name of the man's cousin. It's fifty-fifty.

"I'm not going to presume to know what the higher-ups are doing. All I know is that I was dispatched to New York City Municipal Transportation to secure extra barriers for the perimeter."

The two men exchange a look when the device chirps. "Transponder checks out."

"Special Agent Caylem would have informed us of your arrival," the agent argues.

"Then ask him," Haven says, playing it cool.

"He's on stage by now. Control updated the threat matrix an hour ago," the ICX security officer advises the agent after checking the time. "He must see the benefit of beefing up countermeasures against a vehicle-borne attack."

Three additional heavily armed men join the gaggle at the gate. Each is outfitted with enhanced body armor, ballistic headgear, ear defenders to protect against sonic weaponry, and tactical throat microphones with Wi-Fi transmitters for communications. They're likely a roving patrol, and they mean business.

The ICX guard climbs up onto the flatbed to inspect the load. Haven pays him no attention, but Nyvar keeps an eye on him as he checks the heavy polymer shells filled with concrete. At least, some of them are.

The others are filled with an explosive created over a hundred years ago during World War II. PLX is a hard-to-detect, binary mixture of ethylene diamine and nitromethane. It's extremely volatile, so they stabilized the concoction for transport by using nitrocellulose to turn it into a gel. None of those chemicals are available in the underground.

The barriers in the center of the load contain booster charges. To increase the heat and energy of the explosion, aluminum powder was added to the PLX suspension. These men don't know it yet, but they are already dead. If the plan is foiled, Nyvar has orders to blow the truck. The destructive force would still rock Assembly Hall from here.

"Nothing out of the ordinary," the guard says, climbing down off the flatbed.

"I should have received authorization. Failing to follow the chain of command is unusual."

"Abnormal is a better word," Haven says, correcting him. "Look, guys, we all know the stakes for this summit's success. If this is causing too much confusion, we can pull the truck out while you get it sorted. Every minute you spend with me is a minute you're not watching what you should be."

The offer puts the BCS agent at ease.

"That might be best," the ICX Security agent opines, now flipping his position. They make them soft and impressionable these days. The men Haven once worked with had a stiffer backbone and a lot more grit.

"No, he's right. The interior perimeter should be beefed up. You stay here with us while we contact Control. These men can escort your driver and help drop the barriers."

If one thing can be counted on, it's the Bureau of Corporate Security wanting to do the opposite of what any other security organization suggests. Haven doesn't know if they specifically teach that up at West Point, or it's learned later.

"Makes sense to me. Let's get on with it."

Nyvar fires up the truck and begins to follow the three men of the roving patrol. They slowly creep toward Assembly Hall. With every inch comes an exponential increase in the bomb's damage. Haven represses his excitement at sticking this dagger into their hearts. BCS agents don't get excited about anything, and he's one of them at the moment.

"You ready?"

"Right behind you," Haven says, following the two men into the guard shack.

Shack might not be the best word to describe this structure. Even though violence has largely been stomped out in this world, the sturdy brick building has a large, front-facing bullet-resistant glass window. A long, narrow counter is installed along the back wall for surveillance and drone control equipment, communications gear, active and passive entry denial countermeasures, and a bank of high-definition displays with real-time video feeds.

He scans the rest of the room. A camera mounted in the corner will have to be dealt with. The side entry door will also need securing. Content that he has the layout memorized, Haven turns his attention to the agent and the guard. With the roving guards escorting the truck into place, it's just the two of them to deal with. He glances at an LED readout of the time; his guys are late.

No sooner does he curse under his breath than he hears the muffled popping sound of gunfire.

"All stations, this is Post Seven! We're taking small arms fire from outside the perimeter," the urgent voice cries out. "I say again, small arms fire at Post Seven."

"Seven, this is—"

Haven doesn't let the agent finish the sentence. He drives his knife deep into the intercostal space between the fourth and fifth ribs at a slight angle, deflating both lungs and taking out both heart ventricles in a single motion. Unable to scream, he'll die quietly in a matter of minutes.

The ICX guard freezes in place. He's the lesser threat. Far less trained and too young to have the wisdom that comes with experience, he's slow to process what just happened.

When it finally registers, he reaches for his weapon instead of punching the emergency button on the wall. It was a deadly error. Haven withdraws his knife and swings it in an arc toward him. He glances up, allowing the blade to slice across his neck. The carotid arteries and jugular veins are severed by the steel edge, as is his larynx. He grabs at his throat in horror before collapsing to the ground to bleed out in silence.

Haven wipes his knife on the man's uniform and sheathes it. He moves to the surveillance control console and selects the feed for this entrance. It isn't pointed inward but at the door leading to the access road. Perfect. He wasn't captured on video.

The action playing out at Post Seven is piped to one of the overhead displays. He has access to every camera on campus, allowing him better situation awareness than he thought he would be afforded. The current position and movement of all security forces personnel are tracked down to the meter. It was moronic to provide this capability into a perimeter security post. Then again, stupidity is why he faked his death and left Intercorpex in the first place.

The shooting in the north continues, punctuated by urgent pleas over the comms. He grins and rubs his hands together eagerly. He has his own command center now. This is going to be fun.

CHAPTER THIRTY-ONE
INTERCORPEX

"The Motor Pool"
Hell's Kitchen Geographic District
New York City Municipal Corporation

For a long moment, Zyree stares at the garments Malkor is holding. The ramifications are mind-boggling. The uniforms may be here because Haven opted not to don them, but that wouldn't make sense. Headquarters is swarming with BCS agents. He will blend in perfectly.

"Connect to the ICX Security watch officer, New York Headquarters Control," Zyree commands his biocomp.

"What do you want me to do?" Malkor asks, tossing the uniforms.

"Find a vehicle that runs. Make it a fast one that you can drive."

"Drive?"

"You took the aggressive driving training course. It's time to put it to use."

"Sure. It was only five years ago, so I'm sure I'll remember," the junior inspector adds with a heaping of sarcasm.

Self-driving cars were all the rage before the Great Collapse. That trend restarted when computer networks were restored and manufacturing rebooted in the early days of the Corporate Age. Unfortunately, it is forbidden in this corporation except when on high-speed thoroughfares. Urban driving is manual now.

"This is ICX Security—"

"This is Chief Inspector Zyree reporting an imminent Class A threat to the facility."

Malkor fires up an old two-door coupe and climbs out to open one of the overhead doors leading out of the garage.

"Class A threat? With all due respect, Chief Inspector, this is the most heavily guarded place on earth right now."

"I have actionable intelligence that terrorists are impersonating BCS agents and will attempt to breach the perimeter. Lock the campus down and reinforce vehicular access points."

"Okay, stand by."

Malkor jumps back into the red coupe and eases it up to the door. Zyree climbs in and signals him to punch it. The PSS can secure this site when they arrive. He and Malkor have bigger problems right now.

"Chief Inspector Zyree? This is Special Agent Kenychi of the BCS. I received your report of a Class A threat. The facility is secure. We already have triple the usual—"

"Terrorists are wearing your uniforms, Special Agent!" Zyree asks, becoming increasingly frustrated that his report isn't being taken seriously. "You need to lock down the campus."

"Orders are to grant access to late-arriving patricians."

"You've got to be kidding me! Damn your orders. If you don't deny access, a lot of people are going to die."

"Stand by, Chief Inspector."

Malkor gives Zyree a sideways look, hearing only half the conversation as he snakes through traffic. This corporation strictly enforced speed caps, so getting anywhere in a hurry will be challenging. They don't have strobes to force cars out of their way or an RTCC on the line to change traffic control indicators to green.

"Malkor, you're driving like an old lady. Floor it. Use the sidewalks if you have to."

"Hey, backseat driver, do you want to take the wheel?"

"If it gets us there faster, yeah."

"Chief Inspector, we're getting reports of sporadic gunfire from outside the perimeter at Post Seven."

"That's a diversion! Search everything at the gates. Check for vehicles that have recently entered the premises."

"Vehicular entry has not been reported from any access point. We have gunfire outside the perimeter and it's being handled. That's your terrorist attack unless you can prove otherwise."

Zyree punches and kicks the dash a few times after disconnecting the communications channel. There's nothing more to be gained by arguing. The arrogance of his own security team is mind-boggling. He might have expected that from the BCS. His people are trained to employ some common sense.

"Don't stop," Zyree says, feeling the conveyance decelerating.

"The traffic indicator is crimson."

"Run it."

Malkor takes a deep breath and blesses himself as he heeds the order. His eyes are welded shut as he blows through the intersection at high speed. Cars going north and south stop short or juke to get out of their path. Zyree flips the dash display to the rear-facing camera and surveys the carnage left behind as conveyances collide.

"We won't get there at all if the PSS stops us."

"They can chase us there for all I care. The more people at this party, the better."

Malkor weaves aggressively past Library Park and Grand Central Terminus. He slows enough at one traffic indicator to nudge through the intersection without running down the stream of employees crossing the street. Getting a feel for driving, Malkor guns the engine. Despite his best efforts, this is taking too long.

"Boss, I hate to ask, but what do you expect us to do once we get there?"

"Whatever we can."

"You could be wrong," he says, dodging another vehicle making a right onto the thoroughfare from a cross-street.

Zyree hopes that he is but knows he isn't. After more than a decade of service, he has learned to trust his gut. Right now, it's screaming that Haven is planning a bloodbath.

"Yeah, I could be wrong. If that ends up being the case, so be it. But those BCS uniforms weren't souvenirs, Malkor. Haven isn't planning on attacking the perimeter to kill a few guards."

Malkor glances over, waiting for Zyree to finish his thought.

"He's going *through* the perimeter in hopes of killing everybody."

CHAPTER THIRTY-TWO
THE PATRICIANS

Keating Family of the Gentez-Majorez Estate
Greenwich Geographic District
Southern Connecticut Municipal Corporation

This sprawling estate is the crown jewel in the Keating family empire. The acres of coastline real estate feature a fortress-like mansion, outbuildings and garages, a helipad, and sweeping manicured green lawns. It's majestic, but Denali's favorite place is the east botanical garden. When in bloom, a small army of horticulturists, botanists, and landscapers maintain thousands of fragrant flowering plants and bushes that are a feast for the senses.

Denali comes here for daily constitutionals, which are the only exercise his aging body sees. Walks are good for the body, but also the soul. Sometimes, like now, they provide time to think, reflect, and plan.

Abbot trails behind him at a respectful distance in silence. On most days, Denali walks unaccompanied. This is not like most days. Not by any stretch of the imagination.

"Good morning, sir," a member of his uniformed operations staff says as he approaches from the direction of the mansion.

"What is it?"

"Commander Lacune sent me to inform you that it's time."

Denali turns and stares at the coastline through the bushes and trees. Beyond Long Island Sound is the New York City Municipal Corporation. Nestled on the East River is Intercorpex's headquarters and a summit with the most powerful people on the planet. Well, most of them. He has no intention of joining them. He will watch the world change from here.

"Is everything on schedule?"

"Our teams on the ground have reported that the package is in transit and on schedule for delivery."

Denali nods. That's the easy part. What happens next is what matters.

"Have the commander contact our insider. Tell him to retrieve Sergeant Shaw."

The young soldier cocks his head. "Sir?"

"He'll understand."

Very few other people will. The reference is to the 1959 novel *The Manchurian Candidate* by Richard Condon. It's on the corporate banned list, along with most works from that era.

The novel begins in South Korea in 1952 when a U.S. Army patrol is ambushed and captured. The squad escapes a year later, and Staff Sergeant Raymond Shaw receives a prestigious medal for single-handedly saving their lives. That's what they were brainwashed to believe. Shaw is a sleeper agent programmed to perform assassinations when he hears a post-hypnotic trigger, and then he forgets every detail of the mission. His KGB handler is his overbearing mother, who convinced communist leaders to install her politician husband as president so they could control the American government.

It was a good novel. Too bad corporations don't allow their employees to read the classics. He thought the reference was appropriate for this situation, even if the ending isn't.

"Will you join the commander in Ops?" the young man asks.

"I will momentarily."

"Very well, sir," he says before hustling back down the path.

"Isn't it obvious that not all the patrician families aren't represented at the conference?" Abbot asks, coming up alongside Denali.

"It won't matter an hour from now. They will have bigger concerns. Contact the members of the Trust. Inform them that the wheels are in motion."

"And if they press me for details?"

The corner of Denali's mouth curls. "Explain to them that you don't have any. They can speak to me directly to voice their concerns."

Abbot respectfully bows and moves off. Denali pauses to enjoy the view and inhale a gulp of the fresh air. The next time he visits this garden, the world will be on fire, and he will be that much closer to his goal.

CHAPTER THIRTY-THREE
INTERCORPEX

ICX Headquarters Assembly Hall
Midtown Manhattan Geographic District
New York City Municipal Corporation

Raimius has been prattling on for over fifteen minutes now. Maybe his plan is to win over the patricians by boring them all to death. Most stopped paying attention ten minutes ago. They want answers, and he's offering only meaningless words and platitudes.

The woman next to Lyris stifles a yawn. She looks at him sheepishly when he catches her and grins. Intercorpex employees are forcing themselves to appear interested out of fear of the consequences. Every single one of them would choose to be anywhere else but here right now.

"Director Lyris, you need to come with me," a voice whispers in his ear.

He turns to see the clearly nervous man who somehow managed to materialize at his side. "I'm sorry?"

"We have to go *right now*," he says with unnerving urgency.

"Who are you?"

"A representative for Denali Keating."

"Why do we have to leave?"

"Because those are my instructions," he says, shifting his eyes to study the people around them.

Lyris doesn't continue arguing. He eases out of his seat and follows the man to the corner of the hall before stopping. "Tell me what's going on."

"We have five minutes to leave, and the clock started two minutes ago. Please, sir, we must move *now*."

Lyris has no idea what's going on. Beads of sweat are rolling down the man's forehead. Whatever Denali is planning can't be good. It might be smart to be somewhere else when it happens.

"Lead the way."

"Going dark for the first time in our history has been traumatic for all of the men and women who work long hours to keep this exchange running smoothly," Raimius laments from the stage. "But it has also provided us with unique opportunities – opportunities that we plan to take full advantage of.

"The past month's events have been tragic but also illuminating. We have been provided a chance to pause and reflect on what we've accomplished and what we still need to accomplish. A result of that soul-searching is a new strategic direction that will define the relationship between the exchange, our distinguished corporate members, and the great patrician families."

Lyris wonders how the regents will react to that. He glances up at the stage. The executives flanking the bloviating AG are getting restless. He catches sight of Nevala standing in the corner, patiently waiting to resume her emcee duties.

"Hold on. I'll be right back."

"We don't have time, sir," the escort says, a little too loudly.

Ignoring him, Lyris walks back toward the stage along the east wall. Despite his best efforts, it's tough to be inconspicuous. Nevala spots him and begins walking up the aisle.

"Analysts have been able to evaluate our personnel and resource requirements to determine if we have the right people in the right positions. Intercorpex prides itself on the skill and professionalism of its staff, but sometimes changes must be made to allow the organization to grow."

"I need you to follow me, no questions asked," Lyris whispers when they reach each other.

A confused look flashes across her face, but she complies without argument. They are heading back toward the escort when the tenor of Raimius's voice changes.

"Trust me when I say that we have already begun purging the personnel whose inattentiveness and poor judgment brought this exchange to the edge of calamity."

That comment was directed at Lyris. He pauses at the exit and turns to the stage to see Raimius glaring at him from the podium. He flashes a wide smile and executes a sloppy salute. Whatever is about to happen, he's certain Raimius won't be in a position to retaliate against him.

CHAPTER
THIRTY-FOUR
LIBERTEUM

ICX Headquarters
Midtown Manhattan Geographic District
New York City Municipal Corporation

Now the music is playing. Haven feels like a conductor whose orchestra doesn't need guidance. He can watch Nyvar get escorted to the target and listen as the communications grow more desperate. He has never enjoyed himself this much.

"All stations, this is Control. We have reports of shots fired at Post Seven."

"Control, this is Roving Three. Report confirmed. Post Seven is under attack, and men are down. We have engaged hostile contacts outside the perimeter."

"Six confirms. Targets spotted on the ramp to the East Side Highway opposite the cooling plant."

"Roger. Roving Three, hold your position. QRF is in route."

The words are like a sweet melody. Haven was counting on response teams getting committed to the north. It's reassuring that Intercorpex Security hasn't changed its playbook in the years since he "died." The reaction to the diversion takes that piece out of play. He checks the camera feed to see what's happening with Nyvar.

"Main Gate Two, this is Control. Where did that truck come from?"

"Shit."

Haven searches for the button to establish an audio reply but can't find it. Then the feed cuts out, and the display fills with the image of someone he assumes is in charge. Wearing the close-cropped hair of an archetypal BCS agent, the Asian man stares at him with competent eyes.

"Main Gate Two, what's going on?"

"Nothing, sir," Haven states. "The vehicle was dispatched here on orders from the Pentagon with extra barriers."

"Who are you?"

"Special Agent Hyven," Haven says, altering his name just enough so he'll respond to it immediately if it's ever used.

"Hyven? You're not assigned to this detail. I personally oversee the roster. Where is the ICX security guard manning that post?"

"He's escorting the vehicle."

"I see, very well."

The video clicks off, and the camera feed returns to the display. Haven grimaces. He didn't buy it. They're out of time.

A group of men approaches Nyvar from the north, barking orders for him not to move. Haven secures the dead agent's rifle and moves to the side door. Using a concrete barrier for cover, the terrorist kneels and takes up a supported firing position. He needs to buy Nyvar a few seconds to arm himself. Aligning his digital sights on the lead ICX guard, Haven breathes, pauses, and then squeezes the trigger.

The shot echoes off the concrete and glass buildings that make up the main structures of the ICX complex. The man drops before the sound even registers. His counterparts stare at him for a moment too long. When they realize he's down, it's already too late. Haven takes aim and lets loose several rounds in succession. Three more men drop, forcing the truck's escort to dive onto the ground.

Nyvar wastes no time retrieving his rifle. He abandons the vehicle and breaks into a full sprint toward the gate. Haven lays suppressive fire, but it isn't enough. Security forces begin materializing everywhere, guided by overhead drones now taking a keen interest in their presence. One of them dives at him and pulls up before moving off. He notices why with mere seconds to spare.

Haven ducks behind the concrete barrier just before an explosion nearly engulfs him. Cement chips are blasted from the barrier as bullets from another drone's automatic weapon rip it apart. He's pinned down, and the jaws of the vise are closing.

The fire ceases, and Haven hazards a look. The drone is sputtering smoke and struggling to maintain altitude. It loses the fight and craters into the ground. Behind it, a kneeling Nyvar lowers his rifle. Good man. He stands and is starting to run when a pink burst erupts through his shoulder, spinning him and sending him tumbling hard to the ground.

"Nyvar!"

He lifts his weapon and fires behind before taking another bullet for the effort. He's not going to be able to move.

Haven lays down a desperate salvo of suppressive fire. The return volleys force him to dive back into cover. There are just too many to fight off. He'll be cut down before making it ten steps.

Nyvar knows it, too. He lifts his head and stares at his boss with a face that betrays his actions before Haven notices him clutching the detonator. This was the mission, and he will see it through no matter the cost. Haven nods, and Nyvar returns it. What needed to be said between them was uttered long ago.

"Goodbye, old friend," Haven mutters. "See you in hell."

He dodges rifle fire as he moves around the front of the guardhouse. They are closing in, but their time is up. Haven dives to the ground and covers his head and ears. The building won't offer much protection, but it's better than nothing. Whether he survives this or not, he's going to win. The thought causes him to smile.

The overpressure from the blast hits him before the sound of the explosion. The guard shack crumbles around him an instant before a deafening roar overwhelms his ears. The air is replaced by searing heat as the fireball expands. The earth shakes from the concussion. Air sucked back into the vacuum carries dirt and debris with it.

Day turns into night as Haven holds his breath to avoid inhaling the superheated air. Lives were extinguished more quickly than the men and women in that building deserved. After all the planning and training, he finally has his vengeance. The angry roar of sheer destruction fades fifteen seconds later. The only thing punctuating the eerie silence is the sound of his laughter.

CHAPTER THIRTY-FIVE

RYKOS

"Valhalla"
Midtown Geographic District
New York City Municipal Corporation

This is an interesting place. Quarren constructed this stronghold deep underground to avoid detection. For all intents and purposes, it's a fancy tomb. Being sealed off from the world makes it nearly invisible but comes with a few downsides. There are no windows to see the city, and the lack of natural light makes Valhalla feel claustrophobic. The air is filtered, so no aromas waft through to tickle the nostrils. Sounds bounce off the walls, making even whispers sound like they are run through a speaker system.

When nobody is talking, the two loudest sounds are and people typing on keyboards. When the hackers aren't working or the fans cut out, Valhalla is deathly still, even during the daytime.

That's one reason they leave AME News on at least one of the displays that line the walls of the operations room. It's a lifeline to the outside world that makes me feel a little less out of touch down here. I was raised to check our stock price every couple of minutes. It's what good executives do, or until recently, did. It's not a skill that anybody is using now.

I'm moving around better now, but my abdomen is still sore. I need rest, but the lack of appreciable exercise is taking the biggest toll on me. I am standing to stretch when the lights suddenly cut out. The operations center plunges into pitch darkness as the room begins shaking. I reach out for anything to steady myself as the floor vibrates. The effect only lasts a few seconds, but the lights haven't come on.

"What the hell was that?" Jasper asks through the darkness.

"Are we getting breached?" I ask.

"Adiz, find the flashlights," Michele commands. It turns out to be unnecessary.

The lights flicker back on, and the computers in the room begin rebooting. We all look at each other in confusion as Michele snatches an old two-way radio from its charging base.

"Koltayne, report. Are you okay?" Michele asks into the handheld radio they only use for emergencies.

"I'm fine. I think the cathedral may be missing a few windows, though."

"Do you know what that was?"

"Not exactly. It felt like a shockwave."

"Stay on alert. Adiz, Jasper…we need those computers up."

"They're coming online now," Jasper says.

Everyone watches the display as the boot sequence ends. Adiz types some commands, and a video player launches. He switches the feed to an AME News long shot of Manhattan's East Side. Everyone's eyes grow wide, and Michele covers her mouth.

"What…the…hell?" I don't know what else to say. The devastation at the Intercorpex campus is astounding. "You guys have bombs capable of that?"

"No."

I react to the quick denial. "What do you mean? Haven did that! Is that what you planned—"

"No! We don't have anything nearly that powerful."

I want to believe her, but I've learned not to underestimate this group. They are capable of almost anything. They make their own weapons, gunpowder, and explosives. There is no reason to believe they couldn't build a bomb that destructive.

"Then where did he get it from?"

"That's a good question," she says, turning to Jasper. "Get Narik in here."

Jasper does as he's instructed. The patrician is escorted into the operations center and is as surprised as we were when he sees the plume of smoke on the news feed.

"Talk."

"Damn," he says, ignoring the demand.

Michele gets his undivided attention when she holds her knife to his throat. "I said talk."

"Whoa. What do you want to know?"

"Where did Haven get the materials for a bomb that powerful?"

"How the hell would I know!"

"Someone is supporting him. Haven is a brilliant tactician but a lousy chemist. His men are loyal and fierce but not that bright. Who gave him the bomb?"

"Not me. I tried to have him killed, remember?"

Michele studies him and then removes the knife from his jugular. He's right. Narik is down here because he sold Haven out to the PSS and then pulled a gun on Michele. It doesn't make any sense that the Covingtons would materially support him.

"Sit him down."

Narik is forced into a chair as the feed changes to a shot much closer. People covered in cuts and blood-soaked clothing are wandering the streets. Debris from what used to be Assembly Hall is everywhere.

The world has changed. If Michele thought that the manhunt for her, Haven, and Liberteum was bad before, she hasn't seen anything yet. The BCS will flood thousands of agents into this city. They will scour every inch of the underground with every available piece of technology. There is no hiding and no escape. Haven just put Liberteum squarely in the middle of everyone's crosshairs, and I am standing there with them.

CHAPTER THIRTY-SIX

AMERICA, INC.

NYCMC Waterside Advanced Trauma Center
Gramercy Geographic District
New York City Municipal Corporation

She wasn't expecting hugs and warm greetings. Hers isn't that kind of family. It has never been, even when times were good. What Ilaria didn't expect were angry glares and open hostility from her spouse and his adoring daughter.

"Shouldn't you be heading off to your fancy new corporate job?"

Ilaria is used to her husband being a condescending ass. It amazes her that he still finds a way to make her feel insignificant while he's laid up in a medical center. She wants to explain that Safmor granted her permission to visit him while he was at the Intercorpex summit. She doesn't bother. He won't care.

"Varella, give me a minute alone with your father, please."

"Mother, I'm a part of this fam—"

"Now, Varella!" Ilaria snaps.

Teman nods when her daughter appeals to him. Ilaria can *feel* the resentment as Varella glowers at her until reaching the door. There is no doubt where her loyalties lie. She has always been daddy's little executive.

"You didn't have to dismiss her like that. She's hurting too."

"This is a conversation between a husband and wife. Our daughter doesn't need to be here for it."

"That's what this is? A husband-*wife* conversation? You're not acting like my wife. You haven't shown an ounce of compassion for what I've been through."

"Compassion? You *hit* me, Teman," Ilaria says, futilely fighting back the tears welling in her eyes. "Is that your idea of compassion?"

"I'm sorry for that."

"Are you? Or are you just ashamed because your guardians intervened?"

"Both, I guess."

She shakes her head, wishing he hadn't answered that question honestly.

"I was stressed. You were pushing my buttons and...."

The tears win the battle and stream down her cheeks. He doesn't get it. The years of being chief guardian have made him callous and jaded. When the stress becomes overwhelming, she's his most convenient target.

"I'm sorry, Ilaria, for everything. Tell me what to say to make this better. To make us better."

"You can't *say* anything. You hit me. You shot our son. Do you think either of those is forgivable?"

"Rykos was working with terrorists," he barks. "What part of that don't you get?"

"He is your *son*, Teman. What part of giving him the benefit of the doubt don't *you* understand?"

"You weren't there."

"I didn't need to be. You shot him while he was rescuing you."

He stares at her blankly. "You weren't there."

The silence grows from short and tense to uncomfortably long. Neither of them knows what to say. Twenty-plus years of marriage, and they feel like complete strangers.

"You'll never forgive me, will you?" Teman finally asks in a voice a shade above a whisper.

"You took my son from me."

Ilaria doesn't give him the news about Rykos. A man without a shred of regret for what he did doesn't need to know that he's still alive. Teman has been perpetually locked in a winner-take-all battle between loyalty to his job and his obligation to his family. It's a conflict that has defined his entire adult life. The battle was decided in a dark crypt under an old Manhattan church. He was faced with the choice and made it.

"You need to know something. The entire time I was tortured, I thought of you, Rykos, and Varella. All the things I've done wrong...the mistakes I've made. My family got me through that, even when I wanted to break. I was so close to giving up. Then I saw Rykos...."

Tears form in Teman's eyes.

"I don't know what I was thinking. Maybe I wasn't. I guess what I'm trying to say is—"

The door is thrown open, and two giant guardians violently burst into the room. Ilaria and Teman stare slack-jawed as a third guardian with the rank of captain enters. He nods at his chief guardian before turning to her.

"You need to come with me, ma'am," he decrees.

"I'm having a—"

"Right now, ma'am," he demands.

Each burly man hooks Ilaria under an arm. The captain holds the door open as she's hauled out without explanation.

"What's going—?"

"Move now!" the guardian shouts as Varella is pushed out of the way.

Ilaria's feet skip across the floor as she's carted down the corridor toward the elevators. Another group of guardians in full tactical gear form a protective shield around them. Anyone in their path gets brushed aside. A doctor, intently studying a patient record, doesn't notice the train bulldozing towards him. His lack of awareness is rewarded with a shove into the wall.

The convoy swerves into the stairwell and descends it like a river cascading down a waterfall. Once on the ground floor, Ilaria is ushered into the foyer, where another phalanx of guardians keeps watch over stunned employees. The escort crashes through the front doors and stuffs her into a waiting conveyance. The two men from the room join her in the back while the captain rides up front with the driver.

"Can somebody tell me what the hell is going on?" Ilaria demands as they tear out of the entryway, followed by a tactical vehicle providing escort.

"I'm sorry, ma'am, we didn't mean to frighten you. Your safety is our primary concern. We need to secure you at One Guardian Plaza immediately."

"Why? What's happened?"

"There's been an explosion at Intercorpex Headquarters."

"Oh my God! How bad? I-I mean, are there any injuries?"

The men exchange weary glances.

"Assembly Hall is gone. We are assuming the worst."

Gone. Ilaria struggles to understand what that means. How can an entire building just be gone? Then she remembers the Broad Street explosion and the resulting crater in the middle of the street.

"Safmor…the top executives…."

"They were present at the meeting. There are likely no survivors."

The news hits her with the force of a brick. She's too numb to comprehend much of anything right now, much less what the loss of the entire corporate executive structure means.

"Who's in charge of the NYCMC right now?"

He turns and looks Ilaria in the eyes. "You are."

* * *

A summons to the Situation Room usually comes by way of internal communication. Not this time. Two BCS agents retrieve their CEO and escort her down here. Whatever is happening is not the usual crisis.

"I'm spending more time here than in the Oval Office," Zeykala says after arriving. "This had better be good."

"It's anything but good, I'm afraid. There has been an explosion at Intercorpex Headquarters," Virtari declares in a voice devoid of emotion on the VidLynk display from the Pentagon. "Intercorpex's Assembly Hall has been leveled. There has also been significant damage to the tower building."

Zeykala stares at him blankly. Did he just say "leveled?" She's trying to imagine what that looks like and can't.

"Ma'am, I'm pulling up live drone footage from the scene and putting it on the main display," an agent at the table says.

The video is dark because of something obscuring the camera and not due to a problem with the drone's feed. When it shifts position, she realizes it was flying through smoke pouring from what's left of the building. After it repositions, everyone in the room gasps in unison.

Assembly Hall has been reduced to rubble. Only the southeast corner of the structure closest to the tower remains standing. Nobody could have survived. The smoke would have asphyxiated the survivors if the blast or flying debris didn't kill them.

Windows are blown out on the tower's lower floors. Pieces of Assembly Hall are strewn across the campus. It reminds her of the archived images of the September Eleventh attacks in the financial district that started the United States on its downward spiral.

"Was there any warning?" the CEO asks quietly.

"No, ma'am. Medical and fire services have responded, but no survivors from inside the building have been located. There are hundreds of casualties within the blast radius."

"Do we have an official list of attendees to the summit?" Zeykala manages to ask while staring in disbelief at the footage.

"We have a working list that Special Agent Caylem provided," Virtari says. "Administrator-General Raimius, the entire Intercorpex Board of Regents, top executives from the New York City Municipal Corporation, and hundreds of patricians are presumed dead."

Zeykala's mouth hangs open. Politics be damned. She doesn't care how many agents and officers the BCS and Intercorpex deployed to secure the site. The decision to hold the summit there was reckless. Raimius's ego just got him killed, and now she will pay the price.

"Director Virtari, how the hell was this allowed to happen?" Zeykala demands, feeling her shock morph into anger.

"We're still working that out, Chief Executive."

"Working it out?" she shouts. "There's a crater where the building once stood, and you don't know how it got there? Where's the agent you put in charge up there? What the hell was his name?"

"Special Agent Caylem. He's dead. He was on the stage while Raimius was addressing the patricians. Special Agent Kenychi has assumed command and is coordinating with ICX Security to determine what happened."

"Tell him we need answers. If Raimius is dead, who's leading Intercorpex?"

"It's mass confusion right now. Zurich is scrambling. Nobody is in charge."

Zeykala slowly lowers herself into her seat. She needs to get ahead of this. Whoever ends up running the exchange will immediately blame America Incorporated, which will reflect on her.

"Get me a VidLynk with anybody you can find. What about the NYCMC?"

"Same problem. Most of the leadership was at the meeting. Executives need to gather to determine who was lost and reconcile that with the succession plan."

"Get to New York, Virtari," Zeykala says, rubbing her temples. "I someone to take charge. We need to catch whoever did this."

"With all due respect, ma'am, I'm short on manpower up there."

In only the third full day of her tenure as acting chief executive officer, she is weathering a catastrophic storm. This crisis is an opportunity for her to show leadership. The world will be watching, and more importantly, so will the shareholders and board of directors.

"Assume full control of Public Safety and Security personnel and facilities. You'll have the order on your tablet by the time you arrive," she says, turning to one of the executives in the room. "Get it drafted."

"Yes, ma'am."

"Where's my VidLynk with Intercorpex?"

"All requests to Zurich, Wall Street, and ICX Headquarters are being declined."

"Keep trying."

This crisis is an opportunity but also a liability. Valen was removed for his incompetence in stopping attacks on Intercorpex. Now, part of their headquarters has been destroyed and their leadership murdered. Zeykala knows that to escape Valen's fate, she needs to find a scapegoat fast.

CHAPTER THIRTY-SEVEN
THE PATRICIANS

Keating Family of the Gentez-Majorez Estate
Greenwich Geographic District
Southern Connecticut Municipal Corporation

The aftermath is stunning. Denali has never seen an explosion that size in real-time. When nuclear Armageddon gripped the Middle East during the Valentine's Day Holocaust, it wasn't beamed into his mansion as it happened. The world didn't see the footage of the mushroom clouds leveling ancient desert cities until hours or days later.

The carnage at Intercorpex is beamed onto these displays in high definition. The explosives that his men supplied Haven with packed a punch. Assembly Hall has been erased from existence. The only hope for survival was not being in there.

"Anything?" Denali asks, not taking his eyes off the display.

"No, sir. Our asset still hasn't checked in," Commander Lacune says, standing over near the communications console in Denali's underground command center.

"What is he waiting for?"

"I can't be sure. He had instructions to check in when he and Lyris were clear."

Denali grumbles. He doesn't appreciate delays. "Is it possible they didn't get out in time?"

Lacune checks the console again. "He had enough advance notice. Any explanations about his radio silence would be pure speculation, sir."

"Then confirm it."

Denali is navigating through the various feeds from Manhattan. He has more angles of the destruction than anyone else on the planet. Lacune posted scouts in adjacent buildings with cameras pointing at the Intercorpex campus. He watched Haven breach the gate and engage in the ensuing firefight. Then the fireworks started. His driver was making a run for it when he got hit from behind. There was no cowardice in that man. He detonated the bomb, and then Denali didn't see much of anything. Now that the initial blast effects have cleared, he has a better idea of the situation on the ground and the damage inflicted.

"Sir, our teams don't have Lyris in their line of sight. If he's alive, he's likely in the tower."

"Do you have any teams in plain clothes?"

"Yes, sir. They were deployed in America Incorporated employee uniforms to blend in."

"Are any in PSS or ICX Security uniforms?"

"No, sir," Lacune says, his tone low.

Denali scowls. That was an oversight. The outcome of this mission was always going to require a massive security response. They should have been carrying those uniforms.

"What about Haven? Did he survive?"

"We're awaiting confirmation. The building he was sheltering behind was decimated."

"Then it shouldn't be that hard if he's a corpse. You had a team tracking his movements."

"The team was injured in the blast."

Denali looks at his commander with a raised eyebrow. "Injured?"

"Windows were shattered for blocks from the epicenter. They reported serious injuries from flying glass."

"Didn't they duck?" Denali grumbles.

Lacune doesn't say anything. He doesn't need to. They knew what would happen and should have taken the necessary precautions. The men he hired are supposed to be the best-trained in the world. They need to start acting like it.

"Commander Lacune, I have questions that need answers. Find them for me. I will be in the study."

"Right away, sir."

Denali retreats upstairs to the only room he spends any appreciable time in. The video feeds streaming into the operations center will be piped up to the large display so he can watch from the comfort of a leather sofa with a drink in his hand. He also tunes into AME News. He wants to see how America Incorporated tries to spin this coverage. It's impossible to ignore a blast that makes what happened on Broad Street look like a cherry bomb.

Abbot slips into the room. As Denali's *de facto* gatekeeper, all requests to speak to the esteemed patrician must go through him. There is no doubt that a list is forming.

"Sir, several patricians have requested VidLynks with you."

Denali nods. Members of the Trust, no doubt. The problem with a conspiracy is dealing with the co-conspirators. Some things they know. Other things they have been kept in the dark about. This is one of the latter. He will answer for that later but now is not the time.

"I'm indisposed. I will contact them when I'm available."

Abbot nods and disappears as stealthily as he arrived. Denali rubs his chin. Loose ends must be tied before he can celebrate. Haven needs to be found and killed. His capture by the BCS would be catastrophic. Lyris, as useless as he is, needs to have survived to take the reins of control at Intercorpex.

This part of the plan is out of his control. What happens, happens. He can only adapt to the moves of others. Every chess master plans a dozen moves ahead, but the rules of chess are finite and understood. Life isn't like that. He has mapped out countless courses of action but needs to be ready to deviate from them. So long as he keeps his eyes on his destination, it doesn't matter what path he blazes to get to it.

CHAPTER
THIRTY-EIGHT

INTERCORPEX

ICX Headquarters
Midtown Manhattan Geographic District
New York City Municipal Corporation

The air is so thick with smoke that a chainsaw couldn't cut through it. Lyris rolls onto his back and coughs and hacks, struggling to pull into his lungs what little oxygen isn't displaced. He rolls back to his stomach and climbs to his knees, feeling every muscle and bone in his body protest the movement. He struggles to clear his vision, first by blinking and then by scraping off the dust cementing his eyes shut.

He senses someone move next to him, and he gropes around to remove the debris. Nevala regains consciousness, and he helps sit her up. They are staggering to their feet when he nearly trips over a body. It must be Denali's representative. He checks for a pulse and doesn't find one.

He pulls her toward the main building. When they reach the foyer, his lungs get their first breath of better air. The area is still hazy and smoky, but nothing like what he just experienced.

"Are you okay?" he asks between coughs in a voice loud enough for him to hear over the ringing in his ears.

"I think so," Nevala says, checking herself over as she violently coughs.

Lyris lifts his head and stares in amazement at what he sees. The foyer is covered in shattered glass. Some people are in a frenzied panic, while others wander around in a daze. A few have managed to keep their senses and are helping evacuate the wounded. Everyone is covered in pulverized concrete dust and bloody clothing.

"Director Lyris? Is that you? You-you're alive!" an agitated man shouts as he approaches, shining a torchlight directly into his face.

"Yeah, barely. Calm down and tell me what happened."

"It's gone!" he says, pointing back the way they came. "The whole building is gone!"

"Where's Raimius?"

"He's gone! They're all gone," he wails before sobbing uncontrollably.

The man is in shock. Getting details out of him will be impossible. Lyris is desperate to find someone who has information.

"Hey! Hey!" he shouts, getting the attention of two bunker gear-clad rescuers who enter the building with fire axes.

"Sir?"

"This man is in shock. Take care of him," Lyris orders one man before turning to the other. "You, follow me."

The duo complies, and Lyris heads to the elevator, with Nevala struggling to keep pace. Millions of glass shards crunch under his feet. No wonder Denali's representative was in a hurry to get him out of there. He was nervous because he knew what was about to happen.

"You have an elevator override, right?" Lyris asks the rescue professional.

"Yes, but this is an emergency—"

"Open the doors. I will help you coordinate the evacuation from the security control center."

The man begins to protest but stops. Nodding, he pulls a device out of his pocket and signals the elevator up from one of the subfloors. The trio climbs aboard and rides up in silence. Everyone in the control center stops what they're doing to marvel at them when they enter the room.

"Holy sh— Director Lyris, are you okay?" an ICX inspector asks.

"I've been better. Someone assist this gentleman in coordinating an evacuation. Who's in charge of the exchange?"

"Nobody. Leadership was in Assembly Hall for Raimius's remarks."

"Nevala, you work in the AG's office. What's the disaster recovery plan?"

Lyris stares at her intently, hoping she reads his eyes. This is the moment they have been waiting for. Raimius is gone. The regents are gone. There is only one person standing in his way.

"The regents would choose a successor, but that's not an option. In a crisis, one of Raimius's direct reports would assume control, but they're also gone. The only person left is the EDGO, but there's a problem with that."

"What problem?" the inspector asks.

"Raimius was in the process of firing Executive Director Wyeth for insubordination. The paperwork is being processed by human resources. He's not necessarily...legitimate."

Lyris smiles to himself. He loves this woman. Nevala knew exactly what she needed to say without any prodding. To keep up appearances, Lyris exhales loudly.

"Okay, fine. Listen up, everybody. In the absence of any clear successor per the DR plan, I'm taking charge of Intercorpex. Does anyone have an objection?"

The heads in the room shake a collective no. They look relieved that someone is taking the reins of leadership and providing guidance.

"No, sir," the ICX inspector concurs.

"Good. First things first: what's the damage to the rest of the campus?"

"Unknown, sir. The tower building somehow still has communications and power. There are shattered windows on the lower floors up to ten, but we will need an engineering team to inspect for major structural damage."

"Evacuate the entire building. Start with the wounded from the lower floors," Lyris directs the facilities manager and fire rescue guardian. "All non-essential personnel can exit the grounds via the south accesses to avoid the blast area."

Lyris walks over to a display showing real-time aerial video footage of the site. He's aghast at the destruction. The scene is as incredible as it is horrifying. This bomb wasn't a small device.

"How the hell did this happen?"

"An NYCMC Transportation truck containing barriers was passed through the perimeter," an Asian man wearing the uniform of America Incorporated's Bureau of Corporate Security says as he emerges from the far side of the room.

"Who the hell are you?"

"Special Agent Kenychi, Second Agent in Charge, America Incorporated Bureau of Corporate Security."

"Second agent in charge? Where's the first agent in charge?"

"He was standing ten feet away from your administrator-general."

Lyris doesn't appreciate the glib response. "In other words, he was incinerated by an explosion from a truck you admitted into our campus."

"We are still ascertaining—"

"You either let a truck in, or you didn't, Agent Kenychi. Which is it?"

The man does not fluster easily. He knows he's in a hostile environment considering the attack that just murdered a thousand people happened in his sphere of influence.

"One of our perimeter posts came under fire. We responded with roving units and the QRF to neutralize the threat. During that time, a vehicle was passed through the auxiliary gate. We don't know how or why. When it was discovered, I contacted the gate, but the agent manning it didn't match our personnel roster. The patrol I dispatched to investigate was engaged. They returned fire, and drones responded, but…you know what happened next."

Everyone in the room stares at Lyris. He's seething at the dispassionate tone of Kenychi's narrative. This was a gruesome attack that shouldn't be treated with such apathy. Everyone in the room must feel the same way.

"Escort Special Agent Kenychi and his people off our campus."

"That's a mistake," he protests.

"No, the mistake was thinking America Incorporated could keep the promise it made to protect the exchange or its people. Now," Lyris says, moving within inches from his face, "get the hell out of my building."

The man doesn't flinch. He doesn't respond at all. After a tense moment, he turns and nods at his fellow agents. Lyris watches them leave the control center and turns to the ICX inspector.

"Has the attack he mentioned been neutralized?"

"We believe the shooters near Post Seven withdrew. There has been no contact with hostiles since the blast."

"Then they're still out there. Contact One Guardian Plaza. I want the PSS to establish a hard perimeter around this campus. In the meantime, organize a security overwatch with whoever is left to cover evacuees leaving the area. I don't want our employees gunned down in an ambush."

"Yes, sir."

"Good man," Lyris says with a reassuring pat on the shoulder. "Someone get me a VidLynk to Zurich. I want to speak with Commandant-General Jurghen to find out if he had any intelligence on this."

"You need medical attention, Administrator-General."

Lyris tries not to smile at hearing the title. "It can wait. We have work to do."

The room begins to buzz with activity as Lyris pulls Nevala aside. He checks to see if anyone is listening, but they're all preoccupied.

"Well played," she whispers.

"You did a fantastic job. Now we need to make your story hold up before Wyeth learns that he should be running things. Can you fabricate the order firing him?"

Nevala purses her lips. "I think so. Will he believe that?"

"I know he will," Lyris says with a nod. "Just get it done. I'll take care of the rest."

CHAPTER THIRTY-NINE
AMERICA, INC.

Shareholder Hall
Corporate Hill Governance District
Washington-Arlington Municipal Corporation

Fiolla is a woman on a mission. Despite having several opportunities to adjourn Valen's hearing before the board, Chairman Hammond stayed the course. The two men have known each other for decades, and Valen was as shocked as she was that he continued it and cast the deciding ballot. Valen may have laid himself in the coffin, but Hammond nailed it shut.

The chairman has made no public announcements or appearances since the hearing. It's hard for a man of his importance to spend even a few hours off the grid. She storms into his office to uncover the reasons and isn't leaving until she gets answers.

"Is the Chairman in?" Fiolla asks the executive assistant seated at her desk in Hammond's outer office.

"I think so," she says, glancing over at the closed door after checking the biographical information of their guest when it pops up. "He was here when I arrived and instructed his digital assistant not to disturb him."

"Does he do that often?"

"I've been assigned here for years. I've never seen him do that. He hasn't been acting himself since the hearing."

Fiolla presses her lips together. He betrayed one of his friends and closest allies. He ought to feel guilty about that.

"Do you know how long he'll be?"

"No, I'm afraid not, Executive Fiolla. You're welcome to wait while I post a message to his display."

"Thank you."

Fiolla takes a seat in the waiting area when she hears a VidLynk request chime at the assistant's workstation. Her hand gestures to open the connection.

"Chairman Hammond's Office."

"This is Washington Public Safety and Security, Medical Response Unit. We received a notification from the Executive Monitoring Directorate that there is a communications cutout on Chairman Hammond's biojack. Can you confirm there is no medical emergency?"

The blood drains out of his assistant's face. EMD notifications are treated as routine by the WPSS during business hours. Executives interact with staff, who would immediately sound the alarm in an emergency. She hasn't seen her boss this morning, so this may be anything but routine.

"Well…uh…no, he's been locked in his office all morning."

"We're sending an emergency response team," the guardian informs her. "They'll be there in two minutes."

Fiolla doesn't plan on waiting that long. She rushes over to the office door and bangs hard on it with her fist. "Chairman Hammond? Chairman Hammond? This is Executive Fiolla. Open up, please!"

She doesn't hear a response. This door is thick but not that thick. She slams her fist into it a couple more times. Again, there's no response. Frustrated, she backs up a couple of steps and launches forward, throwing her shoulder into it. She weighs one hundred and twenty pounds. It was an act of desperation more than a practical solution.

"Ma'am, that's a steel core door with top-of-the-line magnetic locks."

"Then open it."

"I can't. The access is computer-controlled."

"You have an override code, right?" Fiolla asks, growing annoyed.

"I do, but Chairman Hammond gave me strict instructions—"

"You just received a report of a medical emergency! He could have suffered a heart attack at his desk. To hell with his instructions. Override the computer and open the damn door!"

Cowed into compliance, she returns to her workstation and calls up the access window. She taps a hexadecimal code on her virtual keyboard and enters a numeric admin password. Fiolla hears the magnetic locks disengage, and she swings the doors open.

Chairman Hammond is slumped over at his desk. Fiolla inches closer until she sees that he didn't suffer a heart attack or stroke. Blood gushed from a puncture in his neck until his heart stopped beating. The culprit is an antique letter opener in his right hand.

"Oh, my God! No!" the assistant shrieks in terror.

Fiolla stands petrified in the middle of the office. The world goes on around her, yet she's oblivious. Emergency rescue workers arrive, breezing past her to confirm what is already known. This isn't a medical emergency; it's a crime scene. Chairman Hammond is dead.

Guardians arrive and begin securing the scene. They could suspect foul play, or it could be a standard operating procedure. Regardless, they're treating his death as suspicious. That's exactly what she thinks it is.

"Ma'am? You work at the White House, right?" a woman on the medical team asks as she comes up alongside Fiolla.

"Yeah."

"Then you should see this," she says, gesturing over her shoulder.

Fiolla follows her back into the outer office, where she points at the large wall display. AME News is showing drone footage of billowing smoke from Midtown Manhattan.

"What the hell?"

She is captivated by the sight, and it takes Fiolla a moment to hear her tablet's incessant chirping. Recognizing the priority alert tone, she accesses the comms and opens the emergency communication. The message is succinct:

Attack in New York. Return to the White House immediately.

CHAPTER
FORTY

INTERCORPEX

ICX Headquarters
Midtown Manhattan Geographic District
New York City Municipal Corporation

With traffic at a dead standstill, Zyree and Malkor abandon their vehicle and trek on foot to what's left of Intercorpex. They were too late, and their warnings went unheeded. The resulting devastation is unimaginable. The power of the explosives used to level Assembly Hall was massive. Either Michele didn't tell them, or she didn't know the bomb existed. Zyree doesn't like the thought of either conclusion.

The two men navigate around the rubble littering the street that runs past the campus. Windows in buildings hundreds of yards away from the detonation site were shattered from the force of the blast. People covered with severe lacerations are everywhere. Many are seeking medical attention that is in short supply. With all the commotion, it's hard for Zyree to get a sense of anything down here at ground level.

"What are you hoping to find?" Malkor asks, surveying the bedlam around them.

"Haven."

"You know, boss, there's a good chance he's dead."

Malkor has a knack for wishful thinking. "Then that should make him easy to find."

"Not if he was sitting in the truck," Malkor grumbles as they press forward.

"Haven is a lot of things, but suicidal isn't one of them. He wants to keep killing. Any plan would have included several exfiltration options."

"No plan ever survives first contact with the enemy," Malkor says. "I don't know how you expect to find anything in this mess. I'll be lucky to find you if we get separated."

Their positions are tracked via the biocomps, but Malkor has a point. The sheer number of PSS emergency services personnel and wounded will make identifying anyone difficult. They need a different approach.

Zyree signals Malkor to walk north. They scan the faces of the survivors without expecting to find much. Haven will try to blend in, assuming he's still alive and in the area. There is a chance. If he concludes that everyone thinks he's dead, he'll assume nobody is searching for him during an active triage operation.

"Where are we going, boss?"

"The North Gate. There are only two ways they got that truck in there. The south entrance was reserved for patricians. I'm betting he entered through the auxiliary," Zyree says, turning the corner to find the foundation of the destroyed guardhouse.

There isn't anything left. The overpressure wave disintegrated it. His contacts zero in on a concrete barrier behind the structure. It is pockmarked with bullet holes.

"We're in the right place," Malkor observes.

"Any luck reaching ICX Security?"

"No response. Control could be offline," he says, looking up at the damaged tower largely obscured by smoke.

Zyree kicks a piece of debris. They are going about this all wrong. If Haven was engaged by security forces, he could have been wounded. In a BCS uniform, he would get immediate medical attention. Zyree scans the chaos in front of him.

"Look around, Malkor. Tell me what you don't see."

"Daylight?"

"Corporate security. I don't see a single BCS agent. Look for anyone wearing one of their uniforms," Zyree orders.

They make their way across the street toward a hasty triage area. The PSS has set up casualty collection points to funnel the injured to one central location to make efficient use of on-site medical personnel. Once diagnosed and treated, they are shipped off to area medical centers. That's how Zyree would try to escape if he were planning this.

An armored PSS truck is causing a commotion by trying to make its way toward the triage area. It's not a rescue vehicle, so he doesn't know why they're pushing into the disaster area. They might know something about the terrorists.

Zyree begins walking in that direction when a uniform catches his eye. It's dirty and ripped, and the man wearing it appears injured. Then he turns his head.

"Son of a bitch…Haven!"

The sharp shout has the desired effect. He reflexively turns, and they make eye contact. He grins and bolts to the north.

"Stop him!" Zyree shouts as Malkor breaks into a sprint.

He doesn't make it far. The footing is treacherous, and Malkor trips on a piece of shattered concrete and falls hard to the ground. Zyree looks for a clean shot and finally gets one. His contacts indicate the backdrop is clear, and he squeezes the trigger twice.

The first shot misses, but the second grazes Haven's upper arm. He reacts to the pain, slowing his gait. Zyree is retraining his weapon in the center of his back when the PSS truck veers right and barrels toward him. The big tires fight for traction as it climbs over rubble strewn over the street. Malkor recovers from his tumble and joins Zyree in pinning Haven between them and the PSS. There is no place for him to run.

Haven is only forty feet away. They approach him carefully with weapons raised. The driver's door to the armored truck opens, as does the rear hatch. Men materialize with shouldered rifles and open fire. Zyree realizes almost too late that it isn't aimed at Haven. He and Malkor hit the ground just in time as people around them are hit and fall to the ground.

"What the hell?" Malkor shouts, slithering over to cover behind a chunk of concrete.

The men continue their withering fire, keeping them pinned down. A couple of intrepid guardians see what's happening and engage them but are quickly forced to take cover. Zyree lifts his head and spots Haven climbing into the hulking vehicle.

The truck buttons up and revs its engine. People frantically dive out of its path as it plows through the intersection and lumbers around the corner. Ten seconds later, it disappears down the side street.

"Now what?" Malkor asks, climbing to a knee.

"We follow them. Let's commandeer a vehicle of our own."

CHAPTER FORTY-ONE

RYKOS

"Valhalla"
Midtown Geographic District
New York City Municipal Corporation

I'm going to be sick to my stomach. We're all gathered around one display, despite every one of them being tuned to AME News. Maybe we all just need to lean on each other for support right now. I knew Haven was capable of this—he's a psychopath. But this scale of destruction....

Smoke is billowing out of the destroyed building. The chyron reads *Terrorists Strike Intercorpex*. The video then shifts to medics treating the wounded at a makeshift triage station. I have some experience with that after being "rescued" from Broad Street. Some of the wounds are lacerations. Others are more traumatic. The images are poignant.

"Haven just erased what little goodwill we had," Farron moans, refusing to peel his eyes off the scene.

"Partially true," I say, turning to the patrician. "Most employees won't mourn the loss of patricians. No offense."

"None taken. I don't like most patricians either."

"Farron's right," Michele mumbles. "The problem is perception. They will use these images to fuel anger and then unleash it on us."

"Michele, I don't know what you're waiting for," Narik prods. "This is the perfect time to strike. Finish Archimedes. You couldn't have planned it better."

"You call the murder of a thousand people a *distraction*?" I ask, turning to face him. I want to smack the impassive expression off his face.

"I personally knew many of the people that died in that building. Farron's right. It isn't a loss to the world."

"I said I didn't like them, not that they deserved to die! What happened to you, Narik?" Farron asks, aghast at the callous comment.

"Don't play innocent with me. Your father killed three patricians, remember?"

"That was part of a plan."

"And this can be too. Haven gift-wrapped the perfect opportunity for us. Intercorpex is shut down, and now it has no leadership. The patricians lost the heads of most major families. The New York City Municipal Corporation has been decapitated. There is chaos in the streets. There will never be a better time to act."

Michele looks over at Jasper, who shrugs. Adiz is next to him, shaking his head. The others in the room don't offer an opinion. They're just here to execute decisions, not participate in making them.

"Our chances of success are no better than they were an hour ago," Jasper says.

"I agree," Adiz chimes in. "Narik is right in saying that the situation is perfect. But if the intrusion fails, as it's likely to, everything we've worked for is for nothing."

"You people are unbelievable," Narik screeches.

"And you're getting on my nerves," Adiz admonishes. "You need to shut up and brood in silence."

"Whatever," Narik says, pouting.

"What's the problem, Michele? You look perplexed," I say.

She motions Farron and me to the planning area. It's not private but far enough away from Narik's prying eyes and ears.

"How did he know?"

"How did who know what?" Farron asks, confused.

"We assumed that Haven would learn the true date of the summit. We were right, but how did he breach their security? And even if he figured out a ruse, where did he get explosives capable of that?" Michele asks, pointing at the display. "We don't have anything close to being that powerful."

"You think he had help?"

Michele shrugs. "Haven planned this in advance, and I mean *well* in advance. It must have been."

"Who would help him do that to Intercorpex?" I ask, not seeing where she's going with this.

"Who has the most to gain?"

I follow her eyes over to Narik. It makes sense on some levels.

"You think Narik is working with Haven?" Farron asks.

"It's a theory, but it's worth investigating."

"Not possible," the patrician argues. "He's been locked down here with us since the end of phase two. He couldn't have warned him."

"His father could have. The two men who hate Intercorpex the most are Denali Keating...."

"And Shalius Covington."

"I think we're being played, Farron. Something bigger is going on."

I rub my chin. It's a theory, but not a bad one. Narik has been pushing hard to complete phase three. He displayed little shock at the bombing. It's like he knew it was going to happen. It makes sense.

"How do we find out for sure? It's not like Narik will tell us," I surmise.

"Not willingly. We could torture the information out of him, but I have a better idea. Find Koltayne and have him meet us in the small kitchen in fifteen minutes."

I look at Farron and then back at Michele. We're both wondering the same thing.

"Are you going to share whatever plan you're cooking up?" I ask.

"It's better if I tell you when Koltayne gets here. It will give you less time to try talking me out of it."

CHAPTER FORTY-TWO

AMERICA, INC.

One Guardian Plaza RTCC
Municipal Governance District
New York City Municipal Corporation

Out of all the times she's been in this building, Ilaria has never been on this floor. Her visits to One Guardian Plaza were usually to Teman's office or the auditorium for some ceremony that the chief guardian's wife was expected to attend. Visitor passes don't permit access to sensitive areas in the facility.

The Real-Time Crime Center is modeled after what the New York Police Department used to combat the city's criminal elements. The room is an interface to the servers that analyze every video feed and Maester system. The computers do the heavy lifting, and the problems they flag are investigated by analysts here.

The RTCC is fifty feet in diameter, with three sets of tables forming concentric rings around the room. A large circle of light in the ceiling above provides illumination for the entire room, with accent lights on the walls for added ambiance. Along the front wall past the dais are three large, curved displays. The state-of-the-art room is unlike anything she has ever seen.

Ilaria is escorted into the center. She studies the uniformed men and women as she passes. Their faces show a range of emotions, from sadness and shock to anger and rage. Public safety and security is a proud organization, and they've suffered yet another attack on the city they've pledged their lives to protect.

Violence like this was common in the decades before the collapse. Corporations eradicated much of it when they consolidated power. This city has now endured a half-dozen explosions in just a couple of weeks. This was the worst of them. Her biggest fear is that this terror will become commonplace. She also hopes that Rykos has nothing to do with it.

"Attention in the RTCC!" the incident commander bellows. At once, every person in the room stops what they're doing and trains their eyes to the front.

"Guardians, we've witnessed an unspeakable tragedy today," Dzamko says. "We take measures to ensure continuity of leadership should the worst happen despite our vigilance. Many of you may know Ilaria as Teman's spouse. What many of you may not know is that she was recently appointed to an executive position in the New York City Municipal Corporation. She's now the acting chief executive officer. Ma'am," he says, gesturing her forward.

Ilaria swallows hard as she steps forward. She never expected to be in this position. Her wanting to return to the executive ranks didn't include any aspirations to become chief executive. She wanted to support Safmor, not assume his role.

"Thank you, Constable Dzamko. This would be awkward under normal circumstances, but there's nothing normal about what happened this morning. As the constable stated, many of you know me only as Teman's wife. I understand your reluctance to look at me as your CEO. I'd be hesitant in your position.

"I'm untested and don't have a proven track record. But a true leader turns weaknesses into strengths. I'm going to rely on you like no executive ever has before. Your knowledge will move us forward; your actions will restore order to the chaos; you will bring the terrorists who declared war on this city to justice. The strength of the men and women in this room, and that of your brothers and sisters serving this city, will be critical to emerging from this dark time.

"You are all well-trained and competent. I know that because my husband never would have entrusted you otherwise. Focus on your jobs. We've been punched in the gut. We need to regain our footing because we're *going* to start punching back."

The guardians stand and applaud. It's strange to hear their enthusiastic response on such a dark day. Some of them are even crying. Everyone is caught up in the emotion of the moment.

"You heard the lady. Let's get to work!" the incident commander says from her left when the applause finally dies down. The room instantly buzzes with activity.

"Very inspiring, ma'am," Dzamko leans in and says into her ear.

"Don't humor me, Constable."

"I'm not. Are you sure you've never done this before? That was amazing."

Ilaria is buoyed by the compliment. She hopes it's as sincere as it sounds. It's been a long time since she's been paid a genuine one.

"I just spoke from the heart."

"And that's exactly what we needed. In forty-five seconds, you turned doubts into fortitude. You're going to be very good at this job."

"Maybe," Ilaria says, turning to him. "Assuming I'm allowed to keep it."

CHAPTER FORTY-THREE

LIBERTEUM

Surface Streets
Midtown Geographic District
New York City Municipal Corporation

Loghun takes the corner hard, nearly tipping the top-heavy armored vehicle over. That maneuver would rattle most drivers, but not this kid. He bites his lower lip and floors it, determined not to lose control of the beast he's driving.

"What happened to Nyvar?" Tielur shouts from the back.

"He did his duty. What happened to Symun?" Haven asks, only now realizing that they are short a man.

"He caught a round to the head from the perimeter guards," Tielur says.

"He was a good man."

The armored vehicle handles like a pig, but it's also the biggest thing on the street. Loghun attempts to weave through traffic but plows through conveyances more often than he dodges them. Haven glances back to see Tielur laughing as he watches the onboard video feed of the carnage left in their wake.

"You're pretty good at this," Haven observes as Loghun crunches another vehicle with the audacity to be in his way.

"I was a delivery driver before going underground."

"That explains it."

Haven winces as he repositions in his seat. He was fortunate his guys showed up when they did. It was a gutsy move that wasn't part of the plan. You can't put a price on loyalty. The explosion pummeled his body, and he was in no condition to run for it. He never would have escaped Zyree.

Haven opens the vehicle's first aid kit and uses a quick seal bandage to dress his shoulder wound. Zyree only grazed him. If that bastard could shoot straight, he'd be dead right now. He digs through the bag and finds a pain inhibitor. Just what the doctor ordered for his battered body. He plunges the autoinjector into his thigh and feels a relieving warmth course through him.

Loghun makes a series of turns, and Haven isn't sure where they are. Signs are whizzing by faster than he can read them.

"Guardians are laying spike strips ahead," Tielur announces, using the digital zoom of the roof-mounted camera to scan the area around the vehicle and warn them of obstacles.

"Where the hell are we?"

"Heading west on Forty-ninth between Lexington and Park," Loghun shouts.

Haven grimaces. "We'll never make it back to the Motor Pool. Half the guardians in this city will be chasing us in the next two minutes. Turn down the next avenue."

"Roger," Loghun says as he rips around a corner. The top-heavy vehicle feels like it's going up on two wheels.

"Damn, man."

"Now what?"

"Head to Grand Central."

"We have company," Tielur announces, hanging on for dear life in the back of the armored truck as he moves his face closer to the display. "A guardian vehicle is coming up fast behind us. Their uniforms are different."

"It's Zyree. This guy doesn't quit," Haven mutters, unfastening his restraints and climbing into the back.

He pulls a rifle off the weapons rack positioned in the center of the vehicle between the two benches. Tielur does the same, and the men check the chambers. Both weapons have magazines and are loaded. The PSS is nothing if not prepared.

"Go easy for a second, Loghun," Haven shouts.

Tielur gives a three count and opens the heavy back hatch of the vehicle. Steadying himself with the hand grasping the edge of the door, Haven leans out with the rifle. Tielur does the same from the opposite side of the hatch, and they start spraying.

The PSS vehicle veers onto the sidewalk as their unaimed fire causes the conveyances behind them to swerve. Pedestrians scramble like chickens fleeing a butcher. In a matter of seconds, the weapons run dry, and Tielur closes the hatch to protect them from any return fire.

"Hang on, guys! This ain't gonna be subtle!"

Loghun yanks the truck around another corner. The vehicle groans as its massive body strains against its frame. Inertia carries its occupants forward, and it takes every ounce of their strength to avoid pancaking into its aluminum side.

"Haven, get up here!" Loghun calls out from the front.

Haven moves forward, almost teetering over during one of Loghun's swerves. They are on Forty-Second Street and are facing a problem. A swarm of PSS vehicles and overhead drones are blocking the street ahead.

"They're boxing us in at the Park Avenue Skybridge!"

"The hell they are. Accelerate."

Loghun complies without question. The men who joined Haven are soldiers for the cause. The misfits and whiners are all either dead or with Michele. She can have them. He wouldn't trade these guys for anyone.

"We're not making it through that barricade," Tielur shouts from behind them.

"We're not going to try. See the doors at the southwest corner of the terminus?" Haven asks, pointing ahead. "Can you punch through them?"

Loghun turns to him and smiles. "I like the way you think. You might want to brace yourself."

Haven complies, climbing into the seat and fastening his four-point seat restraint for good measure. Tielur is left to hang on in the back as they barrel down the four-lane street.

"Aim for the retractable vehicle barrier next to the Vanderbilt pedestrian plaza."

This truck can't breach the permanent barriers around Grand Central. Retractable ones are designed to prevent access but won't protect a structure from damage. It'll give if Loghun hits it hard enough.

"Here goes nothing."

The truck veers across the oncoming lanes and smashes into the barrier. They lose velocity but manage to plow through the green steel supports of the building's entryway. The ancient wood doors splinter and fly off their hinges.

Loghun cuts the wheel hard to the left, keeping most of the vehicle on the ramp that leads down to the main level. The right-side tires slip off it, shredding the steel railing and bowling over people as they slide.

"We don't have the clearance. Hang on!"

Metal scrapes against metal as the truck wedges itself between the beam supporting the restaurant on street level and the ramp. The sudden stop racks Haven's already sore body. He unfastens the restraint and turns gingerly.

"You okay?"

"Ugh. I busted a couple of ribs," Loghun says, grimacing.

"Tielur?"

"Yeah," he moans.

Haven climbs in the back to find Tielur gushing blood from a gaping wound over his eye. He grabs an assault pack from the forward rack and helps the man to his feet.

"It's time to go, brother. We'll patch you up later."

"What's this?" Loghun asks after Haven hands him the pack full of ammunition and non-lethal crowd control devices.

"Some toys that could come in handy. Contact!"

Guardians materialize at the entrance of the Forty-Second Street SpeedRail station. Haven and Loghun open fire, forcing them to retreat. He checks their rear just in time. Two more guardians appear between them and upper-level tracks. They aren't heavily armed but don't have to be.

"Contact left!"

"We're pinned down!"

Tielur barely gets the words out of his mouth before his chest explodes. His lifeless body drops to the ground. Haven fires to drive the attackers back behind cover to avoid joining him.

"Go down the ramp to the lower level," Haven shouts to Loghun.

They move quickly as they fire, sweeping for targets and firing at anything that moves. Two guardians emerge along the railing of the overpass that leads from the main space in the terminus to the hall in the front of the building. Haven fires and misses, but the shots keep them from engaging.

They move into an alcove in front of the Oyster Bar, one of the city's most iconic pre-collapse restaurants. They take up positions at the corners, with Loghun covering the ramp heading west while Haven covers the east.

"Down?" he asks, pointing to one of the two stairwells located on either side of the restaurant entrance.

Haven considers his options. There aren't any good ones. If they go to the lower level, it will be easier to hem them in. They'll be sitting ducks fleeing through the tunnels unless….

A man pops his head up in the restaurant, and Haven blows it off with a quick burst. That should give anyone in the restaurant second thoughts about intervening. He changes magazines. He needs time. Hostages are an option, but they'll never negotiate. Employees are expendable for the good of the corporation.

Loghun fires at targets up the ramp. "We have to move, boss."

"We're going into the Dining Concourse. Ready?"

He looks over his shoulder and nods. They hustle through the kill zone where the ramps converge, and sprint down to the dining level. Two guardians emerge on opposite sides of the information booth, their weapons drawn. Loghun drops to a knee, and Haven stops short. They fire at the same time, hitting both men square in their chests.

"Go! Head for the East Side Commuter Access."

They veer left past countless shell-shocked employees cowering in fear and charge through the portal, taking the escalator steps two at a time. People are huddled around displays flashing warnings about an incident in the terminus, waiting for instructions. Haven walks over to a trash receptacle thirty feet away.

"We need to keep moving. If they seal the exits, we'll be trapped."

"I don't intend to get trapped anywhere."

Haven spins Loghun around and digs through the assault pack. He pulls out five grenades and flips open the safety guards. Handing them to Loghun, he reaches in and secures three more.

"Set ten-second timers. We arm them and casually head back the way we came."

"You got it."

They press the activation buttons on all eight devices and dump them into the bin. They walk back towards the escalators but don't get far before the grenades detonate. Smoke and gas pour from the trash can. People panic, just as Haven knew they would. Now he urges them along.

"Evacuate! Evacuate! This way!" he bellows to the stunned people, pointing up the escalator.

Nobody questions a man wearing a BCS uniform. People begin running past him until it becomes a herd.

"Evacuate! Clear the level. Head up the escalators. Stay calm and exit the concourse," Loghun adds, looking like he's enjoying this.

The mixture of smoke and gas forms a thick layer that activates the fire suppression system. The resulting mist obscures visibility, just like Michele did to them back at NYU. This opportunity is a long shot, but it's all they've got. Haven leans the rifle against the side of the escalator, signaling his comrade to do the same.

As the panicked crowd bottlenecks, Haven unfastens his tunic and strips it off. Loghun follows suit. They don't blend in with uniformed employees, but the dark undershirts won't make them obvious. Loghun stashes the rifles and tunics under some belongings that the frightened employees left behind. They won't easily be found.

Haven drops his handgun into a cargo pocket and tries to look frightened as they mingle with the crowd up the escalators. At the top, they turn left out the sally port. An overwhelmed guardian is trying to check everyone in the river of humanity, but he's searching for a BCS uniform. So far, so good.

Haven and Loghun peel off to one of the portals leading to the train platforms. He looks around, trying to determine their next move. The tunnel is too risky right now.

"There's surveillance everywhere down here. What's the plan?" Loghun asks.

Haven smirks. "We hide."

CHAPTER
FORTY-FOUR
AMERICA, INC.

The White House
Corporate Governance District
Washington-Arlington Municipal Corporation

Fiolla opens her office door and leans up against it after it closes. She relishes the solitude. Part of her wants to cry. The other part wants to celebrate because Hammond betrayed Valen and got what he deserved. The need to cry is winning.

"Welcome back, Executive Fiolla," Rosie says when Fiolla pushes off the door and makes her way to the desk. "You have three VidLynk requests that require responses and twenty-five unread e-notes. One of them is marked 'urgent.'"

"Who is it from?" she asks.

"Chairman of the Board Hammond."

Fiolla freezes. "When was it sent?"

"It was delivered at ten thirteen a.m."

She rushes to log in to her system. That was sent only a few minutes before she arrived at his Corporate Hill office. The camera above the display authenticates her using facial recognition software. The display glows to life, and with a few hand gestures, she selects Hammond's e-note and opens it.

The computer prompts her for additional credentials. The note is marked classified and requires double authentication to access. She scans her biojack and feels her stomach tighten at the thought of reading a dead man's last communication. The uneasiness becomes full-blown nausea by the end of the second line.

Fiolla,

I have always tried to live a life of integrity and loyalty, and I owe you an explanation as to why I can no longer see those traits in myself. You see, I was forced to remove Valen as CEO by Zeykala and Prima Bettancourt.

I'm ashamed. It's not something I could have imagined myself doing, regardless of the threat. Business is rough at this level, and I have endured corporate politics for decades now. They knew I would never cave to their demands, which is why their threats were leveled against my family.

My wife, children, and grandchildren mean the world to me. I know that's a strange thing to say in a society that places corporate service above all else, but it's how I've always felt. I can bear many losses, but family is not one of them. They were in mortal danger and still are.

I'm telling you this now because they will never be safe while my heart still beats. Bettancourt and Zeykala will continue to use them as leverage. I'm a pawn in whatever scheme they have planned. Therefore, I have but one option to ensure my family's safety and escape the prison I find myself in.

This is a dangerous time, Fiolla. I understand the peril I have placed you in by sending this message. Please forgive me for that, but I needed you to know the truth. I hope you will relay the contents of this e-note to Valen. He needs to know that I never intended to harm him. I may be departing this world now, but what happened on Saturday is what really killed me.

So, this is goodbye. Please take care of yourself during the coming storm.

With my deepest apologies,
Hammond

Fiolla leans back in her chair. She instantly regrets all the bad things she thought about the man since the hearing. The thought of corporate executives sinking to the level of threatening a man's family for political gain is unconscionable. That's not how business is conducted in the modern age. What's the world coming to?

She rereads the e-note four or five times to commit it to memory. This message can't be saved on a server or downloaded to a device. Hammond was right – she is in danger and having this communication in her possession exacerbates that.

The WPSS or the BCS will check for outgoing messages sent from the workstation in Hammond's office during their investigation. If investigators uncover this message's contents, they'll bury the information and her along with it. Anything to cover up the truth and protect America Incorporated's newest CEO.

As this is personal correspondence, a copy won't be stored once it's deleted. Composing herself, she deletes the e-note. Anyone searching her workstation history will know Hammond sent a message but not know its contents. At least, she hopes that's the case.

"Executive Fiolla?" Rosie chirps. "You are being summoned by Chief Executive Zeykala to the Situation Room. You are to report immediately."

A shiver of fear runs up and down her spine. Could she know about the visit to Hammond? Is she aware of his e-note? Her stomach, already sour and churning, twists into a tighter knot.

"Inform her I'm on my way."

Fiolla leaves her office and heads for the first sublevel to an uncertain meeting.

CHAPTER FORTY-FIVE
INTERCORPEX

ICX Headquarters
Midtown Manhattan Geographic District
New York City Municipal Corporation

The young ICX Security communications specialist looks up at Lyris hovering over his shoulder after his workstation chimes for the tenth time. It's another urgent VidLynk request from the White House. They're growing more insistent.

"Don't accept it. There's nothing Zeykala can say that changes anything."

"Administrator-General Lyris, the evacuation is almost complete," the facilities manager informs him. "Engineers surveying the lower floors have concerns about the tower's structural integrity. They're advising we evacuate as well."

"If the building hasn't collapsed by now, what the hell makes them think it will?" Chiana asks as she storms through the door.

The woman knows how to make an entrance. Moreover, she knows how to crawl under people's skin. It makes her an effective chief inspector and annoying to the point of being offensive.

"Are you an engineer?" one of her security colleagues asks with stress-induced sarcasm.

"Do I look like a damn engineer to you?"

"No," he says, cowering at the force of her retort.

"No, *ma'am*," she corrects, "unless you hold the rank of chief inspector."

"No ma'am," he rasps, sinking back into his seat.

She sees Lyris grinning at her near the communications console. "Good. You're not dead."

"And you're not on a plane to the SEU."

"There are two chief inspectors in New York, and one of them is Zyree. Do you want me to go back to Zurich or find the bastards that did this?"

"Easy choice," Lyris says with a smile. "One of your men can get you up to speed. As of right now, I'm the acting AG. I will leave what security and investigative capabilities we have left in your capable hands."

"As you wish, Administrator-General," she says with a wink.

"Contact Executive Director Wyeth at the NOC," Lyris orders the comm specialist. "Tell him that we're moving all operations to Wall Street and to start making accommodations for our arrival."

"Yes, sir."

"Sir, I have a VidLynk with the Office of Exchange Security in Zurich."

"You may want to hear this, Chiana. Connect us."

"Executive Director Lyris?" Commissioner-General Jurghen asks when the communication establishes. "I didn't know—"

"It's acting Administrator-General Lyris now, Commissioner."

He wrinkles his brow. "On whose authority?"

"Mine, and the fact that everyone else is dead."

"This is highly irregular. You aren't in the line of succession after being fired from your position. Leadership should transfer to Executive Director Wyeth."

"Wyeth was removed from his position. His administrative assistant found the order affixed with Raimius's digital approval code."

The commissioner-general stares at him impassively. He can't refute that the order exists without demanding to see it. He also knows they have more to deal with than a power struggle.

"If Wyeth's legitimacy is in question, administrators in Zurich—"

"Are four thousand miles away. I was *there*. I barely escaped that explosion with my life. Now I'm trying to put the pieces back together. Ask the men and women in this room that lost friends and colleagues today who they want in charge."

"Sir, our regulations are—"

"Irrelevant," Lyris interjects. "No regulation, edict, doctrine, or disaster recovery plan covers the simultaneous loss of everyone who perished today."

Lyris folds his arms. Jurghen can complain all he wants. There is nothing he can do to challenge his leadership. It's time to change the subject before he tries.

"I don't think—"

"Why was there no warning about the bombing?"

"What?"

"You run the most competent and professional security organization on the planet," Lyris says for the benefit of the inspectors in the room. "Where was the intelligence about this attack?"

"A warning was issued," Jurghen confesses, realizing he has a problem. "Inspector Malkor informed us via VidLynk of a possible attack, and Chief Inspector Zyree informed Executive Director Wyeth in person at the NOC."

Lyris is thrilled that the report didn't mention Lyris's presence. "Let me get this straight: He told you that there was going to be a bombing, and yet somehow—"

"He didn't mention a bombing."

"Don't you dare interrupt me, Commissioner-General!" Lyris screeches. "What exactly were you told?"

"Chief Inspector Zyree uncovered direct intelligence about a threat to the facility."

"And how would Chief Inspector Zyree know that?"

"He didn't divulge his source."

"I see. Commissioner-General, we've been attacked four times in less than a month. Many people think the terrorists have someone on the inside. It's hard to refute that after today."

The accusation was as subtle as a chainsaw. Lyris fights the urge to smile as he catches Chiana grinning out of the corner of his eye.

"There's no evidence that Chief Inspector Zyree or any other Intercorpex employee is complicit in the attacks."

"Then ICX Security's position is that these are coincidences that should be dismissed without even a cursory investigation."

"I didn't say that!" Jurghen snaps.

Lyris springs the trap. "Then you shouldn't be opposed to finding out. Unless you're protecting Zyree."

"I have no interest in indulging your paranoia."

"Raimius was paranoid. Maybe he'd still be alive if you shared some of his concerns. If the chief inspector has nothing to hide, proving his innocence shouldn't be an issue. We have over a thousand dead people here that deserve justice and billions globally who deserve answers."

He's out of arguments. Lyris expected more of a fight from the old codger. Germans are supposed to be tough. All the years behind that desk have made his heart soft and his mind dull.

"History will judge us based on this moment. Don't be on the wrong side of it, Jurghen. I'll be waiting for you to issue the order."

Lyris signals the communications tech to end the VidLynk. Chiana is almost bubbling with excitement. The only person she despises more than Zyree is Jurghen.

"Zyree isn't going to come in," she says, meaning it for public consumption.

"Then go find him, Chiana."

"What if he resists?"

"Take appropriate action," Lyris says with a wink of his own.

CHAPTER FORTY-SIX

INTERCORPEX

The White House
Corporate Governance District
Washington-Arlington Municipal Corporation

The withering glare Fiolla gets when she enters the Situation Room must have been expected because it doesn't faze her. Instead, she strides up to Zeykala and clasps her hands behind her back. None of the other executives in the room bother looking at her.

"It's about time you arrived. Where were you when the alert went out?"

"Shareholder Hall. I went to see Chairman Hammond."

"I see," Zeykala says, feeling her blood pressure spike. "I can't imagine what duties took you there, but I hope you enjoyed your time with him."

"Not really, ma'am. He's dead."

Her revelation causes Zeykala to recoil and earns the attention of everyone in the room. The CEO attempts to recover. Hammond dying was not part of their plan. She needed a chairman who could be controlled. Talya is not going to be happy.

"How?"

"Suicide. Or, more precisely, an *apparent* suicide."

Zeykala takes a deep breath. She doesn't like the way this insolent little tart said that. The implication hangs heavy in the air. Unfortunately, there are other matters to handle first. Fiolla will get hers in due time.

"Hammond's death is unfortunate, but we have more pressing business. We're waiting to be connected to what's left of the NYCMC's executive leadership. I understand you have some familiarity with the executives up there."

"Yes, ma'am. I know most of them personally."

"I assume you're up to speed about the Intercorpex bombing, so I want you here for this meeting."

"The VidLynk is active, ma'am," the communications technician robotically announces.

"This is Chief Executive Officer Zeykala from the White House. To whom am I speaking?"

"Acting Chief Executive Officer of the New York City Municipal Corporation Ilaria. This is our acting chief guardian, Constable Dzamko."

"Do you know the status of CEO Safmor or any of the other senior executives?"

She hangs her head, and Zeykala frowns. What a weakling. She's getting weepy talking to the CEO of the parent corporation. Municorp executives should be tougher than that.

"No," she says, reestablishing eye contact, "but they're assumed dead."

"Then it appears you're in charge. What position did you previously occupy?"

"Managing director of business development."

"Okay," Zeykala says, unimpressed at her title. "How long have you held that position?"

"I reported yesterday but officially assumed the title this morning."

Zeykala falls speechless. It takes her a moment to force the words out of her mouth. "Did you say you started this morning?"

"Ilaria, I'm Executive Fiolla, the White House liaison from Corporate Affairs. Is your husband Chief Guardian Teman?"

Zeykala glares at her subordinate for not letting Ilaria answer her question. A novice is running their most important city, and Fiolla is asking about her dating history. Unbelievable.

"Yes, he is."

"You assumed control of our largest municipal corporation with no executive experience?" Zeykala asks before Fiolla can inquire about Ilaria's favorite color.

"No, I have—"

"What was your previous position?"

"I was raising my children."

Zeykala leans into her chair. A homemaker. This woman is barely an executive. This won't do.

"Well, thank you, Ilaria. We'll be in touch."

"Ma'am, I have been—"

The technician ends the VidLynk, cutting Ilaria off mid-sentence. Zeykala isn't going to invest a second more in that conversation. That woman needs to be shown the door.

"Who the hell is Teman?"

"The municipal corporation's chief guardian. He was involved in the siege of the old Broad Street subway station and was taken hostage by Liberteum after being ambushed during a raid."

"Are you telling me that the acting CEO is the wife of the man who failed to track down the terrorists in the first place?"

"I don't think that's a fair characterization."

"I didn't ask for your analysis, Fiolla," Zeykala warns. "A yes or no will suffice."

"Yes, she is."

Zeykala glides her hands across the edge of the table. This could be an opportunity. With municipal leadership gone, and a woman with no executive experience in charge, she's justified in installing whomever she wants as CEO without pushback.

"Fiolla, return to your office and create a list of top parent company executives working in New York."

"Ma'am?"

Zeykala squints. At least she addressed her properly. "What part didn't you understand?"

"Municorps traditionally choose their own leadership."

"Desperate times require desperate measures. Carry out my instructions."

"I'll make it my top priority," Fiolla says before spinning on her heels and marching out of the Situation Room.

"I would hope so," Zeykala mumbles.

She wonders why Valen thinks so highly of her. Fiolla may be well-liked, but she sees a maverick who questions everything. That's a liability.

Everyone at the table stares at her in silence. Fiolla challenged her authority, and Zeykala wonders if the men and women here are contemplating something similar. She needs a display of decisive leadership.

"Get me Virtari," she commands. After a moment, the VidLynk connects. "Where are you?"

"On final descent into Bettancourt International Airport," he says, his head oversized from holding his tablet too close to his face.

"Good. Are you familiar with the RTCC?"

"It's the Real-Time Crime Center. The PSS operates—"

"I don't care," Zeykala says. "Get over there and personally relieve their acting CEO and chief guardian of their duties. Take control of the NYCMC. All resources and departments will report to you until new executive leadership is installed. Then you will maintain control of public safety and security until this crisis has subsided."

"Okay, I get the second part, but why remove the acting CEO?" Virtari asks.

She feels her blood pressure spike again. What part of her being the chief executive officer don't people understand? This is how it should work: She speaks, they listen and then execute. Valen did more damage to this office than she thought.

"Just do it, Director. You'll have the order before you reach their facility."

"Consider it done, ma'am."

Zeykala leans back in the chair and watches the people in the room desperately avoid eye contact with her. This will be so much easier when everyone starts obeying her without question.

CHAPTER FORTY-SEVEN

INTERCORPEX

Grand Central Terminus
Midtown Manhattan Geographic District
New York City Municipal Corporation

The mass of humanity streaming out of the dining level slows to a trickle. Zyree has found getting information out of PSS impossible. Every on-scene guardian they speak to has a different perception of what is happening. None of them seem to have coherent orders.

Haven is racking up quite a body count. It appears that nobody was killed in this part of the terminus, but dozens were killed and countless injured when he rammed the armored vehicle through the entrance. Five more guardians were killed or wounded as he fled. Now the guardians are after blood – Haven's.

"I need a hard lockdown of every entrance and exit in this building. Seal access to all platforms and the mezzanine for the Long Island-bound trains. Get more eyes in the control room and scour every video feed on the East Side Mezzanine and platforms. He must be down there, so find him."

The man walking down the ramp carries an air of authority. He also seems to be the only person with a clue about what's going on. Malkor joins Zyree in walking up the ramp to greet him.

"Who the hell are you?" he asks, noticing their uniforms.

"Chief Inspector Zyree of Intercorpex Security. This is Inspector Malkor."

"You need to leave."

"With all due respect, you could use every man you can get down here right now."

"Not for this operation. Leave now."

It's clear Zyree won't get anywhere with him. Professional courtesy is a foreign concept these days. "Let me talk to Constable Dzamko. He'll explain—"

"I'm not talking to anybody. I don't report to the constable. We aren't under his control. The Bureau of Corporate Security is running the terrorist manhunt."

"Fine. Then get them on a VidLynk."

"Even if I wanted to – and I don't – it won't make a difference. Now, out of respect for your position, I'm asking you politely to leave. If I'm forced to ask again, guardians will drag you out of here in restraints. What will it be?"

This guy wants to be the big dog. Any challenge will be seen as usurping his authority. There's nothing more to be gained here. Zyree needs to find another way.

"Come on, Malkor."

"That was being respectful of our positions?" he asks as they trek past a swarm of newly arrived guardians.

"Apparently."

The pair strides briskly in silence past the destroyed armored vehicle and up the damaged ramp to street level. Tactical teams are on the scene, receiving instructions just outside the gaping hole in the terminal entrance. They walk across the small pedestrian plaza and into the gleaming glass foyer of the Vanderbilt Center. Zyree surveys the inside and heads over to the East Side train access. It's already locked down. If Haven plans on escaping, it won't be this way. It was worth checking.

An anonymous VidLynk request pops up on his contacts. Zyree smirks. At least he isn't pretending to be someone else this time.

"Connect, audio only. This isn't a good time, Ortan."

"It never is with you. You need to know—"

"Find me an access point to the rail lines leading out of Grand Central Terminus."

"Zyree, you are—"

"Focus on the ones heading north. Haven has used those before."

"Zyree—"

"There is no way I'm letting Haven get away—"

"Zyree!"

"What?" He didn't realize that he was talking over him.

"ICX Security just issued orders for your immediate apprehension and detention pending an investigation into your activities."

Zyree recoils. If this is one of Ortan's jokes, it's not funny. Something in the tone of his voice leads Zyree to believe he isn't kidding this time.

"Why?"

"They think you were involved in the bombing."

"I *warned* them of the attack. Who issued the order?"

Ortan sighs. "Commissioner-General Jurghen."

That was the last name he expected to hear. Loyalty is the coin of the realm among ICX inspectors. They operate knowing that they have each other's backs. A man he considers a friend more than a superior issuing that order is unthinkable.

"There's no way in hell Jurghen did that on his own accord."

"You're right. I did some digging. It was submitted after a VidLynk session to what's left of our headquarters with the acting administrator-general."

"Who is the acting AG?"

"Lyris."

Zyree throws his head back and stares up at the ceiling. The patients are now running the asylum.

"How did a man relieved for cause pull that off?"

"Maybe because everyone else is dead? All I know is that he's calling the shots. This can't be good news for you."

"I'll deal with it later. I need you to find me an access point to the Park Avenue train tunnel."

"Already done. I'm sending you and Malkor a couple of options now. The Fifty-Ninth Street maintenance access is your best bet." The man multitasks more easily than most people breathe.

"Got it. What about the backtrace to Liberteum?"

Malkor is gesturing wildly, dying to know what's going on. Ignoring his pleas, Zyree signals to follow him out of Vanderbilt Center. He walks north, following the guidance projected onto his contacts.

"Ugh. They routed that call through less-secure corporate networks all over the world. They're good, but I'm better. I'll find them, but it's going to take time, even with Huldufólk helping."

"Tell the elf to work faster, Ortan. Time is something we don't have."

"Then stop distracting me by pointing out the obvious. I'll get back to you when I know something. And Zyree?"

"Yeah?"

"Stay safe, my friend," he adds before terminating the link.

"What did he say?" Malkor asks as soon as he sees Zyree blink hard to disconnect.

"That I'm a fugitive, and Lyris is our new boss."

"What?"

"I'll explain later. We need to get into that tunnel."

Reaching the spot on his navigation, Zyree spots the unmarked service entrance and jogs over. It's locked, but there are ways around that. Nodding at Malkor, he gets to work.

"What makes you think Haven is going to use this tunnel to escape?" he asks as he sets another EMP device.

"Call it a gut feeling. Haven rammed that truck into Grand Central for a reason. He knows this area well, and this stretch of tunnel leads into Harlem. There are a lot of ways to slip away without being tracked."

"I hope you're right about this. What do we do when we find him?"

Zyree stares at Malkor as he thumbs the guard off of the detonator's button.

"Put a bullet in his head."

CHAPTER FORTY-EIGHT

LIBERTEUM

"Valhalla"
Unknown Geographic District
New York City Municipal Corporation

Koltayne understands his role. Success hinges on him. Michele also warned him that Narik can be unpredictable and to be prepared for that. With her young sentry briefed, it's time to put the plan in motion and hope for the best.

"Where are we, Adiz?" Michele asks, coming up behind him in the operations center.

"Same as before: nowhere."

"Jasper?"

He shakes his head. "I know you're eager, but it could be weeks before we're ready."

"A lot of people died today, guys. We're just trying to add meaning to their sacrifice," Farron says, joining the conversation.

"Then launch phase three and finish Archimedes," Narik presses from his spot in the corner.

"We've been through this, Narik," Michele sighs.

"And I don't think the decision is yours to make."

"Excuse me?"

"You heard me," he says, rising from his chair and commanding the attention of everyone in the room. "If you're unable to make the tough choices, then it's time for new leadership."

Michele scans the room and sees anger on her people's faces. Narik is inciting a coup. Or trying to.

"Are you sure you want to go there, Narik? Haven tried that once and barely escaped with his life."

"This is our chance, Michele," he pleads. "Everyone in this room knows it. Just because you're a coward—"

"Watch yourself!"

"Or else what? What are you going to do? What more *can* you do to me?"

"Open your mouth again, and I'll need to figure out the best way to dispose of your body."

The tough talk is meant to rattle him. Narik is used to getting his way. Michele plans on using that to her advantage. Once she's inside his head, it's up to Koltayne.

"Is that how it is now?" Narik squeals. "Squelch all dissenting opinions that don't conform to your worldview? Isn't that what you're trying to change?"

"Koltayne, escort our guest back to his room. Drag him there if you need to."

"Come on," Koltayne says, giving the patrician a shove.

Koltayne pivots, exposing the holstered weapon on his hip. Narik sees the opportunity and makes his move. He grabs the gun and shoves the young man into Jasper, who is seated nearby. Both men tumble to the ground. Adiz instinctively reacts with a sloppy haymaker, but Narik deftly moves inside the slow-developing swing and pops Adiz in the head with the butt of the weapon.

Adiz collapses as Michele misses wide right with a punch. Narik grabs her and turns, cinching his arm around her neck and pressing the weapon against her temple.

Farron, Rykos, and every other person in the operations room train their weapons on Narik. He uses Michele as a human shield. If they fire, she dies.

"Drop them."

The team looks at her for instructions. She's in no position to resist. When the others don't flinch, Narik's grip tightens.

"I'm sorry," Koltayne moans. "I screwed up."

"It's okay."

"Drop the weapons now!"

Michele fights to loosen the hold around her neck. "They don't take orders from you, Narik. They take them from me."

"Fine. Order them to disarm, or your next breath will be your last."

"If you kill me, they'll kill you. Phase three still won't happen any faster," she warns him.

"Nah. They won't let you die."

"He's right, Michele. We're not sacrificing you for this bastard," Jasper says, having climbed up off the floor.

"Please, Michele," Rykos adds with pleading eyes.

"Fine, lower them."

Every weapon is slowly lowered.

"Jasper, Adiz, start phase three."

The two hackers again look at Michele. The moment she gives the order to begin the intrusion, the countdown to stop before being discovered begins. After that threshold is met, they all die. Right now, there's no alternative.

"Go ahead. Do it."

"You heard her. Move!" Narik barks, prompting the reluctant men to begin pecking commands on their virtual keyboards. "I need to get word to my father."

"And how do you suggest we do that without implicating him?" Farron asks.

"Simple. You're going to call your girlfriend."

CHAPTER FORTY-NINE

AMERICA, INC.

One Guardian Plaza RTCC
Municipal Governance District
New York City Municipal Corporation

Dzamko and Ilaria watch fire and medical personnel provide aid and assist in the evacuation of buildings surrounding the Intercorpex campus. The PSS has established a porous perimeter. Support requested from the Bronx and Brooklyn hasn't arrived in Manhattan. Dzamko is concerned about another attack, but if further violence was planned, it likely would have happened by now.

"We have a transportation problem," a guardian in the room announces. "The East Side Autoway is closed between Thirty-Fifth and the fifties. Bridges and tunnels are secured, and Grand Central Terminus is shut down. A lot of employees are going to have a hard time getting home tonight."

"We have a few hours to worry about that," Ilaria says, staring at the main display. "You have the message instructing employees to shelter in place still up, correct?"

"Yes, ma'am."

"Good. The fewer people on the streets, the better. What's happening at Grand Central?"

"Not much. We have unconfirmed reports that the terrorists fled there, but responding guardians are op-con to the BCS. They aren't sharing information."

That's not surprising. Rivals never cooperate, and guardians under operational control of the BCS were likely ordered not to communicate with their commanders. Sometimes Ilaria thinks that the BCS forgets they're all on the same team.

"Where do we stand with the senior executives from the municipal divisions?"

"They're assembling now," the incident commander says. "The acting heads of transportation, finance, city services, human resources, sanitation, and municipal infrastructure are at the NEC. The others are still being contacted."

"Okay. We're going to need their help putting the city—"

Two BCS agents plow through the doors and take positions on either side of them in a strange show of force. A second group of men parades into the center of the oval room.

"Who's in charge here?" the gaunt, balding man demands.

"Who's asking?" Dzamko challenges, barking back in a similar tone to show he's not intimidated. He knows who this is. Even Ilaria recognizes him.

"Director Virtari of the Bureau of Corporate Security," he mutters through his teeth. "Now, answer my question."

"I don't give a damn who you are. You have no authority to make demands in this facility."

"Don't be so sure about that."

"Settle down, gentlemen," Ilaria says, intervening before this gets ugly. "I'm Acting Chief Executive Officer Ilaria."

"Not anymore. I'm assuming control of the New York City Municipal Corporation effective immediately."

"Excuse me?"

"Under whose authority?" Dzamko demands, now visibly angry.

"Chief Executive Zeykala."

"You mean *Acting* Chief Executive."

"Who exactly are you?" Virtari asks.

"Constable Dzamko. I'm the acting chief guardian."

"I see. You're relieved of your position."

The response in the room is instantaneous. Almost at once, everyone in uniform stands and begins closing in around their gathering. The woefully outnumbered BCS agents collapse in closer to their boss, ready to protect him.

"I suggest you tell your people to stand down, Constable," Virtari says, looking around the room.

"I would love to help you, Director, but you just fired me."

"What gives Chief Executive Zeykala the right to relieve me of my duties?" Ilaria asks, pivoting away from the impending melee.

"She's the CEO of the parent company. She can do as she pleases."

"And since when has any CEO in Washington ever taken such a dramatic step with a municorp?"

He gives her a sarcastic smirk. Virtari strikes Ilaria as the kind of man who doesn't appreciate being challenged. It explains why he hated her husband, who in many respects is the same way. She knows that they've locked horns at least once during the search for Liberteum.

"To my knowledge, no CEO ever has. Then again, we've never had the senior leadership of an entire corporation wiped out by a truck bomb that they failed to prevent."

"Oh, Director Virtari, you're smarter than that, I'm sure. The BCS was responsible for summit security at Intercorpex and assumed the responsibility of searching for Liberteum. That's not one colossal failure – it's two."

"Are you getting sassy with me, honey?"

His sexism makes Ilaria's blood boil. For all of society's advances, it's regressed as much as progressed. Women enjoyed improving levels of inclusion pre-collapse. Gender discrimination has accelerated since then.

"I'm stating a fact. It's not my problem that you can't handle it."

He smirks at the insult. "Let me show you how I handle things. Everyone in this room is now under my command. Follow my orders or face punitive action. Escort these two from the building."

The BCS agents grab their arms, causing the phalanx of guardians surrounding them to tighten. Dzamko's subordinates aren't about to let this go down. At least Ilaria has confirmed their loyalty. That may come in handy later, but it's a losing battle right now. Virtari has the upper hand. Taking this further could result in terminations. Zeykala's order is inappropriate, but she has the authority to issue it.

"It's okay. Stand down, everyone," Ilaria instructs the men and women ready to rip the agents to shreds.

"Wise move," Virtari says. "I am assuming full control of this corporation's departments and assets. Control will be relinquished once a new chief executive is named. Right now, our priority is Liberteum. I want a full briefing in five minutes. Get back to your posts."

Everybody remains frozen like statues with defiance carved into their stony faces.

"Do not make me utter the directive again. If you're not capable of following commands, I will replace you with people who are."

Dzamko nods, and the guardians reluctantly return to their workstations. Ilaria has been around guardians for most of her adult life. If she had asked them to shed blood, they would have. If the day she does ever comes, it's because something important will be gained by it. She won't waste their lives over ego.

"Get these two out of my sight."

The two agents accompany them to the elevator, down to the lobby, and out into the street. Once they're deposited on the sidewalk, the agents stand guard at the door. Virtari probably has the RTCC monitoring a feed from outside One Guardian Plaza to ensure Ilaria and the chief guardian go on their merry way.

"Now what?" Dzamko asks, looking back at the facility. "You're not planning on taking this lying down, are you?"

"Hell no. We're going to the Executive Center. Virtari may fancy himself a god, but he's human. That means he can't be in two places at once."

CHAPTER

FIFTY

THE PATRICIANS

"Valhalla"
Midtown Manhattan Geographic District
New York City Municipal Corporation

Jasper did whatever it is that hackers do to mask the route of the call. It's bad enough that it will only be a matter of time before Archangyl detects their intrusion and traces them. There is no point in making it easy for the BCS to do the same.

"Hello? Farron?" he hears Fiolla say after she accepts the audio-only VidLynk request.

"Get somewhere private you can talk."

"I'm in my office. Where the hell have you been? I've been trying to reach you forever."

"I know, and I'm sorry. It's…complicated."

"Complicated?"

Her tone betrays her anger and disbelief. He abandoned her. He's been using her at his father's behest. It's also not the whole story.

"Yes, as in hard to explain and not something I want to go into right now."

"Valen was removed as CEO, terrorists have turned New York into a bloodbath, and your family is suspected of abetting their attacks against Intercorpex. Could that have anything to do with it?"

"Yes, it does."

There is a long silence before Fiolla speaks. "Are you calling about what happened in New York?"

"No."

"Do you even care?"

"I knew most of the patricians in Assembly Hall. I care."

Farron winces. He didn't have any emotion in his tone. He's so afraid of giving something away that he's causing her to become more suspicious.

"Yeah, you sound real broken up about it. Zeykala gave me an assignment, and I can't afford to fail to deliver it. What do you want?"

"Is Zeykala as bad as you feared?"

"Worse."

"Do you want to do something about it?"

He hears Fiolla sigh. "I'm not doing this with you anymore, Farron. I can't deal with everything being an enigma. If you have something to say, just say it."

"If you want to cripple Zeykala, you need to force Talya Bettancourt out. For that to happen, you need Shalius Covington to forcefully assert his claim as *prima*. He can force Hammond to convene the board."

"Hammond's dead!" Fiolla shouts.

Farron looks at Michele, who shrugs. From the look on Narik's face, he didn't know either. The hackers immediately begin checking the GlobalNet, but there is no reason for Fiolla to lie about that, even if it isn't public knowledge.

"What? How?"

"Suicide. Bettancourt and Zeykala were extorting him. That's how they got Valen removed."

"How do you know that?" Farron asks.

"Because he sent me an e-note explaining the whole thing."

Farron can hear her pacing around her office like a registrant on Career Day. She's under incredible stress. He can't help but feel guilty over being responsible for much of it.

"Tell Shalius Covington that."

"Sure, that's a great idea," Fiolla says after scoffing. "I'll just waltz right into a patrician's office without an appointment. You must think he'll throw open the door for a rank-and-file executive. I'm not an elite, Farron."

"Go to his office. When the gatekeeper asks your name, just say, 'Call me Ishmael.'"

"Ishmael?"

"No, use the full line: 'Call me Ishmael.' Say it, and you'll get in to see him."

Narik nods. Most patricians have a rarely shared and often changed code that allows access to whoever utters it. It's not surprising that the Covingtons have a nautical-themed passphrase.

"You're sure he'll help?"

Farron glances at his childhood friend. "Narik is right here. Use that line and tell his father that we sent you. I promise that he'll help in any way he can."

The patrician stares blankly at the far wall. It's another lie. Farron couldn't make that promise even under the best of circumstances. Even with any other patrician. That's not how the world works. They rarely do favors for anyone.

"What's in this for you?"

"Nothing."

"I don't believe you," she snaps.

Farron closes his eyes. "You spend a lot of time not believing me and then regretting it later."

"Yeah, I guess I do," Fiolla says in a near whisper. "Have you ever given me a reason to believe you?"

"I'm trying to help, Fiolla," Farron argues. "Accept that or don't. You know what you need to do. I'll leave it up to you to make the decision."

Farron pulls a finger across his throat, and Jasper kills the VidLynk. That was harder than he thought it would be. A lot harder.

"Bravo, Farron, bravo," Narik chides, still holding Michele by the throat. "That went better than I thought it would. She is the scorned lover you promised the world, after all."

"Screw you, Narik."

"Touchy, touchy. Now, we get comfortable and wait."

Farron glances at Michele, who frowns. Wait for their deaths is what he should have said. Whatever plan Michele had for Narik has derailed in dramatic fashion. If the hack fails, none of them will live long enough to regret it. And the time until that failure is winding down.

CHAPTER
FIFTY-ONE
LIBERTEUM

Grand Central Terminus
Midtown Manhattan Geographic District
New York City Municipal Corporation

This utility area is cramped. When the terminus was rehabilitated following the collapse, much of it was restored to its original antique glory. From the old pictures Haven had seen, the platforms were gloomy. They were completely remodeled with marble to match the rest of the structure's interior. The facility's maintenance and custodial equipment were obscured behind facades to avoid an eyesore. Fortunately, none of those spaces, including the garbage collection point hidden behind one of those false walls, has cameras.

"How long has it been?" Loghun asks, getting noticeably antsy. "I feel stupid just waiting here."

"About twenty minutes. You can feel stupid, or we can rush and get caught. Which do you prefer?"

"What makes you think we won't get caught anyway?"

Haven smiles. "Because corporate employees are dumb. They're still looking for us in the East Side Access Concourse."

"Not if they check the surveillance footage."

"Which they are, but the smoke and fire suppression system obscured the video. They think we used the crowd to slow pursuit, not escape. The guardians will report that everyone was checked even though they were overwhelmed. They won't realize we aren't down there until the perimeter is airtight and they breach."

Loghun stares at Haven. "You sound sure about that."

"I am," Haven says with another smile. "Lessons from past lives."

"Then they need to get on with it," he says, rubbing his nose to block the stench emanating from the trash behind them.

Another ten minutes pass before the sounds around them change. Boots. Lots of them. The echoes are faint, but he can make out voices through the sealed portal door and the façade they're hiding behind.

"Get ready," Haven warns. "There are cameras and sensors every fifty feet down the tunnel. We have to move fast."

Loghun nods and gets his feet under him. Then he checks his weapon.

"Go! Go! Go!" someone shouts from the other side of the closed portal door.

"Okay, let's move."

Haven can hear all manner of non-lethal measures being deployed. With the portal closed, nobody sees them climb out of the garbage area. The two men jump down to the magnetic track bed. Haven looks up at a surveillance camera. The platform area has the highest density of them outside the main terminal. He hopes his assumptions are right. They're dead if he isn't.

The pair moves briskly north up the tunnel. The bright lights of the platforms yield to darkness. The few LEDs on the railbed barely provide enough illumination to see the track incline to the Park Avenue tunnel. Once they reach it, Haven begins to relax. There are several accesses leading to the underground. They can use one if they're being pursued.

Haven stops and listens. Nothing. If the PSS or BCS is onto them, they're using their rubber-soled tactical boots to good effect. They press on, stopping once more to listen before quickening their pace.

"There," Loghun says and points, not wanting to press their luck by traveling farther.

The maintenance access and power substation on the right side of the north tunnel is their best escape opportunity. It was designed to provide a quick means to repair trains that break down in the tunnel, and it serves as an emergency evacuation route in the event of a problem.

It's heavily monitored, but Haven has used it before. There are several travel options from the basement of the adjoining building. None of the routes are ideal, and many are likely monitored. It won't matter. Haven has the upper hand down here.

Loghun climbs up the short ladder to a maintenance platform housing tool storage lockers and generators to power trackside lighting. He helps Haven, who is still feeling the effects of the Intercorpex blast.

"We made it."

"Somehow."

Loghun turns to the arched exit and the freedom it represents, and a shot rings out. Its report bounces off the concrete walls of the dimly lit tunnel. The bullet catches Loghun square in the forehead. He falls backward in slow motion, teetering off the platform and collapsing lifelessly on the track bed a few feet below. Haven watches him but doesn't have time to mourn. He drops to a knee and sweeps left and right down the platform, looking for the shooter.

"You *almost* made it," the voice corrects Loghun's previous conclusion.

Haven recognizes the cadence and tenor of Zyree's voice before he appears with his gun drawn. His partner emerges from the electrical equipment behind him with the same "shoot first" posture.

"If you so much as twitch, Haven, you'll join him. Drop it."

CHAPTER FIFTY-TWO

INTERCORPEX

Park Avenue Rail Tunnel
Midtown Manhattan Geographic District
New York City Municipal Corporation

Haven stands and tosses his weapon on the track bed. He doesn't bother raising his hands, not that Zyree cares. One flinch will be the last move he ever makes.

"I should have known you wouldn't fall for my diversion," Haven says.

"The tragic part for you is that I might have, had the PSS not thrown us out of the terminus."

Haven chuckles. "That figures. The only time the bureaucracy does something right is by accident. So, what now? Are you going to turn me over to the BCS?"

Zyree adjusts the grip on his weapon. What he should do is kill this maniac right now. It's what Malkor is expecting. There is something he needs to know first, as cliché as that appears.

"Why did you fake your death, Haven?"

"Oh, Zyree, I don't think it's fair that I answer your question until you answer mine."

"Life isn't fair. What did you say on that SpeedRail about me lacking imagination? Well, this doesn't require any. I pull the trigger if the next words out of your mouth don't answer my question."

"You're wondering whether I faked my death to join Liberteum. No, I didn't. I wanted to be free, Zyree. Free from regimen and orders. Free from the idiots running the exchange. Free from the pressures of gaining higher rank or more prestigious positions. That wasn't for me. So, since I couldn't fit into the system, I left it for good. Can you think of a better way to do that than dying?"

"And Liberteum?" Zyree asks.

"I struggled in New York's urch community. It's cutthroat and has a far more sophisticated social order than you think. Then Quarren found me. I had the skillset he was looking for, and the rest is, as they say, history."

"And the people you murdered?"

Haven smirks and shakes his head slowly. "You're a hunter. I remember you heading down to Lucerne and venturing into the Alps to stalk and kill small game. I did the same thing here – only my prey isn't as smart."

Zyree inhales. This is a sick man. The Haven he once knew was never this jaded or perverse. Modern society may have its problems, but the mass killing of people is hardly a solution to them. No, the Haven he knew did die in that training accident. This man only inhabits his body.

"Your turn," he continues. "Are you going to take me in now or not?"

Malkor remains locked on Haven. It's a safe bet that he has a plan to escape custody. Zyree swore he would end this to provide justice for all those who died, but that's not the way Intercorpex Security does things. Haven knows that.

"Well?" he prods with a sarcastic grin, his wrists held out in front of him. "Are you going to slap on the electromag cuffs and haul me out of here?"

"No."

Zyree squeezes the trigger three times, catching Haven twice in the center of his chest and once through his forehead. He tumbles off the platform, joining his soldier on the track bed. The chief inspector lowers his weapon and moves to the edge.

Haven stares back with hollow eyes. A trickle of blood creeps out of the corner of his mouth. The bastard was smiling.

"It looks like he's dead this time," Malkor says, joining Zyree. "Now what?" Malkor asks.

"We deal with our second problem. I don't know why you're trying to sneak up on me," Zyree calls out. "You know our biocomps see everything."

"It's a force of habit, I guess," Chiana says, emerging from the access corridor with her weapon trained on him.

"Are you here to execute the detention order on us?"

"Something like that. Why don't you two go ahead and disarm yourselves?"

Malkor shakes his head. "You know, boss, the ninja can't get us both."

"Are you willing to bet your life on that, Malkor?" Chiana asks. "Do as I say, or you die first."

Zyree runs the math in his head. Chiana has the angle on them. The time it would take for them to raise their weapons is long enough for her to get two shots off. One of them will be dead and the other wounded, or worse.

"Toss it, Malkor."

"Boss?"

"Do it," Zyree says, not taking his eyes off his nemesis. "You're not taking us into custody, are you?"

Chiana laughs as they set their weapons on the ground and kick them off the platform. "You didn't surrender, Zyree. You were helping Haven escape. I tracked you here, and you fired at me. I had no choice but to kill you both."

"The facts will show otherwise."

"You're showing your age again, Zyree. Since when does the truth ever spoil a good story? The world is changing. I'm helping it along. The things you believe in no longer have value."

If she means honor, courage, and loyalty, then she's correct. They don't exist anymore, anywhere. Humanity has lost them. If that's permanent, then this is a world he doesn't want to live in.

"Did Lyris promise you Jurghen's job?"

"I can't presume how the new administrator-general might reward me for killing two inspectors who aided Liberteum in killing a thousand of the world's most important people today. I can't wait to find out, though."

Chiana takes a step closer. Zyree wonders if she's not as good a shot as she boasts. With the computer-assisted aiming, any respectable marksman doesn't need to be this close. It's how he tagged Haven's soldier square in the forehead from behind a storage locker twenty-five feet away. Her insecurity provides him an opportunity to let Malkor escape. If she inches a little closer....

Malkor lunges. Chiana fires her weapon twice before Malkor can reach her. He lowers his shoulder and shifts to the left, using his momentum to carry them off the platform.

They both hit the track bed hard. Malkor rolls off her, clutching under his body armor where at least one of Chiana's bullets caught him.

"Malkor!"

"Aw, damn it. Get out of here, Zyree."

Chiana sits up and shakes her head to regain her senses.

"I'm not leaving you!"

"You have to! Go!"

She finds her weapon and fires twice in Zyree's direction. The shots go high and wide, and he takes cover behind the arched exit to deprive her of a third opportunity. He's desperate to reach Malkor, but it's no use.

"Get out of here, boss! Go now, before she—"

Another shot ends his sentence. Zyree fills with rage. He wants to storm out on that platform and kill this bitch, but he's unarmed. Any rash action, and he'll be joining Malkor in the afterlife. But does it matter? Everything is already lost. He clenches his teeth and makes his decision.

Zyree bolts into the service area and diverts into the building's basement instead of taking the stairwell back up to the surface. He finds an urch access and crawls through it. He has no idea where this goes, but anyplace is better than here.

His head start on Chiana is tenuous at best. She can track his location as easily as he can hers. This race is a marathon, and whoever's stamina fails first loses. As long as he's transmitting his position, there's no hiding place where she won't find him.

CHAPTER FIFTY-THREE
THE PATRICIANS

The White House
Corporate Governance District
Washington-Arlington Municipal Corporation

The Oval Office is being set up for the address to the employees. She could have chosen the East Room, but the gravity of the moment requires an address from behind a desk. Podiums are for good news, and nothing that has happened today qualifies.

With technicians going about their business, Zeykala temporarily relocated to the Charter Room to collect her thoughts. It's hard to do, and not because of the chaos in her office. The weight of the world is resting on her shoulders.

"Chief Executive Zeykala? The speech is loaded into the prompter," a staffer says as she enters the Charter Room and hands over a copy loaded on the tablet. Zeykala ordered everyone to drop the "acting" from her title.

She accepts the device and scrolls through the speech to check the language. "Hold on. This speech is completely different. What happened?"

"I changed it. Leave us, and close the door behind you," Talya Bettancourt commands from the door.

The staffer scurries out. Zeykala stands but walks over to the credenza along the back wall instead of offering the customary formal greeting.

"You're writing my speeches now, *Prima* Bettancourt?" Zeykala says as she pours a glass of spring water.

"Hundreds of patricians were murdered. Intercorpex has been decapitated. It's time for America Incorporated to assert itself. If we are to be a leader in that change, we need to have our own house in order. You're squandering an opportunity."

"Have you not been paying attention to my actions?"

Talya smirks. "I have. They're not enough. I'm helping you to be the leader you need to be, Zeykala. If you want to recite your speech, go ahead. You're the CEO. Although I suggest you carefully reflect on that decision."

There's a gentle knock at the door. "They're ready for you, ma'am."

"I think I'll listen in," Talya says.

They exit the Charter Room without a word. They were allies in the struggle to remove Valen, but now that she occupies the Oval Office, things are turning adversarial. Talya wants to exert her influence, and Zeykala wants to set strict boundaries. There is going to be a clash of agendas.

The Oval Office is buzzing with activity. A single camera with a teleprompter is set up for the address, and lighting has been added on either side to eliminate shadows. The AME News producer orders his people to make their final preparations as an executive from Public Relations approaches her.

"Ma'am, we will be cutting into all AME channels at exactly noon. The address is being broadcast to the world's media organizations. Most of the planet will hear what you say."

Zeykala nods and sits at her desk. Powder is applied to her face, and a tiny microphone is affixed to the collar of her tunic. She checks to ensure the logo pin over her heart is straight. She doubts this procedure has changed much over the century and a half's worth of television addresses.

"Here we go, ma'am, in five, four, three…" the producer says, counting the last two using only his fingers. He points, and the light over the camera illuminates.

"Employees of America Incorporated, you have all heard by now about the terror that has once again gripped one of our proudest cities. In what has become an all-too-common occurrence, the New York City Municipal Corporation has fallen victim to violence and bloodshed. It is a stark reminder of a far more dangerous time that preceded the peace and serenity of the Corporate Age.

"It is that chaos, that anarchy, and that violence that these terrorists seek to return us to. They cannot adapt to the peaceful, prosperous world we have created. Instead, they seek to destroy it…and they will fail. The corporatist system that has ushered in a brighter future for mankind is a resilient one. It will take more than attacks from thugs and murderers to collapse it."

Those thugs are useful idiots for destroying a career, though. Valen can attest to that. Intercorpex will live on, but these attacks are embarrassing and are tarnishing her image on the world stage. Zeykala needs the threat to be neutralized. She is determined to not meet Valen's fate after working so hard to get here.

"The assault on Intercorpex is reprehensible. That institution is the single greatest keeper of the peace in human history and an invaluable asset to the global corporate community. Intercorpex is not only a marketplace – it is the glue that binds us together.

"The capture of the perpetrators is our highest priority," she continues. "To achieve that end and restore order in the absence of competent executive leadership, I have decreed through executive fiat that Director Virtari of the Bureau of Corporate Security assume control of all municipal corporate functions.

"This assignment is temporary while America Incorporated executives work to identify and interview talented candidates from the ranks of the parent corporation to assume the chief executive position. I am confident that replacements for Chief Executive Safmor and the senior executives who perished with him will be identified in short order."

This speech lacks any of the empathy she wrote into it. She will come across as cold and unfeeling, but the worst is the next few paragraphs. These words will define her tenure as chief executive. She makes a show of lowering her eyes, trying to create the perception of remorsefulness. This pronouncement will not be received well. Unfortunately, crossing Talya Bettancourt is more dangerous.

"Times are challenging, but America Incorporated is strong, and we will endure. For too long, we have been a corporation divided. Past decisions have handicapped our growth. The labor class is the foundation on which our proud corporation was built. It was once concluded that they should be excluded from the benefits employees enjoy. What was passed off as independence was merely a justification to leave them behind. That ends today.

"As of midnight, all labor unions will be immediately integrated into the corporate structure. Detailed guidance to human resources divisions throughout the sphere of influence will be forthcoming from the Office of Corporate Affairs representatives.

"We will turn today's unspeakable tragedy into an opportunity to enhance our strength. While we grieve the losses of so many patricians, we will rely on their heirs for continued guidance and support. Tragedy has befallen the Intercorporational Exchange, and we pledge to do whatever is in our power to assist in their recovery."

Zeykala stares menacingly into the camera. She won't accept threats to her leadership. This is her corporation to run, and she will demonstrate what happens to anyone who crosses her, starting with these terrorists.

"Finally, we will use the full power of this corporation to bring the Liberteum terrorists to justice. It is my solemn pledge that they will be wiped off the face of this Earth. That work begins now. May we all continue to be blessed in enjoying the productivity and wealth of America Incorporated."

CHAPTER

FIFTY-FOUR

RYKOS

"Valhalla"
Midtown Manhattan Geographic District
New York City Municipal Corporation

Zeykala's speech was a revelation. I watch as AME News begins the analysis of her newest executive decree. They can justify it all they want. Now that I know more about the qulis and their relationships with urches, I understand how that will backfire.

Nobody else in the room has time to care. Michele is at gunpoint, and Farron is ready to rip Narik's throat out. The hackers are busy infiltrating Intercorpex and wondering how long it will be before they're discovered. This standoff needs to end soon.

"You've had forty-five minutes," Narik says to Jasper and Adiz, fidgeting with the gun pressed against Michele's temple. "Why is this taking so damn long?"

"What's the matter, Narik? Is your weak little arm getting tired of holding that heavy gun to my head?"

Under normal circumstances, everyone would laugh at Michele's mockery of the uptight patrician. Nobody finds this hostage situation a laughing matter.

"Shut up. You have three minutes to finish the hack. At three minutes and one second, she dies."

"We can't work any faster without detection," Jasper complains.

"Two minutes, fifty seconds. I suggest you try."

"Learning the network takes time. Do you want us to be fast or successful?"

"It needs to be both. We're committed, assuming Farron's plaything contacts my father."

"Call Fiolla that again, and you'll regret it," Farron says through clenched teeth.

"Don't be so dramatic, Farron. Remember who's holding the gun."

I watch Michele roll her eyes. She's tired of this charade. Narik is fatiguing, so it's time to press for answers.

"Taking Michele hostage is a dramatic step just to get us to launch phase three," I say, taking a step closer to the patrician. "Why is it so important that we launch it now?"

"Two and a half minutes. You don't understand what is happening, do you, Rykos? You're in the dark about what phase three is, aren't you?"

I glance at Michele before returning my gaze to Narik. "Educate me."

"Jasper and Adiz are hacking into the Bytecoin network. Archimedes' goal was never to destroy Intercorpex. It's about seizing control of global monetary transactions and halting circulation. Currency supports the economic system. Without the ability to use it, everything comes crashing down."

I'm stunned. I had no idea that this was their plan. Everything with Intercorpex was smoke and mirrors. Liberteum isn't destroying the exchange. They're trying to destroy the corporations listed on it.

"Don't look so shocked. Michele believes people will rise up against their corporate overlords. Nothing is further from the truth. After the chaos, corporations will restore order, and people will become even more dependent on them."

"You're wrong," Michele whispers.

"My father and I are betting everything that we aren't. In two minutes, we'll start proving it."

"You son of a bitch. You've been playing us all along," Farron seethes.

"You're too trusting for your own good, Farron. When your father approached mine with his grand plan, it was meant to only benefit him. We played along until we could flip the script. You would have done the same to us."

"If you destroy the global economy, you won't have anything left," I say, still not seeing the big picture.

"That's where you're wrong. My family has been accumulating gold for decades. With Bytecoin crippled, we have enough purchasing power to dominate America Incorporated and a few other key global corporations."

"It will take more than a stockpile of gold to restart the global economy," Farron argues.

"That's not going to be your concern, buddy."

"All that talk about supporting what we were doing," Michele interjects, "about returning the power of government to the people was a lie."

Narik presses the weapon more firmly into her temple. "The Covingtons have been wealthy since long before the collapse. Did you think we'd give that up for your populist crusade?"

"So, this is about power?" I ask.

"It's about *control*. It's always about control. Intercorpex, corporations, patricians…other than the names, it's no different than before the Great Collapse. It's all people care about because it's all that matters."

Farron is ready to tear this man limb from limb. Narik committed the most personal of all crimes. I open my hands at Michele, wondering if that gave her the answer she needed. She nods.

"I've heard enough. End the simulation, guys," she orders.

Adiz and Jasper immediately terminate their sessions and turn to her. Narik stares at them with bewilderment.

"What the hell do you think you're doing? Do you want to see her die?"

"Please, let me do the honors," Farron says after walking over to me.

I retrieve the weapon from the small of my back and hand it to the patrician. Narik didn't expect that. When he ordered everyone to disarm, he couldn't search us without letting Michele go.

Narik's eyes grow as wide as dinner plates when he sees the gun. "Stay back! I'll kill her! I swear I will."

"Go ahead."

"Don't test me, Farron. Last chance to back away, or I blow her brains out."

Farron closes to within two steps of him. I hear the click of the weapon when he squeezes the trigger, and then another and another. This bastard was really going to shoot Michele in the head. He pulls the gun away from her temple and stares at it in disbelief. Michele slips out of his grip and slides over to Farron's side.

"It's empty, Narik. It was always empty."

"H-How?" Narik stammers.

"We knew you were up to something, just not what. Now we know. Have you ever read Dante's *Inferno*?"

"What?"

"I know you've read the classics," Farron says. "The story where the poet Virgil guides Dante down through the nine circles of hell. Do you know what the last one was? Treachery. It's saved for the worst of the betrayers…Cassius, Brutus, Judas, and now the Covingtons."

Narik's eyes begin darting around the room. He's panicking and looking for a way out. There isn't one.

"W-wait! We can make this right. Farron! We've known each other since we were kids!"

The patrician is unmoved. "I warned you not to call her a plaything."

Farron levels his weapon and fires twice. Narik takes both rounds to the chest and crumples to the ground. He stares up in disbelief until the light flickers out from his eyes.

CHAPTER FIFTY-FIVE

AMERICA, INC.

NYCMC Executive Center (NEC)
Municipal Governance Geographic District
New York City Municipal Corporation

It's amazing just how much things have changed since the last time Ilaria stepped into this building. Safmor and the senior executives are all dead. Intercorpex has been bombed. The BCS controls the city per order of an insecure chief executive. And Rykos…if he's alive, he could be involved.

"Chief Executive Ilaria, I'm Manager Dyllon. I run the NEC."

"Pleased to meet you," she says, shaking his hand.

"Constable Dzamko, it's good to see you again, sir."

"Thank you, Dyllon."

They walk down corridors toward Safmor's office. There are more guardians posted inside the Executive Center than outside it. Dzamko must figure that if Liberteum can hit one high-priority target, they can hit another. He's not taking any chances.

"We heard what happened over at One Guardian Plaza and just finished watching Zeykala's address," Dyllon says. "I trust you know about the new quli policy?"

"Yes. She was full of surprises in that speech."

"There are a lot of upset people in this municorp right now."

"I'm counting on that," Ilaria says.

Nothing galvanizes people better than a common purpose. It's uniting, stirs passion, and provides safety in numbers. The golden rule of public service is never to underestimate a motivated populace. Zeykala should have united the corporation against Liberteum. Her heavy-handed tactics and unpopular decrees will have a different effect.

"You should know, ma'am, that there are…doubts…from the directors about your assumption of chief executive."

"She's perfectly capable, Dyllon," Dzamko argues.

"Yes, sir, but it's more about the process," he clarifies.

"Because I just got named to the position," Ilaria says as Gotham automatically swings the large doors to the office open.

"That's correct, ma'am."

She steps over the threshold. It's a strange feeling. She went from homemaker to running America Incorporated's largest municorp. At least she did until Virtari seized control. It's overwhelming.

"Thank you, Manager Dyllon. Are all the directors assembled?"

"They're in the main conference room."

"Let's not keep them waiting."

"Don't take the directors' reluctance personally," Dzamko says, reassuring her as they step back into the corridor. "They were all deputies until a few hours ago and had been for a long time."

"I'm not. It's politics. I discussed this being a fast-track position with Safmor. We never considered the possibility that I would ascend to his job."

"Well, it's yours now. I'm not sure how you combat these opportunists eager to climb the ladder themselves."

"I am. Go handle your duties, Dzamko. I will take care of this. Keep me apprised of any developing situations."

"Wilco," he says, guardian-speak for "will comply."

She doesn't want Dzamko in the room. The PSS serves a different function than the business units. He needs to remain neutral in power struggles.

Ilaria takes a cleansing breath and strides into the conference room. Everyone stands, and she waves them into their seats, assuming a position at the head of the table. She recognizes most of the faces. Introductions are made quickly, and then it's right into the pressing business at hand.

"Why are we here? We report to the director of the Bureau of Corporate Security now, not you," the finance director asks in an inflammatory tone.

Municipal divisions don't use the traditional C-level naming convention that the parent company does. There is no chief financial officer or chief operations officer. Services such as sanitation and transportation are run by managing directors who report to the CEO.

"You sound like you're willing to accept that without a fight."

"We saw the CEO's address. Zeykala runs America Incorporated. We must obey her directives," she reaffirms.

Ilaria cocks her head. "Why?"

The simple question causes confusion. Challenging the authority of the chief executive isn't done. They will think it's her executive inexperience and are about to learn differently.

"Chief Executive Ilaria, they are our *parent* company. They give the orders. That's how it works," the cultural affairs director argues.

"Since when? We're not an energy producer or a retailer. We're a municorp that supports the subsidiaries that do business here. We're a critical cost center, and because what we do is specialized, we choose leadership from within our ranks."

"This situation is unprecedented."

"The circumstances are, but the process is not. Chief executives have been replaced in Charlotte, Los Angeles, Detroit, Cleveland, and Denver over the past decade. The successor was chosen from within each time."

"Those were ethics-related removals. This is different," the director of family and support services objects.

"Yes, it is. Our leadership was murdered. Chief Executive Safmor was more than our CEO. He was a personal friend. I suppose that's why many of you think he appointed me to my position."

That struck a nerve. Ilaria watches the directors silently look at each other, letting their body language do the talking. That's precisely what they were thinking.

"Zeykala doesn't think I'm qualified to lead this municorp. Many of you probably agree. I can live with that. But turning executive control over to the director of the BCS until they promote an outsider? No, I'm sorry, I won't accept that. None of our colleagues lost today would want us to."

"What do you suggest we do?"

"Reject their authority."

The grumbles travel around the conference table like ripples on a pond.

"That's sedition."

"Call it what you like. We must challenge Zeykala's unprecedented power grab."

"I've heard enough," the director of sanitation cries. "You all can listen to this treasonous speech, but I did not work to climb the executive ranks to throw it all away."

Ilaria stares at the burly man. "That's what you're about to do."

"Excuse me?"

"When a new CEO is chosen, do you think you'll be retained? Or you? Or you?" Ilaria asks, pointing out individuals in the room. "You can't be that naïve. The new boss will bring in his or her own people. What happens to your careers then?"

The silence is deafening. These are good people but career-oriented like all executives. They value their stations in life and won't jeopardize them. Now they realize that their futures are already in peril. Any outsider will clean house.

"Tell me, Ilaria, what's your real motivation?" the finance director asks. "You weren't even an executive forty-eight hours ago. Isn't this high-minded devotion to the NYCMC really a ploy to stay in the powerful position you stumbled into?"

"She's right," the sanitation director says, the hostility dripping in his voice. "You didn't earn your appointment to CEO, and there are directors here far more capable and experienced than you are."

Every set of eyes around this table is locked on Ilaria. The next sentence out of her mouth will define her leadership. She searches for the perfect words, but they don't come. When that happens, there's only one appropriate route: honesty.

"That's true. I'm outclassed by everyone here. If any of you want the job, it's yours. Step forward, and you can decide whether to consent to this hostile takeover. You will be the one that history judges. So, who wants it?"

Every executive in the room is in a stunned state of disbelief. She expects one of the more ambitious among them to raise a hand. None do. Feeling the momentum shift, Ilaria seizes the moment.

"This is about the future of our corporation, not me. It's about reckless decisions from an *acting* CEO in Washington. Most of all, it's what living under the thumb of corporate security means for our employees.

"I'm willing to make hard choices and accept the consequences. The last couple of weeks has already been hell for me. My husband was captured and tortured by terrorists. My son is missing and was last seen in those same terrorists' custody. I have nothing to lose and will take the fall if it goes bad. Who else here is willing to do that?"

The room is again gripped in an eerie silence. Modern executives are groomed to not commit career suicide. That's the likely outcome of her going against their masters in the parent company.

"That's what I thought. I welcome dissenting opinions and different lines of thinking. I will not, however, accept disloyalty to the people who live and work in this city. Anyone willing to is free to tender a resignation."

Ilaria stands and walks out without a further word. She's satisfied that she got her point across. It's a small victory on a day of stunning defeats. It's also just what she needed.

CHAPTER FIFTY-SIX

THE PATRICIANS

Office of Patrician Shalius Covington
Corporate Hill Governance District
Washington-Arlington Municipal Corporation

The buildings on either side of Corporate Hill once held offices for members of the United States government's legislative branch. They were subsequently burned to the ground by an irate public during the Great Collapse. Those people are turning over in their graves knowing who moved in after the rise of corporations.

Patricians position themselves close to the seats of power in the world's corporations. The major patrician families have offices anywhere a board of directors or a chief executive officer calls home. In Washington, modern structures were erected on the foundations of the old House and Senate office buildings. Patricians of the *gentez-majorez* moved in before the paint was dry.

Shalius Covington is at home behind his large, beautifully ornate wooden desk. He comes here dressed in a crisp shirt featuring the silver coat of familial arms patricians wear in lieu of a necktie. The Covingtons have been major stakeholders in America Incorporated since the birth of Intercorpex. Despite his best attempts, he could never purchase enough shares to overtake Talya Bettancourt as *prima*. That may have changed last Saturday. Not that it will matter if Liberteum succeeds.

The thought makes him smile as a chime indicates that someone has entered his reception area. He watches the video feed when it pops up on his display. Most patricians don't care about visitors. He likes to manage every iota of his operation.

"Can I help you?" his well-dressed assistant asks the young woman who approaches the desk.

"Yes, I'm here to see Patrician of the *Gentez-Majorez* Shalius Covington."

Shalius smiles. She's educated and used the proper title. This isn't someone walking in from the street.

"I'm sorry, he's not taking meetings today."

"He'll take mine."

The man stares at his display. The visitor has undoubtedly been identified by facial recognition by now. He makes a few gestures with his hand and brings it up.

"Listen, I'm not sure who you are—"

"You can call me Ishmael.

Shalius freezes. He wonders if he heard that right. He was hoping to hear those words but didn't expect them from an attractive redhead standing in his foyer. He punches the intercom.

"Send her in." He rises, and his office door opens a few moments later. "Please have a seat."

Shalius gestures at the chairs in front of his desk. Fiolla looks around at the nautical paintings and décor before following his instruction.

"Thank you, sir."

"Have we ever met?"

"Once or twice. I'm—"

"I know who you are, Executive Fiolla. You're the White House liaison for Corporate Affairs and close confidante to the former chief executive officer of America Incorporated. How is Valen these days?"

"Fine, under the circumstances."

Shalius steeples his hands in front of his face and leans forward. "He's taking it better than I would. Tell me, how did you know to use that line?"

"Farron Keating told me. What does it mean, if I may ask?"

Shalius smiles. "It's the opening line of an old novel called *Moby-Dick*. My family has a long sailing history, so we're partial to nautical-themed literature."

"It's some sort of a special access code?"

He grins. "Yes, something like that."

It's far more than that. When communications are unsecured and sensitive messages need to be sent between family members, patricians use a series of codes. This one is of the utmost importance. "Call me Ishmael" means that Liberteum has launched its final phase to seize control of the global currency system.

"What can I do for you, Executive Fiolla?"

"The crest around your neck is the wrong color. You are the *Prima* of America Incorporated. It should be gold. Farron and your son have suggested I seek your help in reining in our new CEO."

"My status as *prima* is still pending. Considering recent events, I'm not sure when we should expect Intercorpex to decide that."

Shalius gestures at the display on the wall. It is still the same long camera shot of the smoke plume emanating from what's left of Assembly Hall that's been airing since the bombing. The news director must be relishing the fact that Public Affairs can't cover this up.

"Then take unilateral action as a major shareholder."

Shalius studies her through his old, experienced eyes. "I intend to. How do you know Farron Keating?"

Fiolla lowers her eyes. "We have a history."

That could only mean one thing. Farron is a lucky man. Even if his affair with her was only to advance an agenda, there are worse ways for a man to spend his time.

"Then I must compliment him on his taste in companions. I'm hoping you can confirm something for me. There are rumors that Chairman Hammond is dead. AME News has yet to report anything. Is it true?"

Fiolla locks eyes with the patrician. "He was found dead at his desk this morning. Suicide."

"You're sure?"

She nods. "I found him."

Shalius raises an eyebrow. He didn't expect that. "That's unfortunate. Are you certain it was suicide?"

"I'm not an investigator. Are you implying that there may have been foul play?"

Shalius offers a shrug. "His actions at Valen's hearing were uncharacteristic. Hammond and Valen were close. Somebody was exerting influence over him and could have silenced him. Dead men tell no tales."

She nods slowly several times. There is no doubt that he was coerced by Talya Bettancourt. She would have made an effective mob enforcer in the early twentieth century.

"Can you convene the board without Chairman Hammond?"

"His death makes calling a session easier. Upon notification of the passing of a member, the board of directors must convene within twenty-four hours to choose a successor. When the chairman passes, nominating a replacement becomes the board's first order of business."

"Have they been notified yet?"

"Not to my knowledge," he says, rising gingerly from his chair.

"Where are you going, sir?"

"The same place you are – the White House. I'm going to drop in on the newly minted CEO and the woman pulling her strings."

"How do you know Talya Bettancourt is there?"

"It's my business to know, Executive Fiolla. If you'll excuse me, I need to place a VidLynk. Then I will see what I can do about showing Zeykala out into the street and restoring Valen to his rightful position."

"Thank you, sir."

Fiolla leaves, and Shalius watches the door close behind her. He checks the display to see her make her way past his admin and through the foyer. Then he connects a VidLynk he has been waiting years to establish.

"Yes, sir."

"The collapse of the currency system is imminent. Secure our gold depositories and have the vehicles prepped for transport. Alert all security personnel to report to their posts. The world is about to be bathed in fire. We need to be ready to drag what remains of it from the ashes."

CHAPTER FIFTY-SEVEN

INTERCORPEX

Global Network Operations Center
Manhattan Financial District
ICX New York Exchange

The small convoy pulls up to the main entrance of the Wall Street NOC. Lyris exits one of the vehicles with Nevala and stops to stare up at the iconic façade of the centuries-old building. He may be the administrator-general with an office in Midtown, but this place will always be home.

Exchange personnel and ICX Security staff pour out onto the sidewalk. The convoy's occupants are beginning their march into the facility when a lone figure walks toward Lyris, resplendent in his blue uniform.

"You look like hell," Wyeth says theatrically.

Lyris subconsciously checks the bandages on his face. "And to think I made an effort to clean up."

"It's good to see you alive and well, Administrator-General Lyris. I feared you were lost when we saw the…."

Wyeth stops and gets a little choked up. Everybody here knows someone who perished in that blast.

"I know, buddy, I know. We need to grieve later. We have work to do. Is everything ready for us inside?"

"Yeah," he says, turning and gesturing toward the door.

They bypass security and head immediately for the NOC floor.

"We began assigning workspaces when your transfer of operations order was received. Manager Nolirah will augment headquarters staff with NOC personnel. Operations are spread throughout the building but all tied into the communications system."

The NOC floor is a hive of activity. There's a lot to be done, and that's before even bringing the exchange back online. They need to conduct an engineering inspection of the tower, identify and replace lost personnel, restore faith in the exchange with the patricians…the list goes on. It will be a long climb back.

"This is excellent work, Wyeth."

"It's ugly and overcrowded, but it's the best we can do for the moment. I'm looking into options for setting up people in the museum but acquiring the necessary equipment will take time."

"Hopefully, an extended stay here won't be required. If the damage to the tower isn't catastrophic, we can be out of your hair in a week or two. Let's get that determination before worrying about additional space."

"Yes, sir, I will inform facilities. I have also posted myself down here so you can have my office."

"Thank you, Wyeth. Why don't you follow me up there?"

The two men are joined by Nevala and take the elevator up to Wyeth's office. Lyris is going to need the EDGO to back his claim to the administrator-general position if it's going to stick. The bureaucrats in Zurich won't concede it without a fight.

"Is it true?" he asks, getting a quizzical look from Lyris. "I was told you found a memorandum in Raimius's office relieving me of my post."

Nevala stifles a smirk. Lyris won't need to broach this subject after all.

"Nevala drafted it per Raimius's order and found it digitally authenticated. Are you thinking about asserting your claim to become AG? You're next in line unless fire rescue teams miraculously pull Raimius out of the rubble."

"We both know that you're more deserving of that position than I am. I don't care what the org chart says."

"It was just a question. I don't want you to think that I'm squeezing you out. I will revoke Raimius's order. You're the permanent executive director of global operations. Congratulations."

"Thank you, Administrator-General."

"If you can support me with the staff in Zurich, I would appreciate it. The bureaucrats there are lining up to make their claim."

"I can release your statement of support to global media outlets, Executive Director Wyeth," Nevala says.

"Whatever you need, consider it done."

The two men shake hands. "What do you say we get to work?"

"Gladly. I'll be down in the NOC if you need me."

"Sounds good. We're going to need to accept a VidLynk from Washington soon. I'll want you up back here for that."

Wyeth nods and leaves the office. Nevala gives Lyris a devilish smile.

"Very smooth. You removed your only competition by promoting him to the position he was never removed from in the first place."

"All in a day's work, my dear. Only Wyeth isn't the only threat. Let's hope Chiana finds Zyree before he finds a way to interfere."

CHAPTER
FIFTY-EIGHT
LIBERTEUM

"Valhalla"
Midtown Geographic District
New York City Municipal Corporation

After removing Narik's body and cleaning up the mess, Michele and the hackers spent time scouring the GlobalNet for information on the bombing and watching the footage on AME News. Two questions need to be answered: How much danger are they in when the BCS responds and did Haven survive the attack?

Michele hopes he has perished but knows there is an upside to his survival. A protracted manhunt would keep security forces distracted. There is little doubt that any escape plan would have made it difficult for the BCS or PSS to track him.

"Can we talk?" Rykos whispers in her ear.

"Sure," she says without turning to face him.

"In private."

Michele presses her lips together. This can't be good. Rykos has willingly come along for the ride, but his trepidation is catching up with him.

She follows him to the small kitchen located off the operations room. He immediately sits, eager to get something off his chest. Michele opens the cupboard and removes a mug and a bag of loose tea leaves.

"Would you like some tea?"

"No, thank you. Why didn't you tell me what phase three was about?"

Michele pauses before continuing to ready the brew. "Would it have mattered?"

"I thought your war was against Intercorpex."

"Our fight is against the system, Rykos. You said yourself that most people don't care about Intercorpex."

"So, you're going to destroy the corporate system by taking down Bytecoin? Force millions of people into starvation? Deprive them of medications? Make everyone scratch for survival? Is that the plan?"

"We're not going to collapse the currency system. We're taking it hostage."

"Hostage?"

She realizes that might not have been the best choice of words. It wasn't long ago when he was confined to a utility room in the Broad Street Station and then chained to a column.

"Do you know how Bytecoin distribution works?"

"Probably better than you do."

"Tell me," she says, removing the leaves from the boiling water and taking a seat at the table in the middle of the kitchen.

"It was based on pre-collapse electronic money called 'Bitcoin,' which used peer-to-peer technology to operate a currency system with no central authority or banks. They called it 'open-source,' meaning it was a public network not owned by anybody and available to everybody."

"That's right," Michele says. "After the Great Collapse, corporations didn't want to make the same mistakes governments did. Currency manipulation and over-printing exacerbated the problems inherent in fiat money. They needed a stable platform utilizing the security of blockchain to conduct transactions that they could *control*. Obviously, an open-source model was out of the question, so...."

"Bytecoin was created. I get it, but the currency is managed by an independent organization based in Geneva. If taking that down was always your goal, why bother attacking Intercorpex?"

"Deception. Bytecoin has no central physical presence. It's a computer network in its purest form. Each corporation has dedicated connections to it. If corporations and Intercorpex conclude we're only capable of physical acts, they would have no reason to believe the currency network is in jeopardy."

Rykos lowers his eyes in thought. Men his age are usually preparing themselves for their advanced schooling, not contemplating strategies and tactics once reserved for generals commanding militaries. It's a leap for him, and to his credit, he's holding his own.

"There are easier ways to create diversions."

"Yes, there are," Michele admits. "Bytecoin is protected by the Archangyl network defense system. It's the most advanced cyber defense tool ever conceived. Do you want to take a guess who wrote the code for it?"

"Intercorpex."

"They have a backup data center in Iceland specializing in research and development. We learned a lot about the system in the last hack."

Rykos is in the inner circle now, whether he likes it or not. If he can't accept what she's telling him, he will find himself a prisoner again. Michele is becoming quite fond of him and hopes it doesn't come to that.

"I still don't understand why you would take the risk unless…unless you're using the patricians' access to the Bytecoin network to take it down," he says, working through the details in his head.

"The patricians and financial staff stare at Bytecoin transactions all day. We can't piggyback on their traffic with them watching, so we gave them a reason not to look."

"Thus, the window of opportunity you were discussing and the need for another distraction," Rykos concludes, shaking his head.

He gets up and starts pacing around the room nervously. Many people need to be in motion as they work out problems. She isn't sure which problem he's working on.

"What's wrong, Rykos?"

"This world went through a collapse once. It was one of the darkest periods in human history. Why would you want to repeat that?"

"I don't. I have no intention of returning humanity to the Dark Ages despite the warnings of corporate propagandists. This is a revolution, Rykos. In any revolution, there is a change in political power, not an absence of it."

"Revolutions occur in relatively short periods when the population rises up against the current authorities."

"That's what the history books say."

"You want the people to rise up so you can show them a better way."

Michele knew this conversation was coming. She also knew it would be better if he worked out their motivations. He has been bombarded with propaganda since he was old enough to speak and understand language. This could be interpreted as more of the same.

Words have power, but they are empty without truth. Society has forgotten how to tell the difference. Rykos is a product of that society, regardless of his enlightened ability to question it.

"You're correct, except it can't be me who shows them. I'm not one of them. The corporation poisons its employees' minds to reject us and our motives. No matter how sincere I am, people will never accept my reasoning."

"Then who?"

She stares at Rykos with soft eyes and watches his face change when it dawns on him. Michele told him he was essential to their cause. That he had a purpose. It's why she risked everything to save his father. She needs his cooperation, and now he understands why.

CHAPTER FIFTY-NINE

INTERCORPEX

Somewhere Underground
Midtown Geographic District
New York City Municipal Corporation

It's a maze down here. After an hour of trying to navigate the subfloors and basements of Midtown Manhattan buildings, Zyree finally put enough distance between himself and Chiana to rest. It was touch and go for a while. He doesn't know how the urches have the stamina for this.

He slides down the wall in the pitch-dark subbasement, exhausted. The respite will need to be brief. Chiana closes the distance with each passing second. There is only one way this ends without drastic measures being taken. He makes the decision.

Zyree reaches for the knife strapped to his left thigh and extracts the blade from its sheath. He flips on and adjusts his body armor's torchlight to illuminate his lower torso. Fishing through a utility pocket, he retrieves his electric arc plasma lighter and rolls the knife blade's edge over the white-hot flame.

Satisfied it's as sterile as it's going to get, Zyree opens his tunic and pulls up the temperature-controlled undershirt. He moves the edge of the glowing blade to the slight bulge above his left hip and takes a deep breath.

"Okay, this is going to hurt a little."

He makes an incision, extending it by two inches for good measure. After several sharp inhales and exhales, he inserts his thumb and index finger into the sliced skin and tries to grip the device. Zyree pauses to debate whether to jerk it out or go slowly when he grasps it. He chooses the latter.

His legs start to tingle. The biological computer is integrated into his nervous system and charges itself using body heat and circulation. Nobody explained what would happen should it ever need to be removed in the field. That's probably because it's a horrible idea that no sane man would ever contemplate.

His contacts flicker as the signal is disrupted. He grimaces at the pain and pulls the computer out with a final tug. He rests his head against the wall, panting. With no sutures, he's stuck with an open incision in the dingy underground for the foreseeable future.

Zyree sets the device on the ground and crashes the butt of his weapon into it several times. The data displayed in his vision flickers off. He removes the now-useless contact lenses with a couple of swipes to his eyes. It's a strange feeling. Zyree has used technology-augmented vision for so long that it feels unnatural to be without it.

"All right, Zyree," he mumbles, "I guess we're going to find out how good you are after all."

He climbs to his feet, muscling through the searing pain shooting up the left side of his body. He searches for another exit and, finding one, flips the torchlight off and climbs through the narrow gap in the wall.

Zyree knows he bought himself time, but nothing more. Chiana can't track him, but that works both ways. She also has the benefit of her augmented vision system to guide her. He didn't level the playing field. He only extended the game.

Nobody can run indefinitely. It's only a matter of time before the BCS or PSS catches him on one of their sensors. Zyree can't survive down here on his own. He's going to need help. The question is, with the world now against him, who can he turn to?

CHAPTER
SIXTY
THE PATRICIANS

The White House
Corporate Governance District
Washington-Arlington Municipal Corporation

The aging patrician struts into the Oval Office like a peacock. Most executives believe that patricians think the world revolves around them. That's because it does. Global society owes them a debt that they have only begun repaying. Executives would be best served to remember that. This occupant of this office most of all.

"I didn't think I would need to be so insistent to see the CEO of America Incorporated, considering my position as *prima*," Shalius says after being shown into the office.

"That's because you're not *prima*," Talya snipes from her seat on the sofa, not bothering to stand to greet him.

"Well, isn't this cozy? Good afternoon, Talya."

Zeykala moves around her desk and stands between the two warring patricians. "Until Intercorpex makes their determination, I consider you both valued shareholders. *Prima* Bettancourt is here because I requested her counsel regarding the tragic events in New York."

"That's sensible, although seeking advice from a woman who has turned insulating herself from her peers into a science is a questionable choice."

"They're not my peers. My family has been *gentez-prima* for generations. They are below my station."

"See what I mean?" Shalius says, offering Zeykala an "I told you so" grin.

Talya glares at her nemesis. It doesn't faze Shalius any. He has known the Bettancourt heir for a half-century. Her bark is worse than her bite.

"What can I do for you, sir?" Zeykala asks.

"I've come to inform you that I've called for an emergency board of directors meeting."

"You don't have the authority," Talya snaps.

"I thought that was yet to be determined," Shalius concludes, appealing to Zeykala.

"With all due respect to both of you, we're in the middle of a crisis. Now is not the time to worry about who the *prima* is."

"Are you saying you won't support my request?"

"I don't think it's prudent at this juncture," Zeykala says, causing Talya to grin.

"I see. Thank you for your time," Shalius says before turning toward the door.

He knows what they're thinking: That was too easy. No patrician has ever ceased pursuing something they want after encountering token resistance. While they are lost in their thoughts, he decides to play his hand.

"Oh, Chief Executive Zeykala, before I forget, I believe the corporate charter dictates that the board must be convened within forty-eight hours of the death of one of its members."

Zeykala doesn't say anything, and neither does Talya. Shalius studies their faces before continuing.

"You know that Chairman Hammond was found dead in his office this morning, don't you?"

"Yes, I'm aware."

"Of course. It's the CEO's responsibility to know such things. That must mean you're willfully withholding a statement about his death."

"I'm doing no such thing," Zeykala argues.

"Okay...when *are* you releasing a statement and calling for the board to convene?"

"Have you not been paying attention to what's happening in Manhattan, Shalius?" Talya asks, trying to regain control of the situation.

"Valen was removed, in part, for his inability to safeguard Intercorpex. I just watched them have their campus...remodeled...under Zeykala's leadership."

"You have some nerve!" Talya barks.

"I'm stating facts. I know that you're both familiar with the term 'incompetence' considering its brazen use last Saturday."

"You don't get to waltz in here and say that," Talya screeches, now standing face-to-face with Shalius.

"You're right, Talya. That will be something for the new chairman to decide, which brings us back to my question," he says, turning to Zeykala. "When should I expect to see your statement and call for an emergency session?"

The CEO looks like she's about to have a stroke. Whether Zeykala recognizes it or not, she's nothing more than Talya Bettancourt's favorite lapdog. She is bought and paid for and is expected to advance her benefactor's agenda. Her issue is that she still must operate under a defined set of parameters and procedures. She violates them at great peril.

Shalius waits for an answer as Talya glares at her newest indentured servant. What does she expect Zeykala to do? Other than relent, that is.

"I will release a statement immediately."

"Excellent. I expect the board to convene first thing tomorrow morning. Until then, ladies."

Shalius leaves with the same swagger he arrived with. He can't help but smile all the way to the door. He got his victory and made Zeykala and Talya look like clowns in the process. That fact isn't lost on them. He would love to know what will transpire on the other side of the Oval Office door after he leaves the building.

CHAPTER
SIXTY-ONE
AMERICA, INC.

The White House
Corporate Governance District
Washington-Arlington Municipal Corporation

Talya Bettancourt charges out like a bull locked on a red cape and nearly bowls Fiolla over. She expects the patrician to stop and scream at her insolence, but the woman continues her charge into the corridor. Whatever just happened in there wasn't good for Zeykala. That could only mean Shalius Covington made his move. This summons is bad news.

"You wanted to see me, Chief Executive Zeykala?" Fiolla asks, standing in front of the desk as the CEO stares at the display on her desk.

"I did. You've been busy."

"I'm not sure what you mean."

"Yes, you are," she says, glancing up. "I expected more of you, Fiolla. I was hoping you meant what you said about being loyal to whoever was the chief executive officer. And then I learned about your visit with Shalius Covington."

Fiolla's anxiety kicks into high gear. That was put together fast. Too fast.

"I didn't—"

"The BCS handed me your biojack information, Fiolla. Don't deny it."

"I wasn't going to deny it," she says, shifting gears. "I was about to say that I didn't think that was a problem. It falls to the Office of Corporate Affairs to brief major shareholders on policy changes that could affect future share prices. I went there to fulfill my obligation."

"You gave him a briefing?"

"The contents are on my workstation should you care to review them."

Zeykala leans back in her chair. She isn't buying that for a second. Everything about her body language screams disbelief. If not for Fiolla's relationships with their subsidiaries, Zeykala would have terminated her moments after assuming this office.

"Nothing came up about Hammond's death?"

"He already knew about it. He asked if I had further details, and I said I didn't. Then he asked when we would release a statement, and I told him to contact Public Affairs. Then we commenced with the briefing."

"Would Shalius Covington attest to what you just told me?"

"I can't see why he would contradict the truth."

Zeykala spins her chair around so Fiolla can't see her. "He was just here demanding that the statement be released. Is that a coincidence?"

Fiolla doesn't like talking to the back of a chair. Valen would never do something so rude. She wants to make an obscene gesture, but Zeykala probably had cameras installed here for that reason.

"Perhaps he found my explanation unsatisfactory and came searching for answers."

That sounded better than Fiolla thought it would. Zeykala already had her mind made up about what happened in that meeting. She expected denials and then a confession. She was mistaken, and now she's doubting her conclusion. Shalius could have received that information from a hundred different people on Corporate Hill alone.

"You shouldn't have gone there without authorization."

"It's a standing directive, ma'am."

"I will revoke it. I don't appreciate having to constantly question your loyalty. Your meetings with Valen and the errands you run on Corporate Hill are all too…convenient."

"Ma'am, I have no desire to go back up there after what I saw in Chairman Hammond's office. As for seeing Valen, he has been a mentor to me. I wasn't sure when he would leave town and didn't want to miss my chance to say goodbye."

It's a lie but a hard one to disprove. Zeykala already knows she had a good working relationship with Valen. She also knows that seeing Hammond slumped over his desk would have a severe emotional impact.

"You have said your goodbyes, so there's no reason to see him again, correct?"

"That's correct, ma'am."

"Good. Given your fragile emotional state, I will refrain from sending you to Corporate Hill unless necessary."

"Thank you for that," Fiolla says with a slight bow.

"You're dismissed. Know that I'm watching you closely. Do you understand what I'm telling you?"

Fiolla nods. The message is loud and clear, and the weight of the words hits her hard, despite being expected. It's a thinly veiled threat to have her terminated if she steps out of line.

"Yes, ma'am."

"Chief Executive Zeykala, you have a secure VidLynk request from the administrator-general of Intercorpex."

"It's about time," she proclaims. "Get out of here, Fiolla. Remember what I just told you."

* * *

Zeykala waits for Fiolla to leave. She will have to deal with her later. This upcoming conversation is far more critical.

"Contact Director Virtari and tell him to hold. Connect the administrator-general and put it on the large display."

The CEO straightens her tunic and sits erect in her chair. The link establishes, and a handsome blond man stares back at her. He looks rough, and she wonders how close to the blast he was.

"Good afternoon, Administrator-General."

"Pardon me, Chief Executive Zeykala. I fail to understand how anyone could characterize anything that's happened today as 'good.'"

"That was a poor choice of words. I'm afraid we've never been formally introduced."

"No, we haven't. My name is Lyris. I was previously Intercorpex's executive director of global operations."

She knows the name but has never seen the face. Her understanding is that he was a superb DGO who ran afoul of Raimius. The final nail in his coffin was ordering the exchange to shut down. He managed to endure Raimius's reign of terror, so he must have excellent survival instincts.

"I would have assumed you were at the summit."

He leans forward slightly. "I was. I'm lucky to be alive, no thanks to you and your corporate security."

Zeykala exhales. The first shots have been fired. "Administrator-General, words cannot begin to express our regret over this unfortunate—"

"Save your regrets. They are as hollow as your promises to safeguard our facilities."

"I assure you that this incident was not foreseeable. We implemented every practical security measure at the summit."

"And yet I witnessed its failure firsthand. Would you like to know what explosive overpressure feels like?"

"No, sir, that won't be necessary," Zeykala says, mustering as much sympathy as she can.

"Fortunately for you, I have received some information that may relieve your corporation of some culpability."

The admission was the last thing she expected from him. It makes her question if she even heard him correctly.

"I'm afraid I don't know what you mean."

"Liberteum may have had help from within the exchange itself."

"Forgive me, Lyris, but that doesn't sound like something ICX would ever admit to."

"It wouldn't have been under Raimius, but that neurotic bastard is dead now. I want to usher in a new relationship with our member corporations and hope that begins here."

"Administrator-General, Director of Corporate Security Virtari is currently in New York and taking charge of the search for the terrorists personally. Would you mind if I conference him in?"

"Go ahead."

Zeykala's digital assistant merges the VidLynks. "Can you repeat what you told me, Administrator-General?"

"We've come across information that implicates a member of ICX Security in the recent attacks. His name is Chief Inspector Zyree."

"That name sounds familiar," Virtari says.

"He was tasked with hunting down Liberteum before the Broad Street Station explosion and engaged in a firefight on your SpeedRail last weekend."

"In both cases, the terrorists escaped," Zeykala says.

"And now we know why. Zyree provided false information to members of ICX Security and exchange leadership by leading us to believe the gunfire at our perimeter post was the main attack. He diverted our attention away from a possible truck bombing. He was then spotted with the terrorist Haven by Chief Inspector Chiana. It appeared that he was helping the man flee Grand Central Terminus."

"Haven hasn't been found," Virtari interjects.

"He's lying dead on the track bed near the Fifth-Ninth Street maintenance platform."

Virtari snaps his fingers and directs his people. This is news to him, and that's embarrassing. It also makes Zeykala more inclined to help Lyris with whatever he needs.

"If Haven is dead, how did Zyree escape?"

"His partner, an inspector by the name of Malkor, attacked Chief Inspector Chiana and bought the time he needed to disappear into the underground. Malkor was killed, but Zyree is still at large."

"I thought you could track him with that computer inspectors have," Virtari says.

"We lost contact with his biological computer. He likely removed it. It's become impossible for our asset to track him through your underground by herself."

"And you are asking for our help?"

Virtari is pissed. Intercorpex cannot run operations within a corporation's sphere of influence without informing them. He's willing to overlook that transgression since they killed Haven. If assisting them in rounding up a rogue inspector helps lessen the embarrassment of failure, it's a small price to pay.

"I am. Zyree's capture will help us both move past the events of the past several weeks."

"We'll do whatever we can," Zeykala says, doubting this inspector will be taken alive. His death is more convenient for everyone.

"I will send over his dossier. There's also something that I think Director Virtari will find very interesting."

"What's that?" he asks.

"Zyree worked closely with Chief Guardian Teman. We're wondering if he could also be involved."

Virtari smirks. "We'll be sure to investigate and share our findings."

"Thank you. We have temporarily moved all headquarters functionality to the Wall Street NOC. You can reach me there."

"Understood. Thank you, Administrator-General Lyris."

He signs off. Zeykala verifies that the VidLynk to Intercorpex has been terminated and she leans back in her chair. She wonders if this is all too good to be true.

"The channel is clear, Virtari. You can speak freely."

"He's hiding something."

"Of course he is. Find out why he wants this man Zyree."

Just because Zeykala is willing to work with Lyris doesn't mean she trusts him. Intercorpex has a long history of doing whatever is in its best interests. The leader of the exchange may be new, but their corrupt culture is as old as their charter. Knowing the real reason for this manhunt may be useful later.

"I will. I find it hard to believe that they're willing to assume any blame for this."

"Whatever the reason, assist in Zyree's apprehension. If it helps repair our relationship with Intercorpex, it's worth it. What about Chief Guardian Teman?"

"The man is a buffoon. He mismanaged the sweeps in the search for Liberteum and allowed transponder codes to fall into terrorist hands. Valen protected him when any competent chief executive would have had him terminated."

"Did he assist Zyree and the terrorists?"

"It would explain his failures."

That's a typical Virtari answer. "Wasn't Teman captured by the terrorists?"

"He was rescued during the raid at Old Saint Patrick's Basilica. We don't know the whole story. Teman hasn't been properly interrogated."

"Make that happen. If he was involved with Zyree, we need to know. It would be distressing if he was playing for the other side. Are we clear?"

"Crystal."

Teman…Zeykala heard that name recently but can't put her finger on the context. She recalls the details of the countless meetings to no avail. When Fiolla pops into her head, she remembers hearing the name.

"Wasn't Teman's wife the one who took over control of the NYCMC?"

"Yes, ma'am. I relieved her of her duties myself."

Zeykala smiles. "Then it's possible she's involved as well. Make sure she has been fully stripped of all corporate authority and keep a close eye on her."

"Consider it done," Virtari says, signing off.

This conversation with Lyris couldn't have gone better. If she can repair their fragile relationship with the exchange, Shalius will have a hard time convincing the board of anything. It also justifies her removal of Ilaria for something more substantive than her inexperience.

Everything is coming together now. She's finally getting the breaks she needs. It's the first time in days she's allowed herself to be optimistic.

CHAPTER SIXTY-TWO

INTERCORPEX

Global Network Operations Center
Manhattan Financial District
ICX New York Exchange

Lyris disconnects the VidLynk to the White House. He didn't like playing peacemaker. Zeykala, and her stooge Virtari, deserved far different treatment. At least he got what he wanted.

He brings up the other VidLynk. He didn't conference it in to avoid unnecessary questions. He did have the audio forwarded to ensure there was a witness to the conversation.

"You heard all that, I presume?"

"Yes, thank you," Chiana says, her image filling the display. "That will help exponentially. Tracking Zyree's movements down here was hard enough when his biocomp was relaying his position. It's impossible without it."

Lyris shakes his head. "You should have killed him when you had the chance."

"I would have, had Malkor not intervened."

"I don't need excuses, Chiana. I need results."

"I'm aware of that."

Chiana doesn't appreciate the lecture, but Lyris doesn't care. The key to fixing everything revolves around Zyree: his taking over as AG, promoting Chiana, the exchange's reputation, and even their relationship with America Incorporated. Failure isn't an option. Pinning these attacks on him will only work if he's dead. Corpses can't defend themselves.

"Then don't waste any more time talking to me. Contact the BCS and determine your next steps."

She nods, and Lyris disconnects.

"The carrot and stick approach. Nice," Wyeth says.

"Too much carrot and not enough stick, if you ask me," Nevala gripes.

Lyris knows the Nevala-Chiana relationship dynamic is going to become a headache. He's already sore, his head hurts, and this day is still long from over. That's a problem for another time.

"Do you have my list?"

Nevala's fingers dance on her tablet, and the document pops up on his display. "Here are the names and positions of Intercorpex personnel who are unaccounted for. Some of them may still be alive. We're contacting the PSS to get admittance information from area medical centers."

"Let's assume they're all lost. Start identifying personnel that can be elevated into the key roles. Ask Manager Nolirah for assistance. She runs personnel operations here."

"Will do."

"Thanks, Nevala. We'll talk later," he says with a wink before she excuses herself.

"What a crazy day. It feels like we've been working for a week, and it's only early afternoon," Wyeth says.

"It's only going to get longer, I'm afraid."

"I can't believe this is happening. The shock is wearing off, I guess."

"We lost a lot of good people today. That's why we need to turn these events into a positive by succeeding when everyone expects us to fail. I need you to redouble efforts to get the exchange back online."

"What about determining the source of the anomaly? We both know it wasn't the patricians' trading activity."

"Assign a team to work on that. Run twenty-four-hour shifts and ensure their findings stay between us. I want an answer before we're ready to restart operations."

"You got it."

Lyris rubs his head as Wyeth departs. The wheels are in motion. He has an opportunity to put the pieces back together in the way he has always wanted them to fit. Intercorpex can be stronger than it ever was under Raimius or his predecessors.

He will be known as the AG who saved the exchange. Their newfound strength will force corporations to bend to his will. Patricians will grovel as he holds the key to their acquiring more wealth. Intercorpex will become the epicenter of world power. That causes Lyris to smile. He's going to be a god in this place.

CHAPTER SIXTY-THREE

RYKOS

St. Patrick's Cathedral
Midtown Geographic District
New York City Municipal Corporation

I join Michele and Farron in ascending the long spiral staircase. By the time we reach the top of our climb, I wish I had passed on this outing. As much as I want to see the Emissary again, my abdomen isn't ready for this much strain. I'm about to stop when we reach a small chamber. A ray of light pours into the darkness from above. That's an appropriate metaphor considering we're under a church.

The Emissary already has a heavy trap door open. We climb the ladder into the archbishop's sacristy and find him waiting for us. Located off the ambulatory, his office is small and simple compared to the scale and majesty of this iconic cathedral. The door that leads down to Valhalla is cleverly disguised in the room's mosaic flooring and hidden under a rug for good measure.

"Hello, my children," the Emissary says, bowing. "The sanctuary is empty as we ready it for Mass. Your guests are waiting in the Lady Chapel. Please follow me."

We exit his office, turn right, and follow the curvature of the ambulatory to its apex. Located at the easternmost point of the cathedral is a small chapel. The three men waiting there for Michele greet her with hugs.

"I will leave you now. Services are in ninety minutes, and the doors will open in thirty. It would be best if your business is concluded by then."

"We'll be brief. Thank you, Cardinal," Farron says before he departs.

"You guys all know Farron," Michele informs them before gesturing at me. "This is Rykos."

"Hero of the corporation, whatever that means," one of them says as he looks me up and down.

"Not so much anymore, I think," I say, feeling compelled to defend myself.

"This cynic is Prano. The other two are Andanz and Phylep."

"You're qulis?"

"He doesn't miss much," Andanz says with a sneer.

"You'll have to forgive my friends, Rykos. They're apprehensive of outsiders and don't like anyone associated with executives. It comes from being the unofficial leaders of New York City's unions," Michele explains.

"'Leader' is probably not the right word," Phylep says, correcting her. "When we talk, people sometimes listen."

I nod. The men and women in the labor unions are a unique lot. They are looked down on by employees and have developed their own subculture to compensate for that. Although shop bosses interact with executives, the influencers in these unions are the individuals with real leadership capacity.

"You operate outside of the quli union structure?" I ask, causing the three men to laugh.

"Executives are a paranoid lot. Our shop bosses are under constant surveillance by the BCS. Those guys can't take a dump without the Pentagon knowing the color, consistency, and volume."

"That's…disgusting," Farron groans.

"Oh, yeah, I forgot that patricians are above taking a shit," Prano says, earning a glare from Farron.

"What brings you guys here?" Michele asks before this really gets out of hand.

"You heard about the explosion?"

"We live underground, Andanz. We're not buried in it."

"Then you also heard the CEO's directive about forcing the qulis to become full employees?" Phylep asks.

"We figured you guys wouldn't be fans of that. Are you planning to protest?" Farron asks.

The three men look at each other. The level of conviction in their eyes is something I've never seen before. Whatever they are planning, it's serious.

"Protests may only be the beginning," Prano says. "My guys are ready to go to war over this. The word around the sphere is much of the same."

"This is the one line we won't let them cross," Andanz adds. "It's the last insult we're going to endure from these people. We're gonna fight."

"The BCS will tear you guys to pieces," I say.

"Then we'll die fighting for what we believe in. We're already indentured servants, Rykos. Now they propose to make us slaves," Phylep argues.

"I'm worried about what that will mean for you," Michele says.

'That's why we're here. We came to say goodbye."

"Part of me wants to talk you out of this," Michele says, lowering her gaze briefly. "But I would feel the same way. Please take care of yourselves. Don't be reckless with your lives."

They share hugs again. Even Farron and I get respectful nods. These men may despise employees and patricians, but anyone who runs with Michele earns a modicum of their respect.

"Interesting characters," I observe after the three men leave.

"That they are. They help maintain Valhalla. Many of their men helped build it in the first place."

"Aren't you afraid the BCS could get that information out of them?"

I would think that's a legitimate concern. Valhalla's strength is secrecy, or so Michele said. I can imagine scenarios where qulis could bargain information on Liberteum's headquarters away for immunity or preferential treatment. Most employees would consider that in a heartbeat.

"The BCS and PSS know that urches and qulis sometimes work together, but they've never made the connection to Liberteum," Farron says. "Nobody would ever think they could have built Valhalla in the first place."

"They don't have to be under duress to sell you out," I warn.

Michele smirks. "You don't know too many qulis, do you?"

"The unrest means that we have no choice but to leave," Farron says.

"You mean leave Valhalla? Why would we want to do that?" I ask, now really confused.

"Valhalla needs to be protected. This new CEO will order the BCS to descend on the city in numbers we've never seen. The labor class keeps us stocked with food, water, and basic necessities. If Phylep, Prano, and Andanz are embroiled in a conflict with security forces, we'll either need to get it ourselves or risk running out."

"Neither of those options is pleasant," Farron concludes.

Michele looks around the chapel. "My father and I moved around the underground, but Valhalla was always my home. I feel safe there. That feeling will be more of an illusion than reality if we stay. Can you arrange for us to leave?"

"I can send a message to my father through the Emissary. His men can extract us, but it will be tricky, and the timing will need to be perfect."

"We'll never make it out via a bridge or tunnel," Michele warns. "It has to be by air or over water."

"I will have Commander Lacune choose the method with the least exposure and margin for error."

"Arrange it quickly, Farron."

The patrician heads toward the archbishop's office, leaving me alone with Michele. She has the weight of the world on her shoulders. I wish I could say or do something to help with that.

"Have you ever attended services here?" she asks.

"Once or twice a year when the chief guardian needs to be visible. My family isn't overly religious."

"I've always wanted to go in person. I watch the internal feeds sometimes. The pageantry, the music…it's beautiful."

I nod slowly. "Are you sure you want to leave Valhalla? You don't look like you have your heart in it and the decision feels…rushed."

"It was always part of the plan, but after the final phase. Narik was right in that we lost our opportunity. I don't know what the consequences of Haven's attack will be other than bad. The BCS won't stop until every member of Liberteum is identified and captured. Staying here is too much of a risk."

"Okay."

"Are you getting cold feet?"

I shake my head, but I honestly don't know what to feel. Things are happening too fast, and there isn't enough time to process the decisions being made.

"I guess I still don't understand my role in all this."

"I wish I could help you, Rykos. The situation is fluid. I think we'll know when the time is right. Come on, let's get back down to Valhalla before parishioners start arriving."

I follow her to the trap door and meet up with Farron, who finished making his arrangements with the Emissary. We descend back into the chamber and start the trek down the spiral staircase. A downward spiral. I only hope that isn't a metaphor for things to come.

CHAPTER SIXTY-FOUR

INTERCORPEX

Somewhere Underground
Midtown Geographic District
New York City Municipal Corporation

No wonder the PSS could never find the urches in this city. There are subterranean access routes everywhere. You would think the corporation would compel building managers to be more diligent in monitoring the conditions of their underground facilities.

Zyree stumbles into a subbasement through a boiler room access. He pokes his head out around a corner and enters another maintenance space. When he spots the sign next to the door, he hangs his head.

"All that, and I've only made it here?" he mumbles.

The Waldorf Astoria Hotel isn't more than ten blocks from where he started. With adequate light for the first time in hours, he takes measure of himself. Covered in dirt and grime, he can't travel through public spaces unnoticed. The hotel gives him the option to steal clothing and possibly find a tablet to contact Ortan. Maybe he is willing to help.

The building is bound to be monitored by a Maester, or the hotel's version of that system. Spending time here is a huge risk. Urches steer clear of hotels for a reason. Unfortunately, he's running out of options.

Zyree climbs a seldom-used stairway up to the first basement level. The accommodations aren't much better, but it's apparent that the area is used. He checks the various utility rooms and storage closets before finding what he's looking for.

The medium-sized lounge has pre-collapse-era lockers lining the wall and a rickety table with unmatched chairs in the middle. He starts methodically searching for anything useful in the lockers.

"You don't belong here."

Zyree is startled by the voice behind him and jumps into a fighting stance. He has good senses, but they are dulled by fatigue. He also relied on his contacts to warn him when someone was sneaking up. If that had been Chiana, he'd be dead.

The young man in work coveralls holding a tablet doesn't flinch. If anything, he looks amused by Zyree's aggressive stance.

"I'm not going to fight you. It doesn't look like it would do me much good to try."

"Who are you?" Zyree demands.

"The name's Phylep. I'm a laborer assigned to the renovation here."

"You're a quli."

"And you are definitely not an urch, despite trying your best to look like one."

"What makes you say that?" Zyree asks, curious.

"Urches don't call us qulis and don't point out the obvious. Then there's your clothing. That tunic hasn't been modified to urch goth. So, you're either Intercorpex Security, or you killed someone who was."

Zyree allows himself to relax. This guy is sharp. More importantly, he's not skittish or afraid. He decides to take a risk and be honest with him.

"My name is Chief Inspector Zyree of Intercorpex Security. Or at least, I was with ICX Security. Now they're hunting me."

"Does it have to do with the explosion?"

"Indirectly. Let's just say that the guy running Intercorpex now doesn't like me."

"That explains all the guardians and BCS agents combing the Midtown underground."

That's news to Zyree, although he isn't surprised. Chiana must have asked Lyris for reinforcements after he removed his biocomp. It must have killed her to make that call. There's no doubt she wanted to take care of him on her own.

"How did you—"

"Laborers in this city talk to each other. A lot."

"Well, if you'll forget we had this conversation, I'll be on my way."

He starts to move past him when Phylep holds up a hand. "You can't go back down there. It's only a matter of time before they catch you."

"I don't have much choice."

"You do. I can get you some clothes and find a shower. You can blend in topside."

"I appreciate the confidence, Phylep, but I don't think I'll last very long on street level with all the drones and facial recognition in this city."

"It's a risk, but they're not looking for you on the streets. Come on," he says, pulling a gray jumpsuit out of a locker. "Control, this is Phylep."

"Go," the voice replies from his beat-up tablet.

"I'm here to make two more runs of fixtures up to the reno for tomorrow's installs. Clear it with the management system."

"Okay, done."

"Thanks." Turning to me, he says, "Everything we do has to be cleared through the system. So long as we check in, they never probe further."

The two men move through the basement to an underground loading zone with a huge freight elevator that leads to the surface. America Incorporated, like many of the world's corporations, prefers to keep its cities tidy. All construction and maintenance materials are hidden from view or shipped to a site when needed. The hotel keeps theirs in here.

"Take these and follow me," he says, handing Zyree some new light fixtures.

They travel up to a floor under construction. Tools, buckets of paint, saws, and construction debris litter the corridor. He turns into one of the unfinished rooms and sets the fixtures down on the ground.

"This room has the plumbing installed, so you can shower. Just make it quick. The computer will get suspicious if we stay up here too long. I'm going to look productive and meet you back here in fifteen minutes."

Zyree disrobes and basks in the steaming hot water for as long as he dares. He could have stayed in that shower for an hour. Heeding Phylep's warning, he changes into the new clothes and is waiting for him when the laborer returns.

"I found this in our lost and found cabinet. You should be able to connect to public wi-fi and place VidLynks. We need to leave now," he says, handing Zyree the old tablet.

They take the elevator back down to the maintenance area. Instead of heading to the lounge, he walks Zyree to a small utility area. The shelving has been cleared out, and the space turned into a bunk room with a few cots.

"We use this place to crash out sometimes. Nobody will bother you here. If anyone asks, say you're with the day crew, and you're having a problem with your miserable wife."

Zyree snickers. Marital distress is a universal problem that garners immediate understanding and sympathy. It's something both men and women understand and a better lie than he could have come up with.

"Just be out of here by nine a.m.," he continues. "It will be awkward if you're here when my guys show up."

"Where are you going?"

"I was in the area and only stopped in to check work orders. I have to meet back up with some friends now. Have you heard about the parent company's new directive regarding laborers?"

Zyree shakes his head. "I've been too busy running for my life."

"You will," he says with a slap on the shoulder.

"Thank you for your help, Phylep," Zyree says, shaking his hand.

"Good luck to you."

He leaves, and Zyree powers on the old device. It boots and connects to the hotel's public wi-fi, much to his surprise. He opens the VidLynk application and punches in the code for Ortan.

"Yes?"

"It's me."

"Thank God," Ortan whispers, hanging his head. "I thought you were a goner. Are you someplace safe?"

"For now. I'm at the—"

"Don't tell me! This connection is unsecured, and it's better if I don't know. I'm working to get you out of Manhattan. Can you hang tight there for a while?"

"Until morning."

"Then I had better get to it. Keep whatever device you're using powered on. I'll contact you when I have an escape plan."

"Thanks, Ortan."

The VidLynk ends, and Zyree lies down on the cot, cradling the device against his chest. It was good to see Ortan. It's hard to imagine that the quirky bastard is the only friend he has left. If he can even be called a friend. Zyree feels himself drifting off. There's no point in fighting it. He needs to rest while he can.

CHAPTER SIXTY-FIVE

AMERICA, INC.

NYCMC Executive Center (NEC)
Municipal Governance Geographic District
New York City Municipal Corporation

It's still hard for Ilaria to think of this office as hers. Safmor was a friend as much as a colleague, and she's had no time to deal with his loss. With the city in crisis, executives and managers have been coming and going. They are all turning to her to make decisions. It's an incredible weight to bear.

Doubts creep into her mind. She hasn't stopped asking herself if she is up to this. Chief Executive Zeykala doesn't think so. Some of her directors agree despite their reluctance to fill the role. It's not that she can't do the job. She's just been out of the game for so long. Twenty years is an eternity in the business world. Things change. She hasn't changed with them. Maybe that's what she can bring to the table.

"Tell me some good news, Dyllon," Ilaria says as he steps into her office.

"I have good and bad. Which do you want first, ma'am?"

"The bad."

"Your husband has been trying to contact you."

Ilaria groans. There hasn't been an opportunity to contact Teman since she was escorted from his room. It may have only been ten hours ago, but it feels like it's been a lifetime. He might not even know, considering AME News never mentioned her assumption of CEO duties. Maybe that's the reason she's avoiding him. Technically, he works for her now.

"What's the good news?"

"Do you want me to arrange a VidLynk with him?"

"The good news, Dyllon, please."

"I've spoken to the directors. Two thirds of them are prepared to support you publicly. The remainder quietly agrees with your rejecting BCS rule. They're adopting a 'wait and see' approach."

"Do any of them want this job?"

He shakes his head. "It's all yours. At least until you get the city on its feet and they step in to take the credit after the BCS hauls you away for sedition."

"You're quite the optimist, aren't you?" she asks sarcastically.

"I'm a realist, ma'am. I've been watching the political game here since graduating from Princeton. That's the most likely outcome."

"Something to look forward to."

"We have a problem, ma'am," Dzamko says, charging into the office.

"Oh, thank God! We haven't had a fresh crisis in the last ten minutes. Let me guess: The BCS is here to evict us."

"We're not that lucky. The qulis are organizing."

"That didn't take long," Ilaria laments.

Dzamko calls up an interactive map on his tablet and sends it to the main display. He zooms in and then overlays real-time population density tracking. The hot spot is clear, and it's growing.

"The CEO's pronouncement has them pretty worked up. It started with a few hundred laborers. Now at least a thousand have taken over John Jacob Astor Park."

"More will be coming," Ilaria says, standing and moving closer to the display. "The park is south of quli domiciles on the East Side."

"Have they turned violent?" Dyllon asks.

Rioting qulis have caused major headaches in metropolitan areas around the sphere in the decades since the Great Collapse. They cause massive damage when objecting to corporate overreach. Stripping their autonomy will unleash a rage never seen before.

"No, it's peaceful so far."

"Has One Guardian Plaza issued any orders?"

"Not yet. I'm sure the RTCC is monitoring them, but the PSS is still at Grand Central and involved in some manhunt for a rogue ICX inspector."

"What?" Ilaria asks. That's news to her.

"I'm sorry, it's a BCS thing. I don't have any more details," Dzamko says.

Ilaria returns to her chair and stares at the map. This will turn into a bloodbath with Virtari running the city. Men armed with hammers and screwdrivers won't fare well against men equipped with body armor and automatic rifles.

"How many guardians are loyal to you?"

"All of them," the constable answers, offended at the question.

She gives him a look of apprehension. No leader commands the loyalty of an entire organization. There are always naysayers and opportunists.

"I served with these men and women for decades. They'll follow my orders over Director Virtari's."

"How much of the force is involved in the manhunt?"

"In Manhattan? About thirty percent."

"Nobody has been called in from Brooklyn, the Bronx, or Queens?"

Dzamko rubs his chin. "Not to my knowledge. They may be tasked with extra security for critical infrastructure. What are you thinking, Ilaria?"

She rubs her hands before pressing them together in front of her mouth. She knows what she wants to do. It's the right thing. The only problem is convincing anyone to go along with it, starting with these two men.

"Would a couple of legions venture into Manhattan if you ordered them to?"

"Sure. To what end?"

"To protect the qulis."

"Protect them?" Dyllon asks. The tone of his voice implies that he thinks she's crazy. He may be right.

"Look at what's going on around us. How long before the BCS marches in and guns them down? How many people will die when they do?"

"They'd be doing us a favor," Dyllon mumbles.

"I hate to admit it, but he's right, Ilaria. The qulis are trouble. You've been married to Teman long enough to know that."

"They live in this city, right?"

"Yes, ma'am, but—"

"And guardians are charged with protecting all the city's residents?"

"All of the city's *employees*, yes. The qulis aren't employees."

She smiles. "As of midnight, they will be."

The two men look at each other. She has a point, and they know it. Dzamko offers the first argument against it.

"I see where you're going with this, but they don't have the right to assemble. Any gathering over ten people requires a permit."

"Then we'll issue one."

"Ma'am, you want your first official act as a rogue CEO to be the sanctioning of a quli protest?"

"It's a crazy world, Dyllon. Can you think of a more righteous act of corporate disobedience?"

"No, ma'am, but it's unprecedented."

Ilaria nods. "So is relieving a municorp's CEO and turning control over to the director of corporate security."

He doesn't like this but is running out of objections. She can't blame him. Dyllon gets paid to run the NEC and offer sound advice to the chief executive. This course of action runs contrary to everything he's ever been taught. No sane person would think this was a good idea.

"This is a good way to lose the support of the directors," he warns.

Ilaria stands and places her hand on his shoulder. "This is bigger than my assuming this office. It's about the office itself. If we're not going to do the right thing, then why are we here? We've been relieved of our duties. Are we pretending to be in charge, or are we willing to take charge?"

"They could terminate us for this," Dzamko claims.

"Let them try. I'm done genuflecting to executives in Washington who change policies whenever it suits them. If you didn't feel the same way, you wouldn't be here now."

"You're right – I wouldn't," he says before turning to their young manager. "Dyllon, you're caught in the middle of all this. I'm old and have nothing to lose. You have a whole career ahead of you. If you want out, say the word. I'm sure Chief Executive Ilaria will understand."

Ilaria nods. She wants him with them, but only if he wants to stay. There are enough edicts forced on the people in this corporation. Executives have forgotten an axiom that has endured through the ages: There's nothing stronger than the heart of a volunteer.

"You may be the first executive I've ever seen willing to take bold action. I might as well be a part of it."

"Good man," Dzamko says, giving him a slap on the shoulder.

"It doesn't mean I'm not terrified," he says with a smirk before spinning on his heels. "I'm going to go draft the permit before you find more ways to get me in trouble."

"Thank you, Dyllon," Ilaria calls out, eliciting a sharp wave in response before he disappears around the corner.

"At least now I know where Rykos got his rebellious streak from," Dzamko says, grinning.

She hadn't even thought of Rykos. "I never encouraged that. I pledged my full allegiance to the corporation. Only now am I realizing that my son was right to question the world around him."

Dzamko takes her hands in his and stares at her like her late father used to.

"You know that this isn't going to end well for us. Are you sure you want to go down this road? Once you do, there's no turning back."

Ilaria gives his hands a squeeze. "I'm tired of being on the sidelines. After twenty years of raising children, I'll be damned if I'm going to spend the rest of my life toiling in a dead-end job until a manager decides I'm no longer useful and HR orders me killed. You're damned right I'm going down this road."

"Okay. I'll go call some of the legions," he says with a nod.

"Dzamko? Tell them to protect those people at all costs."

He smiles and leaves her alone in her office. She stares at the display and the growing red dot in Astor Park. She's about to find out if she's up to this job before this week is over.

CHAPTER SIXTY-SIX

LIBERTEUM

"Valhalla"
Midtown Geographic District
New York City Municipal Corporation

Michele sits alone in the kitchen with her hands around the warm mug of tea. She finds the sensation of the heat relaxing. She needs that right now. The footage on AME News has become unbearable to watch. It is a parade of victims to show every employee the horror of Liberteum's attack. They are showing body parts and medical trauma centers to document the horrific human cost of Haven's rampage. It's effective propaganda because it's not built on a lie. Just not the whole truth.

Farron slips into the kitchen and pours himself a coffee. Michele hasn't said much about Narik. The two used to be close. That couldn't have been easy for him, but she figures that he will talk about it when he's ready.

"Are the arrangements finished?"

"Not yet," Farron says. "Soon."

"Did you talk to your father?"

Farron shakes his head. "He can't be happy with me, and I don't want to deal with that right now. I spoke directly to the commander. He'll inform my father."

"You're going to need to face him sooner or later," Michele warns.

"I prefer later. Where's Rykos?"

Michele presses her lips together. "He wanted to be alone for a while."

"That's hard to do in this place."

"Don't I know it," she moans.

"You told him, didn't you? About Archimedes," Farron says, pulling out a chair and sitting.

"It was time."

"What did he think?" Michele shrugs, causing Farron to cock his head. "You told him why he's here."

"He figured it out. I wasn't going to lie to him about Archimedes or his role in our plans. I'm surprised it took this long to have the conversation."

"Did he agree to it?"

"He didn't disagree."

It was a non-answer, and Farron knows it. "You took a lot of risks for him."

Michele violently leans back in her chair. She knows where this is going. For all of Farron's support, he doesn't really understand the endgame. She needs the support of the people for Archimedes to succeed. Farron lives in a different world. He doesn't understand why that's necessary.

"We've already had this conversation."

"And we're going to have it again. Michele, Archimedes is a weapon more powerful than a nuclear arsenal. They destroy cities. If phase three works, you could destroy the global economy with a single keyboard command."

"That's why we need Rykos. The corporations will turn our revolution into the specter of Armageddon. My father recognized a long time ago that we needed someone to tell our side of the story. Rykos is perfect for that."

"You're assuming that people will listen."

"And you're assuming they won't," Michele snaps.

"You've never lived in the corporate world, Michele. You can't understand what it's like. Most employees aren't like Rykos. They don't question what they're told. They are raised from the time they speak their first words to be allegiant and compliant."

The side of Michele's mouth curls up. "You're right. But if that was universally true, there would be no urches. Not everyone accepts their programming. What will happen when another truth is presented?"

"It won't matter," Farron argues.

"Are you sure? You watched me do it on that SpeedRail."

Farron can't argue with that. When the employees learned who Michele was in the aftermath of the raid on the Alamo under Old St. Patrick's Basilica, they should have acted. They could have detained the four of them. At a minimum, they should have reported them to the PSS. They did neither of those things. Instead, they let them pass. Rykos is only alive because they did.

"You're asking a lot from Rykos, especially in light of what happened this morning."

"I know," Michele admits, "and we did a lot for him in return."

"So, this is a quid pro quo?"

"No. It's also not a one-way street. He isn't a disciple of the cause. If we're asking him to do the impossible, we should be willing to do the same."

"What if he calls it quits? What are you going to do if he walks in here and says that he can't do this anymore?"

Michele hasn't put much thought into that. It's not because it's unlikely. She just doesn't know what she would do. It would put all of them in a horrible position. She doesn't want to make Rykos a prisoner again.

"Then he's free to go."

"The BCS will grab him the moment he leaves. They'll learn where Valhalla is, even if they are forced to beat it out of him. It will be the end of this."

"Free will, Farron. Rykos understands what leaving means. If he wanted to, he'd already be gone. As for helping us, it's a decision that he needs to make. I can't coerce him."

"You already have," Farron says, standing. "You just don't realize it."

"Someone gave Haven high-powered explosives," Michele says, eager to change the subject. "If it wasn't Narik, then who was it?"

"You had better not be implying it was me."

"I'm not, but it was someone powerful. He didn't get explosives from the corporation and didn't mix them himself. That leaves patricians. We need to find out who. We can't afford to get blindsided again."

CHAPTER
SIXTY-SEVEN
THE PATRICIANS

Global Network Operations Center
Manhattan Financial District
ICX New York Exchange

Denali understood long ago that power is as much psychological as it is political or physical. A man can have an army or occupy a position that wields it, but bending others to your will without using those tools is the true power.

That started when he had Lyris "escorted" to Greenwich. Then Denali showed up unannounced at his domicile. Now, he's invaded the new administrator-general's temporary Wall Street office without notice. He is daring the young man to push back, knowing he won't.

Denali instructed his man in Intercorpex to evacuate Lyris only minutes before the building was leveled. That act saved his life and made him the administrator-general of Intercorpex, just as he promised. The mass murder of over a thousand people was all it took. Now, with his stooge in place, it's time to exert another level of control.

"What's this?" Lyris asks as he's handed a tablet computer.

"It's the statement you will release to the global media first thing tomorrow morning declaring yourself Raimius's permanent replacement with the full support of the *gentez-majorez*."

"When did I get that?"

"*You* didn't. I got it for you. The bureaucrats in Zurich are about to make a move. You need this."

"This announcement suspends the Zurich Canon," Lyris says, further scanning the announcement.

Denali flashes an amused smile. "It's an antiquated document that places undue restrictions on patricians. That bargaining chip secured their support for you. Keep reading."

Lyris complies, probably wishing he hadn't. His face changes with each paragraph.

"This announcement scraps all of Raimius's market expansion plans."

"Keep reading," Denali advises.

Lyris leans over the tablet. "All trades prior to the market closing on Saturday will count as executed. What about the trading anomaly?"

"What anomaly? They were authenticated trades made by patricians. That's the end of it."

"Our investigation isn't complete," Lyris argues.

"You learned that Raimius completed it and withheld the results as leverage. You will instruct your team to employ circuit breakers to ensure a monumental collapse doesn't happen again when you open the exchange next week."

Lyris reads the last paragraph and leans back in his chair. "I'm disbanding the Board of Regents and rewriting the Intercorpex charter."

"It's going to be a brilliant document. You'll be praised for ushering Intercorpex into a new era. The first draft is already quite good."

"First draft? I don't understand."

"My people are writing it for you."

Lyris fidgets, rubbing his chin and running a hand through his hair. He doesn't like this. Too bad. This is the price of membership in this league. He wanted to be AG, and now he is.

"Denali, with respect, I can't release this," Lyris says, handing the tablet back to him. "This isn't the direction I want to take Intercorpex."

"I'm sure. It's the direction I want to take it."

"Sir, I'm the one in charge now."

Denali laughs in a tone that's more sinister than jovial. "Because I made it happen. I promised that you would become administrator-general. I never said the position didn't come with strings attached. Now, I'm pulling them."

His marionette metaphor isn't lost on him. "I appreciate everything you've done, and I look forward to partnering with you to usher Intercorpex into the next century. But I can't go along with this."

"Mark Twain was right," Denali says with a deep sigh.

"I'm sorry, who?"

"Mark Twain. He was a nineteenth-century author. He said, 'If you pick up a starving dog and make him prosperous, he will not bite you. This is the principal difference between a dog and man.' I expected more gratitude from you, Lyris. Perhaps I was mistaken about your loyalty. That's an unfortunate mistake on my part. There were other promising candidates I could have chosen."

"I'm very grateful for the opportunity—"

"Unfortunately, I can't undo my choice and must resort to other measures."

"Other measures?"

"Lyris, if you cross me, I will take away everything you care about, starting with the Asian whore sitting in the outer office."

His face is a mix of shock and surprise. Lyris's mouth is moving, but no words flow from it. There is satisfaction in making someone speechless. It's another exercise in power.

"I know about your late-night trysts with Nevala. She's a beautiful woman. It would be a shame if she vanished one day. You know how these urches are. They would ravage a woman like that until she was dead."

"You wouldn't—"

"Dare?" Denali leans forward. "You watched me kill three patricians and murder their families in cold blood. Are you certain that I wouldn't 'dare?'"

He didn't just kill Namyn, Nygehl, and Yannen – he *enjoyed* killing them. Leadership is the act of doing what must be done, and that includes killing when necessary. If Lyris doesn't comply with his every demand, he wouldn't think twice about eliminating Nevala, or him for that matter.

"I'm leaving for Greenwich," Denali says, standing. "This municorp is going to hell. Administrator-General Lyris, please accept my sincerest congratulations on your new role. You've earned it. If I don't hear the media reporting this statement before eating my breakfast, you've been warned of the consequences. Have a good evening."

CHAPTER
SIXTY-EIGHT
AMERICA, INC.

Fiolla's Domicile
Foggy Bottom Geographic District
Washington-Arlington Municipal Corporation

Fiolla crashes on her sofa in front of the large crystal display. She waves her hand to flip through the channels, searching for any programming that doesn't include an AME Breaking News banner. Every channel has been preempted. Public Affairs wants employees focused on the horrors in Manhattan.

She would love to find a sappy drama but would settle for a documentary. Anything other than the footage that's been playing on a continuous loop. She needs this day to be over.

"Fiolla, someone is approaching the front door," the Maester system informs her.

She struggles off the overstuffed couch and identifies the visitor. Her mouth is still hanging open in surprise when she opens the door.

"Chief Executive Valen?"

"Valen will suffice. We're way past titles, and you don't work for me anymore."

"Of course. Would you like to come in?"

"Yes, thank you."

Valen enters and checks the place out. Fiolla gets subconscious, wishing she had tidied up a little. She doesn't sacrifice her little free time for cleaning.

"Your domicile is very nice."

"Thank you. I'm surprised Zeykala let you out of the White House."

"I'm not on house arrest or anything," he says, pulling out his disruptor and setting it on the table. "I can come and go as I please. I had no reason to until now."

"Have they assigned you new housing?"

"From what I was told, I will be living somewhere near San Diego. The estate won't be ready for another two weeks, so my stay in the White House Residence has been extended."

"I guess Zeykala wants you as far away from Washington as she can get you."

"Absolutely, only she may not get the chance to see me off. The board of directors is convening in the morning. Rumor has it that you were the one who put Covington up to it. Thank you."

The man never ceases to surprise her. Valen still has his finger on the pulse of the corporation despite no longer running it. That can only mean executives in the West Wing are still loyal to him.

"Hammond sent me a message," Fiolla says, causing Valen to cock his head. "He asked me to explain that he was extorted by Zeykala and Talya and tell you he was sorry."

Valen stares off into space, slowly nodding. The two men were close, and his betrayal is still an open wound. That information may answer some questions in his mind, but he'll never completely forgive his old friend.

"Did you save the message?"

"No, and I deleted it off the server."

"That's too bad. It would have been useful to present it at the board of directors meeting."

"I know they're going to pick a new chairman. Is there any chance you'll be reinstated?"

"Probably not. Zeykala has supporters on the board who won't move against her without more outcry following the disaster in New York. Although Shalius is full of surprises, so you never know."

"Is there anything I can do to help?"

"Are you sure you want to?" he asks, leveling his eyes at her.

A part of Fiolla wants to take the words back. Her anger towards him vacillates with her mood and stress level. She wants the old Valen back—the one she admired before she learned too much.

"Yes."

He reaches into his pocket and hands her a slip of paper. That's a rarity. In the age of digital assistants and immediate communications, there's no need to handwrite a note.

"This GlobalNet address is a forum economists use to exchange information. Use it to get my contact in Liberteum a message."

"Is this what you meant in the theater about needing my help?"

"Yes."

Fiolla shakes her head as she stares at the paper. "Why? Why now? Haven't your dealings with this guy cost you enough?"

Valen presses his lips together and exhales. "If I could go back and undo my mistakes, I would without hesitation. Unfortunately, regrets don't change the stakes. My asset will find a way to contact the new administration. You see the problem if Zeykala finds out about any of this."

His words stir up her anger. Fiolla's emotional pendulum swings hard in the other direction. Valen's recklessness has cost far more than his position. People died – a lot of them.

"Did you know? About today, I mean," Fiolla asks, terrified to hear the truth.

"I had no idea that Liberteum would attack the summit."

"But you knew they would try something. That there was a plan, yet you didn't warn anyone. Why?"

"Zeykala wanted my job, and now she has it. I'm not helping her."

"Forget Zeykala. Or Virtari. You have a responsibility to the employees—"

"Everything I've ever done is for our employees!" he says before standing and walking across the room.

Fiolla wrings her hands. The road to hell is paved with good intentions. Valen might have been doing this for the corporation's good, but it had the opposite effect. Either he doesn't fully grasp the ramifications or is too arrogant to acknowledge them.

"Valen, you're asking me to commit treason."

"I'm asking you to trust me one last time," he says, his back still turned to her.

"Why should I?"

"The plan was always to stop Liberteum when we got what we wanted. We need to stop them now or…."

"No, finish that statement," Fiolla demands.

"It could mean the end of our society."

More dire words have never been spoken. She didn't live through the Great Collapse but studied it enough to understand that only anarchists would relish the chaos. The world could never recover from another collapse. They were lucky to survive the last one.

"How?"

"The code you're holding instructs the asset to disclose their location. Liberteum's apprehension will end the threat for good."

"Won't that hand Zeykala the win you're desperate to avoid?"

"I'll deal with her later."

Fiolla closes her eyes and shakes her head. This whole request is self-serving. He doesn't want to save corporatism. He wants to save himself from a treason charge, which makes him no different than anyone else in this world.

"I never wanted to ask this of you, Fiolla. I have no choice. Will you do it?"

She stares at the note in her hand. Fiolla has wanted to make a difference in this world since she was a child. She dedicated her life to achieving that goal. Now she's at a crossroads and facing separate paths to unknown fates. Her decision could shape events that affect the world. She alone will shoulder the burden of that outcome.

CHAPTER
SIXTY-NINE

RYKOS

"Valhalla"
Midtown Geographic District
New York City Municipal Corporation

I wander into the operations room with my steaming cup of coffee. It's very early, the lights are turned low, and it's quiet. I expected to see Jasper or Adiz pecking away at a keyboard in here. I was wrong. The sight is far better.

"You're up early," Michele says.

"I could say the same about you. Couldn't sleep?"

"No. You neither?"

"There's too much on my mind. Has Farron finished the arrangements for us to leave?"

"Almost," Michele says before pointing at the display. "The qulis went on strike last night across the sphere. They've taken to the streets to protest yesterday's policy announcement. Every time they get dispersed, larger and more intense protests pop up."

"Where?"

"Everywhere, from the looks of it."

I stare at the display and see footage from gatherings in a half-dozen cities. AME News wouldn't be showing this unless it suited the parent company's agenda. That means they are gearing up for a major operation.

"This is bad."

"Why do you say that? This many protests will stretch the BCS thin. They can't respond to all of them."

Michele nods. "You're right. They can't. That's what makes this dangerous. The Pentagon will employ alternative measures to subjugate the qulis. This could be worse than the Catharsis."

Nearly thirty years ago, the BCS executed an operation to round up and execute the corporation's urch population. Tens of thousands were murdered in only a few weeks, and those are only the official numbers. If I've learned anything from Liberteum, it's that any information the corporation puts out should be questioned. I'm betting that the actual numbers are much higher.

"What do you think they'll do?" Michele asks.

"I don't know."

"Rykos, you are the chief guardian's son. You have a better idea than I do."

I probably do, but not as much as she might think. My father kept me insulated from his work. I was never on a path to follow in his footsteps and join the ranks of public safety and security. That doesn't mean I didn't pick up a few things. Just because my father never took me to work doesn't mean he didn't take it home with him.

"They'll start with non-lethal measures to show employees that they tried to spare lives. If the rest of the qulis share your three friends' resolve, those measures will inevitably fail. Then they'll start shooting until they run out of bullets. Once enough of them have died, the qulis will capitulate."

Michele rubs her temples. That wasn't what she wanted to hear. I can't see the future, but it's better than an educated guess. It's the playbook. My father never had to delve that deep into it.

"How bad is the protest in New York?" I ask.

"It's the largest and the most determined. I've never seen one this size. That's saying something considering the past problems in Boston and Philly."

She's remarkably well-informed for someone who lives underground. Quli uprisings aren't a rare occurrence. Most protests are small and quickly dispersed. The most frequent and worst uprisings happened in those two northeastern cities. The quli populations there are considered extremist and earn the BCS's undivided attention.

"Director Virtari is in control of the NYCMC. He'll start here and hope the other cities get the message."

"That's what I'm afraid of," Michele murmurs. "Why did the CEO do this? It doesn't make any sense."

I shake my head. "I don't know. She's responding to one crisis by creating another. I could see a smaller distraction, but this is huge. All I know is that it's about power. That's all they care about."

Michele calls up another feed. "There is a board of directors meeting in Washington this morning. Something about the chairman dying. Do you know what that means?"

"When a board member dies, there is a set amount of time to appoint a replacement. It's in the charter."

"What about appointing a *prima*?"

"You're thinking about Narik's message to his father?" I ask, getting a nod. "He may have something planned. I don't know."

"Too many questions and not enough answers," Michele says.

"You threw a wrench in the Covingtons' plans when you killed Narik. They needed phase three for some reason."

"That's what I'm afraid of. Narik was using us. Is he the only one?"

"You mean Farron?"

Michele shrugs. "Or his father."

I fold my arms. Farron has been involved in this from the beginning. He has a vested interest in Liberteum's success. Is it because he believes in their cause, or is he as duplicitous as his best friend was? It's a legitimate question.

"Then why leave Valhalla? Why put our faith in the hands of the Keatings if there's doubt?"

Michele offers a slight smile. "When you're damned if you do and damned if you don't, you might as well do."

"That's not good enough."

"Farron knows about this place. If we're being played, we aren't safe here anyway. We cannot be trapped down here if the BCS locks down the city."

I'm not sure I agree with that. I want to believe Farron is being straight with us. I'm sure the executive he was manipulating is thinking the same thing. If he's capable of deceiving her, why should we be any different? There are too many competing agendas. Too many people are making moves. How long before someone makes the wrong one? What happens then?

CHAPTER SEVENTY

LIBERTEUM

"Valhalla"
Midtown Geographic District
New York City Municipal Corporation

The quiet calm that Michele and Rykos shared in the operations center faded once Valhalla's other inhabitants began stirring. Jasper was the first to arrive, along with some technicians who assist him. Adiz finally rolled out of bed to join him at the bank of workstations along the wall. The last to arrive was Farron. Patricians are known for sleeping in.

Michele retreated to the planning area, despite there being nothing to plan. The timeline is at the mercy of her two hackers, and there hasn't been much progress since yesterday. All she can do is sit back and watch the clock.

"Whoa! What the hell!" Jasper throws his hands up in the air and away from the keyboard. An image simultaneously appears on every display in the room.

"Hel-lo!" the gaunt, unshaven man says as he leans in to his camera. His proximity makes his pale face unusually large.

"Who the hell are you?" Adiz demands after recovering from his shock.

"I'm the guy who just hacked into your network. Aren't you impressed?"

"We may have company. Go stand guard upstairs," Michele orders Koltayne. "Be ready for anything."

"Got it," he says, charging out of the operations center.

"I'm locked out of my workstation," one of the techs in the room informs the group.

"Me too," another says.

Whoever this man is, he's savvy enough to locate them and skilled enough to pop their firewalls. If they need to defend Valhalla from an assault, it's better if they don't know their numbers.

"That camera he's accessed has a narrow field of view," Michele explains to Farron and Rykos, who look around in shock. "Stay out of it."

"How did you find us?" Jasper demands.

"You guys are remarkably good at masking network routes. Unfortunately for you, I'm better at uncovering them."

The man steps back from the camera. Michele can't help but stare at the exoskeleton strapped to his legs.

"I asked who you are, other than some alien freak show," Adiz says.

"Tsk, tsk…such bad manners. No wonder everybody hates urches. I don't answer to you, minion. If you think I'm an alien, fine," he says, leaning in to the lens again. "Take me to your leader."

"I'm right here." Michele steps into the camera's view.

"Oh. Hi there."

"Congratulations, you found us. Can you at least tell us who you work for?"

"Intercorpex."

"Good. Next time I'm downtown, I'll swing by and slit your throat," Jasper threatens.

"Good luck with that. I don't work in the NOC."

"Well, wherever you are, then."

"You don't have the reach from that hole under the cathedral, my friend. If you decide to visit, bring a winter parka. I work in Iceland."

Jasper and Adiz both recoil. It's not his location that has them spooked. They're reacting to what caused Michele's heart to skip a beat. He knows where they are.

"Should we be expecting goons from Intercorpex to arrive soon?" Michele asks.

Something feels off about this. If Intercorpex was conducting a raid, why announce it by hacking their communications network?

"Nobody knows that I've contacted you. Consider this a private conversation."

Michele is intrigued, not that she completely believes him. "Fair enough. May I ask your name and your business with us?"

"Hey, minions, you should take politeness lessons from your boss."

"Screw you," Adiz mumbles.

"My name is Ortan, and I need a favor."

"A favor?"

"Yes. A mutual acquaintance is in a touch of trouble. He's being hunted by ICX Security and the Bureau of Corporate Security."

"Mutual acquaintance?" Rykos asks, joining the conversation as he comes up to Michele's side.

"You must be Rykos."

"You're talking about Chief Inspector Zyree, aren't you?"

Ortan cocks his head and offers an amused smile. "I heard that you knocked him unconscious. I had a good laugh about it. Not many people have gotten the better of him."

"It was beginner's luck. Why are your own people after him?" Rykos prods.

"Politics."

"What do you think we can do about it?" Michele asks.

"I want you to try to save him."

"Have you lost your mind? Why should we?" Farron joins Rykos and Michele.

"Farron Keating. I guess the gang's all there."

Michele gives Farron the same dirty look she rewarded Rykos with when he joined the conversation.

"Sorry," Farron says, reading her expression.

"How does this work, Ortan? We help, and you return control of our network? If we don't, you report our location?"

"Blackmail is messy and unprofessional. I was just going to ask nicely and hope you agree."

"If I may ask, why do you care? You work for Intercorpex. Why do you want us to save Zyree from your own organization?"

"Because he's…a friend. The only real one I have."

Michele nods her understanding. There's sincere desperation in his voice. It's haunting…and real. Whatever his bond with Zyree is, it's strong.

"You're not seriously considering this, are you?" Farron asks.

"Why shouldn't she?" Rykos counters. "We asked Zyree for help trying to stop Haven. Are you saying we shouldn't reciprocate?"

"It's not the same," Adiz argues.

"The principle is. Zyree saved my life at Broad Street Station. We should return the favor."

"You returned it when you didn't kill him in that SoHo basement," Farron angrily concludes.

"Talk about things not being the same."

Michele silences them with a hand. "Where is Zyree now, Ortan?"

"I don't know. He's on the run somewhere in Midtown. I can relay his location when I know it. Does this mean that you agree to help?"

Other than ending this hack, there is no reason to embark on something so risky. The reason they came to Valhalla was to reduce their exposure. If Michele agrees to this, it could compromise their mission. That is more than enough reason to say no, but every fiber in her body is screaming to say "yes." She has learned to trust that feeling even when it doesn't make sense.

"I can't make any promises. We don't have the resources to mount a rescue operation. If you return control of our network, you have my word that we'll do what we can."

Everyone stares at Michele. It's her call, but nobody outside of Rykos agrees with her.

"Done. Control of your network has been restored."

"What makes you think I won't just change the firewall to block you?" Adiz asks.

"First, nothing short of cutting the hard line will keep me out of Valhalla. You won't do that."

The guys take turns looking at each other. He also knows the name of this place. What else did he learn by poking around their network before announcing his presence? Could he also know about Archimedes?

"Second," Ortan continues, pointing at Michele, "I trust her. I'll be in touch soon."

CHAPTER SEVENTY-ONE
AMERICA, INC.

John Jacob Astor Park
Alphabet City Geographic District
New York City Municipal Corporation

They made the decision first thing this morning. Nobody slept well in the NEC. Not the guardians, not Dyllon, and definitely not Ilaria or Dzamko. Their anxiety grew when they saw the size of the quli protest on the heat map. Coming here was a no-brainer.

Even with lights blazing and sirens wailing, it took Dzamko twenty minutes to reach the south end of John Jacob Astor Park. He parks a block away, and Ilaria joins him for a walk along its southern edge. They earn nasty looks from the qulis, but there isn't a violent reaction to their presence.

Wedged between Avenues A and B and spanning three blocks from north to south, the park is a recreational and relaxation area for laborers. Like most public spaces, it's a gorgeous green area with gardens, stone sidewalks, courts for games, and large shade trees. Right now, it's jammed with angry people.

They meet up with a contingent of guardians at Seventh Street, keeping an eye on things. Quli protesters have gathered fifty feet away to square off against them. They're serious about fighting anyone who moves to break this gathering up.

"What do we have, Captain?"

"Virtari ordered the protest dispersed. We're to round up the leaders for termination. Anybody who resists or fails to leave is to be shot on sight."

Ilaria rubs her temples. The BCS is determined to turn the streets into rivers of blood. It will be a massacre.

"How many personnel do you have?" Dzamko asks.

"I have three hundred men posted in squad-sized elements around the park and an additional hundred mustering in Brooklyn. The BCS and a guardian detachment are approaching from Tenth Street in convoy. They'll be here in a matter of minutes."

"Okay. Order the guardians all to the northwest corner of the park. Form them into a line two ranks deep. Form a wedge, one leg running between Ninth and Tenth Streets and the other extended down Tenth."

"Wilco," the captain says before issuing orders.

The men march up Avenue A to the rally point. Seeing the guardians' movement, the protestors begin to move parallel with them, the crowd increasing in size. They're bracing for a fight.

Within minutes, two long single-file lines form, bending ninety degrees at the corner near the sports courts. Insults are hurled from the unruly crowd as the guardians stoically face them. On command, the guardians turn their backs to the qulis, placing themselves between the crowd and the approaching convoy.

Men and women ready for a brawl suddenly find themselves staring at the backs of the men they were expecting to fight. The bubbling hostility simmers down to quiet confusion. The barrage of insults ceases.

Ilaria and Dzamko pass through the lines of guardians into the park. Three men break off from the crowd and approach them. They aren't armed with anything that can be used as a weapon, but that does little to put Dzamko at ease.

"Who are you?" Ilaria asks when the three men stop in front of them.

"I'm Phylep. These guys are Prano and Andanz."

"Are you the leaders of this gathering?"

The three men eye her with suspicion. "We're all leaders in this protest."

"Fair enough. Let me show you something. Do you see that column of men and vehicles?" Ilaria asks, pointing up the street. "The BCS has orders to disperse this protest by any means necessary. They will shoot anyone who doesn't comply with their orders."

"How do you know that?" Phylep asks.

"Because I'm the acting CEO of the NYCMC. This is Constable Dzamko. He's the acting chief guardian."

"You're here to disperse us before they can?" Prano asks, his voice laced with anger and defiance.

"No. We're here to protect you."

The three men fall quiet. Ilaria stays silent to let them process that information. Considering their history with the PSS, she has a better chance of convincing them the sky is purple with pink polka dots.

"I don't believe you. It's a trick," Andanz says. "The PSS hates us."

"I know your history with them better than most. My husband is Chief Guardian Teman."

The three men look at each other with trepidation. They hated him, and probably with good reason.

"Words won't convince you of anything. Let me show you."

The three men follow Ilaria through the line of guardians. Dzamko orders five guardians to join them as they walk up Tenth Street. The column of vehicles halts fifty yards away, and three BCS agents walk toward them. A PSS captain in charge of the guardian detail follows, looking like this is the last place he wants to be.

"What the hell do you think you're doing?" an irate agent demands.

"Protecting the citizens of this city."

"Citizens? You're living in the wrong era, lady. Clear out of the way or face discipline for obstruction."

Ilaria crosses her arms. She wants to say something witty or condescending but is too nervous. She's determined to stand her ground and simultaneously terrified about what will happen.

"Fine. Have it your way. Deploy your men," he says to the guardian.

"Belay that order, Captain," Dzamko countermands, ratcheting up the tension.

"I know who you are, Constable," the agent says, drawing closer. "You've been relieved of your post and have no authority to reverse my commands. The PSS reports to Director Virtari, and I'm acting on his orders."

"No guardian has or will ever report to corporate security."

"I said deploy your men!" the agent barks.

The captain doesn't acknowledge the order. He stares blankly at his "superior" without moving a muscle. Aggravated at the disobedience, the agent draws his sidearm and points it at Dzamko's head.

The guardians jump into action, drawing down on the BCS agents. The captain pulls his weapon and points it at the agent's head. It's a standoff, and the crowd behind them responds to it with cheers.

"You are defying a corporate edict. I'm authorized to use deadly force and will kill you right here in this street, old man."

"You're not going to want to do that, sonny. I'm ready to die for what I believe in. Are you? Because the moment you pull that trigger, you and your fellow agents die with me."

"I'm counting to three."

"I'll be impressed if you can," Dzamko retorts.

Ilaria would smile at the insult if she weren't shaking uncontrollably.

"One...."

"Let's see if he gets the next one right," Dzamko says.

"Two...."

"Oh, look at that!"

The qulis accompanying them jerk Dzamko away. Before anyone can react, Phylep stands in his place. The agent's muzzle is only inches from his forehead.

"Your quarrel is with us, not him."

"Yes, it is. Detain them," he orders his agents.

The two agents move, and the guardians shove them backward. Not willing to be brushed back so easily, they launch themselves forward and begin grappling with the guardians. Ilaria stands back, trying to stay out of the melee. Then the world changes.

The report echoes off the buildings. One of the guardians clutches his shoulder as he collapses to the asphalt. Everyone stops moving. All eyes are locked on the man writhing on the ground. Time stands still. The image is processed. The cause is determined. Then all hell breaks loose.

The response is intense. The guardians raise their rifles and gun down the three BCS agents. Ilaria drops to the ground and watches the men in the convoy turn on their PSS cohorts, who return fire from only feet away.

The crackle of gunfire punctuates shouts coming from the protesters. The qulis hold their ground behind the phalanx of guardians despite having no weapons. Several men in the line aim their rifles and fire at the convoy, but most don't have clean shots.

After the sounds of the final shots dissipate, the groaning and wailing of the injured fill Ilaria's ears. She lifts her head to peek down the street. Both guardians and BCS agents are down. She crawls over to find Dzamko uninjured.

"Are you okay?"

"I'm getting too old for this."

"Go see to your men in the column," Ilaria says, helping him to his feet. "I'll handle things here."

Dzamko and a handful of guardians lumber down the street while she helps Prano and Andanz off the ground. They're joined by Phylep, who seems unshaken by the bloody confrontation.

"Are you guys okay?"

"We've been through worse," Prano says. "Thank you for standing up to them."

"Not that we aren't appreciative, but do you know what you just did?" Phylep asks.

"What we should've been doing all along – protecting the people. All the people, not just the ones deemed worthy."

A large group of qulis sifts through the line of guardians and forms a gaggle around them. They're curious about what they just witnessed. It's the first time anyone has fought for them instead of against them. It must be confusing.

"You've signed your death warrant," Andanz says.

"Probably. I didn't ask for this job," she says, loud enough so those gathering around her can hear. "I never wanted to be a chief executive. I was thrust into a position that executives in Washington don't think I should have. They want to make the decisions and leave us to deal with the consequences.

"They need to keep all of us under their thumbs so they can live comfortable lives and enrich the elites. Meanwhile, you're the ones who do the work. You're the ones who suffer. I'm sick and tired of it."

There is universal agreement from the qulis around her. Their fates are now intertwined. She needs them to understand that.

"It wasn't always like that. Corporations valued their employees once. Some considered them their most valuable assets. America Incorporated believed that once, too. This city was rebuilt on the backs of qulis. All of them were.

"When did you stop mattering? When did we all stop mattering? The parent company only values itself. We're expendable and irrelevant. I refuse to accept that any longer. We need change. I need good people to help me bring that change. I will stand beside you. The guardians will stand beside you.

"I have authorized this protest. You may assemble in this city. Shout at the top of your lungs until you're heard. I don't care what the BCS says."

Cheers go up from the guardians and qulis alike. Ilaria was a housewife. Now she has an army behind her. Zeykala may have power, but she doesn't have what these people do: passion. To silence them, it will take more than a few BCS agents.

News of her speech spreads through the crowd like wildfire. Their frenzied excitement feels like a surge of electricity. For better or worse, Ilaria has become a revolutionary. Her thoughts drift back to Teman lying in his hospital bed. She wonders what he'll think of all this.

CHAPTER SEVENTY-TWO

THE PATRICIANS

Keating Family of the Gentez-Majorez Estate
Greenwich Geographic District
Southern Connecticut Municipal Corporation

Abbot informed Denali of Lacune's request for an audience so that he could provide an operational briefing on the unfolding situation in America Incorporated. The patrician is quite certain that his commander didn't phrase it that way. Soldiers are a gruff bunch. His commanders and team leaders are only slightly more cultured. The request was more likely, "Tell the old man to get down here."

Denali chuckles at the thought as he makes his way down the stairs to the mansion's sublevel. He doesn't care what Lacune says as long as it isn't to his face and he accomplishes his missions. After all, he is an old man.

"What's the situation, Commander?"

Lacune waits for Denali to take his position in front of the displays.

"I have confirmed that Haven is dead. He was found in the Park Avenue Tunnel along with the body of an Intercorpex Security inspector."

The patrician grins. That solves one of his problems. It's bad enough that there is a video linking his son to Liberteum. The last thing he needs is the most wanted man on Earth spilling his guts to the Pentagon.

"Good. Any news on my son or Liberteum?"

"No, sir. I'm afraid not."

"Okay. What else?"

"The quli protest in Jacob J. Astor Park is growing."

He changes the display to show a feed from the park. The qulis are packed in. How this hasn't already turned into a riot, he will never know. Most of the block should be on fire by now.

"That's hardly news."

"Except they are being protected by the PSS," the commander explains. "Chief Guardian Dzamko ordered the three hundred men there to stand their ground between the qulis and the BCS."

He changes the images to show lines of guardians. Instead of facing the qulis in a threatening manner, they have their backs to them. That's a first.

"That's interesting."

Lacune smiles. "Not compared to what happened twenty minutes ago. A BCS tactical detachment moved in to disperse the protest. Gunfire was exchanged."

The video is filmed from a bad angle, but he can make out what's happening. "Who fired first?"

"We aren't sure, but the BCS agents are dead, and several guardians were shot."

Denali runs his hand through his hair. Moves and countermoves. The PSS has made theirs. Now it's the BCS's turn. They will need special powers that this fool Zeykala will be compelled to give them. Things will spiral out of control quickly. Both sides used to act with restraint. Now, the gloves have come off.

"Have all units placed on alert. We may need to move up the timeline for the next phase of our operation."

"Yes, sir."

"Keep me apprised of any developments in the NYCMC."

"I will. There is one more thing, sir. I have a request from our technicians at the airfield. One of the planes is ready, and they want to conduct a test flight. They say they cannot verify flight worthiness without one."

Denali rubs his chin. "When?"

"As early as tomorrow or the day after."

He shakes his head. "America Incorporated will likely be under martial law by then. They'll close the airspace, and any flight will draw unwanted attention to this project."

"How do you know Zeykala will declare martial law?"

Denali only grins. "The opportunity for a test flight will present itself. Until then, all testing must be done on location. Those planes are grounded until I say otherwise. Make that clear."

"Yes, sir."

"What's the status of White Lotus and the other groups?" Denali asks, broaching the next order of business.

"Their training is nearing completion. Our team commanders have growing confidence in their capabilities."

"Order them to make their final preparations. We may need to execute sooner than anticipated."

Lacune grimaces and rubs his hands. "They won't react well to that."

"I don't care how they react," Denali says with a dismissive wave as he stares at the display showing unit readiness. "Proper timing was a condition of our assistance. If they need to be reminded of that, we will rethink our relationship."

"Very well, sir."

Denali makes his way back up to the mansion and heads to the patio. Being a visionary means having a plan. Being a leader means being able to adapt that plan. Strategies need to change when the circumstances do. It is a shame that so few people realize that, although fools make his life easier. He is always five steps ahead of everyone. He should be rewarded for that handsomely. And he will be. He is Denali Keating of the *Gentez-Majorez*. He always gets what he wants.

CHAPTER SEVENTY-THREE

INTERCORPEX

Global Network Operations Center
Manhattan Financial District
ICX New York Exchange

Wyeth parks himself in a chair across from Lyris. He looks more rested than the new AG does, but that isn't saying much these days. Their situation is taking a toll on everyone. The trauma of the attack added to the push to bring the exchange online is creating an unbearable strain.

"Morning," Lyris says, not looking at his subordinate. "What can I help you with?"

"An explanation. Rewriting the charter? Disbanding the regents?" Wyeth asks. "What are you thinking?"

Lyris sighs. "Neither was my idea."

"I don't understand."

"It's better that you don't. There are other forces at play calling the shots."

Wyeth is a smart man. He'll put the pieces of the puzzle together. Lyris prefers to have plausible deniability if Denali ever asks if he told anyone about their conversation.

"Forces with the power to dictate to the administrator-general how Intercorpex is governed? That's disconcerting."

"You don't know the half of it," Lyris grumbles.

Denali has him by the balls, and he can't explain to Wyeth why. His loyalty would be tested if he knew about their arrangement. Everybody has their limits.

"What are you going to do?"

"Play along for now. I have no other choice."

Wyeth grimaces. "Lyris, with all due respect, an AG needs to rise above that."

"What do you expect me to do?" Lyris snaps.

"You're resourceful. Find a way to deal with whoever this is."

"Even if that person is Denali Keating?"

So much for keeping the secret. He realizes that he may have just placed Wyeth's life in danger. One thing is apparent: his stunned reaction is too genuine to be faked. At least Lyris knows that his EDGO hasn't been bought off.

"When you said powerful forces, you weren't kidding. You can't run Intercorpex with him holding an ax over your head."

"I know. I need you to get the exchange ready to be brought back online. I'll figure out what to do. It should go without saying that this stays between us."

"You're right," Wyeth says, standing. "It goes without saying. I'll be down in the NOC if you need me."

Lyris moves to the window and looks out over the city. Constant stress made Raimius paranoid and ineffectual. He's starting to understand why. The difference is that his predecessor would fold under an ounce of the pressure Lyris is feeling.

The burden of restarting trading is monumental. Add the bureaucrats in Zurich clamoring for his position, angry patricians, and power-hungry corporations…it's too much.

And then there's the wildcard. By claiming Zyree collaborated with the terrorists, he's found the perfect scapegoat. He can reforge a relationship with America Incorporated and the elites. For that to work, Chiana needs to locate and eliminate him. Unfortunately, he's become a ghost.

That's a problem, but not his biggest. Denali was correct in stating that they never discussed the strings attached to his "promotion." Lyris didn't want to. He was blinded by his ambition, and now he's paying the price. There's only one way to extricate himself from this mess: Denali Keating must be eliminated.

CHAPTER SEVENTY-FOUR

AMERICA, INC.

The White House
Corporate Governance District
Washington-Arlington Municipal Corporation

Zeykala is already angry and looking for someone to take her frustration out on. She finds her way downstairs to the Situation Room, expecting to be greeted by a room full of people. A young BCS agent is the only one there to greet her.

"Who the hell are you? Where is everyone?"

"I am Special Agent Dvarkin with the Special Activities Directorate of the BCS. You are the only person cleared to see this."

"Special Activities? Do you arrange the badminton games and three-legged races at the Pentagon's summer picnic?"

He smiles at the attempt at humor. "My responsibilities are a little more…covert than that, ma'am."

Dvarkin calls up a map of Washington with a conveyance being tracked by a drone in real-time and sends it to the main display. It's boxed in yellow for easy identification. The other display shows static surveillance of a random intersection.

"Intercorpex just announced unprecedented changes and didn't bother giving chief executives the courtesy of a heads-up. That bastard AG unilaterally suspended the Zurich Canon, disbanded the Board of Regents, and is rewriting their charter. All of that happened without a shred of intelligence from the BCS. Why the hell do you have me down here watching the damn morning traffic report?"

"Because you need to see what happens to that car," Virtari's voice bellows over the speakers.

"Since when do you not announce your presence?" Zeykala asks, annoyed that she was caught off-guard by his appearance via VidLynk.

"Since I'm about to remove one of your problems," he says, gloating. "That conveyance belongs to Shalius Covington, future *prima* of America Incorporated. He's being driven to this morning's board meeting, where he plans on pushing the new chairman for your removal. The intersection is a quarter of a mile from his present location."

"Okay, so what?"

"Just watch," Virtari says, barely masking the glee in his voice.

Zeykala is about to lose her patience as the conveyance enters the video. A municipal sanitation truck screams down the cross street. It doesn't slow down despite the red traffic control indicator. Covington and the steel behemoth meet at the intersection. What happens next is catastrophic.

The truck slams into the passenger side rear door with the force of a locomotive. The violent collision folds the conveyance in half and causes it to spin. Zeykala watches the energy from the crash dissipate, and the patrician's vehicle comes to a rest.

It's a mangled mess. Bystanders try to pull the driver from the front seat. No effort is being made to help Covington.

"Mission accomplished," Virtari says.

"Do you know he's dead?"

"It has been arranged for him to die on the way to the medical center if he somehow survived that collision," Dvarkin says.

"What about containment?" Zeykala asks. The last thing she needs is a scandal.

"The sanitation truck experienced a complete braking system failure. On-board data has been manipulated to prove that should there be an independent inquiry."

"And the truck's driver?"

"He's one of ours," Virtari interjects. "Although sanitation employment records show he's been an employee there for seven years. It's just a tragic accident on the streets of Washington."

Zeykala smiles. "Well done, gentlemen."

"With that out of the way, there's something else that demands your immediate attention," Virtari says. "There has been an incident here in Manhattan. BCS agents tasked with dispersing the protest in Astor Park have been killed."

"What! The qulis killed them?"

"No, ma'am. Guardians were protecting the qulis. We have overhead drone footage of them engaging our agents. My men were killed by the PSS."

The BCS and PSS are rivals, but this level of treachery is unheard of. Maybe pinning the terrorist murders of the BCS agents on them had a more profound impact than anticipated.

"You said that you had everything under control up there, Virtari."

"I have complete control of the RTCC and One Guardian Plaza. The city will take longer to subdue, especially with Acting Chief Executive Ilaria and Acting Chief

Guardian Dzamko moving against me. They were present at the park during the incident."

Zeykala shakes her head. "This is an insurrection."

"I concur. Guardians have formed protective lines around the qulis with heavy vehicles and defensive positions at cross streets."

"I want Ilaria and Dzamko detained and referred to a tribunal for high treason. Anyone standing in your way will be terminated. Is that understood, Virtari?"

She expected him to do cartwheels at the order. Instead, he lowers his eyes.

"That's going to be a problem."

"Why?"

"I lack the manpower. Unarmed qulis I can handle. If even ten percent of the guardians join her rebellion, we're outnumbered and outgunned by several orders of magnitude. It will take me two or three days to bolster our force here to a level capable of direct action."

Zeykala throws her hands in the air. "That won't do! These protests need to end! The leaders need to be hauled in front of Human Resources and found guilty in a public spectacle. I want AME News playing Ilaria's and Dzamko's termination on a continuous loop as a message to anyone who stands against the parent corporation."

"Then I recommend a different approach. Ilaria's husband is being treated at Waterside Trauma Center."

"You're talking about Chief Guardian Teman?"

"Yes."

Zeykala wrings her hands. She has no love for a man as ineffectual as Teman was. Maybe he can make himself useful for once in his miserable life.

"All right, Virtari, tell me what you have in mind."

The director smiles, and it's enough to send a shiver down even Zeykala's spine.

CHAPTER SEVENTY-FIVE

LIBERTEUM

"Valhalla"
Midtown Geographic District
New York City Municipal Corporation

The planning area in the operations room is being put to good use. Complete with multiple displays and a center console, it allows for collaboration on a scale that rivals most corporate organizations. It was used a lot for the planning of Archimedes but hasn't seen much action since before they launched the first attack.

Rykos stares in awe at the displays. They contain a three-dimensional depiction of Midtown Manhattan with a series of red lines bisecting and traversing buildings and down streets. The thicker ones denote the main avenues of urch travel, with the medium and thinner lines representing crawl spaces or narrow tunnels. It's the picture of the underground transit system that the PSS only wishes they had.

"You guys mapped all this?"

"Not exactly. There have been maps of the underground since the first urches left the corporation. We digitized them over the years and created a navigation application to make them more useful."

"This is amazing," Rykos gushes.

Michele smiles at the compliment. "They're not one hundred percent accurate. Urches create new accesses every day, and the corporation locates and closes old ones. The underground is as dynamic and ever-changing as the weather."

"This is never going to work," Farron complains for about the eighth time.

"It has to. Zyree can't have gotten far. He doesn't know the underground and isn't used to navigating down here."

"And it's exhausting," Rykos says. "I speak from experience."

"It doesn't matter. We don't know where this chief inspector was going or where he's hiding. Even if his robotic friend manages to find him, we'll never reach him with so many agents and guardians combing the underground. He could be a block away, and it doesn't change the math. A rescue attempt is suicide, end of discussion."

Michele looks at Rykos, who shrugs. "He has a point."

"You're on his side now?" she moans.

"No, but you told me that there weren't enough people to protect Valhalla if it was breached. If that's true, how can we possibly launch a rescue mission?"

"We reached your father, didn't we?" Michele argues.

Rykos nods. "Yeah, but that was different, and you know it."

Michele sighs and braces herself against the center console as she studies the map. For as good as it is, it doesn't have the real-time geolocations of the BCS or PSS. That would be useful right now. She might be able to determine Zyree's location within a couple of blocks, but she has no idea how many agents and guardians would be between them.

"Farron, how will you get us out of Valhalla?" Rykos asks.

"My driver is picking us up, just like he did before going to the Alamo. He will ferry us to the east side of the island. I've arranged for a boat and a helicopter to be on standby to whisk us away. We can use whichever one makes more sense. The boat is less noticeable, but air transport has the benefit of speed. Commander Lacune isn't taking chances by limiting our options."

Michele smacks her hand on the console. "We don't have to look for him underground. Ortan needs to tell Zyree to get to street level. We can pick him up on the way to the rendezvous."

"Are you insane?" Farron asks, his mouth hanging open.

"That could work," Rykos offers.

"No, no, no! It won't work at all."

"Have you ever willingly taken a risk in your life, Farron?"

Farron straightens and crosses his arms and stares at Rykos. "I'm standing here, aren't I?"

"And Ortan knows you're here," Michele interjects. "He can get into our systems. If that isn't enough reason to help Zyree, here's another: I made him a promise."

"You said you'd try."

"And I meant it. I'm not going to sit back and watch everything we've worked for fall apart because we were cowards."

Farron scoffs. "This isn't about courage!"

"No, it's about conviction!" Michele exclaims, her voice increasing in pitch and volume. "It's about doing what we must do to complete our mission. This has become one of those things."

The patrician doesn't like that reasoning one bit. "This is a mistake."

"Then go, Farron," Michele says, gesturing at the spiral staircase that leads up to the cathedral. "Have your driver take you to your helicopter and leave us here."

He shakes his head. "I'm not doing that. I'm asking you to think about what you're risking. How many more times will the BCS need to search the church before they stumble upon the access hatch to Valhalla? You know I'm right. We need to leave, and soon. Greenwich is the safest location for us to weather the coming storm."

"I'm not arguing against that."

"Then why add more risk?" Farron asks, lowering his voice. "Tell Ortan when he calls – if he calls – that we had to evacuate, and the chief inspector is on his own."

Michele shakes her head slowly. "No."

The tension in the room has become as thick as concrete. The hackers and technicians are trying to look like they are paying no attention, but they are tuned into the conversation. Even if they weren't listening, the whole vibe in this subterranean stronghold has changed.

Rykos decides to play peacemaker. "Is the extraction time flexible?"

"No. Things are falling apart fast. My father's men can't operate with impunity anymore. Our extraction time is set. If we miss the boat, that's it."

"Then we don't miss it. But we'll wait as long as possible for Ortan to get back to us."

"And when he does?" Rykos asks.

"We're going to try to rescue Zyree, just as we promised. That's the end of this discussion."

Michele glares at Farron, whose face tightens. He looks like he ate bad sushi. The patrician usually defers to her judgment. This time is different. His argument had a sense of urgency to it. Is it fear or something else? It gives Michele something to think about as she and Farron head in different directions. That's the funny thing about compromises – nobody gets what they want.

CHAPTER
SEVENTY-SIX
INTERCORPEX

Park Avenue
Midtown Geographic District
New York City Municipal Corporation

His luck was bound to run out. Zyree has been wandering the streets of the most monitored city in the world since leaving the bunk room. Drones buzz overhead, relaying all sorts of data back to his pursuers.

The bland quli garb and work boots would help him remain inconspicuous any other day. Employees typically ignore laborers, just as the lower class has been ignored throughout history. With the protests erupting, everyone is getting extra scrutiny.

Despite the underground search for him, the PSS and BCS still maintain a strong street presence. Eluding them has been tricky, and now he finds himself on Park Avenue a couple of blocks north of the hotel with two agents bearing down on him. Reversing direction will raise suspicions. Cutting across the tree-lined boulevard outside a pedestrian crossing is a punishable offense, so that's out.

Zyree is left with either ducking into an office building or talking his way past the agents. Office security will be less inquisitive, so he walks to the small flight of stairs leading to the building's elevated sidewalk.

"You, quli! Where are you going?" an agent shouts.

Zyree points at the office without saying anything. It seemed like an appropriate thing to do. He was wrong.

"Are you a mute or something? I asked you a question. Present your biojack."

Zyree holds up his hand, fingers extended, palm facing in. One agent stands directly in front of him with a scanner while the other moves a half step to his right. That was his first mistake.

The first scan fails to register any data. Intercorpex personnel don't have biojacks. He will only have one shot at escape. The agent begins to recheck, as is their protocol, and Zyree makes his move.

His knife-edge hand strikes the agent on the right, hitting him flush in the throat. He drops, gasping for air as the second agent presses a panic button on his wrist tablet. When he looks up, Zyree catches him square in the face with a hard punch. The whole assault takes only a few seconds, but the damage is done. The alarm has been sounded. When they do a facial recognition scan, they will swarm into this area.

Zyree doesn't wait around for that to happen. He grabs one of the men's weapons and extra ammunition and breaks into a trot. With no need to care about jaywalking now, he cuts across traffic and sprints down a side street.

Two guardians exit a retail store fifty feet away and draw their weapons. Zyree purposely fires high to force them back into the shop. A pair of BCS agents makes the turn from Madison and opens fire. He takes cover behind a parked conveyance as bullets punch holes in the glass and hood.

Zyree fires off a couple of rounds and bursts into a small courtyard between office buildings. He knocks an employee down as he charges through the lobby to the sounds of shouts and shrieks. The corporate concierge manning the information counter stares at him blankly until Zyree points his weapon at the man's head.

"Where's your main exit?"

"Th-that way," he says, pointing to Zyree's right.

"Much obliged."

He moves just in time. The windows explode, and people dive for cover as the gunfire chases Zyree out of the foyer. The BCS isn't messing around, which means they've already identified him. He knows the odds of his survival just got long.

The entry connects to a larger foyer on the other side of the elevator banks. Zyree blasts through the exit onto Madison Avenue and sprints across the street west down Fifty-Fifth. Then he catches a break. Trucks full of catering equipment line the sidewalk, offering him cover from another ambush.

He stops and peers around the corner up Fifth Avenue. Panicked employees are fleeing in all directions as agents and guardians bark orders. Zyree glances up and sees a drone hovering overhead. The noose is tightening.

He needs a place to hide that will make it impossible to find him until Ortan sends help. There's one place that fits the bill, and it's five hundred meters away. It might as well be five hundred miles, but it's his only shot. Zyree takes off, hoping that the BCS agents' aim hasn't improved.

CHAPTER
SEVENTY-SEVEN
INTERCORPEX

John Jacob Astor Park
Alphabet City Geographic District
New York City Municipal Corporation

Ilaria is beginning to worry about Dzamko. The sight of his wounded and dead guardians shook him up. It may have steeled his resolve, but it's taking an emotional toll. He knows there is a chance that none of these guardians will survive the day.

"How are we looking?" Ilaria asks.

"The perimeter is solid, but if the BCS is determined to break through it, there won't be much we can do to stop them. The casualties will be astronomical on both sides."

"You've already done more than we could've expected," Phylep says. "The BCS will have to deal with us, too. We don't expect you to fight our battles for us."

"Thank you, Phylep, but I need you to do something for me," Ilaria says, putting her hand on his shoulder. "Promise that, whatever happens, you won't start rioting."

"That's a tough sell," Prano warns.

"This fight is against the parent company, not the residents of this city. When you riot, you hurt them instead of the decision-makers in Washington."

"What's the difference?"

"Bigger than you think. If you want this new policy rescinded, you need people on your side. Rioting will turn them against you."

"We'll spread the word," Andanz says before following Prano into the crowd.

Dzamko checks his wrist tablet and steps away. Ilaria eyes him wearily for a long moment.

"It's weird working with guardians," Phylep says. "They're the ones we usually clash with. Chief Guardian Teman is your husband?"

"We've been married for over twenty years."

"Does he know you're here?"

Ilaria feels another pang of guilt. She's still angry and doesn't want to hear what he has to say. He wouldn't support this, and there's no place for doubt in her mind right now.

"I don't know."

"Can I ask you a question? Why are you helping? I mean, your speech was amazing, but that passion is something I only see from people the corporation has wronged."

Ilaria is about to answer his question when her tablet chimes. Any explanation to her new ally will have to wait.

"Let's just say our interests are aligned. Please excuse me for a moment. What's wrong, Dyllon?"

"I just heard from a friend in Human Resources. An emergency termination request was just submitted by the parent company for processing."

"Is it for Dzamko or me?"

He sighs. "Neither. It was issued for your husband."

Ilaria's heart jumps, and tears begin welling in her eyes. "Teman? Why?"

"I don't know," Dyllon whispers, a moribund tone demonstrating the gravity of his words. "The directive came directly from Washington, and it's being expedited."

"How long do we have?"

"An hour or two. It's being personally handled by the director of corporate security. I'm so sorry, ma'am."

Ilaria closes her eyes. Virtari. That means the order came from Zeykala. It also means that her actions have placed her husband's life in jeopardy. She should have gotten him out of that medical center as a precaution.

"Thank you for letting me know. Contact me if you hear anything else."

"Good news!" Dzamko shouts, buoyant after his own conversation. "Virtari cleared out of the RTCC, so now we have…what's wrong?"

"He left because he's going to the medical center with orders to terminate Teman."

"Oh, God," he says, the blood draining from his face.

"We have to stop them."

"Ilaria, you know that I have the greatest respect for Teman…but if we do this, we're liable to end up in the same predicament."

"I don't care."

"You need to care. You're the CEO now. The people in this park have placed their trust in you. The people of this city need you to lead them. It's all for nothing if you walk right into the BCS's arms. Your duty is to the people now, not just those you love."

Ilaria knows he's right, but she's replaceable. There are countless executives in the NYCMC. She's the only one who can claim to be Teman's wife. Her commitment has been to him and their family for decades. She should have contacted him the first chance she had. She doesn't want to regret not clearing the air with him.

"I will not stand back and watch my husband get murdered, Dzamko. These people are in your capable hands. I'm going to try to save him, whatever the consequences are. That's my decision."

Dzamko nods. "You and you – get that vehicle and bring it over here."

The guardians comply without protest.

"Let's go get Teman."

* * *

With strobes blazing, the trip to the medical center took only minutes. Dzamko confirmed Teman's condition with the front desk. He's stable and still under observation. They may have beaten the BCS here only by a matter of minutes. Dzamko opens the door before the vehicle even stops.

"Wait here," he commands the driver as Ilaria climbs out.

A small complement of guardians exits the trail vehicle, and the group bounds into the foyer together. It's clean and modern, but it's not the physical appearance that's bothering her. The place feels…off. Nobody is making eye contact with them.

"This is weird," Ilaria whispers to Dzamko as they slow to a walk.

"Too weird."

"We're here to see Chief Guardian Teman. I know the room number," she says to the woman at the counter.

"You can go right up."

She doesn't scan their biojacks as is the procedure. Dzamko shakes his head. Something is wrong. They flinch when a man bursts into the large foyer from an adjacent hallway. Her entourage might have shot him if he wasn't dressed in a guardian uniform.

"You don't want to go up there," he says. "Teman isn't here. They moved him a half hour ago."

"We contacted the admissions office. They said he was resting comfortably," Dzamko argues.

"They're lying. I watched the BCS leave with him, sir. The only thing in his room is a half-dozen BCS agents waiting to take you all into custody."

"It's a trap," Ilaria mumbles, realizing she almost led them right into it. That explains the reaction to their arrival.

"Who are you?"

"Deyago. I'm assigned to the Department of Domestic Intervention and Arbitration."

"I know you," Ilaria says, placing the name and face.

"Yes, ma'am. I responded to your last…." He looks at Dzamko, unsure of how much to say. "Incident. I was here following up on an abuse case when I saw the BCS wheeling the chief guardian out to transport. When the tactical team didn't follow them, I thought I would stay behind to see who they were waiting for. Then you showed up."

"We have to go," Dzamko says, the urgency of their situation now sinking in. He waves his finger in a circle over his head, and they head back to the entrance.

"Where did they take him, Deyago?"

"I don't know," the man says, shaking his head.

Dzamko grimaces. "There's only one logical place. We need to get to Rikers."

CHAPTER SEVENTY-EIGHT

RYKOS

All Farron has done since Obvir picked us up from the cathedral is complain. Not that I think his objections are entirely wrong. Every second we sit here increases the chances that some BCS agent or guardian investigates. Electronic countermeasures draw attention from anyone monitoring static video and drone feeds. Michele doesn't think that they will harass a patrician. Considering what's going on in this city, she's being optimistic. That's what Farron is arguing about.

"My family is under investigation for associating with known terrorists. They know my domiciles and conveyances, and in case you haven't noticed, the city is crawling with BCS agents and blanketed by drones."

"You're not telling me anything I don't already know, Farron," Michele says, continuing her gaze out the window.

"How long are you willing to wait?"

"As long as we can."

Michele stares out the heavily tinted window. I forget that this is still a new experience for her. For my entire life I've watched people on the sidewalks going about their business. She has spent hers under them.

"Fine," Farron says, relenting. "Obvir, get the commander on the line."

The VidLynk connection opens. A man appears dressed in a uniform emblazoned with the Keating coat of arms and two swords. He adjusts his headset.

"Where are you, sir?"

"In our staging area…waiting," Farron says, glaring at Michele.

"Waiting? Farron, the timing of this operation must be perfect. Airspace has been closed. We can't hover outside it without drawing attention. The BCS may be distracted, but they're not oblivious."

"Understood, Commander. We've had an unavoidable delay."

I catch a glimpse of the VidLynk in the center console. The commander isn't pleased. This is a man who expects precision and doesn't like adapting operations without good cause.

"If the bird returns without you, your father will ask questions. Can you justify your delay?"

"I'm hoping it doesn't come to that."

"Hope is not a plan," the commander announces. "The bird will need to refuel soon. You have—"

Ortan's face appears in the center of the conveyance's dashboard.

"We interrupt this tedious broadcast to bring you an important announcement from our sponsors."

"What the hell?" their driver shouts, caught off-guard by the virtual intruder.

"It's okay, Obvir," Farron says. "We're used to this. How did you manage to hack into *my* network?"

"And a hello to you, too, Farron," Ortan says. "Your firewalls are a joke. The cybersecurity experts that you patricians pay are morons. It's laughably easy to penetrate your secured communications."

"You know, I'm getting tired of—"

"Zyree needs you now."

"Where is he?" Michele asks, poking her head up front.

Ortan glances away from the camera. "Uh…Fifth Avenue. He was spotted on Park and is being chased north. They're closing in on him."

"How do you know that?" I ask.

"I'm watching him from above. Maintenance needs to clean the lenses on these drone cameras."

"How…? Never mind," Farron says.

"Do you know where he's heading?"

"They're going to corner him in the southeast corner of Central Park."

"Glory of the Sphere Plaza?" I ask Michele.

She nods. "He's trying to get to one of the underground access points. There are SpeedRail tracks, old subways, utility infrastructure, and caves under the park. The list of hiding spots is long, but he needs to get there first."

"Tick tock, tick tock," Ortan prods.

"Obvir, head west to Sixth Ave and go north," Farron orders his driver, who immediately complies.

A few moments later, we make a right turn onto Fifty-Ninth Street and slam into a wall of traffic. The road runs along the southern edge of the park, and people along the walkway are peering up the street. This runs parallel to the park path I took to and from Dinsmore Academy. I've never seen it like this.

"They are tightening the noose," Ortan says. "He won't last long."

Glory of the Sphere Plaza used to be called Grand Army Plaza. It was an unremarkable area featuring an old statue of an American Civil War general. The plaza was rebuilt into a magnificent garden featuring an elevated fountain at one end and a huge gold-inlaid silver globe on a marble pedestal at the other. It's a popular gateway to Central Park and is always full of people. If Zyree gets pinned down there, he's in big trouble.

"This is a bad idea, Michele," Farron warns.

"Not the first time you've said that," Michele says, checking her weapon.

"What does that tell you?" he grumbles.

"Only that we're going to find out if the armor on this thing was worth the price. Let's roll."

CHAPTER SEVENTY-NINE

AMERICA, INC.

The White House
Corporate Governance District
Washington-Arlington Municipal Corporation

The strip of paper Valen gave Fiolla lies unfolded on her desk. She doesn't need it. After agonizing over this for so long, she committed the information scrawled on it to memory.

GlobalNet is open on her workstation. Corporations restrict access to the world's internet and monitor its usage. It's a one-stop source for propaganda, speculation, innuendo, and rumors. Under that wrapper is an inner core of what could be considered truth.

There are thousands of forums for experts and executives to discuss every conceivable subject. She found the one the note referenced and she typed out a message. She just hasn't been able to bring herself to post it. She's still angry with Valen.

Decisions at this level are still a mystery to her. There is an axiom about leadership that states, "nobody understands any job unless they've done it." Everyone criticizes the decisions made in the Oval Office, but few can relate to the process and responsibility of making them.

Zeykala certainly didn't. Valen was right about what would happen if she ever took his job. His biggest fear was realized. Her arrogance will destroy this corporation and every employee working for it. Is that her problem? And does sending this message change any of that?

She barely understands the consequences of getting caught. Maybe no one would ever know the intended recipient or the post's meaning. She doesn't even have those answers, and that's another problem. She could be sending a message directing Liberteum to end the world.

"Screw it," Fiolla mumbles, posting the response in the forum.

She closes her terminal window and shreds the paper into tiny, unreadable confetti. Fiolla tries to concentrate on her tasks, but focus eludes her. Her head is swimming.

"Executive Fiolla," Rosie says. "Your presence has been requested at Shareholder Hall."

Fiolla cocks her head. Zeykala already said she doesn't want her anywhere near that place.

"At whose request?"

"I'm sorry, the requestor is anonymous. The chief executive officer approved the schedule deviation for the "earliest possible time.'"

Fiolla is surprised. Zeykala wants her to go after all. "Okay. Please arrange transportation."

"Due to enhanced security measures, a conveyance is not available."

"What? According to whom?"

"Further information is unavailable."

Fiolla purses her lips. Curious. She knows that all travel is restricted to official corporate business, but that's what this is.

"Forward all contact requests to my tablet."

Fiolla isn't about to walk back up to Corporate Hill. Nobody pays her attention as she exits the main foyer and passes through the gate. Crossing the street, she feels compelled to look back at the grand and elegant building.

She thought getting out of the White House would help her uneasiness subside. It didn't. She heads to the MetroLev station with another thought rattling around her head. Whether it's because of the events in New York or the reaction to Zeykala's radical policy changes, there's something very wrong with America Incorporated.

CHAPTER
EIGHTY
THE PATRICIANS

Keating Family of the Gentez-Majorez Estate
Greenwich Geographic District
Southern Connecticut Municipal Corporation

Denali rests in his chair with his eyes closed. The stress of the day is taking its toll on his aging body. There isn't much for him to do until his son returns. That is a conversation he's eager to have and needs to have his energy for. That doesn't mean his respite is immune from interruption.

"What is it, Abbot?" Denali grumbles.

His loyal servant is as stealthy as they come, but Denali is old, not deaf. He heard the man open the big oak door to the study and tiptoe in.

"I'm sorry to disturb you. I have news."

Denali wonders if it is about Farron's extraction from New York. He doesn't want to assume incorrectly.

"What news?"

"Shalius Covington is dead."

Denali opens his eyes. That's a surprising development.

"How?"

"A traffic accident while traveling to the board of directors meeting in Washington. According to the WPSS, his conveyance was struck by a malfunctioning sanitation truck. He was pronounced dead at the scene."

He scoffs. "There was nothing accidental about that."

"Should we ask for an investigation?" Abbot asks.

Denali leans back against the headrest. "No. His family will do that. It's a waste of time either way. The BCS covers their tracks."

"If you'll pardon my asking, sir, how do you know it was them?"

"Because it's something I would have arranged. The truck driver was likely an agent, although he'll have a fat personnel record that says otherwise. I bet anyone who interviews his colleagues will say they've never seen him before."

"The murder of a patrician is a bold move for the BCS."

"They were acting on orders."

"Chief Executive Zeykala?" Abbot asks.

Denali shakes his head. "Talya Bettancourt, most likely. She had the most to gain. With Shalius gone and Narik missing, the Covingtons' *prima* claims won't be pursued."

"I'm sorry for your loss, sir. I know you were close friends."

They were, so far as patricians in rival families can be. It's not something he cares to discuss.

"What's the status of my son and Liberteum?"

"Commander Lacune is coordinating their evacuation from Manhattan. The situation in the municorp is deteriorating. Things are tense since the PSS and BCS traded fire at the quli protest."

Lacune has two teams near the park watching things closely. Timely intelligence is a necessity for his plan to work. The two security operations need to be distracted, not shooting at each other.

"It could lead to a civil war," Denali concludes. "The BCS will overreact. They don't like not being in control and will seal off Manhattan to restore order. Tell Commander Lacune that I don't care how much force needs to be applied or against whom. I want my son returned to Greenwich immediately."

"Yes, sir."

Denali stares at the chess board as Abbot excuses himself. There are no lights illuminated since it isn't an active VidLynk game. It will never be finished, at least by Shalius.

He was only supposed to distract Talya, not threaten her position as *prima*. Greed and pride are the two most powerful deadly sins. Shalius took things too far, and it got him killed.

Denali makes a move. "Check."

Making a move is the easy part. Anticipating counter moves is more difficult. In this case, Shalius only has only one, so Denali moves a bishop to protect the king. That exposes his flank. Denali makes another move.

"Check."

Haven was more successful than he could have imagined. Intercorpex is in turmoil. The BCS and PSS engaging in open combat could end up working to his advantage when the time comes. That's another reason life is like chess. You need to be patient and make your move at the right time.

He moves Shalius's pawn to block. Again, it's the only available move. He leaves the pawn alone. You don't need to take all the pieces off the board to win. Sometimes they're more valuable alive.

Denali threatens the king with his knight. Shalius was an excellent player who liked to be aggressive. He would think the move is an exploitable mistake. He moves the rook, not seeing the trap that was set. That was Shalius's way. He never saw the big picture in the real world.

The queen gets moved to a commanding position. Shalius would see the threat too late and counter in a panic. That's what he does. Sees things too late and panics. Denali moves in for the kill with his rook. He leans back and stares at the board.

"Checkmate, old friend. Checkmate."

CHAPTER
EIGHTY-ONE
AMERICA, INC.

The White House
Corporate Governance District
Washington-Arlington Municipal Corporation

A notification from the BCS agent manning the desk in the foyer arrives, informing Zeykala of Fiolla's departure. The CEO is amazed that she followed instructions without questioning them.

She was hoping Fiolla would come around. With all her relationships and likability, she would be a valuable resource. There could have even been a promotion on the horizon for her. It's such a waste of talent.

"Chief Executive Zeykala, you have an incoming VidLynk request from Shareholder Hall."

"Connect us. Good morning, Chairman Joakeen," Zeykala says after the session establishes. "Congratulations on your selection."

"Thank you," the big black man says, beaming. "I appreciate your endorsement."

"It was my honor. If you're looking for recommendations for a new board member, there are some great executives in the energy and tech sectors to choose from. I'd be happy to discuss options with you."

"I appreciate that, Chief Executive Zeykala. I will take you up on that. In the meantime, I wanted to let you know that we recertified Talya Bettancourt as the *prima* of America Incorporated."

Zeykala nods. That's impressive. The board moved faster than she expected.

"Did you have any problems?"

"News of Shalius Covington's untimely death and our inability to locate his son sped things up. The issue isn't entirely settled. Anyone from Shalius's family could still make a claim, and Intercorpex has yet to render a decision on the trades."

"Of course, I understand. Is there anything else?"

"Yes, unfortunately, there is," he says, his expression turning grim. "How long have we known each other, Zeykala?"

Those are the words a friend uses before dropping an anvil on your head. Zeykala shifts uneasily in the seat behind her desk. With Joakeen named chairman of the board and Talya confirmed as *prima*, she should have nothing to worry about. Yet, she's worried.

"A decade or so. Why?"

"You know I'm one of your most ardent supporters."

Zeykala scowls. "Dispense with the disclaimers, Chairman. What's on your mind?"

"There is a growing number of board members who are unhappy with your performance. I wanted to introduce amending the charter to make your ascension permanent during new business, but that door slammed shut quickly. There are loud whispers about replacing you."

"I wanted you in the chairman's position because you can handle them, Joakeen."

"And I will do what I can to tamp them down. Unfortunately, if they assemble a majority, it will be impossible to stop or delay a vote."

The danger of breaking a rule is that others will exploit the trail you just blazed. The charter was written to ensure board members couldn't use their positions to sabotage a chief executive and elevate themselves to the Oval Office. It was a prudent precaution considering the turmoil Intercorpex's Board of Regents experiences. She shredded the rule when she ousted Valen.

"How close are they to a majority?"

"You're hemorrhaging support. The explosion at Intercorpex headquarters, the policy change with the qulis…they have reasons to believe you aren't a suitable CEO."

"There is no better candidate! I should have been named to this position over Valen years ago."

"I agree, but—"

"But nothing! I *deserve* my shot at this. How can the board of directors, in good conscience, be considering a move in such a short time period?"

Joakeen doesn't have an answer for that. He looks down at his hands before speaking.

"Zeykala, you need to regain control. AME News can gloss over events, but there's a sense that things are falling apart. If this strife continues unchecked, the pressure on the board will mount when Intercorpex reopens trading."

Zeykala takes a cleansing breath to calm down. He's doing her a favor by providing this information. He's the chairman of the board, not omnipotent. Business is war, and battle fatigue is a sign of weakness she can ill afford to show.

"I understand. Thank you for the warning, Joakeen. Congratulations again on your new position."

"Thank you, Chief Executive Zeykala. I'll be in touch again soon."

The display returns to the corporate logo when the VidLynk ends. Zeykala leans back in her chair and contemplates what to do next. Regaining control over the sphere of influence is not as simple as it sounds. The discord will burn itself out over time, but that's a luxury she doesn't have. The voices on the board need to be silenced. That leaves her only one option.

"Assemble all available liaisons in the Oval Office in ten minutes," she orders her digital assistant. "I have an announcement to make."

CHAPTER EIGHTY-TWO

INTERCORPEX

Glory of the Sphere Plaza
Midtown Manhattan Geographic District
New York City Municipal Corporation

Bullets nip at Zyree's heels and snap over his head as he charges up the steps on the backside of the fountain on the southern end of Glory of the Sphere Plaza. He's exhausted and is being encircled. He won't make it to Central Park. He needs to make his stand here.

The ornate fountain places a barrier between him and his closest pursuers. Unfortunately, the front of it features a series of tiered pools and cascading waterfalls that are impossible to quickly climb down. Bullets whiz over his head from the left, forcing him to dive into the water in the top tier. Surfacing, he returns fire at the advancing BCS agents.

Zyree spots a group of guardians moving between the long lines of conveyances stuck immobile on the street to his right. He peers past the globe monument and doesn't see anything. The escape route is still open, but that may be more of an illusion. It's obviously where he's going.

"Chief Inspector Zyree! You're surrounded. There's no place left to run," a familiar voice shouts.

Chiana is nothing if not persistent. Employees and visitors have taken cover in the plaza's gardens. Those closest to him are gripped in panic and fear two dozen meters away. They've found themselves smack in the middle of a maelstrom.

There is movement again to his right, and he fires to send a guardian scurrying back to cover. The slide locks to the rear, and he inserts his last magazine. It won't hold them off long.

"Be reasonable, Zyree. This can only end badly for you."

Men are moving to surround the small park. It's only a few hundred feet to the short wall that separates Central Park from the sidewalk. Under fire, that will feel like miles. He has no choice; if he doesn't make it to East Drive, it's over.

"Last chance, Chief Inspector," Chiana sings out.

Zyree fires three rounds in the direction of her voice. The return fire is immediate and intense. Marble chips from the bullet strikes fly around him, and he hears a piercing scream.

A man in the garden has been shot and is bleeding as his wife wails over him. Panicked, the people huddling with them begin to flee. One of the men races past him and is cut down by the indiscriminate fire. The BCS doesn't seem to care who or what they hit.

Zyree slides down into the lower level of the fountain. When he surfaces, none of the gunfire is directed at him. The shouting is indecipherable, but the guardians are firing at…he turns his head…the BCS? What the hell is going on?

There is no time for rationalizing. He uses the window of opportunity to climb out of the water and sprint across the stone and brick patio and street that bisects the plaza. He enters the wine bottle-shaped granite walkway leading up to the Glory of the Sphere monument, stops, and fires behind him. An advancing agent dives to the ground.

Zyree's waterlogged clothes and boots are slowing him down. Winded, he takes cover behind the monument. That's when he sees the men hidden behind trees and bushes. Chiana's tactic is to drive him right into them – hounds to the hunters, as Jurghen would say.

He checks his ammo count: three rounds left. It's over. Zyree begins to resign himself to his fate. The thought of Chiana winning causes his stomach to turn. What she will do to Intercorpex Security…he's almost glad he won't live to see it.

Zyree takes a breath and prepares to step out into the open to make this as quick and painless as possible. Then he hears a commotion off to his right.

CHAPTER
EIGHTY-THREE
AMERICA, INC.

Brooklyn-Queens Express Autoway
Woodside Geographic District
New York City Municipal Corporation

"All guardians, all guardians," a dispatcher announces over the conveyance's communications system. "This is a broadcast message from the RTCC."

Dzamko shakes his head and turns the volume up. Deyago, seated next to Ilaria, perks up as their driver divides his focus between listening and navigating the side streets leading to the Midtown Tunnel. They all think this announcement will pertain to their failure to fall into the trap set at the medical center.

"This can't be good," the CEO concludes.

"We have confirmation that the PSS and BCS are involved in a shootout at Glory of the Sphere Plaza. Several guardians are down. Immediate assistance is required."

"They're shooting at each other? What the hell?" Deyago asks.

"Constable Dzamko, we've been looking for you," the battle captain at the RTCC says after Dzamko establishes a VidLynk with the RTCC.

"Did I hear your last message correctly?"

"Yes, sir. BCS agents chasing a rogue ICX inspector opened fire on him south of Central Park. Employees in the plaza were caught in the crossfire. The agents were ordered to stop firing but ignored our demands and ended up hitting three innocents. The on-scene commander instructed his men to intervene, and the BCS opened fire on them as well."

"He did the right thing," Dzamko assures his subordinate. "What's happening now?"

"There's a lot of confusion. Additional guardians were dispatched. We're going to force the BCS to stand down."

"That's the right call. Detain those agents, if practical."

"Yes, sir, I'll relay the directive. RTCC out."

Dzamko disconnects the VidLynk and looks out the window. He's thinking about the situation, worried about his guardians. Ilaria is concerned for them, too.

"I'm surprised the BCS left the RTCC," Deyago says, interrupting the long, tense silence.

"Virtari knows they're loyal to me. He's likely going to transfer their operations to the EOC. That facility has better capabilities."

"Dzamko, you need to lead your guardians. This fight with the BCS over Teman is mine, not yours."

"It's all our fight now, ma'am. The RTCC can manage the situation in the plaza without me micromanaging them. I need to be here. Teman isn't just my boss. He's a friend, and so are you."

"Thank you. Do we have a plan?"

"Get to Rikers, find Teman, extricate him, and try not to get ourselves killed in the process. Outside of that, no, I don't have one. We're not going to outman or outgun them."

"Can we sneak in?" Deyago asks.

Dzamko shakes his head. "Rikers is a secure facility. By design, there's only one route in and out. There's no way we can enter undetected."

"We could steal a boat," the driver says.

"Approaches are monitored, and it would take too much time. They aren't going to waste any time marching Teman into that courtyard," Dzamko counters.

"So, what are we going to do?"

"Rely on the element of surprise. If we lose it, we're going to have big problems."

CHAPTER
EIGHTY-FOUR

LIBERTEUM

Near Glory of the Sphere Plaza
Midtown Manhattan Geographic District
New York City Municipal Corporation

Michele joins the others in staring out the windshield in awe. Muzzle flashes burst around the plaza before the reports travel to their ears. It's bedlam. She has never seen street violence this up close and personal. She was on the run with Rykos, Farron, and Koltayne when Haven tore the city apart, escaping from the Alamo. Very little of his flight from the Intercorpex bombing scene made it to AME News. The whole scene in front of her is surreal.

"Zyree is caught in a crossfire," Ortan informs them. "It looks like the guardians and corporate security are…shooting at each other."

Everyone in the conveyance exchanges confused stares before turning to Rykos. He's the recent employee among them and would understand the relationship between the BCS and PSS. He only offers a shrug.

"They don't like each other, but that's never happened before."

Michele glances out the windows. Traffic is at a standstill, and they're boxed in. It's bumper to bumper with no sign they'll move anytime soon with a raging firefight a hundred meters away.

"Obvir, this thing's a beast. Ram your way out of here and use the sidewalk," Michele suggests. "We didn't come up here for a front row seat to Zyree's death."

Farron nods, and Obvir takes a deep breath before slamming the conveyance in reverse. He pushes the vehicle behind them out of the way as a horn blares. The same is done to the conveyance in front of them. Jerking the wheel hard, Obvir finds space to squeeze through. The shrill sounds of metal on metal fill their ears as he muscles the vehicles traveling in the opposite direction out of their way. Employees climb out and start shouting as Obvir jumps the curb and guns it down the walkway.

The wide promenade runs along the entire southern edge of the park. Obvir plows through tables and chairs set up near a street vendor as they reach the corner.

"Drive right up to the monument."

"Okay. Hang on," he says, barreling through protective fencing and tearing up hedges and flower beds.

Bullets begin pinging off the armored behemoth. It could be the BCS or PSS, but it doesn't matter. Whoever it is isn't friendly.

"Avoid killing anyone if you can," Michele says as Obvir slams on the brakes only feet from the base of the monument.

He exits the driver's side and opens fire in the direction of the agents. Farron rolls down his window and does the same from the safety of the car's front seat as Koltayne steps out the driver's side and covers their rear.

"You again?" Zyree asks from the prone position when Michele opens her door and swings her legs out. "What are you doing?"

"You're a chief inspector with Intercorpex and don't recognize a rescue when you see one?"

"Why?"

"Because you have a very convincing friend." He looks at her with puzzlement but says nothing. "I don't like getting shot at, Zyree, so we're leaving. You can stay here and die, or you can come with us. It's your choice, so make it now."

He's conflicted. Michele is one of the terrorists he was hunting. Now she's here offering to save his life. The only question left to answer is whether he'll let them.

CHAPTER EIGHTY-FIVE

AMERICA, INC.

The White House
Corporate Governance District
Washington-Arlington Municipal Corporation

Zeykala is not going to sugarcoat this. Executives can see it for themselves on AME News. Things are bad, and they won't be inspired by a chief executive who pretends that everything is business as usual. She needs to take bold action.

"You are probably wondering why you're all here," Zeykala says, addressing the gathering in the Oval Office. "It's been a tough couple of days, and it's only going to get harder. We're facing serious challenges, and it will require constant effort to overcome them. Today's events in New York and the growing quli protests require drastic action. I've decided that there is no alternative but to declare martial law."

The shocked look on everyone's faces says it all. Despite their constant problems with qulis and urches, martial law has only been declared once since the signing of the corporate charter. It was done in the early days of the Catharsis and was used to justify the extermination of hostile urches.

"You're transferring control of municipal corporations to the BCS?" one of her executives asks.

"Yes. It will be temporary until order is restored."

Zeykala didn't expect enthusiastic support but hoped for more than confused stares. These people are here to ensure her success as CEO. They should be eager to solve problems so that the corporation can thrive once again.

"Ma'am, there are only a few hotspots right now. Declaring martial law throughout our sphere of influence is excessive."

"Corporate security suggests the uprisings will become more widespread," Zeykala says, glaring at him. "This is not a time for half-measures."

"With all due respect, ma'am," her legal counsel interjects, "I don't think you have the authority. Acting CEOs aren't entitled to the full benefits of the office. That is clearly stated in the corporate charter, as is the clause that a board member cannot become chief executive."

"The board is changing that," Zeykala argues.

"Yes, but they have not changed it *yet*. Strictly speaking, exercising powers not bequeathed to you is not permitted."

Zeykala glares at him. America Incorporated needs a strong CEO, and she isn't going to be forced into inaction out of fear of a fifty-year-old charter. Her legal counsel should be searching for ways to justify her actions.

"Are you saying that I'm not permitted to take measures to secure the safety and prosperity of this corporation in a time of crisis?"

"If your course of action is decreeing martial law, that's what I'm saying."

"That's your opinion," Zeykala says, losing her patience with the man.

"My *expert* legal opinion as counsel."

Zeykala nods. "If my decision isn't legal, then I need executives willing to find loopholes. Since you aren't willing to do that, your services are no longer required. You are relieved of your duties."

"It doesn't work that way, ma'am."

"It does now," she says, moving inches from his face. "You're dismissed."

The man is about to protest and thinks twice about it. Lawyers are still required to broker intercorporational deals and write contracts. That should be the limit of their involvement in business affairs. The elimination of lawyers plaguing pre-collapse society was one of the corporation's greatest achievements. Zeykala made a career out of ignoring lawyers. She isn't about to let one impede her now.

The stare-down lasts longer than it should. He turns and leaves the Oval Office before Zeykala can have him escorted out. She has set the tone of how business will be conducted in this building. Now she needs to capitalize on it.

"Does anyone else want to express their opinion?" the chief executive challenges. Nobody even flinches. "Good. I need Public Affairs to draft a statement, and I want it reported on AME News at the top of the hour. Begin filtering the directive down the ranks. Make it happen."

The office clears out, and Zeykala moves to the window overlooking the Rose Garden. Alone with her thoughts for the first time today, she can finally take a moment to reflect. Everything is happening quickly. Her actions are more reactive than strategic. Martial law is a Draconian measure designed to get quick results. That paradigm will need to change for her to be successful.

CHAPTER EIGHTY-SIX

INTERCORPEX

Glory of the Sphere Plaza
Midtown Manhattan Geographic District
New York City Municipal Corporation

This is not the rescue Zyree had in mind. There isn't any time to ponder Liberteum's motives. The math is simple: Go with them or stay and die. He can figure out later why they're risking their lives to rescue him, assuming they all survive.

"Oh, what the hell," he mumbles loudly enough to be heard.

He pops up, hoping not to get shot in the back. He stops at the door, seeing the crowded back seat.

"We don't have room for four back here," Rykos says to Michele.

She slides onto his lap, and Zyree climbs in and slams the door. Koltayne and Obvir jump back into the conveyance as Rykos's cheeks redden. He grins from ear to ear.

"Don't get any ideas," she admonishes when she sees his smile.

The conveyance is turning into a bullet magnet. The number of rounds hitting the armored body makes it sound like they're in a driving rainstorm.

"Get us out of here, Obvir," Farron says, bracing himself.

The driver peels out, blasting through the garden opposite the monument and back onto the street. BCS agents furiously scramble to get a better shooting angle.

"Not to sound unappreciative, but what the hell is this about?" Zyree demands.

"Glad to see you alive and still cranky," the voice over the VidLynk announces.

"Ortan?" Zyree asks, straining his neck to see the center dash display.

"You asked for help, my friend," the engineer says with an impish grin. "Beggars can't be choosers."

"A rescue by the terrorists I'm accused of helping isn't helping my cause."

"I didn't see anyone else lining up to help you, Zyree."

Well-aimed shots ping off the bullet-resistant windshield. A BCS agent is standing in the middle of the road, holding his ground as he fires his rifle. He doesn't plan on moving.

"Punch it," Michele says.

The response for a vehicle this heavy is impressive. The man freezes at the sudden acceleration and reacts too late. He careens off the hood and over the roof, landing in a pile with two shattered legs.

Zyree turns his attention back to the VidLynk and sees nothing but the bare walls of his Icelandic office.

"Ortan, are you there?"

"I've done all I can," he says, coming back into the frame. "Getting out of the city is up to you."

"Where are you going?"

The engineer wears a resigned expression. "An ICX Security team has been posted here since the explosion. They're obtrusive, which is why I stayed out of contact. Unfortunately, helping you will come at a cost. They're on their way to collect it."

"Ortan—"

"Don't say it. Please. I have no regrets. You're the only real friend I've ever had, Zyree. Whatever happens to me, it was worth it."

"Ortan, get out of there!"

"Best of luck to all of you," he says as the VidLynk suddenly cuts out.

CHAPTER EIGHTY-SEVEN

AMERICA, INC.

Steve Jobs MetroLev Station
Corporate Governance District
Washington-Arlington Municipal Corporation

Executive Park is almost empty. Fiolla strides up the sweeping oval path, determined to get to the station quickly. The park offers a nice view of the north entrance of the White House. She doesn't bother to admire it again as she turns toward the Steve Jobs MetroLev station.

After the collapse, Washington's metro train stations were named after famous tycoons and captains of industry. It was an early move meant to honor the great business leaders of the past. Serving three different lines, this particular station is located on the corner of Seventh and K Streets.

When Fiolla reaches the circular path at the Eagle Fountain, she notices two men out of the corner of her eye. A sudden surge of adrenaline triggers her fight or flight instinct. It may be nothing, but it feels like they're following her.

Moving even faster, she crosses H Street. A block later, she hazards a quick glance behind her as she turns left. She was hoping that the men would veer off in another direction. They didn't.

"It's nothing," she whispers, willing herself to calm down. Both men are dressed in professional attire, not security uniforms.

"You're being paranoid," she mumbles. "There is no reason to panic."

The station occupies the first floor of a small office building. Not wanting to venture down to the platform with two men possibly following her, Fiolla stops to help a pair of Japanese businessmen studying the digital LED route map. Her two stalkers stroll by without paying her any attention. She relaxes. It was a false alarm.

"*Arigato,*" one of the men says after she points them in the right direction.

They head to a different platform, and Fiolla rides the escalator down to the westbound trains that lead to Foggy Bottom. The Silver, Gold, and Pearl lines stop at this station, so trains are as plentiful as they are fast.

Each line is named after a precious metal or stone to project America Incorporated's wealth. The station itself is cavernous. The depth of the platforms allows for high, arched roofs that most cities' mass transit systems can't manage.

This station has two sets of tracks: a pair for each direction of travel. The dual platforms occupy the space between the first and second and third and fourth track beds. Escalators access each from the sky bridge that spans the tracks below. The platforms are long and feature greenery, LED displays, and benches.

Fiolla turns every ten steps or so to check who's behind her. There are a few visitors and employees on the platform. To her relief, there's no sign of the two men she thought were following her.

The change in air pressure and circulation signals the imminent arrival of the high-speed people-mover. The sooner she gets on the train, the better.

"Are you looking for us?"

Fiolla practically jumps out of her skin. She turns and is face-to-face with her two followers. They must have used the emergency exit behind her.

"What do you want from me?"

"Nothing," one of them says with a grin.

"Nothing?"

"That's right. We don't want anything. We're just here to assist with your tragic accident."

Fiolla freezes as she processes those words. The men grab her arms and manhandle her closer to the platform's edge. She struggles against their grasp to no avail. They're too strong.

"Virtari and Zeykala send their regards."

Screaming won't do any good. Nobody is close enough to help, and they would only be endangering their own lives if they did. Fiolla knows the end game. These goons will push her in front of this train if she doesn't act. The wind is being pushed out of the tunnel hard. She only has seconds.

She swings her legs out in front of her and lets gravity do the hard work. The unexpected torque causes them to lose their grip on her as she crashes onto the platform.

Fiolla kicks and flails, fighting for her life as the men struggle to regain their grasp. One of her kicks catches an agent in the lower leg, causing his foot to slip off the platform. Fighting to regain his balance, he loses the battle and teeters off the edge onto the electromagnetic rail bed.

The other agent watches his friend fall. Fiolla scrambles to her feet. Instead of running, she brings her leg up and kicks out. Her foot strikes the second agent's abdomen and sends him careening backward. He runs out of platform and starts his freefall toward the track below.

He never reaches it. The MetroLev plows through both men as it screams into the station. Their bodies evaporate into a pink cloud spewing chunks of flesh and clothing.

"Are you okay?" a woman asks as the train stops and a pair of employees reaches her.

"What happened?" another man inquires, surveying the grotesque carnage on the floor.

She's too shaken to answer. Her legs are wobbly and she's having difficulty breathing.

"Ladies and gentlemen, if I may have your attention, there has been an incident at the station. All travel on the Gold, Silver, and Pearl lines at Steve Jobs Station has been suspended pending a response by emergency services."

Passengers stare at the large LED display suspended over the platform as Fiolla regains her composure. She doesn't want to stay here and explain what happened. The guardians in this city are almost as bad as the BCS. She wills her legs to move and makes a break for the emergency exit her attackers used.

"Hey! Where are you going?" a man bellows from behind her.

Fiolla doesn't turn, not even to check for pursuers. She needs to run as long and hard as she can. She thinks about contacting Farron and asking for help. Maybe he's willing to protect her. It's worth asking, but she needs to get away – first from this city and then from anything to do with America Incorporated.

CHAPTER EIGHTY-EIGHT

THE PATRICIANS

The White House
Corporate Governance District
Washington-Arlington Municipal Corporation

Zeykala is at the end of her rope. Talya sits on the sofa in the Oval Office and watches as her hand-chosen CEO rubs her eyes and presses her fingers against her temples. She knows that Zeykala despises her micromanagement. That's too bad. Until the woman shows some leadership instincts and does what's necessary, Talya doesn't plan on going anywhere.

The liaison from Public Affairs is her next contestant on *The Weak and the Incompetent*. She's standing in front of Zeykala's desk, completely oblivious of her failures. Or, at least, that's how the chief executive is interpreting them.

"The qulis are protesting in almost every major city now. Why is AME News making me look like the bad guy for instituting martial law?"

"I don't think they're doing that," she says, offering her ridiculous and irrelevant opinion. "They were just outlining the quli laborers' complaints."

"Nobody should care about their complaints! AME News works for America Incorporated. In other words, they work for me."

"I can get them on the line for you," the PA executive says, looking like she's about to burst into tears.

"Why do I need to speak to them? You work for Public Affairs, right? Do your damn job."

"I will take care of it, ma'am."

"Good, because if they aren't reporting about how ungrateful the qulis are in the next ten minutes, you'll be packing your workspace. Understood?"

"Yes, ma'am."

Talya shakes her head. Threats are useful only under two circumstances: when used sparingly and when they can be backed up with action. Violate the first, and you're a tyrant. Fail to follow through on the second, and you're inept. Zeykala would probably show the young woman the door. In the process, she would earn the resentment of everyone who works with her. Public Affairs is a group you need on your side. Zeykala needs to learn the definition of the word "nuance."

The executive leaves with her tail between her legs. As she steps out, Special Agent Dvarkin enters. The interruptions are never-ending in this office.

"Is she dead?"

The look on his face isn't celebratory. "My agents tailed her to the station and made contact on the platform. We're unsure what transpired, but they're both down."

Zeykala closes her eyes and grinds her teeth. "There are a hundred cameras in that station. How can you not know? Down how?"

"They were hit by the MetroLev pulling into the station."

Talya scoffs from the sofa. Ever since Covington's 'accident,' it's been a struggle to get anything to go right. Zeykala needs to take care of one thing as directed. Just one thing.

"Fiolla is a petite woman with no training and even fewer street smarts. Instead of getting shoved in front of the train, she somehow overpowered two of your best agents and pushed them?"

Dvarkin puts on a brave face. "We're investigating whether she had assistance."

"Don't make me laugh," Talya barks from the sofa.

"Where is she?" Zeykala demands.

"Heading north on the Ruby Line. Running is futile. We'll get her."

Zeykala interlaces her fingers in front of her mouth. Fiolla has turned into a headache. It's just another distraction that she doesn't seem to be able to handle.

"See that you do. Forget making it look like an accident. Take her into custody and have Human Resources charge her with the murders of your agents. I want to be present when the bitch is terminated."

"Yes, ma'am."

Talya eyes her CEO, almost willing her to take more decisive action.

"No more mistakes, Agent Dvarkin," Zeykala says under her withering glare. "I want this handled today. Don't show your face in here again until it is."

Another threat. The patrician shakes her head. This one is slightly more appropriate but still rings hollow. She needs Dvarkin's guidance while Virtari gets control of the NYCMC. This woman has a lot to learn.

CHAPTER
EIGHTY-NINE
AMERICA, INC.

Human Resources Center
Rikers Island Geographic Area
New York City Municipal Corporation

Their driver slows as they approach the access control point to Rikers Island Human Resources Center. A guardian clad in the uniform of the Corporate Detention Division emerges from his shelter when they stop at the retractable barrier. Ilaria isn't certain how driving up to the entrance is Dzamko's idea of catching them by surprise.

"I'm sorry, sir, I can't permit you access to the facility."

"You're denying the acting chief guardian entry?" Dzamko asks, leaning over to peer out the driver's window.

"I'm sorry, Constable, I didn't see you. We've been given orders by Director Virtari of the BCS to restrict all access to the island."

"I understand. Do you work for the BCS now?"

"No, sir, I'm a guardian," he proudly states.

"And I'm the acting chief guardian. Lower the barrier."

The young guardian looks torn. Virtari likely threatened him with unspeakable things if he didn't follow the order. Now his real boss has put him on the spot.

"Uh…we're under martial law. We all work for the BCS."

Ilaria rolls down her window. "Guardian, my name is Chief Executive Ilaria. I'm the rightful CEO of this city and don't recognize the legitimacy of the acting CEO."

"You're in a bad situation, son," Dzamko interjects before the guardian can crap his pants. "You have conflicting orders and must decide which to follow. To make your decision easier, we're going to that island whether you lower the barrier or we do it ourselves."

Dzamko delivers the threat in a calm, smooth voice. He would have made a great salesman had someone in Human Resources not predetermined that he become a guardian.

The man taps a couple of commands on his wrist tablet, and the barrier retracts. "Thank you, son."

They scream over the Rikers Island Bridge spanning the East River. Ilaria stares out the window at the distant airport and the line of cargo aircraft waiting to be unloaded. Operations there have shut down. The state of corporate emergency is now martial law. Everything is at a standstill except the execution of her husband.

What was once a sprawling prison complex is now much smaller. Some older buildings are still utilized, but much of the work is done in a handful of modern facilities. The rest of the island has been turned into a guardian training center.

"Where to?" the driver asks.

"The Termination Building, probably Delta Wing," Deyago says as gently as possible.

Their driver navigates to the facility located off the main stretch of road that bisects the island. The BCS convoy is parked out front. There doesn't appear to be anyone left watching the vehicles.

The driver pulls up behind them, and everyone in the conveyance piles out. They sprint down the sidewalk and crash through the front doors. Her entourage already has their weapons drawn. She's the only one who is unarmed.

"What's the meaning—?"

"Where are they?" Dzamko shouts at the receptionist.

"Who?"

"They're heading to Delta," another guardian says, pointing.

They move as a group to the corridor and stop dead in their tracks. Men begin shouting in frenzied and urgent voices. When the commotion simmers down, a single, unmistakable voice pipes up from behind a phalanx of BCS agents.

"I was wondering when you all would show up."

CHAPTER NINETY

LIBERTEUM

East Side Autoway
Lenox Hill Geographic District
New York City Municipal Corporation

Obvir screams past Fifty-Ninth Street, bypassing the ramp to the closest bridge over the East River. He makes a hard left and then follows it with a right onto Sixty-Second and the entrance to the East Side Autoway.

"I hope you guys have a plan," Zyree says. "Every bridge and tunnel is closed."

"Who says we're driving off this island?" Michele says with a grin.

"Okay, but this is a bad road to be on. They can easily trap us on a controlled-access roadway."

"We know," Farron calmly says from the front seat.

Zyree leans back into his seat. He's clearly not the one in charge here. They're relaxed, considering the severity of the storm bearing down on them. The BCS won't bother pursuing them—they'll block the escape routes and force them into an ambush. While his rescuers can't be oblivious to that, they aren't concerned about it either.

"Will someone explain how you plan to get off this island since it's likely the last thing we ever try?"

"The BCS agents don't live in this city, Chief Inspector. They won't think to block a footbridge."

Zyree wishes he had his biocomp and contacts to explain what the hell they're talking about. "What footbridge?"

"The Ward's Island Bridge is a pedestrian crossing that leads to the recreational area in the Harlem River," Rykos explains.

"So, you're trading one island for another?"

"Not exactly," Michele says.

"Roadblock!" Obvir shouts as he comes around the corner.

The support columns on either side make this the perfect place for one. Agents open fire with heavy weapons and batter the bullet-resistant glass of the armored vehicle. This conveyance may be akin to a tank, but it's taking an unsustainable beating.

"Ram them!" Michele shouts.

Obvir floors it, and the vehicle lurches forward. He slams into the two conveyances, causing their front ends to disintegrate with the piercing sound of twisting metal and shattering glass.

"Let's hope we don't run into another of those," Farron muses.

"If I have to ram anything else, one of you will have to get out and push," Obvir deadpans.

Feeling helpless isn't something Zyree is used to. He's only along for the ride. The world views these people as terrorists and Farron Keating as a spoiled elite playing with fire. Zyree has long thought there was more to this group despite the accepted narrative. From their name to their actions, the pieces of the puzzle don't fit.

Ortan trusted them to rescue him, and the eccentric engineer doesn't trust anybody. Zyree's employer is now hunting him, and the terrorists he was stalking came to his rescue. The world is upside down. Maybe this is an opportunity to finally learn what is happening around him, assuming he survives long enough to find out.

CHAPTER NINETY-ONE
AMERICA, INC.

Near Isabel dos Santos MetroLev Station
Forest Hills Geographic District
Washington-Arlington Municipal Corporation

Fiolla's hands are still shaking. She can't come to grips with what happened on the platform. Nervous energy rolls up and down her spine, making it hard for her to focus. She was defending herself. Those men were there to kill her and would have, had she not resisted. She still feels guilty about what happened. She killed corporate security agents. What she saw…the train…happened because of her.

She forces the gory image from her mind. She's alive but is a fugitive with a target on her back. She needs to stay a step ahead of corporate security, who are no doubt tracking her. The question is, how?

Fiolla ditched her tablet in a trash receptacle before getting on the Ruby Line. It will do nothing to throw them off her trail. She closes her eyes and takes a deep breath that does nothing to ease the tension. When her eyes open, Fiolla is rocked by another jolt of fear. The hunters stalking her have their prey in sight.

The two BCS agents must have gotten on at the last stop. They're moving forward with hatred in their eyes and the determination of men on a mission. The thought traps Fiolla in the iron grip of panic. They know what happened to their fellow agents and won't offer her quarter or mercy. It's not the corporate way.

She stands when she feels the sudden deceleration. The quick change in velocity encourages most passengers to remain seated until the MetroLev comes to a complete stop. Now isn't the time to abide by the rules. The agents hang on as momentum pushes them forward. When the MetroLev finally halts, the men surge toward her. The race is on.

The doors open, and Fiolla plows through a line of employees looking to board. She sprints toward the escalator that leads out of Isabel dos Santos Station in the

Forest Hills Geographic District. She doesn't look back. She doesn't need to. Fiolla knows they're gaining on her.

The sidewalk outside the station is bristling with people. By the filth on their jumpsuits and skin, they must be qulis protesting Zeykala's latest directive. Forest Hills is heavily populated by the labor class and is home to several technical schools and training academies. Fiolla stands out like a sore thumb, but the congestion will still offer her more concealment than isolation will.

She weaves quickly through the crowd. From the sounds behind her, the BCS agents are drawing the crowd's attention. The qulis are a rough lot and won't take kindly to getting shoved out of the way, especially by corporate security agents.

Fiolla stops to weigh her options. This crowd is a powder keg. WPSS guardians stand watch with heavy weapons and riot equipment. She isn't sure why they didn't disperse the crowd before it grew this large, but that's their problem.

The men and women screaming anti-corporation slogans at the top of their lungs give her disdainful looks as she meanders through their ranks. Fiolla isn't one of them. The AME executive uniform doesn't belong here. They could just as easily turn their anger toward her.

Winded and mentally exhausted, she pauses near the center of the protest to hazard a look back in the direction she came from. There's no sign of the agents. Maybe they thought twice about following her into a volatile crowd.

"You lost?" a gruff, unshaven quli asks, flanked by two very large men.

Fiolla shakes her head, almost bursting into tears. "I have nowhere else to go."

"What d'you mean?"

"I'm being pursued by BCS agents determined to kill me. I'd already be dead if this crowd wasn't here."

"How d'ya know that?" one of the other men asks.

"Because they tried pushing me in front of a MetroLev near the White House."

"You're still alive," the man says, expressing disbelief that she could have somehow avoided an attempt on her life.

"That's because I…got the upper hand on them."

The image of the men being pulverized by the speeding train is overwhelming. Tears flow down her cheeks. Fiolla desperately tries to wipe them away. She wants to appear strong. It's not working.

"Yo, man, I kinda believe her," one of the large men says. The leader turns to his other beefy friend.

"He's right. She ain't lyin'," he adds with a nod.

"What'd you do to get them after you?"

"It's a long story. I work at the White House. Let's just say that the new CEO doesn't like me."

The men smile. That was the right thing to say. Fiolla is certain they don't like her either.

"We can protect you."

"Thanks, but you can't. You'll get hurt if you try. I need to get out of here."

"And go where?" the leader asks.

"New York. I have a friend there who can help me."

"Well, little lady, you're in luck. Bro, you know where Jymmie is?"

The man shrugs. "Around here…somewhere."

"Help me find him. What's your name, doll?"

Fiolla cringes. Sexist language was erased from the corporate culture decades ago, despite Virtari trying to make it cool again. Corporate discrimination and harassment took on other forms.

Qulis play by a different set of rules. He didn't mean it in a derogatory sense. It sounded more like an affectionate term of endearment. Either way, they're offering to help, and she'll take it where she can get it.

"Fiolla, and yours?"

"It has five syllables," he says with a laugh. "My parents were sadistic assholes. My friends call me Dutch. These two big fellas are Jzahn and Boomyr."

"It's nice to meet you, Dutch," Fiolla says, wondering how he earned the unique nickname. "Thank you for offering to help me."

"No problem, love. Let's find Jymmie. He's got a truck and can drive you out of the city."

CHAPTER NINETY-TWO

RYKOS

East Side Autoway
East Harlem Geographic District
New York City Municipal Corporation

There is no sign of pursuit, and we aren't being shot at. Everything is quiet. Too quiet. There is an old expression that says there's calm before the storm. It feels appropriate right now. When Obvir slows down, I begin to hope that we're nearing the end of this chase.

"Are we there?" I ask.

"No," Obvir says, staring straight ahead.

"Then why are we slowing down?" Michele asks, still on my lap with her head cocked to the side to avoid rubbing it against the conveyance's roof.

"Because we're not plowing through those," Farron says, pointing.

Zyree, Rykos, and I bump heads as we strain to look out the windshield. Three large sanitation trucks are blocking the road a tenth of a mile ahead, flanked by BCS agents manning heavy weapons.

"I guess they learned their lesson from the last one," I gloomily observe.

"The ramp to Ninety-Sixth is right there," Farron says. "We can get off the East Side Autoway and go around it."

The roadblock is set up about three hundred feet past the ramp. It's doable if we race full speed down it, although we'll take some fire in the process.

"Do it," Michele commands.

"Don't," Zyree warns. "That's what they want you to do."

"What do you mean?" I ask.

"Think of it like a rock in a stream. It forces water to go around it, right? Those trucks are the rock. If you take that exit, you spring their trap. We won't make it past First Avenue alive."

That makes sense. It also doesn't leave us with a lot of options. We can't go backward, can't go forward, and can't take the ramp. What does he expect us to do?

"Fine, then I'm open to suggestions," Michele says.

"We can make a run for it," I offer. "The footbridge is only a half-mile away."

"That's a long way against snipers who can pick you off from those buildings," Zyree says, pointing. "They can hit targets with ease at three times that distance."

"Do you have a better idea?" I ask.

"Not unless you have an air force."

Farron turns to us from the front seat and stares at our guest. "We have the next best thing. Obvir, get me the commander."

"About time, Farron. Are you in position?" the man asks once the VidLynk establishes. "Your extraction is waiting in the cove at Mill Rock."

"We've literally hit a roadblock, Commander. We're on the East Side Autoway, about a half-mile south of the footbridge. Can extraction pick us up here?"

"Negative," he says, consulting a map. "The flood barrier will make loading impossible. We'll clear the roadblock."

"How long? We just picked up some company."

Farron's comment causes us all to look out the back window at the approaching vehicles.

"We'll be on-station in sixty seconds," the commander says before disconnecting.

I'm not sure we have that long. I can hear the high-pitched rotors of the drones hovering overhead as five vehicles screech to a halt fifty meters behind us. An agent steps out and covers behind the door.

"Exit the vehicle now!" he shouts, with his rifle leveled at us.

"I know you're in there, Zyree," a female voice announces. "You just won't die, will you?"

A slender woman in a different uniform moves up from another vehicle to join the agent. She doesn't have a weapon. I can only stare at her. This may be a life-or-death situation, but…she's beautiful. Michele elbows me on the shoulder, and I close my open mouth.

"Friend of yours?" she asks Zyree.

"Colleague, actually. She's tried to kill me three times so far."

"Talk about a hostile work environment," I mutter, still leering at her.

"I'm giving you ten seconds to surrender, and then we're going to kill all of you," she decrees.

"She isn't bluffing just so you know," Zyree says.

"It's four seconds more than we need," Farron says, staring at the map on the center display.

I don't know what he means until the Asian woman looks ups and dives to the ground. Three of the five vehicles explode behind us. I can feel the heat from the blast through the back window as the deafening roar forces me to cover my ears. I glance out to see two large black helicopters scream over us. It's an impressive sight.

The agent in the nearest intact vehicle scrambles to his feet as the birds bank hard in opposite directions. The gunship on the left peppers him with machinegun fire. To her credit, Zyree's "friend" remains prone on the ground.

The other helicopter fires more rockets that hit the trucks in the blockade before firing at the rooftop of a building just off the highway.

The VidLynk reestablishes. "You are clear to proceed. We'll keep you covered."

"What was on top of that building?" Farron asks the commander.

"They had a rocket launcher," the man deadpans.

We all look at Zyree. He was right. We would have been toast had we gone down that ramp.

Obvir doesn't wait for instructions. He weaves through the remnants of the roadblock and quickly chews up the distance to the footbridge. The choppers are overhead, engaging drones that venture too close. The BCS can still track us, but at least we aren't making it easy.

"Time to go."

We exit the conveyance at the pedestrian footbridge's stairs. I take a moment to look at the outside of our vehicle. Farron didn't get ripped off. The armored beast is pocked by bullet strikes, and the front is mangled from running the first roadblock. The fact that it made it this far is impressive.

We sprint up the stairs. When I reach the top, a loud crack fills my ears as I feel something snap over my head.

"Sniper!" Michele shouts.

We get down, but there's no place to hide up here. One of the helicopters engages a rooftop with Gatling-style mini-guns. The sound is as impressive as the effect. The sniper is either shredded, or he's running for his life.

We scamper across the bridge and down the opposite stairs into the recreational area. Land is at a premium in Manhattan, so athletic fields for local academies were constructed on this island. I watched Dinsmore play sports here. That feels like a lifetime ago.

A sleek black boat streaks up the river toward us. It isn't armored but doesn't really need to be. This machine was built for pure speed.

"I guess the patricians have been gathering armies," Zyree says to Farron while we wait.

"We have tried to do it quietly, but it's the world's worst-kept secret."

"A patrician army and the terrorists you were hunting saved your life twice in the past half-hour," I say, smiling.

He grins. "It's been a surreal day."

We load up on the boat after it arrives. Zyree balks, probably weighing his options. We are only alive because of the air support, and he must know that. He joins us on the vessel as I look over at Michele, who watches him intently as the captain guns the engine and points the bow north.

CHAPTER NINETY-THREE

AMERICA, INC.

Human Resources Center
Rikers Island Geographic Area
New York City Municipal Corporation

Virtari is an arrogant bastard. Ilaria always suspected that, and it was confirmed when they first met in the RTCC. He always thinks he's in complete control. In this case, he might be right. It doesn't mean this is hopeless.

"You're outmanned and outgunned. This standoff isn't going to end well for you."

"You guys can't hit a target taped to the wall in front of you. If your men shoot, you get the first bullet, Virtari."

"I'm prepared to die doing my duty. What do you think the odds are that you'll be alive to relish my death? You didn't think this through, did you, Constable?"

"My job is to protect lives. If I need to go through you to do that, so be it."

"That's honorable. My job is to enforce corporate policy. Teman will be terminated today, per corporate decree. Killing me won't stop that. It's how the system works."

"Then perhaps it's time to begin questioning how things work," Ilaria says.

She moves in front of the guardians. Rifle barrels swing in her direction. Her eyes travel down to see the luminous red dots from laser sights painting her heart.

"I knew you would say something like that, Ilaria. Those are a traitor's words."

"Spoken like a true tyrant," she retorts. The rebuke doesn't faze him.

"I'd love to know how you escaped the trap we set for you at the medical center, but it doesn't matter. This works better. Now I get the opportunity to watch you die."

Ilaria smirks. "You first."

"I almost admire your guts," he says with a chuckle. "You might have made a good CEO."

"Enough talk, Virtari," Dzamko says. "Let Teman go, or you don't walk away from this still breathing."

"Oh, I wouldn't be so sure about that."

Almost on cue, agents rush into the hallway from behind Ilaria and the guardians. Their driver turns and is immediately shot. The rest of them don't have time to react. Everyone is disarmed and pushed down on the tile floor in a matter of seconds.

The agents aren't gentle. They restrain them with electromag cuffs and drag each of them into the foyer face-down. A pair of boots stops in Ilaria's vision. Virtari squats so she can see him.

"I met your husband in the America Building during the search for Liberteum. I knew that day I wanted him dead. You know what? I'm about to make that happen. I could never have known that I want his wife dead even more."

"Sir, we have a priority VidLynk from the Pentagon. Something is happening in Manhattan."

Virtari stands. "Watch them. If any of them tries to escape, kill them all."

CHAPTER NINETY-FOUR

INTERCORPEX

Just South of Commerce Bridge
The East River
New York City Municipal Corporation

The boat heads up the East River with the helicopters covering their escape. The BCS has pulled back the drones, having lost a couple more to the gunships since they embarked. The last thing the BCS expected to face was armed helicopters.

They pass under the Commerce Bridge and loop around the peninsula. Nobody has said a word since leaving the island. When the boat speeds past Kings Point and the American Merchant Marine Training Facility, Michele moves next to the pilot.

"Stop the boat," she orders.

"We're in no position to—"

"Stop the boat," Farron says, eyeing Michele.

These guys don't take orders from Liberteum. Not that Zyree expected a terrorist group to control Denali Keating's army. It does raise the question of how Farron and Michele got involved with each other, though.

The pilot idles the engine. Michele turns to Zyree, causing him to look down at the scummy waters of Long Island Sound.

"Am I going for a swim?"

"Not unless you want to. I wouldn't."

"Then why did we stop?"

"You're conflicted about us rescuing you. It's written all over your face," she observes.

"I didn't think I was being that obvious. Remind me never to play poker with you. I assume that *isn't* illegal in the underground."

"It's one of our favorite activities. You need to decide whether you want to stay with us. We can drop you off on shore and go our separate ways if that's what you want."

Zyree looks at Farron, his driver, Rykos, and Michele's henchman, who hasn't said anything. They all stare back at him.

"You'll let me go just like that?"

"You're not a hostage or a prisoner, Chief Inspector. We rescued you as a favor to Ortan. That's all."

"He blackmailed you, didn't he?"

Ortan's lack of social interactions makes him inept at conversation. He wouldn't have convinced a hunted terrorist to drive into a combat zone to rescue someone from ICX Security on charm alone. Leverage had to be involved.

"He gave us a compelling reason," she says with a bright smile.

It's amazing to see such radiance after the things she's seen…and done. Nothing fazes this woman. It's no wonder Rykos likes her. She's a giant step up from the little chippie he was with that night in Central Park.

It'd be easier for Zyree to think of Liberteum as an evil organization. He's never been able to. He might not agree with their methods, but they aren't the monsters they're portrayed as. Michele isn't, at least. He's betting Rykos noticed that after his "kidnapping." That's why he wasn't afraid to reach out to them after his father was captured.

Farron gives Michele a cautious look. "Are you sure you want to let him stay with us?"

"There are easier ways for Intercorpex to eliminate us than using an elaborate infiltration ruse," Rykos says. Farron looks unconvinced.

"The BCS and his colleague weren't shooting at Zyree because he was on *good* terms with them. For whatever reason, he's persona non grata in the system."

"The enemy of our enemy is our friend," Rykos chimes in.

Zyree's eyes narrow. "So, you're a convert now, Rykos?"

"We want many of the same things. You'll see that for yourself."

"What exactly do you want?"

"Freedom."

Zyree studies him. He doesn't need a biocomp to see that the kid is sincere. There's no hint of deception in his face. He has completely bought what Michele is selling.

"You know that I still owe you for whacking me on the head, right?"

"I changed my mind. We should make him swim after all," Rykos states with a wry smile.

"So, what'll it be, Chief Inspector? Do you want to fend for yourself or find out the truth of what you've been fighting against?"

Zyree looks at the shoreline. He won't last more than a few hours on his own, even in a suburb. There is no returning to Intercorpex with Lyris running it. He needs to move on, even if that's with the terrorists they accused him of working with.

"Let's go."

"Fire it up," Farron commands. "Take us home."

The engine roars to life. They get back underway, moving at a good clip through the choppy sound. Michele touches Zyree on the shoulder.

"For what it's worth, I'm glad to have you with us, Chief Inspector," she says, reaching out her hand.

Chief Inspector – it's a senior title in a security organization responsible for killing Malkor. Zyree considered that man a friend. That friend saved his life. Now Intercorpex is hunting him for something they know he wasn't involved in. The exchange traded a paranoid micromanager for an arrogant opportunist. He may be better off without them.

He takes her hand and gives it a firm shake.

"Do me a favor – just call me Zyree."

CHAPTER NINETY-FIVE

INTERCORPEX

North of Isabel dos Santos MetroLev Station
Forest Hills Geographic District
Washington-Arlington Municipal Corporation

A shrill sound slices through Fiolla's head. It's pure agony, and she drops to her knees as she covers her ears. It feels like her skull is about to shatter into a million pieces. Dutch fights through the pain to pick up the audio grenade and hurl it away from the crowd.

"Stick these in your ears," Boomyr says, handing Fiolla two spongy spheres. "They'll help ward off the effects."

"They're dispersing us!" Jzahn bellows, urgently pointing to the north. "They fired up the quli mover."

Fiolla turns to see an armored vehicle inching forward. Steel panels extend almost thirty feet from its front as it pushes into the crowd like a bulldozer. Guardians launch non-lethal countermeasures from firing ports. It has the desired effect.

Screams erupt from behind them. A mass of humanity surges in their direction. Fiolla has seen quli riots on AME News and always thought they got what they deserved. It's a different experience being in the middle of it.

"Dutch!" Boomyr shouts. "They're also pushing in from the south!"

A thick line of sentries has taken positions to protect the hulking Human Resources facility adjacent to the street. The corporate division is based near the White House, but its operations are conducted from here. The cube-shaped structures that make up the building stick out in this neighborhood. Built nearly fifty years before the collapse, the building was futuristic enough to fit in with the modern architecture.

"They're driving us out of the street so they can isolate us with heat guns," Dutch concludes.

Heat guns are mobile active denial systems that direct thermal energy at a crowd. Mounted on trailers, they work like a microwave ovens by exciting the water and fat molecules in the skin. The sensation is so intense that prolonged exposure can lead to first- and second-degree burns.

Qulis begin throwing rocks at the advancing guardians. A couple of projectiles hit their marks but fail to stop the advance. When the guardians reach a group holding their ground, things turn violent. Men in full body armor begin subduing the protesters with electrified batons. It's a low-tech yet effective solution that provokes an immediate response.

Twenty men rush past Fiolla to attack the guardians. They're joined by another two dozen who overwhelm the security forces. Their formation breaks apart in the ensuing brawl. Their comrades atop the armored vehicles deploy more countermeasures to cease the assault. Tear gas canisters fill the air with pungent smoke as nozzles fire a gooey substance at the rioters. It forces the qulis back but also stalls the guardians' advance south of Union Street.

The angry protest has turned into a riot. Conveyances lining Connecticut Avenue have windshields broken, and construction tools are unleashed on hoods and fenders. Qulis break into the small shops across from the Human Resources building and set them ablaze.

In a fit of rage, a group of qulis jumps the decorative fence of the compound. It was a point of no return. BCS agents and guardians lining the grounds immediately shoulder their rifles and fire, cutting down the trespassers.

Another wave of panic surges through the street. People urgently try to escape the impending massacre. Fiolla is knocked to the ground in the chaos and gets trampled by the mass of humanity stomping over each other for survival. She climbs to her knees only to get knocked back to the ground. Loud shouts erupt above her. She's plucked off the ground and stood up by Boomyr and Jzahn.

"Stay close to us," Dutch shouts once she's upright again. "We'll get you out of here. Where's your truck, Jymmie?"

"Over on Corporate Row. I figured it'd be safer there."

The quintet heads back up Connecticut toward Isabel dos Santos Station. The violence is worse at the facility's main entrance. Fiolla desperately wants to get out of the melee, but her protectors seem intent on getting to Jymmie's truck.

"We can't go down Van Ness," Dutch says, surveying the situation. "We'll have to cut through the tech school."

Once a liberal arts university, the institution was rededicated during the early days of the corporation as a technical college specializing in HVAC systems. The campus lets them bypass the carnage on the streets. That is, it will if they can get to it.

Guardians scuffle with laborers everywhere. Heavily armed men move along the top of a concrete retaining wall bisected by the main staircase. They raise their rifles and take aim. If they fire, this is going to get bloody.

The staccato of gunfire rings out from the crowd. Guardians manning the perimeter take cover behind ballistic shields. The rioters seize the opportunity to storm the entrance. The air is thick with smoke from the fires they set across the street. It provides them concealment but not cover.

The BCS agents open fire. After a moment, the guardians join them. Rioters are cut down into piles of mangled flesh. Dutch pulls Fiolla to the ground. The woman next to them falls, a gaping hole in her chest.

Fiolla stares at the body in horror. That woman was alive and standing next to her only a moment ago. Fiolla's hauled again to her feet and urgently told to move. They don't get far.

The two BCS agents who chased Fiolla off the MetroLev calmly walk up to them. Like a protective father shielding his child, Dutch positions himself between Fiolla and her pursuers. They give him an amused look.

"Step aside."

"Ain't gonna happen."

The two men stare each other down for a long moment. It's a battle of wills – agents of the corporation against the suppressed masses. There isn't a more appropriate metaphor for what's going on in this sphere of influence. Fiolla is pulled from her moment of reflection when the agent draws his weapon and shoots Dutch in the forehead.

Boomyr and Jzahn reflexively arrest the dead man's fall. By the time they realize their mistake, it's too late. Each agent fires a round into their chests.

The qulis around them scream at the sudden new danger and flee. With her new friends dead, she turns to run. Something pinches her back. Fiolla manages to take two more steps before she collapses. A strange sensation creeps down her legs and up her torso. She tries to move her arms, but nothing happens. They won't move. A numbness grips her neck, and it loses the strength to hold her head up. Fear overwhelms her…she can't move.

The two agents are standing over her, shaking their heads. One of them hauls her limp body upright. With no control over her muscles, her head rolls around on her shoulders. Whatever they hit her with has rendered Fiolla helpless.

An agent grabs her hair and yanks her head upright. "Nobody runs from us."

His sadistic smile is terrifying. Fiolla can only stare at the ground as a black bag is placed over her head, plunging her into terrifying darkness. She can't move. She can't resist. She can't even scream.

CHAPTER
NINETY-SIX
THE PATRICIANS

*The White House
Corporate Governance District
Washington-Arlington Municipal Corporation*

Upgrading the sphere's status to martial law is not unprecedented. It was a prudent measure that has backfired spectacularly. Zeykala can't even fathom what these events would have done to their stock price if the stock exchange were open.

"This job isn't as easy as it looks, is it?" Talya asks from her seat on the sofa.

"It's fine."

Talya rises and walks slowly around the office, admiring the portraits on its walls. She's been in here a hundred times, so this theater is for Zeykala's benefit.

"It's fine? So, I guess the qulis have been subdued, our relationship with Intercorpex is restored, and Chief Inspector Zyree is in our custody?"

Zeykala stares at her blankly.

"I thought not. Things are not 'fine.' Why did you agree to capture their rogue agent? What do we get in return?"

"A chance to deflect the responsibility for the attack away from America Incorporated."

Talya shakes her head. "As if that would work. You bargained with the man who almost cost me my position as *prima*."

"I took care of that," Zeykala snaps.

"The non-binding resolution from the board of directors is a temporary solution. It only succeeded because Shalius Covington was eliminated. That was my doing. Intercorpex makes the final determination of shareholders. You demonstrated your ineptitude in dealing with the new AG."

"Excuse me?"

"You gave him what he wanted, and for what? The negotiation wasn't a testament to the business skills you convinced me you possess."

"The board of directors thinks otherwise."

Talya smirks. "You have influence over your former colleagues. I know that you made promises to gain that influence. Greasing palms is a way of life in Washington, but don't confuse leadership with cronyism. Valen never would have let this problem with the qulis happen. Some of his policies were almost as unpopular."

Zeykala looks like she's about to explode. "He never took away their independence under threat from the *prima* of America Incorporated. How did you expect them to react after you rewrote my address?"

"I expected this. Did you? Did you warn the qulis about the consequences of protesting or rioting? Did you issue instructions to security personnel about how they should respond? Did you conduct high-level meetings to—"

"You told me to do it!"

"Do not presume to think you can cut me off mid-sentence!" Talya shouts, glaring at the CEO. "I set policy. You execute it. I said that bringing the laborers under our umbrella would pay long-term benefits, and it will. The way things are going, you won't survive in this position long enough to enjoy them."

"What is that supposed to mean?"

Talya walks behind Zeykala's desk to stare out the window at the Rose Garden. It's a subtle message. She can install anybody in the Oval Office to admire this view.

"You are the chief executive officer. Everything that happens in this corporation is your responsibility. If you're content to blame everyone else for your failures, then this job is too big for you."

"It's not."

"Then prove it!" Talya snaps. "I need a leader in that chair. Step up, or I'll have you removed."

"The board won't do that," Zeykala protests.

"Don't overestimate their loyalty to you. Whatever promises you made will pale in comparison to what I can offer."

Zeykala is speechless. Talya shakes her head and walks to the door, stopping at the threshold.

"Intercorpex wants to resume trading within the next two weeks. I expect you to have the mess you created cleaned up in half that time. If it isn't, then I'm going to borrow your playbook and assign some blame of my own. You wanted this job. Do it. Fail me, and you'll find out firsthand what Valen is going through."

CHAPTER
NINETY-SEVEN
AMERICA, INC.

Human Resources Center
Rikers Island Geographic Area
New York City Municipal Corporation

Ilaria feels like she's been on the ground forever. The agents guarding them are getting restless as they wait for their boss to return. When Virtari finally strides into the lobby, he looks disgruntled. He stares long and hard at Ilaria, Dzamko, and Deyago without speaking.

"What do you want us to do with them, sir? Shoot them?" an agent asks.

"That is the question, isn't it? What do we do with you? You're all traitors to the corporation. I should march all of you out there and have you shot."

"Then do it," Ilaria says.

"If it were up to me, I would," he says. "Against my counsel, Washington thinks making you martyrs will inflame the current crisis."

"Do you think whether we live or die will stop the qulis from protesting?" Dzamko asks.

"Funny, that was my argument. I will tame them one way or another, regardless. Zeykala feels otherwise. She wants to make your trial and execution a spectacle, despite my trying to talk her out of it."

Ilaria strains her neck to glare at Virtari. His arrogance makes her sick. His love affair with corporate-sanctioned murder is detestable. It may be part of his job, but only a psychopath would revel in the thought of doing it.

"We'll keep them under house arrest in Manhattan," he announces to his agents.

"Very good, sir. We'll convoy back into the city."

"Before you do that, there's something our friends need to see. Take them up to the gallery. It'd be a shame if they traveled up here and didn't see the show."

Ilaria's eyes grow wide in horror. "No!"

She fights against the men restraining her as she and Dzamko are dragged upstairs. Even the burly constable has no success against their strength. They're forced to the slanted window overlooking the courtyard. Ilaria would rather be out in that courtyard facing her death than standing here.

DCP personnel march Teman out from the Delta wing. He's bound at the wrists and isn't staggering or sluggish like he's been drugged. He's compliant as they lash him to the trundle. Ilaria can't understand why he isn't struggling.

"He doesn't have any fight left in him, does he?" Virtari asks.

Teman has given up. Despite their problems and arguments, he's still the man Ilaria loves. He's the father of her children.

Old feelings rush back like a movie. The stress from dealing with Rykos, her new job, the demands of Teman's position as chief guardian, and his abuse all fade away. She no longer remembers the bad things. It's only the good memories: their engagement, wedding, children's births…all the happy times they shared.

Ilaria wrestles free from the men holding her and bangs on the glass. She needs him to see her. He needs to know that she didn't abandon him. It's all in vain. He can't hear her and doesn't even look up as BCS agents march into place, and the termination order is read.

"Don't do this," Ilaria pleads, tears streaming down her cheeks. "You don't have to do this."

"Your claws aren't that sharp after all, are they, Ilaria? Orders are orders," Virtari says, swiping a finger across her cheek and tasting her tears. "Even if I didn't have orders, I wouldn't hesitate. Honestly, I want this more than Zeykala does."

His words stab at Ilaria's soul. Not bearing to watch, she turns away.

"Oh, come now, Ilaria. This is the best part," Virtari says, cackling.

He grabs her face and forces her to look forward. She fights him, but he's too strong. Dzamko lunges to intervene and is hauled backward by three BCS agents.

"Let her go!"

"Shut up, Constable. Watch," he whispers into her ear. "Watch what happens to those who subvert the corporation."

The men take aim. Red dots illuminate Teman's chest before coming together right over his heart. On command, the weapons fire simultaneously. The man she loves and gave up so much for slumps against the truncheon.

"No!" she sobs, banging her fist against the glass.

"Nobody is above the corporation, Ilaria."

He releases her face. The icy cold statement is a dagger to the heart. Instead of wounding her further, it triggers something else. Grief transforms into a deep rage that metastasizes. Every cell in her body burns with the intense heat of a thousand suns.

She doesn't acknowledge Virtari. His day of reckoning will come. She lost today, but tomorrow is promised to no one. These people have stolen Rykos's innocence, seized Varella's soul, and taken Teman's life. They destroyed her family. Everything she cherished is gone. There is nothing left for her to lose.

Ilaria closes her eyes and makes a silent pledge. She will get her vengeance if it's the last thing she ever does.

ACKNOWLEDGMENTS

This saga has had an interesting journey of its own. It was released, unpublished, rewritten, and now has a second chance to thrill readers. I could have memory-holed these novels, borrowing a term from Orwell's *1984*, but I believe the message it conveys has modern applications. I appreciate my readers for sticking with it and for all my new readers willing to give this saga a try. There are millions of stories to choose from, and I'm honored and humbled that you spent your time reading mine.

When I wrote the first version of this novel in 2017, it was a year of change for me. That May, I had the pleasure of saying "I do" to an amazing woman. She has endured long hours of me discussing plotlines and character development with her and longer hours of my pecking away at a keyboard. Michele is my rock, encourager, and inspiration, and I hope to bother her with plot development long into the future.

My beloved mother, Nancy, and my sister, Kristina, are always my most ardent fans and vocal cheerleaders. Words cannot adequately express how much your support means to me.

Each novel in the America, Inc. Saga is titled after a business phrase. I liked the idea of using corporate jargon, making book cover creation challenging. How do you take the concept of boiling an ocean and not make it look like an environmental impact study? Simple. I call a great designer. I think every book cover is my favorite, and this one was no exception. Thank you to JD&J Design for an unbelievably great depiction of a difficult concept.

I'm saving the best for last, partly because he will read this and wonder why I haven't mentioned him sooner. Editors are a neurotic bunch that way. They are also critical to the publishing process. Behind every great writer is an editor who painstakingly toils to make a novel the best it can be. It's a thankless job, partly because of a writer's stubbornness but mostly because an editor rarely gets to share the spotlight.

Mike Waitz of Sticks and Stones Editing is that guy. When he isn't trying to explain why I continue making the same grammatical mistakes in my native language, he offers useful suggestions, double-checks research, and, most importantly, maintains consistency in my novels. That's no easy task for a saga set in a post-apocalyptic world with this many characters and plot twists. I am incredibly grateful for everything he brings to the table.

ABOUT THE AUTHOR

Mikael Carlson is the award-winning author of the novel *The iCandidate* and the Michael Bennit Series of political dramas. He also has written two other ongoing series: Tierra Campos Thrillers and Watchtower Thrillers. His newest series, America, Inc., is a retelling of the futuristic dystopian Black Swan Saga that serves as a cautionary tale of life in a world following a global economic collapse.

A retired veteran of the Rhode Island Army National Guard and United States Army, he deployed twice in support of military operations during the Global War on Terror. Mikael has served in the field artillery, infantry, and in support of special operations units during his career on active duty at Fort Bragg and in the Army National Guard.

A proud U.S. Army Paratrooper, he conducted over fifty airborne operations following the completion of jump school at Fort Benning in 1998. Since then, he has trained with the militaries of countless foreign nations.

Mikael earned a Master of Arts in American History in 2010 and graduated with a B.S. in International Business from Marist College in 1996.

He was raised in New Milford, Connecticut, and currently lives in nearby Danbury.